What If I'm Dead? What If This Is What Death Is Like?

It fits. It fits everything with a horrid prophylactic snugness. The dark. The rubbery smell. Nowadays I am Howard the Conqueror, stock broker extraordinaire, terror of Derry Municipal Country Club, frequent habitué of what is known at golf courses all over the world as the Nineteenth Hole, but in '71 I was part of a Medical Assistance Team in the Mekong Delta, a scared kid who sometimes woke up wet-eyed from dreams of the family dog, and all at once I know this feel, this smell.

Dear God, I'm in a body bag.

—From Stephen King's "Autopsy Room Four"

Look for These HWA Titles

Under the Fang
Peter Straub's Ghosts
Robert Bloch's Psychos

Published by POCKET BOOKS

The Horror Writers Association presents

Robert Bloch's
Psychos

Edited by ROBERT BLOCH

POCKET BOOKS
New York London Toronto Sydney Tokyo Singapore

This book consists of works of fiction. Names, characters, places and incidents are products of the authors' imaginations or are used fictitiously. Any resemblance to actual events or locales or persons, living or dead, is entirely coincidental.

An *Original* Publication of POCKET BOOKS

POCKET BOOKS, a division of Simon & Schuster Inc.
1230 Avenue of the Americas, New York, NY 10020

Copyright © 1997 by The Horror Writers Association

ISBN: 0-671-88598-7

First Pocket Books printing January 1998

10 9 8 7 6 5 4 3 2 1

POCKET and colophon are registered trademarks of Simon & Schuster Inc.

Cover design and illustration by Jim Lebbad

Printed in the U.S.A.

Copyright Notices

Contents

CONTENTS

Introduction

Robert Bloch was one of the finest writers of horror and dark fantasy of the twentieth century. He was best known as the author of *Psycho,* but he was far more than that. His writing career spanned more than six decades and encompassed a variety of styles and genres, all of them handled with wit and charm; he was particularly known for twisty, unpredictable endings and his wicked sense of humor. The science fiction community acknowledged his talent by awarding his story "The Hell-Bound Train" the Hugo, that field's highest honor, for the best short story of 1959.

It was in horror, however, that he was best known. Even though HWA did not begin presenting the Bram Stoker Award for Superior Achievement until 1988, more than fifty years into Mr. Bloch's career, he managed to collect four Stokers—the 1990 award for life achievement, the 1994 award for nonfiction for *Coming Around the Bloch,* and the 1995 awards for novelette and collection for, respectively, "The Scent of Vinegar" and *The Early Fears.*

HWA was proud to have Mr. Bloch as a member. When we began producing anthologies featuring stories written by our members, we were delighted to have Mr. Bloch agree to edit one of them for us.

Unfortunately, Robert Bloch did not live to see this book completed, or to write an introduction for it; he died in September 1994, and the finishing touches had to be done without him. We think he'd be pleased with how the book turned out. In lieu of the introduction Mr. Bloch would have written, we will let the stories speak for themselves.

—Horror Writers Association

AUTOPSY ROOM FOUR

Stephen King

IT'S SO DARK THAT FOR A WHILE—JUST HOW LONG I DON'T know—I think I'm still unconscious. Then, slowly, it comes to me that unconscious people don't have a sensation of movement through the dark, accompanied by a faint, rhythmic sound that can only be a squeaky wheel. And I can feel contact, from the top of my head to the balls of my heels. I can smell something that might be rubber or vinyl. This is not unconsciousness, and there is something too . . . too *what?* Too *rational* about these sensations for it to be a dream.

Then what is it?

Who am I?

And what's happening to me?

The squeaky wheel quits its stupid rhythm and I stop moving. There is a crackle around me from the rubber-smelling stuff.

A voice: "Which one did they say?"

A pause.

Second voice: "Four, I think. Yeah, four."

We start to move again, but more slowly. I can hear the faint scuff of feet now, probably in soft-soled shoes, maybe sneakers. The owners of the voices are the owners of the shoes. They stop me again. There's a thump followed by a faint whoosh. It is, I think, the sound of a door with a pneumatic hinge being opened.

What's going on here? I yell, but the yell is only in my head. My lips don't move. I can feel them—and my tongue, lying on the floor of my mouth like a stunned mole—but I can't move them.

The thing I'm on starts rolling again. A moving bed? Yes. A gurney, in other words. I've had some experience with them, a long time ago, in Lyndon Johnson's shitty little Asian adventure. It comes to me that I'm in a hospital, that something bad has happened to me, something like the explosion that almost neutered me twenty-three years ago, and that I'm going to be operated on. There are a lot of answers in that idea, sensible ones, for the most part, but I don't hurt anywhere. Except for the minor matter of being scared out of my wits, I feel fine. And if these are orderlies wheeling me into an operating room, why can't I see? Why can't I *talk?*

A third voice: "Over here, boys."

My rolling bed is pushed in a new direction, and the question drumming in my head is *What kind of a mess have I gotten myself into?*

Doesn't that depend on who you are? I ask myself, but that's one thing, at least, I find I *do* know. I'm Howard Cottrell. I'm a stock broker known to some of my colleagues as Howard the Conqueror.

Second voice (from just above my head): "You're looking very pretty today, Doc."

Fourth voice (female, and cool): "It's always nice to be validated by you, Rusty. Could you hurry up a little? The baby-sitter expects me back by seven. She's committed to dinner with her parents."

Back by seven, back by seven. It's still the afternoon, maybe, or early evening, but black in here, black as your hat, black as a woodchuck's asshole, black as midnight in Persia, and *what's going on?* Where have I been? What have I been doing? Why haven't I been manning the phones?

Because it's Saturday, a voice from far down murmurs. *You were . . . were . . .*

A sound: *WHOCK!* A sound I love. A sound I more or less live for. The sound of . . . what? The head of a golf club, of course. Hitting a ball off the tee. I stand, watching it fly off into the blue . . .

I'm grabbed, shoulders and calves, and lifted. It startles me terribly, and I try to scream. No sound comes out . . . or perhaps one does, a tiny squeak, much tinier than the one produced by the wheel below me. Probably not even that. Probably it's just my imagination.

I'm swung through the air in an envelope of blackness—*Hey, don't drop me, I've got a bad back!* I try to say, and again there's no movement of the lips or teeth; my tongue goes on lying on the floor of my mouth, the mole maybe not just stunned but dead, and now I have a terrible thought, one that spikes fright a degree closer to panic: What if they put me down the wrong way and my tongue slides backward and blocks my windpipe? I won't be able to breathe! That's what people mean when they say someone swallowed his tongue, isn't it?

Second voice (Rusty): "You'll like this one, Doc, he looks like Michael Bolton."

Female doc: "Who's that?"

Third voice—sounds like a young man, not much more than a teenager: "He's this white lounge singer who wants to be black. I don't think this is him."

There's laughter at that, the female voice joining in (a little doubtfully), and as I am set down on what feels like a padded table, Rusty starts some new crack—he's got a whole standup routine, it seems. I lose this bit of hilarity in a burst of sudden horror. I won't be able to breathe if my tongue blocks my windpipe, that's the thought that has just gone through my mind, *but what if I'm not breathing now?*

What if I'm dead? What if this is what death is like?

It fits. It fits everything with a horrid prophylactic snugness. The dark. The rubbery smell. Nowadays I am Howard the Conqueror, stock broker *extraordinaire,* terror of Derry

Municipal Country Club, frequent *habitué* of what is known at golf courses all over the world as the Nineteenth Hole, but in '71 I was part of a medical assistance team in the Mekong Delta, a scared kid who sometimes woke up wet-eyed from dreams of the family dog, and all at once I know this feel, this smell.

Dear God, I'm in a body bag.

First voice: "Want to sign this, Doc? Remember to bear down hard—it's three copies."

Sound of a pen, scraping away on paper. I imagine the owner of the first voice holding out a clipboard to the woman doctor.

Oh dear Jesus let me not be dead! I try to scream, and nothing comes out.

I'm breathing, though . . . aren't I? I mean, I can't feel myself doing it, but my lungs seem okay, they're not throbbing or yelling for air the way they do when you've swum too far underwater, so I must be okay, right?

Except if you're dead, the deep voice murmurs, *they* wouldn't *be crying out for air, would they? No—because dead lungs don't need to breathe. Dead lungs can just kind of . . . take it easy.*

Rusty: "What are you doing next Saturday night, Doc?"

But if I'm dead, how can I feel? How can I smell the bag I'm in? How can I hear these voices, the doc now saying that next Saturday night she's going to be shampooing her dog, which is named Rusty, what a coincidence, and all of them laughing? If I'm dead, why aren't I either gone or in the white light they're always talking about on Oprah?

There's a harsh ripping sound and all at once I *am* in white light; it is blinding, like the sun breaking through a scrim of clouds on a winter day. I try to squint my eyes shut against it, but nothing happens. My eyelids are like blinds on broken rollers.

A face bends over me, blocking off part of the glare, which comes not from some dazzling astral plane but from a bank of overhead fluorescents. The face belongs to a young, conventionally handsome man of about twenty-five; he looks like one of those beach beefcakes on *Baywatch* or

Melrose Place. Marginally smarter, though. He's got a lot of black hair under a carelessly worn surgical greens cap. He's wearing the tunic, too. His eyes are cobalt blue, the sort of eyes girls reputedly die for. There are dusty arcs of freckles high up on his cheekbones.

"Hey, gosh," he says. It's the third voice. "This guy *does* look like Michael Bolton! A little long in the old tootharoo, maybe . . ." He leans closer. One of the flat tie-ribbons at the neck of his green tunic tickles against my forehead. "But yeah. I see it. Hey, Michael, sing something."

Help me! is what I'm *trying* to sing, but I can only look up into his dark blue eyes with my frozen dead man's stare; I can only wonder if I *am* a dead man, if this is how it happens, if this is what *everyone* goes through after the pump quits. If I'm still alive, how come he hasn't seen my pupils contract when the light hit them? But I know the answer to that . . . or I think I do. They *didn't* contract. That's why the glare from the fluorescents is so painful.

The tie, tickling across my forehead like a feather.

Help me! I scream up at the *Baywatch* beefcake, who is probably an intern or maybe just a med school brat. *Help me, please!*

My lips don't even quiver.

The face moves back, the tie stops tickling, and all that white light streams through my helpless-to-look-away eyes and into my brain. It's a hellish feeling, a kind of rape. I'll go blind if I have to stare into it for long, I think, and blindness will be a relief.

WHOCK! The sound of the driver hitting the ball, but a little flat this time, and the feeling in the hands is bad. The ball's up . . . but veering . . . veering off . . . veering toward . . .

Shit.

I'm in the rough.

Now another face bends into my field of vision. A white tunic instead of a green one below it, a great untidy mop of orange hair above it. Distress-sale IQ is my first impression. It can only be Rusty. He's wearing a big dumb grin that I think of as a high-school grin, the grin of a kid who should have a tattoo reading "Born to Snap Bra Straps" on one wasted bicep.

"Michael!" Rusty exclaims. "Jeez, ya lookin' *gooood!* This'z an honor! *Sing* for us, big boy! Sing your dead ass off!"

From somewhere behind me comes the doc's voice, cool, no longer even pretending to be amused by these antics. "Quit it, Rusty." Then, in a slightly new direction: "What's the story, Mike?"

Mike's voice is the first voice—Rusty's partner. He sounds slightly embarrassed to be working with a guy who wants to be Bobcat Goldthwait when he grows up. "Found him on the fourteenth hole at Derry Muni. Off the course, actually, in the rough. If he hadn't just played through the foursome behind him, and if they hadn't seen one of his legs stickin' out of the puckerbrush, he'd be an ant farm by now."

I hear that sound in my head again—*WHOCK!*—only this time it is followed by another, far less pleasant sound: the rustle of underbrush as I sweep it with the head of my driver. It *would* have to be fourteen, where there is reputedly poison ivy. Poison ivy and . . .

Rusty is still peering down at me, stupid and avid. It's not death that interests him; it's my resemblance to Michael Bolton. Oh yes, I know about it, have not been above using it with certain female clients. Otherwise, it gets old in a hurry. And in these circumstances . . . *God.*

"Attending physician?" the lady doc asks. "Was it Kazalian?"

"No," Mike says, and for just a moment he looks down at me. Older than Rusty by at least ten years. Black hair with flecks of gray in it. Spectacles. *How come none of these people can see that I am not dead?* "There was a doc in the foursome that found him, actually. That's his signature on page one . . . see?"

Riffle of paper, then: "Christ, Jennings. I know him. He gave Noah his physical after the ark grounded on Mount Ararat."

Rusty doesn't look as if he gets the joke, but he brays

laughter into my face anyway. I can smell onions on his breath, a little leftover lunchstink, and if I can smell onions, I must be breathing. I *must* be, right? If only—

Before I can finish this thought, Rusty leans even closer and I feel a blast of hope. He's seen something! He's seen something and means to give me mouth-to-mouth. God bless you, Rusty! God bless you and your onion breath!

But the stupid grin doesn't change, and instead of putting his mouth on mine, his hand slips around my jaw. Now he's grasping one side with his thumb and the other side with his fingers.

"He's *alive!*" Rusty cries. "He's *alive,* and he's gonna sing for the Room Four Michael Bolton Fan Club!"

His fingers pinch tighter—it hurts in a distant coming-out-of-the-novocaine way—and begins to move my jaw up and down, clicking my teeth together. *"If she's ba-aaad, he can't see it,"* Rusty sings in a hideous, atonal voice that would probably make Percy Sledge's head explode. *"She can do no wrrr-ongggg . . ."* My teeth open and close at the rough urging of his hand; my tongue rises and falls like a dead dog riding the surface of an uneasy waterbed.

"Stop it!" the lady doc snaps at him. She sounds genuinely shocked. Rusty, perhaps sensing this, does not stop but goes gleefully on. His fingers are pinching into my cheeks now. My frozen eyes stare blindly upward.

"Turn his back on his best friend if she put him d—"

Then she's there, a woman in a green gown with her cap tied around her throat and hanging down her back like the Cisco Kid's sombrero, short brown hair swept back from her brow, good-looking but severe—more handsome than pretty. She grabs Rusty with one short-nailed hand and pulls him back from me.

"Hey!" Rusty says, indignant. "Get your hands off me!"

"Then you keep your hands off *him,*" she says, and there is no mistaking the anger in her voice. "I'm tired of your sophomore class wit, Rusty, and the next time you start in, I'm going to report you."

"Hey, let's all calm down," says the *Baywatch* hunk— Doc's assistant. He sounds alarmed, as if he expects Rusty and his boss to start duking it out right here. "Let's just put a lid on it."

"Why's she bein' such a bitch to me?" Rusty says. He's still trying to sound indignant, but he's actually whining now. Then, in a slightly different direction: "Why you being such a bitch? You on your period, is that it?"

Doc, sounding disgusted: "Get him out of here."

Mike: "Come on, Rusty. Let's go sign the log."

Rusty: "Yeah. And get some fresh air."

Me, listening to all this like it was on the radio.

Their feet, squeaking toward the door. Rusty now all huffy and offended, asking her why she doesn't just wear a mood ring or something so people will *know*. Soft shoes squeaking on tile, and suddenly that sound is replaced by the sound of my driver, beating the bush for my goddam ball, where is it, it didn't go too far in, I'm sure of it, so where is it, Jesus, I *hate* fourteen, supposedly there's poison ivy, and with all this underbrush, there could easily be—

And then something bit me, didn't it? Yes, I'm almost sure it did. On the left calf, just above the top of my white athletic sock. A red-hot darning needle of pain, perfectly concentrated at first, then spreading . . .

. . . then darkness. Until the gurney, zipped up snug inside a body bag and listening to Mike *("Which one did they say?")* and Rusty *("Four, I think. Yeah, four.")*.

I want to think it was some kind of snake, but maybe that's only because I was thinking about them while I hunted for my ball. It could have been an insect, I only recall the single line of pain, and after all, what does it matter? What matters here is that I'm alive and they don't know it. It's incredible, but they don't know it. Of course I had bad luck—I know Dr. Jennings, remember speaking to him as I played through his foursome on the eleventh hole. A nice enough guy, but vague, an antique. The antique had pronounced me dead. Then *Rusty*, with his dopey green eyes and his detention hall grin, had pronounced me dead. The lady doc, Ms. Cisco Kid, hadn't even *looked* at me yet, not really. When she did, maybe—

"I *hate* that jerk," she says when the door is closed. Now it's just the three of us, only of course Ms. Cisco Kid thinks it's just the two of them. "Why do I always get the jerks, Peter?"

"I don't know," Mr. Melrose Place says, "but Rusty's a special case, even in the annals of famous jerks. Walking brain death."

She laughs, and something clanks. The clank is followed by a sound that scares me badly: steel instruments clicking together. They are off to the left of me, and although I can't see them, I know what they're getting ready to do: the autopsy. They are getting ready to cut into me. They intend to remove Howard Cottrell's heart and see if it blew a piston or threw a rod.

My leg! I scream inside my head. *Look at my* left leg! *That's the trouble, not my heart!*

Perhaps my eyes have adjusted a little, after all. Now I can see, at the very top of my vision, a stainless steel armature. It looks like a giant piece of dental equipment, except that thing at the end isn't a drill. It's a saw. From someplace deep inside, where the brain stores the sort of trivia you only need if you happen to be playing *Jeopardy!* on TV, I even come up with the name. It's a Gigli saw. They use it to cut off the top of your skull. This is after they've pulled your face off like a kid's Halloween mask, of course, hair and all.

Then they take out your brain.

Clink. Clink. Clunk. A pause. Then a *CLANK!* so loud I'd jump if I were capable of jumping.

"Do you want to do the pericardial cut?" she asks.

Pete, cautious: "Do you want me to?"

Dr. Cisco, sounding pleasant, sounding like someone who is conferring a favor and a responsibility: "Yes, I think so."

"All right," he says. "You'll assist?"

"Your trusty copilot," she says, and laughs. She punctuates her laughter with a *snick-snick* sound. It's the sound of scissors cutting the air.

Now panic beats and flutters inside my skull like a flock of starlings locked in an attic. The Nam was a long time ago, but I saw half a dozen field autopsies there—what the doctors used to call "tent-show postmortems"—and I know what Cisco and Pancho mean to do. The scissors have long, sharp blades, *very* sharp blades, and fat finger holes. Still, you have to be strong to use them. The lower blade slides into the gut like butter. Then, *snip,* up through the bundle of nerves at the solar plexus and into the beef-jerky weave of muscle and tendon above it. Then into the sternum. When the blades come together this time, they do so with a heavy crunch as the bone parts and the ribcage pops apart like a couple of barrels that have been lashed together with twine. Then on up with those scissors that look like nothing so much as the poultry shears supermarket butchers use— *snip-CRUNCH, snip-CRUNCH, snip-CRUNCH,* splitting bone and shearing muscle, freeing the lungs, heading for the trachea, turning Howard the Conqueror into a Thanksgiving dinner no one will eat.

A thin, nagging whine—this *does* sound like a dentist's drill.

Pete: "Can I—"

Dr. Cisco, actually sounding a bit maternal: "No. These." *Snick-snick.* Demonstrating for him.

They can't do this, I think. *They can't cut me up . . . I can FEEL!*

"Why?" he asks.

"Because that's the way I want it," she says, sounding a lot less maternal. "When you're on your own, Petie-boy, you can do what you want. But in Katie Arlen's autopsy room, you start off with the pericardial shears."

Autopsy room. There. It's out. I want to be all over goosebumps, but of course, nothing happens; my flesh remains smooth.

"Remember," Dr. Arlen says (but now she's actually lecturing), "any fool can learn how to use a milking machine . . . but the hands-on procedure is always best." There is something vaguely suggestive in her tone. "Okay?"

"Okay," he says.

They're going to do it. I have to make some kind of noise

or movement, or they're really going to do it. If blood flows or jets up from the first punch of the scissors they'll know something's wrong, but by then it will be too late, very likely; that first *snip-CRUNCH* will have happened, and my ribs will be lying against my upper arms, my heart pulsing frantically away under the fluorescents in its blood-glossy sac—

I concentrate everything on my chest. I *push*, or try to . . . and something happens.

A sound!

I make a sound!

It's mostly inside my closed mouth, but I can also hear and feel it in my nose—a low hum.

Concentrating, summoning every bit of effort, I do it again, and this time the sound is a little stronger, leaking out of my nostrils like cigarette smoke: *Nnnnnnn*— It makes me think of an old Alfred Hitchcock TV program I saw a long, long time ago, where Joseph Cotton was paralyzed in a car crash and was finally able to let them know he was still alive by crying a single tear.

And if nothing else, that minuscule mosquito-whine of a sound has proved to *myself* that I'm alive, that I'm not just a spirit lingering inside the clay effigy of my own dead body.

Focusing all my concentration, I can feel breath slipping through my nose and down my throat, replacing the breath I have now expended, and then I send it out again, working harder than I ever worked summers for the Lane Construction Company when I was a teenager, working harder than I have ever worked in my *life*, because now I'm working *for* my life and they must hear me, dear Jesus, they must.

Nnnnnnnn—

"You want some music?" the woman doctor asks. "I've got Marty Stuart, Tony Bennett—"

He makes a despairing sound. I barely hear it, and take no immediate meaning from what she's saying . . . which is probably a mercy.

"All right," she says, laughing. "I've also got the Rolling Stones."

"You?"

"Me. I'm not quite as square as I look, Peter."

"I didn't mean . . ." He sounds flustered.

Listen to me! I scream inside my head as my frozen eyes stare up into the icy-white light. *Stop chattering like magpies and listen to me!*

I can feel more air trickling down my throat and the idea occurs that whatever has happened to me may be starting to wear off . . . but it's only a faint blip on the screen of my thoughts. Maybe it *is* wearing off, but very soon now recovery will cease to be an option for me. All my energy is bent toward making them hear me, and this time they *will* hear me, I know it.

"Stones, then," she says. "Unless you want me to run out and get a Michael Bolton CD in honor of your first pericardial."

"Please, no!" he cries, and they both laugh.

The sound starts to come out, and it *is* louder this time. Not as loud as I'd hoped, but loud enough. Surely loud enough. They'll hear, they *must*.

Then, just as I begin to force the sound out of my nose like some rapidly solidifying liquid, the room is filled with a blare of fuzz-tone guitar and Mick Jagger's voice bashing off the walls: *"Awww, no, it's only rock and roll, but I LIYYYYKE IT . . ."*

"Turn it down!" Dr. Cisco yells, comically overshouting, and amid these noises my own nasal sound, a desperate little humming through my nostrils, is no more audible than a whisper in a foundry.

Now her face bends over me again and I feel fresh horror as I see that she's wearing a Plexi eyeshield and a gauze mask over her mouth. She glances back over her shoulder.

"I'll strip him for you," she tells Pete, and bends toward me with a scalpel glittering in one gloved hand, bends toward me through the guitar thunder of the Rolling Stones.

I hum desperately, but it's no good. I can't even hear myself.

The scalpel hovers, then cuts.

I shriek inside my own head, but there is no pain, only my polo shirt falling in two pieces at my sides. Sliding apart as my ribcage will after Pete unknowingly makes his first pericardial cut on a living patient.

I am lifted. My head lolls back and for a moment I see Pete upside down, donning his own Plexi eyeshield as he stands by a steel counter, inventorying a horrifying array of tools. Chief among them are the oversized scissors. I get just a glimpse of them, of blades glittering like merciless satin. Then I am laid flat again and my shirt is gone. I'm now naked to the waist. It's cold in the room.

Look at my chest! I scream at her. *You must see it rise and fall, no matter how shallow my respiration is! You're a goddam expert, for Christ's sake!*

Instead, she looks across the room, raising her voice to be heard above the music. (*"I like it, like it, yes I do,"* the Stones sing, and I think I will hear that nasal idiot chorus in the halls of hell through all eternity.) "What's your pick? Boxers or Jockeys?"

With a mixture of horror and rage, I realize what they're talking about.

"Boxers!" he calls back. "Of course! Just take a look at the guy!"

Asshole! I want to scream. *You probably think everyone over forty wears boxer shorts! You probably think when you get to be forty, you'll—*

She unsnaps my Bermudas and pulls down the zipper. Under other circumstances, having a woman as pretty as this (a little severe, yes, but still pretty) do that would make me extremely happy. Today, however—

"You lose, Petie-boy," she says. "Jockeys. Dollar in the kitty."

"On payday," he says, coming over. His face joins hers; they look down at me through their Plexi masks like a couple of space aliens looking down at an abductee. I try to make them see my eyes, to see me *looking at them*, but these two fools are looking at my undershorts.

"Ooooh, and *red,*" Pete says. "A sha-*vinguh!*"

"I call them more of a wash pink," she replies. "Hold him up for me, Peter, he weighs a ton. No wonder he had a heart attack. Let this be a lesson to you."

I'm in shape! I yell at her. *Probably in better shape than you, bitch!*

My hips are suddenly jerked upward by strong hands. My back cracks; the sound makes my heart leap.

"Sorry, guy," Pete says, and suddenly I'm colder than ever as my shorts and red underpants are pulled down.

"Upsa-daisy *once,*" she says, lifting one foot, "and upsa-daisy *twice,*" lifting the other foot, "off come the *mocs,* and off come the *socks—*"

She stops abruptly, and hope seizes me once more.

"Hey, Pete."

"Yeah?"

"Do guys ordinarily wear Bermuda shorts and moccasins to play golf in?"

Behind her (except that's only the source, actually it's all around us) the Rolling Stones have moved on to "Emotional Rescue." *"I will be your knight in shining ahh-mah,"* Mick Jagger sings, and I wonder how funky he'd dance with about three sticks of Hi-Core dynamite jammed up his skinny ass.

"If you ask me, this guy was just *asking* for trouble," she goes on. "I thought they had these special shoes, very ugly, very golf-specific, with little knobs on the soles—"

"Yeah, but wearing them's not the law," Pete says. He holds his gloved hands out over my upturned face, slides them together, and bends the fingers back. As the knuckles crack, talcum powder sprinkles down like fine snow. "At least not yet. Not like bowling shoes. They catch you bowling without a pair of bowling shoes, they can send you to state prison."

"Is that so?"

"Yes."

"Do you want to handle temp and gross examination?"

No! I shriek. *No, he's a kid, what are you DOING?*

He looks at her as if this same thought had crossed his

14

own mind. "That's . . . um . . . not strictly legal, is it, Katie? I mean . . ."

She looks around as he speaks, giving the room a burlesque examination, and I'm starting to get a vibe that could be very bad news for me: severe or not, I think that Cisco—alias Dr. Katie Arlen—has got the hots for Petie with the dark blue eyes. Dear Christ, they have hauled me paralyzed off the golf course and into an episode of *General Hospital*, this week's subplot titled "Love Blooms in Autopsy Room Four."

"Gee," she says in a hoarse little stage whisper. "I don't see anyone here but you and me."

"The tape—"

"Not rolling yet," she says. "And once it is, I'm right at your elbow every step of the way . . . as far as anyone will ever know, anyway. And mostly I will be. I just want to put away those charts and slides. And if you really feel uncomfortable—"

Yes! I scream up at him out of my unmoving face. *Feel uncomfortable! VERY uncomfortable! TOO uncomfortable!*

But he's twenty-four at most and what's he going to say to this pretty, severe woman who's standing inside his space, invading it in a way that can really only mean one thing? *No, Mommy, I'm scared?* Besides, he wants to. I can see the wanting through the Plexi eyeshield, bopping around in there like a bunch of overage punk rockers pogoing to the Stones.

"Hey, as long as you'll cover for me if—"

"Sure," she says. "Got to get your feet wet sometime, Peter. And if you really need me to, I'll roll back the tape."

He looks startled. "You can do that?"

She smiles. "Ve haff many see-grets in Autopsy Room Four, *mein herr.*"

"I bet you do," he says, smiling back, then reaches past my frozen field of vision. When his hand comes back, it's wrapped around a microphone which hangs down from the ceiling on a black cord. The mike looks like a steel teardrop. Seeing it there makes this horror real in a way it wasn't

15

before. Surely they won't really cut me up, will they? Pete is no veteran, but he *has* had training; surely he'll see the marks of whatever bit me while I was looking for my ball in the rough, and then they'll at least suspect. They'll *have* to suspect.

Yet I keep seeing the scissors with their heartless satin shine—jumped-up poultry shears—and I keep wondering if I will still be alive when he takes my heart out of my chest cavity and holds it up, dripping, in front of my locked gaze for a moment before turning it to plop it into the weighing pan. I could be, it seems to me; I really could be. Don't they say the brain can remain conscious for up to three minutes after the heart stops?

"Ready, Doctor," Pete says, and now he sounds almost formal. Somewhere, tape is rolling.

The autopsy procedure has begun.

"Let's flip this pancake," she says cheerfully, and I am turned over just that efficiently. My right arm goes flying out to one side and then falls back against the side of the table, banging down with the raised metal lip digging into the biceps. It hurts a lot, the pain is just short of excruciating, but I don't mind. I pray for the lip to bite through my skin, pray to *bleed,* something bona fide corpses don't do.

"Whoops-a-daisy," Dr. Arlen says. She lifts my arm up and plops it back down at my side.

Now it's my nose I'm most aware of. It's smashed down against the table, and my lungs for the first time send out a distress message—a cottony, deprived feeling. My mouth is closed, my nose partially crushed shut (just how much I can't tell; I can't even feel myself breathing, not really). What if I suffocate like this?

Then something happens that takes my mind completely off my nose. A huge object—it feels like a glass baseball bat—is rammed rudely up my rectum. Once more I try to scream and can produce only the faint, wretched humming.

"Temp in," Peter says. "I've put on the timer."

"Good idea," she says, moving away. Giving him room. Letting him test-drive this baby. Letting him test-drive *me*. The music is turned down slightly.

"Subject is a white Caucasian, age forty-four," Pete says, speaking for the mike now, speaking for posterity. "His name is Howard Randolph Cottrell, residence is 1566 Laurel Crest Lane, here in Derry."

Dr. Arlen, at some distance: "Mary Mead."

A pause, then Pete again, sounding just a tiny bit flustered: "Dr. Arlen informs me that the subject actually lives in Mary Mead, which split off from Derry in—"

"Enough with the history lesson, Pete."

Dear God, what have they stuck up my ass? Some sort of cattle thermometer? If it was a little longer, I think, I could taste the bulb at the end. And they didn't exactly go crazy with the lubricant . . . but then, why would they? I'm dead, after all.

Dead.

"Sorry, Doctor," Pete says. He fumbles mentally for his place and eventually finds it. "This information is from the ambulance form. Mode of transmittal was Maine driver's license. Pronouncing doctor was, um, Frank Jennings. Subject was pronounced at the scene."

Now it's my nose that I'm hoping will bleed. *Please,* I tell it, *bleed. Only don't* just *bleed. GUSH.*

It doesn't.

"Cause of death may be a heart attack," Peter says. A light hand brushes down my naked back to the crack of my ass. I pray it will remove the thermometer, but it doesn't. "Spine appears to be intact, no attractable phenomena."

Attractable phenomena? *Attractable phenomena?* What the fuck do they think I am, a buglight?

He lifts my head, the pads of his fingers on my cheekbones, and I hum desperately—*Nnnnnnnnn*—knowing that he can't possibly hear me over Keith Richards' screaming guitar but hoping he may *feel* the sound vibrating in my nasal passages.

He doesn't. Instead he turns my head from side to side.

"No neck injury apparent, no rigor," he says, and I hope he will just let my head go, let my face smack down onto the table—*that'll* make my nose bleed, unless I really *am* dead—but he lowers it gently, considerately, mashing the

17

tip again and once more making suffocation seem a distinct possibility.

"No wounds visible on the back or buttocks," he says, "although there's an old scar on the upper right thigh that looks like some sort of wound, shrapnel perhaps. It's an ugly one."

It *was* ugly, and it *was* shrapnel. The end of my war. A mortar shell lobbed into a supply area, two men killed, one man—me—lucky. It's a lot uglier around front, and in a more sensitive spot, but all the equipment works . . . or did, up until today. A quarter of an inch to the left and they could have fixed me up with a hand pump and a CO_2 cartridge for those intimate moments.

He finally plucks the thermometer out—oh dear God, the relief—and on the wall I can see his shadow holding it up.

"Ninety-four point two," he says. "Gee, that ain't too shabby. This guy could almost be alive, Katie . . . Dr. Arlen."

"Remember where they found him," she says from across the room. The record they are listening to is between selections, and for a moment I can hear her lecturely tones clearly. "Golf course? Summer afternoon? If you'd gotten a reading of ninety-eight point six, I would not be surprised."

"Right, right," he says, sounding chastened. Then: "Is all this going to sound funny on the tape?" Translation: *Will I sound stupid on the tape?*

"It'll sound like a teaching situation," she says, "which is what it is."

"Okay, good. Great."

His rubber-tipped fingers spread my buttocks, then let them go and trail down the backs of my thighs. I would tense now, if I were capable of tensing.

Left leg, I send to him. *Left leg, Petie-boy, left calf, see it?*

He must see it, he *must,* because I can *feel* it, throbbing like a bee sting or maybe a shot given by a clumsy nurse, one who infuses the injection into a muscle instead of hitting the vein.

"Subject is a really good example of what a really bad

idea it is to play golf in shorts," he says, and I find myself wishing he had been born blind. Hell, maybe he *was* born blind, he's sure acting it. "I'm seeing all kinds of bug bites, chigger bites, scratches . . ."

"Mike said they found him in the rough," Arlen calls over. She's making one hell of a clatter; it sounds like she's doing dishes in a cafeteria kitchen instead of filing stuff. "At a guess, he had a heart attack while he was looking for his ball."

"Uh-huh . . ."

"Keep going, Peter, you're doing fine."

I find that an extremely debatable proposition.

"Okay."

More pokes and proddings. Gentle. Too gentle, maybe.

"There are mosquito bites on the left calf that look infected," he says, and although his touch remains gentle, this time the pain is an enormous throb that would make me scream if I were capable of making any sound above the low-pitched hum. It occurs to me suddenly that my life may hang upon the length of the Rolling Stones tape they're listening to . . . always assuming it *is* a tape and not a CD that plays straight through. If it finishes before they cut into me . . . if I can hum loudly enough for them to hear before one of them turns it over to the other side . . .

"I may want to look at the bug bites after the gross autopsy," she says, "although if we're right about his heart, there'll be no need. Or . . . do you want me to look now? They worrying you?"

"Nope, they're pretty clearly mosquito bites," Gimpel the Fool says. "They grow 'em big over on the west side. He's got five . . . seven . . . eight . . . jeez, almost a dozen on his left leg alone."

"He forgot his Deep Woods Off."

"Never mind the Off, he forgot his digitalin," he says, and they have a nice little yock together, autopsy room humor.

This time he flips me by himself, probably happy to use those gym-grown Mr. Strongboy muscles of his, hiding the snakebites and the mosquito bites all around them, camouflaging them. I'm staring up into the bank of fluorescents again. Pete steps backward, out of my view. There's a humming noise. The table begins to slant, and I know why. When they cut me open, the fluids will run downhill to collection points at its base. Plenty of samples for the state lab in Augusta, should there be any questions raised by the autopsy.

I focus all my will and effort on closing my eyes while he's looking down into my face, and cannot produce even a tic. All I wanted was eighteen holes of golf on Saturday afternoon, and instead I turned into Snow White with hair on my chest. And I can't stop wondering what it's going to feel like when those poultry shears go sliding into my midsection.

Pete has a clipboard in one hand. He consults it, sets it aside, then speaks into the mike. His voice is a lot less stilted now. He has just made the most hideous misdiagnosis of his life, but he doesn't know it, and so he's starting to warm up.

"I am commencing the autopsy at five forty-nine P.M.," he says, "on Saturday, August twenty, nineteen ninety-four."

He lifts my lips, looks at my teeth like a man thinking about buying a horse, then pulls my jaw down. "Good color," he says, "and no petechiae on the cheeks." The current tune is fading out of the speakers and I hear a click as he steps on the foot pedal which pauses the recording tape. "Man, this guy really *could* still be alive!"

I hum frantically, and at that same moment Dr. Arlen drops something that sounds like a bedpan. "Doesn't he *wish,*" she says, laughing. He joins in and this time it's cancer I wish on them, some kind that is inoperable and lasts a long time.

He goes quickly down my body, feeling up my chest ("No bruising, swelling, or other exterior signs of cardiac arrest," he says, and what a big fucking surprise *that* is), then palpates my belly.

I burp.

He looks at me, eyes widening, mouth dropping open a

little, and again I try desperately to hum, knowing he won't hear it over "Start Me Up" but thinking that maybe, along with the burp, he'll finally be ready to see what's right in front of him—

"Excuse yourself, Howie," Dr. Arlen, that bitch, says from behind me, and chuckles. "Better watch out, Pete—those postmortem belches are the worst."

He theatrically fans the air in front of his face, then goes back to what he's doing. He barely touches my groin, although he remarks that the scar on the back of my right leg continues around to the front.

Missed the big one, though, I think, *maybe because it's a little higher than you're looking. No big deal, my little* Baywatch *buddy, but you also missed the fact that I'M STILL ALIVE, and that IS a big deal!*

He goes on chanting into the microphone, sounding more and more at ease (sounding, in fact, a little like Jack Klugman on *Quincy, M.E.*), and I know his partner over there behind me, the Pollyanna of the medical community, isn't thinking she'll have to roll the tape back over *this* part of the exam. Other than missing the fact that his first pericardial is still alive, the kid's doing a great job.

At last he says, "I think I'm ready to go on, Doctor." He sounds tentative, though.

She comes over, looks briefly down at me, then squeezes Pete's shoulder. "Okay," she says. "On-na wid-da show!"

Now I'm trying to stick my tongue out. Just that simple kid's gesture of impudence, but it would be enough . . . and it seems to me I can feel a faint prickling sensation deep within my lips, the feeling you get when you're finally starting to come out of a heavy dose of novocaine. And I can feel a twitch? No, wishful thinking, just—

Yes! *Yes!* But a twitch is all, and the second time I try nothing happens.

As Pete picks up the scissors, the Rolling Stones move on to "Hang Fire."

Hold a mirror in front of my nose! I scream at them. *Watch it fog up! Can't you at least do that?*

Snick, snick, snickety-snick.

Pete turns the scissors at an angle so the light runs down the blade, and for the first time I'm certain, really certain, that this mad charade is going to go all the way through to the end. The director isn't going to freeze the frame. The ref isn't going to stop the fight in the tenth round. We're not going to pause for a word from our sponsors. Petie-boy's going to slide those scissors into my gut while I lie here helpless, and then he's going to open me up like a mail-order package from the Horchow Collection.

He looks hesitantly at Dr. Arlen.

No! I howl, my voice reverberating off the dark walls of my skull but emerging from my mouth not at all. *No, please no!*

She nods. "Go ahead. You'll be fine."

"Uh . . . you want to turn off the music?"

Yes! Yes, turn it off!

"Is it bothering you?"

Yes! It's bothering him! It's fucked him up so completely he thinks his patient is dead!

"Well . . ."

"Sure," she says, and disappears from my field of vision. A moment later Mick and Keith are finally gone. I try to make the humming noise and discover a horrible thing: now I can't even do that. I'm too scared. Fright has locked down my vocal cords. I can only stare up as she rejoins him, the two of them gazing down at me like pallbearers looking into an open grave.

"Thanks," he says. Then he takes a deep breath and lifts the scissors. "Commencing pericardial cut."

He slowly brings them down. I see them . . . see them . . . then they're gone from my field of vision. A long moment later, I feel cold steel nestle against my naked upper belly.

He looks doubtfully at the doctor.

"Are you sure you don't—"

"Do you want to make this your field or not, Peter?" she asks him with some asperity.

"You know I do, but—"

"Then cut."

He nods, lips firming. I would close my eyes if I could, but of course I cannot even do that; I can only steel myself against the pain that's only a second or two away now—steel myself for the steel.

"Cutting," he says, bending forward.

"Wait a sec!" she cries.

The dimple of pressure just below my solar plexus eases a little. He looks around at her, surprised, upset, maybe relieved that the crucial moment has been put off—

I feel her rubber-gloved hand slide around my penis as if she means to give me some bizarre handjob, safe sex with the dead, and then she says, "You missed this one, Pete."

He leans over, looking at what she's found—the scar in my groin, at the very top of my right thigh, a glassy, no-pore bowl in the flesh.

Her hand is still holding my cock, holding it out of the way, that's all she's doing, as far as she's concerned she might as well be holding up a sofa cushion so someone else can see the treasure she's found beneath it—coins, a lost wallet, maybe the catnip mouse you haven't been able to find—but something is happening.

Dear wheelchair Jesus on a chariot-driven crutch, *something is happening.*

"And look," she says. Her finger strokes a light, tickly line down the side of my right testicle. "Look at these hairline scars. His testes must have swollen up to damned near the size of grapefruits."

"Lucky he didn't lose one or both."

"You bet your . . . you bet your you-knows," she says, and laughs that mildly suggestive laugh again. Her gloved hand loosens, moves, then pushes down firmly, trying to clear the viewing area. She is doing by accident what you might pay twenty-five or thirty bucks to have done on purpose . . . under other circumstances, of course. "This is a war wound, I think. Hand me that magnifier, Pete."

"But shouldn't I—"

"In a few seconds," she says. *"He's* not going anywhere." She's totally absorbed by what she's found. Her hand is still on me, still pressing down, and what was happening feels like it's *still* happening, but maybe I'm wrong. I *must* be wrong, or he would see it, she would *feel* it—

She bends down and now I can see only her green-clad back, with the ties from her cap trailing down it like odd pigtails. Now, oh my, I can feel her *breath* on me down there.

"Notice the outward radiation," she says. "It was a blast wound of some sort, probably ten years ago at least, we could check his military rec—"

The door bursts open. Pete cries out in surprise. Dr. Arlen doesn't, but her hand tightens involuntarily, she's gripping me again and it's all at once like a hellish variation of the old Naughty Nurse fantasy.

"Don't cut 'im up!" someone screams, and his voice is so high and wavery with fright that I barely recognize Rusty. *"Don't cut 'im up, there was a snake in his golf bag and it bit Mike!"*

They turn to him, eyes wide, jaws dropped; her hand is still gripping me, but she's no more aware of that, at least for the time being, than Petie-boy is aware that he's got one hand clutching the left breast of his scrub gown. He looks like *he's* the one with the clapped-out fuel pump.

"What . . . what are you . . . ." Pete begins.

"Knocked him flat!" Rusty was saying—babbling. "He's gonna be okay, I guess, but he can hardly talk! Little brown snake, I never saw one like it in my life, it went under the loadin' bay, it's under there right now, but that's not the important part! I think it already bit that guy we brought in. I think . . . holy shit, Doc, whatja tryin' to do? Stroke 'im back to life?"

She looks around, dazed, at first not sure of what he's talking about . . . until she realizes that she's now holding a mostly erect penis. And as she screams—screams and snatches the shears out of Pete's limp gloved hand—I find myself thinking again of that old Alfred Hitchcock TV show.

Poor old Joseph Cotton, I think.

He only got to *cry.*

Afternote

It's been a year since my experience in Autopsy Room Four, and I have made a complete recovery, although the paralysis was both stubborn and scary; it was a full month before I began to recover the finer motions of my fingers and toes. I still can't play the piano, but then, of course, I never could. That is a joke, and I make no apologies for it. In the first three months after my misadventure, I think that my ability to joke provided a slim but vital margin between sanity and some sort of nervous breakdown. Unless you've actually felt the tip of a pair of postmortem shears poking into your stomach, you don't know what I mean.

Two weeks or so after my close call, a woman on Dupont Street called the Derry Police to complain of a "foul stink" coming from the house next door. That house belonged to a bachelor bank clerk named Walter Kerr. Police found the house empty . . . of human life, that is. In the basement they found over sixty snakes of different varieties. About half of them were dead—starvation and dehydration—but many were extremely lively . . . and extremely dangerous. Several were very rare, and one was of a species believed to have been extinct since mid-century, according to consulting zoologists.

Kerr failed to show up for work at Derry Community Bank on August 22, two days after I was bitten, one day after the story ("Paralyzed Man Escapes Deadly Autopsy," the headline read; at one point I was quoted as saying I had been "scared stiff") broke in the press.

There was a snake for every cage in Kerr's basement menagerie . . . except for one. The empty cage was unmarked, and the snake that popped out of my golf bag (the ambulance orderlies had packed it in with my "corpse" and had been practicing chip shots out in the ambulance parking area) was never found. The toxin in my bloodstream—the same toxin found to a far lesser degree in orderly Mike

Hopper's bloodstream—was documented but never identified. I have looked at a great many pictures of snakes in the last year, and have found at least one that has reportedly caused cases of full-body paralysis in humans. This is the Peruvian Boomslang, a nasty viper that has supposedly been extinct since the 1920s. Dupont Street is less than half a mile from the Derry Municipal Golf Course. Most of the intervening land consists of scrub woods and vacant lots.

One final note. Katie Arlen and I dated for four months, November 1994 through February of 1995. We broke it off by mutual consent, due to sexual incompatibility.

I was impotent unless she was wearing rubber gloves.

HAUNTED

Charles Grant

HE HAD NO NAME.

The good ones never do.

Like ghosts without chains, they haunt parking lots and parks, houses and shops, street corners and alleys, churches and schools, and it doesn't make any difference whether you can see them or not.

No matter where you live, the place you live is haunted. You just can't tell who all the ghosts are.

I saw him for the first time the night after it rained, about a year ago last spring. I was home, and getting ready to do the town like I do most nights when the weather's good, to fill my stomach, stretch my legs.

First thing, I folded the cardboard carefully at the creases, taking care not to rip it because it was a little soggy from that shower. Then I took it and my blankets a little way down the alley, away from the light, away from the Dumpster. You have to do that, see. You don't, when they come to take the garbage, sometimes they take the cardboard, too.

Then I made sure my hair wasn't sticking out like it does sometimes when it gets too dirty, too greasy. You should see

27

me then. Little black swizzle sticks poking out at the air. Silly. Really silly. And I can't look silly if I want to eat.

After that, I make sure my coat doesn't have a whole lot of alley stuff sticking to it. A bum, a real bum, not one of those sickos, doesn't want to look like one unless he has to. My coat, for example, it's a pretty nice dark brown I found the winter before. Fits okay, and it kind of matches my pants. My shoes aren't too bad, either. I try to keep them clean. Doesn't always work, though, and then I have to find a new pair. Once, all I could get was a pair of sneakers, and I damn near starved, I looked so stupid.

Finally, when I was sure little children wouldn't go screaming for their mothers, I went out to the street.

The rain had left a sheen over everything, like thin ice without the cold. Steam slipping from a manhole cover. Streetlights extra bright. Puddles here and there, catching neon like colored stones or sad faces. Sometimes I try to take one and put it in my pocket for luck.

That night there was nothing out there, and it made me kind of nervous. No cars, no one on the sidewalks, no one hanging around the stores or diner or bars or the movie theater up there at the corner. It happens once in a while. A brief moment that lasts far too long, when you're the only one left in the whole wide world.

Times like that, I just start walking, slapping my shoes hard on the pavement, hoping the noise will get everything moving.

It usually does.

It did that night.

Suddenly there were guys hanging at the bar door, a couple heading for the movies, a bus hissing and hitching around the corner, cars slipping along the blacktop through the night and the neon. Pedestrians on their way from one place to another. Not a lot, though, since it was a weeknight. I watched them carefully, watched their faces without looking right at them. Most nights they don't see me; some nights a face creases and lips come together, and that's when I know it's time to head for the shelter over at St. Luke's. It's the only time I go—when I need a shower, maybe a shave. Otherwise, I pretty much stay away. They got counselors there, always asking questions, always making suggestions, always writing things down in these little notebooks of theirs. Nice enough, most of them, and well meaning in their way, but when push comes to fall, most of them don't know what it's like to live at the bottom of a well without water.

My first stop was at Chou Lin's, where the cook usually has something for me. Egg rolls, that night. So I took out the garbage for him, and swept the sidewalk in front of the restaurant. When I was done, I brought the broom back, and he asked me if I had a gun or a knife or something. I smiled and told him I was okay, but thanks anyway. He said I was crazy, I was gonna get killed, all the nuts on the loose. I laughed and moved on. It was nice that he worried, though. It made me feel kind of good.

Next stop was across the street at the Limelight, where I went down the side alley. A couple of the regular waiters had left me leftover sandwiches on top of a trash can; for that I picked up a bucket and a sponge, and washed the front window, not looking at the folks inside, the folks inside not looking at me. When I was done, I ate the sandwiches, drank some coffee, while the owner came out for a smoke, and we talked about the weather and some sports and ain't life a bitch.

I stayed away from the bars.

I'm a bum, not a drunk.

Then, because it was still kind of warm, I decided to head on up to the park, across the street from the theater. I have a bench there, near the bus stop, where I watch the people and the traffic, read the newspaper or a magazine, whatever I've scrounged from the trash, until it's time to go to bed, or until I get restless and have to walk. Just to keep from screaming.

Now this park isn't very big, just a few blocks on each side. No walls, but there's a ten-foot, thick and thorned hedge all around it. The only way in or out, unless you want to cut yourself to shreds, is between two stone pillars on each side. So when I'm on my bench like I was that night, I can hear real interesting things behind me sometimes. Guys throwing up before they go back to the bars, people arguing about stuff, people using the shrubs for a bathroom, and when the night's warm, a little moaning and thrashing now and then.

There hadn't been any of that for a long time now, though.

There was always a couple, three weeks when it was silent in there, right after somebody died.

People got scared, they stayed away.

Then they'd come back, one by one, and pretty soon the night noises were the same as always.

Until the next time.

That night I didn't have anything to read, so I watched the world instead from my seat on the east side. No reflections, though. No beating my breast, demanding answers from the gods. I got over that years ago. So I was just checking the world out, when a voice said, "Hey, Tex."

That isn't my name.

I looked up, smiled politely, nodded a hello to the cop standing there. Mahaffey wasn't young, puffed cheeks and puffy eyes, a paunch and broad hips. He'd heard me whistling a cowboy song one day a couple of years before; damned if he hadn't recognized it, and ever since, I'd been "Tex."

It was better than nothing.

It was better than what he called the other guys on the street.

We didn't talk much. He didn't want to save me, and I didn't want to be saved. I have my job; he has his. When he got bored, he walked on, warning me not to wander off, be alone. I thanked him politely, and snuggled back to keep on watching.

I saw *him* about two hours later.

Most of the street was gone by then. Only a bus every so often, once in a while a car. The smell of more rain. The smell of exhaust and fresh wet leaves.

He came out of the park about a hundred feet from where I sat, hands in his pockets, glitter in his hair until I realized it was droplets of water. He walked up the street, away from me, not looking anyplace in particular, taking his time, and disappeared into the dark up where the streetlamps had gone out.

A couple of minutes later, a man fell out of the park, screaming once as he staggered to the curb, grabbing a tree trunk and holding on for a few seconds before he slid slowly, very slowly, into the street.

He was red.

He was all red and shiny.

I thought about going over there; I thought about trying to find a cop; I thought about the man I had seen, walking away.

I thought about saddling up, ol' Tex on the trail, but by then it was too late.

A car stopped right away, the driver had a phone, and before I knew it, there were cops and ambulances and TV cameras and yellow ribbons and cars all over the place. More noise than I could stand on such a pretty spring night.

No one talked to me.

No one asked me any questions.

I got up and went home.

I dreamed that I could walk through walls.

I dreamed that the colored stones and faces I picked up stayed in my pocket, so I could dream about them some more.

I dreamed about Tex Ritter and Roy Rogers, Clint Eastwood and a dead tree with a branch that held a single empty noose.

The next day I stayed in my cardboard shack, thinking about all the people who had been killed over the last twelve months. At least those I knew about. Newspapers mostly didn't say much except another man or woman had been murdered, probably by muggers.

It's a big city.

People die all the time.

But when I saw that man walking away, hands in his pockets, I knew he had done it. That he had done them all.

And I figured I had to do something; I just didn't know exactly what.

So I did a lot of traveling those next few weeks. Every part of the city that touched the park, that touched my neighborhood. Sometimes I walked, sometimes I saddled up the old bronc and rode, just to show the flag.

I saw a whole lot of things, but I didn't see him.

"No wonder you're so damn skinny," Mahaffey the cop said to me one day. "You never stay still, Tex, you know that? You're always on the move. Man, your legs must be like iron from all that walking."

I sniffed, hitched my gunbelt a little higher, narrowed my eyes at a couple of guys leaving the movie theater. "Gotta keep my eyes peeled, you know what I mean? Ain't healthy around here these days, 'case you hadn't noticed."

"Tell me about it. Chief's on my ass every goddam second." He yanked angrily on the bill of his cap. "Just catch one, that's all they want. Catch one of those bastards and feed him to the press." He laughed, but he wasn't happy. A couple more minutes talking like that, and I realized they would throw him behind a desk, maybe hand him his hat and his pension, if someone else died on his shift. "Just one," he whispered, and walked away, swinging his night stick, glaring at the stores.

I wanted to help, but someone down at City Hall suddenly decided maybe it was one of us. The guys on the street. The ones nobody ever sees.

Before I knew it, on a blue sky Saturday morning, about as fine a late spring day as you're going to get in this world, all these vans come around, cops boil out, TV cameras and reporters dancing around the edges, and we all get hauled in. Vagrancy. Drugs. Prostitution, both sexes. Disturbing the peace. Public nuisance. Everything, anything they could think of to make it legitimate.

Now I hate to say it, but naturally, some of it was true. Some guys do deal a little, do get drunk a lot and piss on someone's brand new shoes, do try to sell themselves for a bottle of red, other disgusting stuff like that. Makes a bad name for the rest of us. Makes it like we're no better than trash, or worse, a bothersome ring around someone's fancy tub. Take a sponge, wipe it away, all gone, all gone.

Until the next time someone decides to take a bath.

So some of us actually ended up staying with the city for quite a while. The rest of us, like me, eventually got hooked up with public defenders, the righteous kind, who eventually pulled and squeezed us through the system and back outside.

It took me two weeks and a couple of days before I saw my neighborhood again.

During that second week, I read in the paper that a woman walking her dog was knifed in front of her apartment house, on the other side of the park. The dog, too.

I never had a dog, I don't think. But I was married once, maybe, so maybe I had a dog then.

I don't know.

But that was pretty low, killing the dog.

It made me mad.

It made me wonder what the world was coming to when a guy goes on vacation for a couple of weeks, comes back, and finds out the bad guys have taken over his town.

It made me madder.

I don't know how long it took me after that. I know I sat in my shack, thinking hard, thinking harder, looking at things a whole new way than I used to.

The cook at Chou Lin's wanted to know if something was wrong, did they beat me up or something when I was in jail; it wouldn't have been the first time.

The owner of the Limelight told me to stop screwing around, get a life, stop living like a damn alley cat, for God's sake. Then we shared a smoke and a tuna sandwich, a hit or two of something throat-burning from a silver flask of his, the city's going to hell and ain't life a bitch.

Mahaffey was gone.

The new cop, a young kid with incredible green eyes and a pair of lips that would shrink a lemon, wouldn't tell me what happened, just snarled a little and told me to get my sorry ass off his beat before he ran me in.

He didn't even call me "Tex."

I knew the kind, though. Looking for a ribbon on his chest, a piece of paper that tells the world what a good cop he is. Looking for another notch on his belt.

I see them all the time.

They never last.

They never do.

That's when I went back to the alley and did some more thinking.

That's when I dreamed of faces in puddles and stars in the gutters and the bronc and me, riding down the street, riding out of the storm.

The next day, I knew what I had to do.

First thing after breakfast, I cleaned myself up real good, even went so far as to get over to St. Luke's for a shower and a shave. Then I went down to the library to check all the old papers. Cops do this all the time, I wasn't stupid, I knew that. Not the library, of course; they had their own papers and reports. So I was surprised when I saw something that maybe they hadn't noticed.

I checked, I double-checked, I tore a blank page from the back of a book and wrote it all down with a pencil I borrowed from the librarian lady. I read it five times. I read the papers again. Then I hurried outside, surprised that the sun had already gone down. It took me a second to get my bearings, remember where I was, what I was doing, then I practically ran all the way back, looking for that cop.

I found him coming out of Diamond Lil's, scowling, just looking for a fight.

"Excuse me, Deputy," I said, respectful as always.

"What the hell do you want?"

I showed him the paper, and he looked at it like it was going to eat him alive or give him some disease. "Read it, please," I said. "It's about those people—"

"Aw, Jesus H." He pushed me aside and headed up toward the park.

"Hey!" I called after him. "Hey, no, really!"

He looked over his shoulder. "Listen, scumbag, you keep bothering me like this, I'm . . ." He shook his head, waved a hand in disgust, and kept on moving.

Pedestrians all around, not looking at me but bumping into me just the same. Turning me a little this way, turning me a little that way. I wanted someone to have the paper, to know what I knew, but no one would take it.

Just like the cop, they kept on walking.

Years ago, I don't know when anymore, I walked out of my house and walked into the sunset.

I don't know why.

I just did.

I don't know; maybe I was haunted.

I dreamed of faces in puddles and wagon trains on dusty trails and faces in the sky that looked down and didn't see me.

I dreamed of Mahaffey and St. Luke's and the filth that I live in every day of my life.

I dreamed of sneaking through the woods and stepping on a twig that snapped in half and woke a lion that charged out of a cave and clawed out my heart.

I dreamed of looking in a mirror, just to see who was there.

Money is something I don't have a whole lot of use for. Been getting along pretty good without it for years, but I do get it just the same. When I do, I keep a few bucks in my pocket for when Chou Lin's is closed, and I bury the rest. Here and there. Mostly there. The farther away it is, the less tempted I am to use it. Once in a while someone finds it and steals it, but that's okay. There's more. Here and there.

I felt strange the next day.

I didn't like it, and couldn't explain it.

I walked a mile or so from the alley, to another park, a strange park I barely remembered. I forced my way through a thicket to a tiny clearing in the center, and dug up a coffee can that had some of the dollars I'm pretty sure were mine.

I walked another mile in a different direction, and I found a man who sold me what I wanted without asking a single question except did I have the money, you old fart, to pay for this thing.

He was pretty surprised when I did.

Then I walked back home, stood in the mouth of the alley, and watched the street get ready for nightfall. I was tired, very tired, and I was so hungry I could barely stand on my aching feet. I couldn't eat, though. I needed to rest. I had stood in front of an appliance store for nearly two hours before I saw the news. Faces talking without sound on the other side of the glass. I didn't need to hear them. Halfway through, I had seen exactly what I wanted.

So when the street emptied of its daytime and filled again with its night, I went back to my shack and shook the blankets out before spreading them on the floor. I took off my shoes, rubbed my feet, took off my coat, and used it for a cover.

The trouble was, I couldn't sleep right away.

All I could do was stare at the strip of sky over my head, looking for stars and seeing nothing but a hazy glow, and beyond that, empty black.

The bronc whickered softly, stamped a hoof once.

A rat scurried by, bumping into my boots and making the spurs sing softly.

I smelled piss and vomit and hay and dust and gasoline and exhaust and leather and trail heat.

"You know something, Tex?" Mahaffey said to me once. "You and me, we ought to chuck it all and move to Montana, buy a ranch, and watch cows eat grass for the rest of our lives." Then he laughed so hard, he nearly fell over.

I closed my eyes, and woke up to a hot sun fighting off the coming of a storm.

I stayed in the shack all day, and no one came near me.

I watched people walk by and not once look in.

I watched a dog root around the Dumpster, then zigzag from wall to stained wall until he saw me, and whined, and ran like hell for the street.

I stood up at sunset and strapped on my guns.

I put on my duster, my hat, and the saddle on my bronc.

I walked to the sidewalk just as the rain began to fall, light and easy, riding a breeze to the street, raising the smell of wet blacktop, dripping off awnings and hats, making a halo around the streetlamp, settling into puddles that caught the neon and held it.

I didn't move.

It poured for about ten minutes, washing the world away, and I still didn't move.

When the storm left, leaving a drizzle behind, I stretched a little to ease my legs and arms, and wondered which direction I should take first.

An easy decision.

He came out of the theater, wearing a light jacket, pressed trousers, good shoes, good shirt. He paused under the marquee to cup his hands around a match while he lit a cigarette.

I moved.

He flicked the match into the gutter and headed for the park.

I moved, but I took my time. I was a little nervous, but I wasn't worried. It had rained, and he was there; that's all I needed to know.

He entered the park through the south gate, around the corner from my bench. I didn't look at him, didn't look at anyone, didn't hesitate at all when I walked through the east gate, following the blacktop path that would eventually meet in a large blacktop circle around a large marble fountain with benches all around.

Once inside, the night was silent.

No cars, no buses, no footsteps, no birds, no calling across the street to a friend or a neighbor.

Just me, taking it slow, taking it easy, hands in my pockets, moving through pools of light that held raindrops like falling diamonds.

I was just about in the middle when I heard a noise in the bushes off to my right. It sounded like someone coughing his lungs out, trying to get a breath, trying not to strangle.

"Hey," I said, not quite yelling, trying to sound like I cared. "Are you okay?"

A man answered, "I . . . oh, Jesus," and coughed again.

I walked over, edged past a high shrub, and saw him down on one knee, a hand pressed hard against his chest.

"Jesus God," he said, gasping a little, looking up at me, tears on his cheeks. "I think I'm having a heart attack."

I stepped closer, and his other hand came up from the ground. It held a knife, and he was grinning as he sprang.

My hand was quicker.

My sideways step was quicker.

My arm was longer.

So was my knife.

It didn't take very long, and there wasn't as much blood as I'd thought there would be.

And when it was over, he lay on his stomach, with his head turned toward me, lying in a puddle.

That was the easy part.

The hard part was taking his face for my pocket.

Now the bronc and me, we've been a lot of places in the past year or so.

Riding from town to town, doing our job, and riding out again.

When my pocket gets filled, I empty it into a can and bury it in a park, or beside a railroad track, or behind a lone bus stop in the middle of nowhere.

The thing is, I'm never in a hurry, even though there's lots to do.

There's always an alley or a bench or a depot or a barn; there's always a Chou Lin's, and there's always a Mahaffey, and a young kid looking to add another notch to his gun.

And there's always a ghost, who's always surprised to see me.

And when he learns, he learns too late: I don't have a name, either.

The good ones never do.

OUT THERE
IN THE DARKNESS

Ed Gorman

1

THE NIGHT IT ALL STARTED, THE WHOLE STRANGE SPIRAL, WE were having our usual midweek poker game—four fortyish men who work in the financial business getting together for beer and bawdy jokes and straight poker. No wild card games. We hate them.

This was summer, and vacation time, and so it happened that the game was held two weeks in a row at my house. Jan had taken the kids to see her Aunt Wendy and Uncle Verne at their fishing cabin, and so I offered to have the game at my house this week, too. With nobody there to supervise, the beer could be laced with a little bourbon, and the jokes could get even bawdier. With the wife and kids in the house, you're always at least a little bit intimidated.

Mike and Bob came together, bearing gifts, which in this case meant the kind of sexy magazines our wives did not want in the house in case the kids might stumble across them. At least that's what they say. I think they sense, and rightly, that the magazines might give their spouses bad ideas about taking the secretary out for a few after-work drinks, or stopping by a singles bar some night.

We got the chips and cards set up at the table, we got the first beers open (Mike chasing a shot of bourbon with his beer), and we started passing the dirty magazines around with tenth-grade glee. The magazines compensated, I suppose, for the balding head, the bloating belly, the stooping shoulders. Deep in the heart of every hundred-year-old man is a horny fourteen-year-old boy.

All this, by the way, took place up in the attic. The four of us got to know one another when we all moved into what city planners called a "transitional neighborhood." There were some grand old houses that could be renovated with enough money and real care. The city designated a ten-square-block area as one it wanted to restore to shiny new luster. Jan and I chose a crumbling Victorian. You wouldn't recognize it today. And that includes the attic, which I've turned into a very nice den.

"Pisses me off," Mike O'Brien said. "He's always late."

And that was true. Neil Solomon *was* always late. Never by that much but always late nonetheless.

"At least tonight he has a good excuse," Bob Genter said.

"He does?" Mike said. "He's probably swimming in his pool." Neil recently got a bonus that made him the first owner of a full-size outdoor pool in our neighborhood.

"No, he's got patrol. But he's stopping at nine. He's got somebody trading with him for next week."

"Oh, hell," Mike said, obviously sorry that he'd complained. "I didn't know that."

Bob Genter's handsome black head nodded solemnly.

Patrol is something we all take very seriously in this newly restored "transitional neighborhood." Eight months ago, the burglaries started, and they've gotten pretty bad. My house has been burglarized once and vandalized once. Bob and Mike have had curb-sitting cars stolen. Neil's wife, Sarah, was surprised in her own kitchen by a burglar. And then there was the killing four months ago, man and wife who'd just moved into the neighborhood, savagely stabbed to death in their own bed. The police caught the guy a few days later trying to cash some of the traveler's checks he'd stolen after killing his prey. He was typical of the kind of man who infested this neighborhood after sundown: a twentyish junkie stoned to the point of psychosis on various street drugs, and not at all averse to murdering people he envied and despised. He also knew a whole hell of a lot about fooling burglar alarms.

After the murders there was a neighborhood meeting, and that's when we came up with the patrol, something somebody'd read about being popular back east. People think that a nice middle-sized Midwestern city like ours doesn't have major crime problems. I invite them to walk many of these streets after dark. They'll quickly be disabused of that notion. Anyway, the patrol worked this way: each night, two neighborhood people got in the family van and patrolled the ten-block area that had been restored. If they saw anything suspicious, they used their cellular phones and called police. We jokingly called it the Baby-Boomer Brigade. The patrol had one strict rule: you were never to take direct action unless somebody's life was at stake. Always, always use the cellular phone and call the police.

Neil had patrol tonight. He'd be rolling in here in another half hour. The patrol had two shifts: early, eight to ten; late, ten to twelve.

Bob said, "You hear what Evans suggested?"

"About guns?" I said.

"Yeah."

"Makes me a little nervous," I said.

"Me, too," Bob said. For somebody who'd grown up in the worst area of the city, Bob Genter was a very polished guy. Whenever he joked that he was the token black, Neil always countered with the fact that he was the token Jew, just as Mike was the token Catholic and I was the token Methodist. We were friends of convenience, I suppose, but we all really did like one another, something that was demonstrated when Neil had a cancer scare a few years back. Bob, Mike, and I were in his hospital room twice a day, all eight days running.

"I think it's time," Mike said. "The bad guys have guns, so the good guys should have guns."

"The good guys are the cops," I said. "Not us."

"People start bringing guns on patrol," Bob said, "somebody innocent is going to get shot."

"So some night one of us here is on patrol and we see a bad guy and he sees us and before the cops get there, the bad guy shoots us? You don't think that's going to happen?"

"It *could* happen, Mike," I said, "but I just don't think that justifies carrying guns."

The argument gave us something to do while we waited for Neil.

"Sorry I'm late," Neil Solomon said after he followed me up the attic and came inside.

"We already drank all the beer," Mike O'Brien said loudly.

Neil smiled. "That gut you're carrying lately, I can believe that *you* drank all the beer."

Mike always enjoyed being put down by Neil, possibly because most people were a bit intimidated by him—he had that angry Irish edge—and he seemed to enjoy Neil's skilled and fearless handling of him. He laughed with real pleasure.

Neil sat down, I got him a beer from the tiny fridge I keep up here, cards were dealt, seven-card stud was played.

Bob said, "How'd patrol go tonight?"

Neil shrugged. "No problems."

"I still say we should carry guns," Mike said.

"You're not going to believe this, but I agree with you," Neil said.

"Seriously?" Mike said.

"Oh, great," I said to Bob Genter. "Another beer commercial cowboy."

Bob smiled. "Where I come from, we didn't have cowboys, we had 'mothas.'" He laughed. "Mean mothas, let me tell you. And practically *all* of them carried guns."

"That mean you're siding with them?" I said.

Bob looked at his cards again, then shrugged. "Haven't decided yet, I guess."

I didn't think the antigun people were going to lose this

round. But I worried about the round after it, a few months down the line, when the subject of carrying guns came up again. All the TV coverage violence gets in this city, people are more and more developing a siege mentality.

"Play cards," Mike said, "and leave the debate society crap till later."

Good idea.

We played cards.

In forty-five minutes, I lost $63.82. Mike and Neil always played as if their lives were at stake. All you had to do was watch their faces. Gunfighters couldn't have looked more serious or determined.

The first pit stop came just after ten o'clock, and Neil took it. There was a john on the second floor between the bedrooms, and another john on the first floor.

Neil said, "The good Dr. Gottesfeld had to give me a finger-wave this afternoon, gents, so this may take a while."

"You should trade that prostate of yours in for a new one," Mike said.

"Believe me, I'd like to."

While Neil was gone, the three of us started talking about the patrol again, and whether we should go armed.

We made the same old arguments. The passion was gone. We were just marking time waiting for Neil, and we knew it.

Finally, Mike said, "Let me see some of those magazines again."

"You got some identification?" I said.

"I'll show you some identification," Mike said.

"Spare me," I said. "I'll just give you the magazines."

"You mind if I use the john on the first floor?" Bob said.

"Yeah, it would really piss me off," I said.

"Really?"

That was one thing about Bob. He always fell for deadpan humor.

"No, not really," I said. "Why would I care if you used the john on the first floor?"

He grinned. "Thought maybe they were segregated facilities or something."

He left.

Mike said, "We're lucky, you know that?"

"You mean me and you?"

"Yeah."

"Lucky how?"

"Those two guys. They're great guys. I wish I had them at work." He shook his head. "Treacherous bastards. That's all I'm around all day long."

"No offense, but I'll bet you can be pretty treacherous yourself."

He smiled. "Look who's talking."

The first time I heard it, I thought it was some kind of animal noise from outside, a dog or a cat in some kind of discomfort maybe. Mike, who was dealing himself a hand of solitaire, didn't even look up from his cards.

But the second time I heard the sound, Mike and I both looked up. And then we heard the exploding sound of breaking glass.

"What the hell is that?" Mike said.

"Let's go find out."

Just about the time we reached the bottom of the attic steps, we saw Neil coming out of the second-floor john. "You hear that?"

"Sure as hell did," I said.

We reached the staircase leading to the first floor. Everything was dark. Mike reached for the light switch, but I brushed his hand away.

I put a *sshing* finger to my lips and then showed him the Louisville Slugger I'd grabbed from Tim's room. He's my nine-year-old, and his most devout wish is to be a good baseball player. His mother has convinced him that just because I went to college on a baseball scholarship, I was a good player. I wasn't. I was a lucky player.

I led the way downstairs, keeping the bat ready at all times.

"You sonofabitch!"

The voice belonged to Bob.

More smashing glass.

I listened to the passage of the sound. Kitchen. Had to be the kitchen.

In the shadowy light from the street, I saw their faces, Mike's and Neil's. They looked scared.

I hefted the bat some more and then started moving fast to the kitchen.

Just as we passed through the dining room, I heard something heavy hit the kitchen floor. Something human and heavy.

I got the kitchen light on.

He was at the back door. White. Tall. Blond shoulder-length hair. Filthy tan T-shirt. Greasy jeans. He had grabbed one of Jan's carving knives from the huge iron rack that sits atop the butcher-block island. The one curious thing about him was the eyes: there was a malevolent iridescence to the blue pupils, an angry but somehow alien intelligence, a silver glow.

Bob was sprawled facedown on the tile floor. His arms were spread wide on either side of him. He didn't seem to be moving. Chunks and fragments of glass were strewn everywhere across the floor. My uninvited guest had smashed two or three of the colorful pitchers we'd bought the winter before in Mexico.

"Run!" the burglar cried to somebody on the back porch.

He turned, waving the butcher knife back and forth to keep us at bay.

Footsteps out the back door.

The burglar held us off a few more moments, but then I gave him a little bit of tempered Louisville Slugger wood right across the wrist. The knife went clattering.

By this time, Mike and Neil were pretty crazed. They jumped him, hurled him back against the door, and then started putting in punches wherever they'd fit.

"Hey!" I said, and tossed Neil the bat. "Just hold this. If he makes a move, open up his head. Otherwise leave him alone."

They really were crazed, like pit bulls who'd been pulled back just as a fight was starting to get good.

"Mike, call the cops and tell them to send a car."

I got Bob up and walking. I took him into the bathroom and sat him down on the toilet lid. I found a lump the size of an egg on the back of his head. I soaked a clean washcloth with cold water and pressed it against the lump. Bob took it from there.

"You want an ambulance?" I said.

"An ambulance? Are you kidding? You must think I'm a ballet dancer or something."

I shook my head. "No, I know better than that. I've got a male cousin who's a ballet dancer, and he's one tough sonofabitch, believe me. You—" I smiled. "You aren't that tough, Bob."

"I don't need an ambulance. I'm fine."

He winced and tamped the washcloth tighter against his head. "Just a little headache is all." He looked young suddenly, the aftershock of fear in his brown eyes. "Scared the hell out of me. Heard something when I was leaving the john. Went out to the kitchen to check it out. He jumped me."

"What'd he hit you with?"

"No idea."

"I'll go get you some whiskey. Just sit tight."

"I love sitting in bathrooms, man."

I laughed. "I don't blame you."

When I got back to the kitchen, they were gone. All three of them. Then I saw the basement door. It stood open a few inches. I could see dusty light in the space between door and frame. The basement was our wilderness. We hadn't had the time or money to really fix it up yet. We were counting on this year's Christmas bonus from the Winsdor Financial Group to help us set it right.

I went down the stairs. The basement is one big, mostly unused room except for the washer and dryer in the corner. All the boxes and odds and ends that should have gone to the attic instead went down here. It smells damp most of the time. The idea is to turn it into a family room for when the boys are older. These days it's mostly inhabited by stray waterbugs.

When I reached the bottom step, I saw them. There are four metal support poles in the basement, near each corner.

They had him lashed to a pole in the east quadrant, lashed his wrists behind him with rope found in the tool room. They also had him gagged with what looked like a pillowcase. His eyes were big and wide. He looked scared, and I didn't blame him. I was scared, too.

"What the hell are you guys doing?"

"Just calm down, Papa Bear," Mike said. That's his name for me whenever he wants to convey to people that I'm kind of this old fuddy-duddy. It so happens that Mike is two years older than I am, and it also happens that I'm not a fuddy-duddy. Jan has assured me of that, and she's completely impartial.

"Knock off the Papa Bear bullshit. Did you call the cops?"

"Not yet," Neil said. "Just calm down a little, all right?"

"You haven't called the cops. You've got some guy tied up and gagged in my basement. You haven't even asked how Bob is. And you want me to calm down."

Mike came up to me then. He still had that air of pit-bull craziness about him, frantic, uncontrollable, alien.

"We're going to do what the cops *can't* do, man," he said. "We're going to sweat this sonofabitch. We're going to make him tell us who he was with tonight, and then we're going to make him give us every single name of every single bad guy who works this neighborhood. And then we'll turn all the names over to the cops."

"It's just an extension of the patrol," Neil said. "Just keeping our neighborhood safe is all."

"You guys are nuts," I said, and turned back toward the steps. "I'm going up and call the cops."

That's when I realized just how crazed Mike was. "You aren't going anywhere, man. You're going to stay here and help us break this bastard down. You're going to do your goddamned neighborhood *duty.*"

He'd grabbed my sleeve so hard that he'd torn it at the shoulder. We both discovered this at the same time.

I expected him to look sorry. He didn't. In fact, he was smirking at me. "Don't be such a wimp, Aaron," he said.

2

Mike led the charge getting the kitchen cleaned up. I think he was feeling guilty about calling me a wimp with such angry exuberance. Now I understood how lynch mobs got formed. One guy like Mike stirring people up by alternately insulting them and urging them on.

After the kitchen was put back in order, and after I'd taken inventory to find that nothing had been stolen, I went to the refrigerator and got beers for everybody. Bob had drifted back to the kitchen, too.

"All right," I said. "Now that we've all calmed down, I want to walk over to that yellow kitchen wall phone there and call the police. Any objections?"

"I think blue would look better in here than yellow," Neil said.

"Funny," I said.

They looked like themselves now, no feral madness on the faces of Mike and Neil, no winces on Bob's.

I started across the floor to the phone.

Neil grabbed my arm. Not with the same insulting force Mike had used on me. But enough to get the job done.

"I think Mike's right," Neil said. "I think we should grill that bastard a little bit."

I shook my head, politely removed his hand from my forearm, and proceeded to the phone.

"This isn't just your decision alone," Mike said.

He'd finally had his way. He'd succeeded in making me angry. I turned around and looked at him. "This is my house, Mike. If you don't like my decisions, then I'd suggest you leave."

We both took steps toward each other. Mike would no doubt win any battle we had, but I'd at least be able to inflict a little damage, and right now that's all I was thinking about.

Neil got between us.

"Hey," he said. "For God's sake, you two, c'mon. We're friends, remember?"

"This is my house," I said, my words childish in my ears.

"Yeah, but we live in the same neighborhood, Aaron," Mike said, "which makes this 'our' problem."

"He's right, Aaron," Bob said from the breakfast nook. There's a window there where I sometimes sit to watch all the animals on sunny days. I saw a mother raccoon and four baby raccoons one day, marching single-file across the grass. My grandparents were the last generation to live on the farm. My father came to town here and ultimately became a vice president of a ball bearing company. Raccoons are a lot more pleasant to gaze upon than people.

"He's not right," I said to Bob. "He's wrong. We're not cops, we're not bounty hunters, we're not trackers. We're a bunch of goddamned guys who peddle stocks and bonds. Mike and Neil shouldn't have tied him up downstairs—that happens to be illegal, at least the way they went about it— and now I'm going to call the cops."

"Yes, that poor thing," Mike said. "Aren't we just picking on him, though? Tell you what, why don't we make him something to eat?"

"Just make sure we have the right wine to go with it," Neil said. "Properly chilled, of course."

"Maybe we could get him a chick," Bob said.

"With bombers out to here," Mike said, indicating with his hands where "here" was.

I couldn't help it. I smiled. They were all being ridiculous. A kind of fever had caught them.

"You really want to go down there and question him?" I said to Neil.

"Yes. We can ask him things the cops can't."

"Scare the bastard a little," Mike said. "So he'll tell us who was with him tonight, and who else works this neighborhood." He came over and put his hand out. "God, man, you're one of my best friends. I don't want you mad at me."

Then he hugged me, which is something I've never been comfortable with men doing, but to the extent I could, I hugged him back.

"Friends?" he said.

"Friends," I said. "But I still want to call the cops."

"And spoil our fun?" Neil said.

"And spoil your fun."

"I say we take it to a vote," Bob said.

"This isn't a democracy," I said. "It's my house and I'm the king. I don't want to have a vote."

"Can we ask him one question?" Bob said.

I sighed. They weren't going to let go. "One question?"

"The names of the guys he was with tonight."

"And that's it?"

"That's it. That way we get him and his pals off the street."

"And then I call the cops?"

"Then," Mike said, "you call the cops."

"One question," Neil said.

While we finished our beers, we argued a little more, but they had a lot more spirit left than I did. I was tired now and missing Jan and the kids and feeling lonely. These three guys had become strangers to me tonight. Very old boys eager to play at boy games once again.

"One question," I said. "Then I call the cops."

I led the way down, sneezing as I did so.

There's alway enough dust floating around in the basement to play hell with my sinuses.

The guy was his same sullen self, glaring at us as we descended the stairs and then walked over to him. He smelled of heat and sweat and city grime. The long bare arms sticking out of his filthy T-shirt told tattoo tales of writhing snakes and leaping panthers. The arms were joined in the back with rope. His jaw still flexed, trying to accommodate the intrusion of the gag.

"Maybe we should castrate him," Mike said, walking up close to the guy. "You like that, scumbag? If we castrated you?"

If the guy felt any fear, it wasn't evident in his eyes. All you could see there was the usual contempt.

"I'll bet this is the jerk who broke into the Donaldsons' house a couple weeks ago," Neil said.

Now he walked up to the guy. But he was more ambitious than Mike had been. Neil spat in the guy's face.

"Hey," I said, "cool it."

Neil glared at me. "Yeah, I wouldn't hurt his feelings, would I?"

Then he suddenly turned back on the guy, raised his fist, and started to swing. All I could do was shove him. That sent his punch angling off to the right, missing our burglar by about half a foot.

"You asshole," Neil said, turning back on me now.

But Mike was there, between us.

"You know what we're doing? We're making this jerk happy. He's gonna have some nice stories to tell all his criminal friends."

He was right. The burglar was the one who got to look all cool and composed. We looked like squabbling brats. As if to confirm this, a hint of amusement played in the burglar's blue eyes.

"Oh, hell, Aaron, I'm sorry," Neil said, putting his hand out. This was like a political convention, all the handshaking going on.

"So am I, Neil," I said. "That's why I want to call the cops and get this over with."

And that's when he chose to make his move, the burglar. As soon as I mentioned the cops, he probably realized that this was going to be his last opportunity.

He waited until we were just finishing up with the handshake, when we were all focused on one another. Then he took off running. We could see that he'd slipped the rope. He went straight for the stairs, angling out around us like a running back seeing daylight. He even stuck his long, tattooed arm out as if he were trying to repel a tackle.

"Hey!" Bob shouted. "He's getting away."

He was at the stairs by the time we could gather ourselves enough to go after him. But when we moved, we moved fast, and in virtual unison.

By the time I got my hand on the cuff of his left jeans leg, he was close enough to the basement door to open it.

I yanked hard and ducked out of the way of his kicking

foot. By now I was as crazy as Mike and Neil had been earlier. There was adrenaline, and great anger. He wasn't just a burglar, he was all burglars, intent not merely on stealing things from me but on hurting my family, too. He hadn't had time to take the gag from his mouth.

This time, I grabbed booted foot and leg and started hauling him back down the stairs. At first he was able to hold on to the door, but when I wrenched his foot rightward, he tried to scream behind the gag. He let go of the doorknob.

The next half minute is still unclear in my mind. I started running down the stairs, dragging him with me. All I wanted to do was get him on the basement floor again, turn him over to the others to watch, and then go call the cops.

But somewhere in those few seconds when I was hauling him back down the steps, I heard edge of stair meeting back of skull. The others heard it, too, because their shouts and curses died in their throats.

When I turned around, I saw the blood running fast and red from his nose. The blue eyes no longer held contempt. They were starting to roll up white in the back of his head.

"God," I said. "He's hurt."

"I think he's a lot more than hurt," Mike said.

"Help me carry him upstairs."

We got him on the kitchen floor. Mike and Neil rushed around soaking paper towels. We tried to revive him. Bob, who kept wincing from his headache, tried the guy's wrist, ankle, and throat for a pulse. None. His nose and mouth were bloody. Very bloody.

"No way you could *die* from hitting your head like that," Neil said.

"Sure you could," Mike said. "You hit it just the right way."

"He can't be dead," Neil said. "I'm going to try his pulse again."

Bob, who obviously took Neil's second opinion personally, frowned and rolled his eyes. "He's dead, man. He really is."

"Bullshit."

"You a doctor or something?" Bob said.

Neil smiled nervously. "No, but I play one on TV."

So Neil tried the pulse points. His reading was exactly what Bob's reading had been.

"See," Bob said.

I guess none of us was destined to ever quite be an adult.

"Man," Neil said, looking down at the long, cold, unmoving form of the burglar. "He's really dead."

"What the hell're we gonna do?" Mike said.

"We're going to call the police," I said, and started for the phone.

"The hell we are," Mike said. "The hell we are."

3

Maybe half an hour after we laid him on the kitchen floor, he started to smell. We'd looked for identification and found none. He was just the Burglar.

We sat at the kitchen table, sharing a fifth of Old Grand-Dad and innumerable beers.

We'd taken two votes, and they'd come up ties. Two for calling the police, Bob and I; two for not calling the police, Mike and Neil.

"All we have to tell them," I said, "is that we tied him up so he wouldn't get away."

"And then they say," Mike said, "so why didn't you call us before now?"

"We just lie about the time a little," I said. "Tell them we called them within twenty minutes."

"Won't work," Neil said.

"Why not?" Bob said.

"Medical examiner can fix the time of death," Neil said. "Not that close."

"Close enough so that the cops might question our story," Neil said. "By the time they get here, he'll have been dead at least an hour, hour and a half."

"And then we get our names in the paper for not reporting the burglary or the death right away," Mike said. "Brokerages just love publicity like that."

"I'm calling the cops right now," I said, and started up from the table.

"Think about Tomlinson a minute," Neil said.

Tomlinson was my boss at the brokerage. "What about him?"

"Remember how he canned Dennis Bryce when Bryce's ex-wife took out a restraining order on him?"

"This is different," I said.

"The hell it is," Mike said. "Neil's right, none of our bosses will like publicity like this. We'll all sound a little—crazy—you know, keeping him locked up in the basement. And then killing him when he tried to get away."

They all looked at me.

"You bastards," I said. "I was the one who wanted to call the police in the first place. And I sure as hell didn't try to kill him on purpose."

"Looking back on it," Neil said, "I guess you were right, Aaron. We should've called the cops right away."

"Now's a great time to realize that," I said.

"Maybe they've got a point," Bob said softly, glancing at me, then glancing nervously away.

"Oh, great. You, too?" I said.

"They just might kick my black ass out of there if I had any publicity that involved somebody getting killed," Bob said.

"He was a frigging burglar," I said.

"But he's dead," Neil said.

"And we killed him," Mike said.

"I appreciate you saying 'we,'" I said.

"I know a good place," Bob said.

I looked at him carefully, afraid of what he was going to say next.

"Forget it," I said.

"A good place for what?" Neil said.

"Dumping the body," Bob said.

"No way," I said.

This time, when I got up, nobody tried to stop me. I walked over to the yellow wall telephone.

I wondered if the cozy kitchen would ever feel the same to me now that a dead body had been laid upon its floor.

I had to step over him to reach the phone. The smell was even more sour now.

"You know how many bodies get dumped in the river that never wash up?" Bob said.

"No," I said, "and you don't, either."

"Lots," he said.

"There's a scientific appraisal for you. 'Lots.'"

"Lots and lots, probably," Neil said, taking up Bob's argument.

Mike grinned. "Lots and lots and *lots.*"

"Thank you, Professor," I said.

I lifted the receiver and dialed 0.

"Operator."

"The Police Department, please."

"Is this an emergency?" asked the young woman. Usually, I would have spent more time wondering if the sweetness of her voice was matched by the sweetness of her face and body. I'm still a face man. I suppose it's my romantic side. "Is this an emergency?" she repeated.

"No; no, it isn't."

"I'll connect you," she said.

"You think your kids'll be able to handle it?" Neil said.

"No mind games," I said.

"No mind games at all," he said. "I'm asking you a very realistic question. The police have some doubts about our story and then the press gets ahold of it, and bam. We're the lead story on all three channels. 'Did four middle-class men murder the burglar they captured?' The press even goes after the kids these days. 'Do *you* think your daddy murdered that burglar, son?'"

"Good evening. Police Department."

I started to speak, but I couldn't somehow. My voice wouldn't work. That's the only way I can explain it.

"The six o'clock news five nights running," Neil said softly behind me. "And the DA can't endorse any kind of vigilante activity, so he nails us on involuntary man-slaughter."

"Hello? This is the Police Department," said the black female voice on the phone.

Neil was there then, reaching me as if by magic.

He took the receiver gently from my hand and hung it back up on the phone again.

"Let's go have another drink and see what Bob's got in mind, all right?"

He led me, as if I were a hospital patient, slowly and carefully back to the table, where Bob, over more whiskey, slowly and gently laid out his plan.

The next morning, three of us phoned in sick. Bob went to work because he had an important meeting.

Around noon—a sunny day when a softball game and a cold six-pack of beer sounded good—Neil and Mike came over. They looked as bad as I felt, and no doubt looked, myself.

We sat out on the patio eating the Hardee's lunch they'd bought. I'd need to play softball to work off some of the calories I was eating.

Birdsong and soft breezes and the smell of fresh-cut grass should have made our patio time enjoyable. But I had to wonder if we'd ever enjoy anything again. I just kept seeing the body momentarily arced above the roaring waters of the dam, and dropping into white churning turbulence.

"You think we did the right thing?" Neil said.

"Now's a hell of a time to ask that," I said.

"Of course we did the right thing," Mike said. "What choice did we have? It was either that or get our asses arrested."

"So you don't have any regrets?" Neil said.

Mike sighed. "I didn't say that. I mean, I wish it hadn't happened in the first place."

"Maybe Aaron was right all along," Neil said.

"About what?"

"About going to the cops."

"Goddamn," Mike said, sitting up from his slouch. We all wore button-down shirts without ties and with the sleeves rolled up. Somehow there was something profane about wearing shorts and T-shirts on a workday. We even wore pretty good slacks. We were those kind of people. "Goddamn."

"Here he goes," Neil said.

"I can't believe you two," Mike said. "We should be happy that everything went so well last night—and what're we doing? Sitting around here pissing and moaning."

"That doesn't mean it's over," I said.

"Why the hell not?" Mike said.

"Because there's still one left."

"One what?"

"One burglar."

"So?"

"So you don't think he's going to get curious about what the hell happened to his partner?"

"What's he gonna do?" Mike said. "Go to the cops?"

"Maybe."

"Maybe? You're crazy. He goes to the cops, he'd be setting himself up for a robbery conviction."

"Not if he tells them we murdered his pal."

Neil said, "Aaron's got a point. What if this guy goes to the cops?"

"He's not going to the cops," Mike said. "No way he's going to the cops at all."

4

I was dozing on the couch, a Cubs game on the TV set, when the phone rang around nine that evening. I hadn't heard from Jan yet, so I expected it would be her. Whenever we're apart, we call each other at least once a day.

The phone machine picks up on the fourth ring, so I had to scramble to beat it.

"Hello?"

Nothing. But somebody was on the line. Listening.

"Hello?"

I never play games with silent callers. I just hang up. I did so now.

Two innings later, having talked to Jan, having made myself a tuna fish sandwich on rye, found a package of potato chips I thought we'd finished off at the poker game, and gotten myself a new can of beer, I sat down to watch the last inning. The Cubs had a chance of winning. I said a silent prayer to the god of baseball.

The phone rang.

I mouthed several curses around my mouthful of tuna sandwich and went to the phone.

"Hello?" I said, trying to swallow the last of the bite.

My silent friend again.

I slammed the phone.

The Cubs got two more singles, I started on the chips, and I had polished off the beer and was thinking of getting another one when the phone rang again.

I had a suspicion of who was calling and then saying nothing—but I didn't really want to think about it.

Then I decided there was an easy way to handle this situation. I'd just let the phone machine take it. If my anonymous friend wanted to talk to a phone machine, good for him.

Four rings. The phone machine took over, Jan's pleasant voice saying that we weren't home but would be happy to call you back if you'd just leave your number.

I waited to hear dead air and then a click.

Instead, a familiar female voice said, "Aaron, it's Louise. Bob—" Louise was Bob's wife. She was crying. I ran from the couch to the phone machine in the hall.

"Hello, Louise. It's Aaron."

"Oh, Aaron. It's terrible."

"What happened, Louise?"

"Bob—" More tears. "He electrocuted himself tonight out in the garage." She said that a plug had accidentally fallen into a bowl of water, according to the fire captain on the scene, and Bob hadn't noticed this and put the plug into the outlet and—

Bob had a woodcraft workshop in his garage, a large and sophisticated one. He knew what he was doing.

"He's dead, Aaron. He's dead."

"Oh, God, Louise. I'm sorry."

"He was so careful with electricity, too. It's just so hard to believe—"

Yes, I thought. Yes, it was hard to believe. I thought of last night. Of the burglars—one who'd died, one who'd gotten away.

"Why don't I come over?"

"Oh, thank you, Aaron, but I need to be alone with the children. But if you could call Neil and Mike—"

"Of course."

"Thanks for being such good friends, you and Jan."

"Don't be silly, Louise. The pleasure's ours."

"I'll talk to you tomorrow. When I'm—you know."

"Good night, Louise."

Mike and Neil were at my place within twenty minutes. We sat in the kitchen again, where we were last night.

I said, "Either of you get any weird phone calls tonight?"

"You mean just silence?" Neil said.

"Right."

"I did," Mike said. "Tracy was afraid it was that pervert who called all last winter."

"I did, too," Neil said. "Three of them."

"Then a little while ago, Bob dies out in his garage," I said. "Some coincidence."

"Hey, Aaron," Mike said. "Is that why you got us over here? Because you don't think it was an accident?"

"I'm sure it wasn't an accident," I said. "Bob knew what he was doing with his tools. He didn't notice a plug that had fallen into a bowl of water?"

"He's coming after us," Neil said.

"Oh, God," Mike said. "Not you, too."

"He calls us, gets us on edge," I said. "And then he kills Bob. Making it look like an accident."

"These are pretty bright people," Mike said sarcastically.

"You notice the burglar's eyes?" Neil said.

"I did," I said. "He looked very bright."

"And spooky," Neil said. "Never saw eyes like that before."

"I can shoot your theory right in the butt," Mike said.

"How?" I said.

He leaned forward, sipped his beer. I'd thought about putting out some munchies, but somehow that seemed wrong given poor Bob's death and the phone calls. The beers we had to have. The munchies were too festive.

"Here's how. There are two burglars, right? One gets caught, the other runs. And given the nature of burglars, keeps on running. He wouldn't even know who was in the house last night, except for Aaron, and that's only because he's the owner and his name would be in the phone book. But he wouldn't know anything about Bob or Neil or me. No way he'd have been able to track down Bob."

I shook my head. "You're overlooking the obvious."

"Like what?"

"Like he runs off last night, gets his car, and then parks in the alley to see what's going to happen."

"Right," Neil said. "Then he sees us bringing his friend out wrapped in a blanket. He follows us to the dam and watches us throw his friend in."

"And," I said, "everybody had his car here last night. Very easy for him to write down all the license numbers."

"So he kills Bob," Neil said. "And starts making the phone calls to shake us up."

"Why Bob?"

"Maybe he hates black people," I said.

Mike looked first at me and then at Neil. "You know what this is?"

"Here he goes," Neil said.

"No; no, I'm serious here. This is Catholic guilt."

"How can it be Catholic guilt when I'm Jewish?" Neil said.

"In a culture like ours, everybody is a little bit Jewish and a little bit Catholic, anyway," Mike said. "So you guys are in the throes of Catholic guilt. You feel bad about what we had to do last night—and we did have to do it, we really didn't have any choice—and the guilt starts to prey on your mind. So poor Bob electrocutes himself accidentally, and you immediately think it's the second burglar."

"He followed him," Neil said.

"What?" Mike said.

"That's what he did, I bet. The burglar. Followed Bob around all day trying to figure out what was the best way to kill him. You know, the best way that would look like an accident. So then he finds out about the workshop and decides it's perfect."

"That presumes," Mike said, "that one of us is going to be next."

"Hell, yes," Neil said. "That's why he's calling us. Shake us up. Sweat us out. Let us know that he's out there somewhere, just waiting. And that we're next."

"I'm going to follow you to work tomorrow, Neil," I said. "And Mike's going to be with me."

"You guys are having breakdowns. You really are," Mike said.

"We'll follow Neil tomorrow," I said. "And then on Saturday, you and Neil can follow me. If he's following *us* around, then we'll see it. And then we can start following him. We'll at least find out who he is."

"And then what?" Mike said. "Suppose we do find out where he lives? Then what the hell do we do?"

Neil said, "I guess we worry about that when we get there, don't we?"

In the morning, I picked Mike up early. We stopped off for doughnuts and coffee. He's like my brother, not a morning person. Crabby. Our conversation was at a minimum, though he did say, "I could've used the extra hour's sleep this morning. Instead of this crap, I mean."

As agreed, we parked half a block from Neil's house. Also as agreed, Neil emerged exactly at 7:35. Kids were already in the wide suburban streets on skateboards and rollerblades. No other car could be seen, except for a lone silver BMW in a driveway far down the block.

We followed him all the way to work. Nobody else followed him. Nobody.

When I dropped Mike off at his office, he said, "You owe me an hour's sleep."

"Two hours," I said.

"Huh?"

"Tomorrow, you and Neil follow me around."

"No way," he said.

There are times when only blunt anger will work with Mike. "It was your idea not to call the police, remember? I'm not up for any of your sulking, Mike. I'm really not."

He sighed. "I guess you're right."

I drove for two and a half hours Saturday morning. I hit a hardware store, a lumber yard, and a Kmart. At noon, I pulled into a McDonald's. The three of us had some lunch.

"You didn't see anybody even suspicious?"

"Not even suspicious, Aaron," Neil said. "I'm sorry."

"This is all bullshit. He's not going to follow us around."

"I want to give it one more chance," I said.

Mike made a face. "I'm not going to get up early, if that's what you've got in mind."

I got angry again. "Bob's dead, or have you forgotten?"

"Yeah, Aaron," Mike said. "Bob *is* dead. He got electrocuted. Accidentally."

Aaron said, "You really think it was an accident?"

"Of course I do," Mike said. "When do you want to try it again?"

"Tonight. I'll do a little bowling."

"There's a fight on I want to watch," Mike said.

"Tape it," I said.

"'Tape it,'" he mocked. "Since when did you start giving us orders?"

"Oh, for God's sake, Mike, grow up," Neil said. "There's no way that Bob's electrocution was an accident or a coincidence. He's probably not going to stop with Bob, either."

The bowling alley was mostly teenagers on Saturday night. There was a time when bowling was mostly a working-class sport. Now it's come to the suburbs and the white-collar people. Now the bowling lane is a good place for teenage boys to meet teenage girls.

I bowled two games, drank three beers, and walked back outside an hour later.

Summer night. Smell of dying heat, car exhaust, cigarette smoke, perfume. Sound of jukebox, distant loud mufflers, even more distant rushing train, lonely baying dogs.

Mike and Neil were gone.

I went home and opened myself a beer.

The phone rang. Once again, I was expecting Jan.

"Found the bastard," Neil said. "He followed you from your house to the bowling alley. Then he got tired of waiting and took off again. This time we followed *him.*"

"Where?"

He gave me an address. It wasn't a good one.

"We're waiting for you to get here. Then we're going up to pay him a little visit."

"I need twenty minutes."

"Hurry."

Not even the silver touch of moonlight lent the blocks of crumbling stucco apartment houses any majesty or beauty. The rats didn't even bother to hide. They squatted red-eyed on the unmown lawns, amid beer cans, broken bottles, wrappers from Taco John's, and used condoms that looked like deflated mushrooms.

Mike stood behind a tree.

"I followed him around back," Mike said. "He went up the fire escape on the back. Then he jumped on this veranda. He's in the back apartment on the right side. Neil's in the backyard, watching for him."

Mike looked down at my ball bat. "That's a nice complement," he said. Then he showed me his handgun. "To this."

"Why the hell did you bring that?"

"Are you kidding? You're the one who said he killed Bob."

That I couldn't argue with.

"All right," I said, "but what happens when we catch him?"

"We tell him to lay off us," Mike said.

"We need to go to the cops."

"Oh, sure. Sure we do." He shook his head. He looked as if he were dealing with a child. A very slow one. "Aaron, going to the cops now won't bring Bob back. And it's only going to get us in trouble."

That's when we heard the shout. Neil; it sounded like Neil.

Maybe five feet of rust-colored grass separated the yard from the alley that ran along the west side of the apartment house.

We ran down the alley, having to hop over an ancient drooping picket fence to reach the backyard, where Neil lay sprawled, facedown, next to a twenty-year-old Chevrolet that was tireless and up on blocks. Through the windshield, you could see the huge gouges in the seats where the rats had eaten their fill.

The backyard smelled of dog shit and car oil.

Neil was moaning. At least we knew he was alive.

"The sonofabitch," he said when we got him to his feet. "I moved over to the other side, back of the car there, so he wouldn't see me if he tried to come down that fire escape. I didn't figure there was another fire escape on the side of the building. He must've come around there and snuck up on me. He tried to kill me, but I had this—"

In the moonlight, his wrist and the switchblade he held in his fingers were wet and dark with blood. "I got him a couple of times in the arm. Otherwise, I'd be dead."

"We're going up there," Mike said.

"How about checking Neil first?" I said.

"I'm fine," Neil said. "A little headache from where he caught me on the back of the neck." He waved his bloody blade. "Good thing I had this."

The landlord was on the first floor. He wore Bermuda shorts and no shirt. He looked eleven or twelve months pregnant, with little male titties and enough coarse black hair to knit a sweater with. He had a plastic-tipped cigarillo in the left corner of his mouth.

"Yeah?"

"Two-F," I said.

"What about it?"

"Who lives there?"

"Nobody."

"Nobody?"

"If you were the law, you'd show me a badge."

"I'll show you a badge," Mike said, making a fist.

"Hey," I said, playing good cop to his bad cop. "You just let me speak to this gentleman."

The guy seemed to like my reference to him as a gentleman. It was probably the only name he'd never been called.

"Sir, we saw somebody go up there."

"Oh," he said. "The vampires."

"Vampires?"

He sucked down some cigarillo smoke. "That's we what call 'em, the missus and me. They're street people, winos and homeless and all like that. They know that sometimes some of these apartments ain't rented for a while, so they sneak up there and spend the night."

"You don't stop them?"

"You think I'm gonna get my head split open for something like that?"

"I guess that makes sense." Then: "So nobody's renting it now?"

"Nope, it ain't been rented for three months. This fat broad lived there then. Man, did she smell. You know how fat people can smell sometimes? *She* sure smelled." He wasn't svelte.

Back on the front lawn, trying to wend my way between the mounds of dog shit, I said, " 'Vampires.' Good name for them."

"Yeah, it is," Neil said. "I just keep thinking of the one who died. His weird eyes."

"Here we go again," Mike said. "You two guys love to scare the shit out of each other, don't you? They're a couple of nickel-dime crooks, and that's *all* they are."

"All right if Mike and I stop and get some beer and then swing by your place?"

"Sure," I said. "Just as long as Mike buys Bud and none of that generic crap."

"Oh, I forgot." Neil laughed. "He does do that when it's his turn to buy, doesn't he?"

"Yeah," I said, "he certainly does."

I was never sure what time the call came. Darkness. The ringing phone seemed part of a dream from which I couldn't escape. Somehow I managed to lift the receiver before the phone machine kicked in.

Silence. That special *kind* of silence.

Him. I had no doubt about it. The vampire, as the landlord had called him. The one who'd killed Bob. I didn't say so much as hello. Just listened, angry, afraid, confused.

After a few minutes, he hung up.

Darkness again; deep darkness, the quarter moon in the sky a cold golden scimitar that could cleave a head from a neck.

5

About noon on Sunday, Jan called to tell me that she was staying a few days extra. The kids had discovered archery, and there was a course at the Y they were taking and wouldn't she please please *please* ask good old Dad if they could stay. I said sure.

I called Neil and Mike to remind them that at nine tonight we were going to pay a visit to that crumbling stucco apartment house again.

I spent an hour on the lawn. My neighbors shame me into it. Lawns aren't anything I get excited about. But they sort of shame you into it. About halfway through, Byrnes, the chunky advertising man who lives next door, came over and clapped me on the back. He was apparently pleased that I was a real human being and taking a real human being interest in my lawn. As usual, he wore an expensive T-shirt with one of his clients' products on it and a pair of Bermuda shorts. As usual, he tried hard to be the kind of winsome neighbor you always had in sitcoms of the fifties. But I knew somebody who knew him. Byrnes had fired his number two man so he wouldn't have to keep paying the man's insurance. The man was unfortunately dying of cancer. Byrnes was typical of all the ad people I'd met. Pretty treacherous people who spent most of their time cheating clients out of their money and putting on awards banquets so they could convince themselves that advertising was actually an endeavor that was of consequence.

Around four, *Hombre* was on one of the cable channels, so I had a few beers and watched Paul Newman doing the best acting of his career. At least that was my opinion.

I was just getting ready for the shower when the phone rang.

He didn't say hello. He didn't identify himself. "Tracy call you?"

It was Neil. Tracy was Mike's wife. "Why should she call me?"

"He's dead. Mike."

"What?"

"You remember how he was always bitching about that elevator at work?"

Mike worked in a very old building. He made jokes about the antiquated elevators. But you could always tell the joke simply hid his fears. He'd gotten stuck innumerable times, and it was always stopping several feet short of the upcoming floor.

"He opened the door and the car wasn't there. He fell eight floors."

"Oh, God."

"I don't have to tell you who did it, do I?"

"Maybe it's time—"

"I'm way ahead of you, Aaron. I'll pick you up in half an hour. Then we go to the police. You agree?"

"I agree."

* * *

Late Sunday afternoon, the second precinct parking lot is pretty empty. We'd missed the shift change. Nobody came or went.

"We ask for a detective," Neil said. He was dark-sportcoat, white-shirt, necktie earnest. I'd settled for an expensive blue sportshirt Jan had bought me for my last birthday.

"You know one thing we haven't considered?"

"You're not going to change my mind."

"I'm not *trying* to change your mind, Neil, I'm just saying that there's one thing we haven't considered."

He sat behind his steering wheel, his head resting on the back of his seat.

"A lawyer."

"What for?"

"Because we may go in there and say something that gets us in very deep shit."

"No lawyers," he said. "We'd just look like we were trying to hide something from the cops."

"You sure about that?"

"I'm sure."

"You ready?" I said.

"Ready."

The interior of the police station was quiet. A muscular bald man in a dark uniform sat behind a desk with a sign that read "Information."

He said, "Help you?"

"We'd like to see a detective," I said.

"Are you reporting a crime?"

"Uh, yes," I said.

"What sort of crime?" he said.

I started to speak but once again lost my voice. I thought about all the reporters, about how Jan and the kids would be affected by it all. How my job would be affected. Taking a guy down to the basement and tying him up and then accidentally killing him—

Neil said: "Vandalism."

"Vandalism?" the cop said. "You don't need a detective,

then. I can just give you a form." Then he gave us a leery look, as if he sensed we'd just changed our minds about something.

"In that case, could I just take it home with me and fill it out there?" Neil said.

"Yeah, I guess." The cop still watched us carefully now.

"Great."

"You sure that's what you wanted to report? Vandalism?"

"Yeah; yeah, that's exactly what we wanted to report," Neil said. "Exactly."

"Vandalism?" I said when we were back in the car.

"I don't want to talk right now."

"Well, maybe *I* want to talk."

"I just couldn't do it."

"No kidding."

He looked over at me. "You could've told him the truth. Nobody was stopping you."

I looked out the window. "Yeah, I guess I could've."

"We're going over there tonight. To the vampire's place."

"And do what?"

"Ask him how much he wants."

"How much he wants for what?" I said.

"How much he wants to forget everything. He goes on with his life, we go on with ours."

I had to admit, I'd had a similar thought myself. Neil and I didn't know how to do any of this. But the vampire did. He was good at stalking, good at harassing, good at violence.

"We don't have a lot of money to throw around."

"Maybe he won't *want* a lot of money. I mean, these guys aren't exactly sophisticated."

"They're sophisticated enough to make two murders look like accidents."

"I guess that's a point."

"I'm just not sure we should pay him anything, Neil."

"You got any better ideas?"

I didn't, actually. I didn't have any better ideas at all.

6

I spent an hour on the phone with Jan that afternoon. The last few days I'd been pretty anxious, and she'd sensed it, and now she was making sure that everything was all right with me. In addition to being wife and lover, Jan's also my best friend. I can't kid her. She always knows when something's wrong. I'd put off telling her about Bob and Mike dying. I'd been afraid that I might accidentally say more than I should and make her suspicious. But now I had to tell her about their deaths. It was the only way I could explain my tense mood.

"That's awful," she said. "Their poor families."

"They're handling it better than you might think."

"Maybe I should bring the kids home early."

"No reason to, hon. I mean, realistically there isn't anything any of us can do."

"Two accidents in that short a time. It's pretty strange."

"Yeah, I guess it is. But that's how it happens sometimes."

"Are you going to be all right?"

"Just need to adjust is all." I sighed. "I guess we won't be having our poker games anymore."

Then I did something I hadn't intended. I started crying, and the tears caught in my throat.

"Oh, honey," Jan said. "I wish I was there so I could give you a big hug."

"I'll be okay."

"Two of your best friends."

"Yeah." The tears were starting to dry up now.

"Oh, did I tell you about Tommy?" Tommy was our six-year-old.

"No, what?"

"Remember how he used to be so afraid of horses?"

"Uh-huh."

"Well, we took him out to this horse ranch where you can rent horses?"

"Uh-huh."

"And they found him a little Shetland pony and let him ride it, and he loved it. He wasn't afraid at all." She laughed. "In fact, we could barely drag him home." She paused. "You're probably not in the mood for this, are you? I'm sorry, hon. Maybe you should do something to take your mind off things. Is there a good movie on?"

"I guess I could check."

"Something light, that's what you need."

"Sounds good," I said. "I'll go get the newspaper and see what's on."

"Love you."

"Love you, too, sweetheart," I said.

I spent the rest of the afternoon going through my various savings accounts and investments. I had no idea what the creep would want to leave us alone. We could always threaten him with going to the police, though he might rightly point out that if we really wanted to do that, we would already have done it.

I settled in the five-thousand-dollar range. That was the maximum cash I had to play with. And even then I'd have to borrow a little from one of the mutual funds we had earmarked for the kids and college.

Five thousand dollars. To me, it sounded like an enormous amount of money, probably because I knew how hard I'd had to work to get it.

But would it be enough for our friend the vampire?

Neil was there just at dark. He parked in the drive and came in. Meaning he wanted to talk.

We went in the kitchen. I made us a couple of highballs, and we sat there and discussed finances.

"I came up with six thousand," he said.

"I got five."

"That's eleven grand," he said. "It's got to be more cash than this creep has ever seen."

"What if he takes it and comes back for more?"

"We make it absolutely clear," Neil said, "that there is no more. That this is it. Period."

"And if not?"

Neil nodded. "I've thought this through. You know the kind of lowlife we're dealing with? A, he's a burglar, which means, these days, that he's a junkie. B, if he's a junkie, then that means he's very suspectible to AIDS. So between being a burglar and shooting up, this guy is probably going to have a very short lifespan."

"I guess I'd agree."

"Even if he wants to make our life miserable, he probably won't live long enough to do it. So I think we'll be making just the one payment. We'll buy enough time to let nature take its course—his nature."

"What if he wants more than the eleven grand?"

"He won't. His eyes'll pop out when he sees this."

I looked at the kitchen clock. It was going on nine now.

"I guess we could drive over there."

"It may be a long night," Neil said.

"I know."

"But I guess we don't have a hell of a lot of choice, do we?"

As we'd done the last time we'd been here, we split up the duties. I took the backyard, Neil the apartment door. We'd waited until midnight. The rap music had died by now. Babies cried and mothers screamed; couples fought. TV screens flickered in dark windows.

I went up the fire escape slowly and carefully. We'd talked about bringing guns, then decided against it. We weren't exactly marksmen, and if a cop stopped us for some reason, we could be arrested for carrying unlicensed firearms. All I carried was a flashlight in my back pocket.

As I grabbed the rungs of the ladder, powdery rust dusted my hands. I was chilly with sweat. My bowels felt sick. I was scared. I just wanted it to be over with. I wanted him to say yes, he'd take the money, and then that would be the end of it.

The stucco veranda was filled with discarded toys—a tricycle, innumerable games, a space helmet, a wiffle bat and ball. The floor was crunchy with dried animal feces. At least, I hoped the feces belonged to animals and not human children.

The door between veranda and apartment was open. Fingers of moonlight revealed an overstuffed couch and chair and a floor covered with the debris of fast food, McDonald's sacks, Pizza Hut wrappers and cardboards, Arby's wrappers, and what seemed to be five or six dozen empty beer cans. Far toward the hall that led to the front door, I saw four red eyes watching me, a a pair of curious rats.

I stood still and listened. Nothing. No sign of life. I went inside. Tiptoeing.

I went to the front door and let Neil in. There in the murky light of the hallway, he made a face. The smell *was* pretty bad.

Over the next ten minutes, we searched the apartment. And found nobody.

"We could wait here for him," I said.

"No way."

"The smell?"

"The smell, the rats. God. Don't you just feel unclean?"

"Yeah, guess I do."

"There's an empty garage about halfway down the alley. We'd have a good view of the back of this building."

"Sounds pretty good."

"Sounds better than this place, anyway."

This time, we both went out the front door and down the stairway. Now the smells were getting to me as they'd earlier gotten to Neil. Unclean. He was right.

We got in Neil's Buick, drove down the alley that ran along the west side of the apartment house, backed up to the dark garage, and whipped inside.

"There's a sack in back," Neil said. "It's on your side."

"A sack?"

"Brewskis. Quart for you, quart for me."

"That's how my old man used to drink them," I said. I was the only blue-collar member of the poker club. "Get off work at the plant and stop by and pick up two quart bottles of Hamms. Never missed."

"Sometimes I wish I would've been born into the working class," Neil said.

I was the blue-collar guy, and Neil was the dreamer, always inventing alternative realities for himself.

"No, you don't," I said, leaning over the seat and picking up the sack damp from the quart bottles. "You had a damned nice life in Boston."

"Yeah, but I didn't learn anything. You know I was eighteen before I learned about cunnilingus?"

"Talk about cultural deprivation," I said.

"Well, every girl I went out with probably looks back on me as a pretty lame lover. They went down on me, but I never went down on them. How old were you when you learned about cunnilingus?"

"Maybe thirteen."

"See?"

"I learned about it, but I didn't do anything about it."

"I was twenty years old before I lost my cherry," Neil said.

"I was seventeen."

"Bullshit."

"Bullshit what? I was seventeen."

"In sociology, they always taught us that blue-collar kids lost their virginity a lot earlier than white-collar kids."

"That's the trouble with sociology. It tries to particularize from generalities."

"Huh?" He grinned. "Yeah, I always thought sociology was full of shit, too, actually. But you were really seventeen?"

"I was really seventeen."

I wish I could tell you that I knew what it was right away, the missile that hit the windshield and shattered and starred it, and then kept right on tearing through the car until the back window was also shattered and starred.

But all I knew was that Neil was screaming and I was screaming and my quart bottle of Miller's was spilling all over my crotch as I tried to hunch down behind the dashboard. It was a tight fit because Neil was trying to hunch down behind the steering wheel.

The second time, I knew what was going on: somebody was shooting at us. Given the trajectory of the bullet, he had to be right in front of us, probably behind the two Dumpsters that sat on the other side of the alley.

"Can you keep down and drive this sonofabitch at the same time?"

"I can try," Neil said.

"If we sit here much longer, he's going to figure out we don't have guns. Then he's gonna come for us for sure."

Neil leaned over and turned on the ignition. "I'm going to turn left when we get out of here."

"Fine. Just get moving."

"Hold on."

What he did was kind of slump over the bottom half of the wheel, just enough so he could sneak a peek at where the car was headed.

There were no more shots.

All I could hear was the smooth-running Buick motor.

He eased out of the garage, ducking down all the time.

When he got a chance, he bore left.

He kept the lights off.

Through the bullet hole in the windshield, I could see an inch or so of starry sky.

It was a long alley, and we must have gone a quarter block before he said, "I'm going to sit up. I think we lost him."

"So do I."

"Look at that frigging windshield."

Not only was the windshield a mess, the car reeked of spilled beer.

"You think I should turn on the headlights?"

"Sure," I said. "We're safe now."

We were still crawling at maybe ten miles per hour when he pulled the headlights on.

That's when we saw him, silver of eye, dark of hair, crouching in the middle of the alley waiting for us. He was a good fifty yards ahead of us, but we were still within range.

There was no place we could turn around.

He fired.

This bullet shattered whatever had been left untouched of the windshield. Neil slammed on the brakes.

Then he fired a second time.

By now, both Neil and I were screaming and cursing again.

A third bullet.

"Run him over!" I yelled, ducking behind the dashboard.

"What?" Neil yelled back.

"Floor it!"

He floored it. He wasn't even sitting up straight. We might have gone careening into one of the garages or Dumpsters. But somehow the Buick stayed in the alley. And very soon it was traveling eighty-five miles per hour. I watched the speedometer peg it.

More shots, a lot of them now, side windows shattering, bullets ripping into fender and hood and top.

I didn't see us hit him, but I *felt* us hit him, the car traveling that fast, the creep so intent on killing us he hadn't bothered to get out of the way in time.

The front of the car picked him up and hurled him into a garage near the head of the alley.

We both sat up, watched as his entire body was broken against the edge of the garage, and he then fell smashed and unmoving to the grass.

"Kill the lights," I said.

"What?"

"Kill the lights, and let's go look at him."

Neil punched off the headlights.

We left the car and ran over to him.

A white rib stuck bloody and brazen from his side. Blood poured from his ears, nose, mouth. One leg had been crushed and also showed white bone. His arms had been broken, too.

I played my flashlight beam over him.

He was dead, all right.

"Looks like we can save our money," I said. "It's all over now."

"I want to get the hell out of here."

"Yeah," I said. "So do I."

We got the hell out of there.

7

A month later, just as you could smell autumn on the summer winds, Jan and I celebrated our twelfth wedding anniversary. We drove up to Lake Geneva, in Wisconsin, and stayed at a very nice hotel and rented a Chris-Craft for a couple of days. This was the first time I'd been able to relax since the thing with the burglar had started.

One night when Jan was asleep, I went up on the deck of the boat and just watched the stars. I used to read a lot of Edgar Rice Burroughs when I was a boy. I always remembered how John Carter felt—that the stars had a very special destiny for him and would someday summon him to that destiny. My destiny, I decided that night there on the deck, was to be a good family man, a good stockbroker, and a good neighbor. The bad things were all behind me now. I imagined Neil was feeling pretty much the same way. Hot bitter July seemed a long way behind us now. Fall was coming, bringing with it football and Thanksgiving and Christmas. July would recede even more with snow on the ground.

The funny thing was, I didn't see Neil much anymore. It was as if the sight of each other brought back a lot of bad memories. It was a mutual feeling, too. I didn't want to see him any more than he wanted to see me. Our wives thought this was pretty strange. They'd meet at the supermarket or shopping center and wonder why "the boys" didn't get together anymore. Neil's wife, Sarah, kept inviting us over to "sit around the pool and watch Neil pretend he knows how to swim." September was summer hot. The pool was still the centerpiece of their life.

Not that I made any new friends. The notion of a midweek poker game had lost all its appeal. There was work and my family and little else.

Then, one sunny Indian summer afternoon, Neil called and said, "Maybe we should get together again."

"Maybe."

"It's over, Aaron. It really is."

"I know."

"Will you at least think about it?"

I felt embarrassed. "Oh, hell, Neil. Is that swimming pool of yours open Saturday afternoon?"

"As a matter of fact, it is. And as a matter of fact, Sarah and the girls are going to be gone to a fashion show at the club."

"Perfect. We'll have a couple of beers."

"You know how to swim?"

"No," I said, laughing. "And from what Sarah says, you don't, either."

I got there about three, pulled into the drive, walked to the back where the gate in the wooden fence led to the swimming pool. It was eighty degrees, and even from here I could smell the chlorine.

I opened the gate and went inside and saw him right away. The funny thing was, I didn't have much of a reaction at all. I just watched him. He was floating. Facedown. He looked pale in his red trunks. This, like the others, would be judged an accidental death. Of that I had no doubt at all.

I used the cellular phone in my car to call 911.

I didn't want Sarah and the girls coming back to see an ambulance and police cars in the drive and them not knowing what was going on.

I called the club and had her paged.

I told her what I'd found. I let her cry. I didn't know what to say. I never do.

In the distance, I could hear the ambulance working its way toward the Neil Solomon residence.

I was just about to get out of the car when my cellular phone rang. I picked up. "Hello?"

"There were three of us that night at your house, Mr. Bellini. You killed two of us. I recovered from when your friend stabbed me, remember? Now I'm ready for action. I really am, Mr. Bellini."

Then the emergency people were there, and neighbors, too, and then wan, trembling Sarah. I just let her cry some more. Gave her whiskey and let her cry.

8

He knows how to do it, whoever he is.

He lets a long time go between late-night calls. He lets me start to think that maybe he changed his mind and left town. And then he calls.

Oh, yes, he knows just how to play this little game.

He never says anything. He doesn't need to. He just listens. And then hangs up.

I've considered going to the police, of course, but it's way too late for that. Way too late.

Or I could ask Jan and the kids to move away to a different city with me. But he knows who I am, and he'd find me again.

So all I can do is wait and hope that I get lucky, the way Neil and I got lucky the night we killed the second of them.

Tonight I can't sleep.

It's after midnight.

Jan and I wrapped presents until well after eleven. She asked me again if anything was wrong. We don't make love as much as we used to, she said; and then there are the nightmares. "Please tell me if something's wrong, Aaron. Please."

I stand at the window watching the snow come down. Soft and beautiful snow. In the morning, a Saturday, the kids will make a snowman and then go sledding and then have themselves a good old-fashioned snowball fight, which invariably means that one of them will come rushing in at some point and accuse the other of some terrible misdeed.

I see all this from the attic window.

Then I turn back and look around the poker table. Four empty chairs. Three of them belong to dead men.

I look at the empty chairs and think back to summer.

I look at the empty chairs and wait for the phone to ring.

I wait for the phone to ring.

PLEASE HELP ME

Richard Christian Matheson

So HOT.

Smells. Exhaust.

Memorize the road. Curves, dips. Ruts. Draw a map in your mind. A way to trace everything for the cops. Take them wherever the hell I'm going.

Five left turns since the Stop 'N Go.

Three rights. Over metal grating. A bridge? The tires buzzed for nine seconds. Maybe the bridge that links Canoga Park with Chatsworth. That narrow one. Remember? Used to fish off it with Dad.

Dad. His smile. Those bad jokes. I'm glad this isn't him. Too old.

So hot.

Why didn't I run? Could've made it. Maybe they would've shot at me.

But I could've gotten away.

Hard to breathe. Ropes tearing my wrists. Ankles. Gag chokes. Tape over it. No way to spit it out. Keep feeling like I'm going to puke. I have to control it. Or I'll choke on my own vomit.

The acrid taste of the rag. Drips down my throat.

What are they going to do with me? Kill me?

I saw their faces. Eyes bloodshot. Wasted on something. Bad skin on the tall one. How tall? The cops'll need details. *Try to remember.* They'll show you a book jammed with a million guys who look just like these three and robbed a hundred other twenty-four-hour markets and shot big holes through the owners.

Kids.

When did they turn into fucking monsters? What the hell went wrong?

Try to remember clothes. What were they wearing? How tall? Jewelry? Scars? All three wearing black head bandanas. Fatigues. One in those baggy gang shorts. Those sleeveless shirts. What are they called? Flannel. Wool plaid? What the hell is it? Goddammit! I used to know that.

Another left. Sharp. I roll to one side, I hear them laugh. Bang on the seat.

"Hey, man! Fucking alive? Don't get too used to it!" They laugh louder, turn up their rap music.

I can hear something metal at my feet. A jack? Guns?

They can't kill me. But I did see their faces. I'll swear not to go to the police. Then why try to remember the road, the clothes? How they looked. Smelled.

I could lie. Swear I won't tell. But maybe they'll know. See it on my face. In my eyes. Smell it on me like dogs. What could I do? They'd kill me just like they killed that store owner. Right in front of his wife.

The blood.

Everywhere. Counter and cash register they emptied. All over the ice cream machine. The white dessert spattered with thick red that sprayed from his face when they shot right into it.

Two women. They ran. Remember? They made it. Why didn't I run? Could've made it. *Why?!* I was afraid. Froze.

Pendletons. That's it! I can't believe I forgot that.

So fucking hot. I'm burning. Middle of August. Must be a hundred out tonight. Makes people crazy.

They're laughing. Deep. Vicious. My God, what are they going to do to me?

A siren! I can hear a siren! Someone reported the car. Saw the three gangbangers throw me in the back, tied up, gagged. Took down the license. Called.

Wait.

If it was the police, the car would speed up. There'd be a chase. Or they'd pull over. Questioning. I could kick at the trunk. They'd hear.

We're driving fast. Going down a bumpy road.

The car stops. What are they doing? Doors open.

Footsteps. A key. The trunk is opening. The air is fresh. Sweet. I'm grabbed by strong hands. I smell tobacco on the clothes. Maybe grass.

I can't speak. They're still listening to the radio. I hear a train whistle. Must be the one that cuts across Chatsworth, behind the big six-screen drive-in. It's a long one, lots of cars rattling on track.

"Leave him." A man.

"No." A girl. Maybe sixteen. She walks closer. I can feel her looking at me. She breathes, close by. Whispers in my ear. "What's your name?"

"You like him. Why don't you fuck him? Huh?"

She laughs. Breathes harder. I can smell her perfume. Then she kicks me in the balls.

They're going to kill me. I can feel it. I can feel it so much. They want to watch me bleed. They'll cut me open and turn up the music and dance around my dying, bleeding body while I squirm.

I hear metal. One has taken something from the trunk.

A gun. They've decided to shoot me. Execution style.

I don't want to die.

My wife and daughter start filling my head like a movie. Smiling and waving to me. Calling to me with no soundtrack.

What's that noise?

Scratching?

Digging.

"Fast, man. We got no time."

More digging. I'm sweating. Scared. I can't hold it anymore and piss my pants. They laugh. She comes over and kicks me in the balls again. Asks me if she's making me hard.

I can smell fresh earth.

They throw me in.

They've been digging a grave.

Their voices are above me. A few feet.

My daughter is swimming to me in our pool with a big smile, front teeth missing. My wife is sitting with her feet in the water, laughing.

Something hits me. Again. Soft. Like heavy snow.

They're throwing dirt on me. I can hear their car music, pounding. Pounding.

I'm on my side. Can't stand.

My daughter is swimming closer. Giggling.

I'm covered with dirt. They keep shoveling in more. One takes a leak on the dirt. I can smell the piss. It gets on my face. They laugh. And then I can't hear them. They're up there somewhere, above all the dirt that covers me.

I feel the soft vibration of more dirt shoveled on.

I'm in blackness.

I can't breathe.

The dirt gets heavier.

I can't see my daughter. Or my wife. The sun has disappeared, and everything is black.

Someone please help me.

Please help . . . me.

THE LESSER OF TWO EVILS

Denise M. Bruchman

THE PROSTITUTE'S HEAVILY PAINTED EYES STILL BULGED OUT OF her pale, stiffening face while her steaming blood spilled onto the dark, fog-enshrouded pavement. Jack liked that the best. As the woman's blood spurted and poured into his skillful hands, he absorbed her evil, tainted soul and consumed her dark energy as he had the others'. He inhaled deeply. A thick, hot, metallic scent mingled with the sharp tang of molding garbage from the nearby Dumpster and the clean wetness of the cool night air. Headlights passed by the mouth of the alley but couldn't penetrate the inky cocoon concealing Jack and his victim from the world. Without fear of intrusion, he savored the experience with all his senses. From the sticky, humming flow of warm blood to the sharp, sweet-sour smell of blood and urine and fear, to the cut-off gasp and cry that ended in a rattling rush of air, and the reddish glow of inner power that vibrated from within her collapsing body up his hungry arms in a current of power flavored with fear, anger, pain, and glory, the all-too-brief orgasm of sensation filled and dazed Jack's feverish mind. The night air sipped at the edges of her heat and dampened the vital warmth Jack sought, leaving an empty, cooling body in his hands. Jack dropped the wrung-out husk still gaping blindly onto the ground, and put away his precious tools. Jack felt him once again sated and strongly bound within his body. The Ripper would require another offering soon, but for now Jack could revel in the heady companionship.

Natasha Borisovna Klimova rubbed a heavily spotted hand over her burning eyes. The dream had emulated the others. Only the woman had changed—a brunette this time with crystal-blue eyes and dark red lips. Different on the outside, but same on the inside, the woman had served the same purpose as the others before and after her.

No matter, thought Natasha Borisovna. She had a shop to run, and foolish American and foreign tourists to impress and amuse. Some actually believed in her work. Others scoffed. But Natasha Borisovna's routine remained the same as when her *babushka* had trained her in the ways of gypsy magic as they traveled through Russia and the Ukraine to make their living. She got out of her soft, hand-stuffed goosedown bed, the same one she'd slept in every night since her wedding night all those years ago, and unwound her steel-streaked, coarse hair, combed it out with long, smooth strokes, and replaited it into a thick braid. She would cover it with a colorful scarf once she had dressed in her peasant skirt and blouse. Someone who had known her in her youth would note only a few differences in her appearance—the thickening of her body and the sagging of her face. Her dark eyes still held their secrets, but bags and wrinkles softened their intent. Her lips still smiled without humor but lacked the lush fullness that had once captivated men. Her life passed one day after the next without much excitement. The faces changed, but the events remained the same.

The simple breakfast she'd eaten since youth nourished her, but she didn't taste it. Her mind did not wander as the morning TV news confirmed her dream; it catalogued what the experts thought they knew about the killer they called the new Jack the Ripper and his motives. Their theories amused her with their total lack of insight.

"Foolish pup. They will catch him soon enough. He cannot control the power of that one," she said. Her thick voice clipped and strung out the English vowels and consonants still strangely shaped for her Russian tongue. "His hunger grows."

Her window shades went up with the first morning light. The small shop behind which she lived held trinkets and charms, crystals and herbs, and icons and other treasures she had collected. Those who came to the shop to browse would not arrive until much later in the morning and afternoon, but Natasha Borisovna's true customers quickly appeared once she turned the heavy lock on the front door. They came for her elixirs and potions or a card reading.

"Spacibo bolshoya, Natasha Borisovna," Nadezhda Ivanovna said. "Thank you so much for the powder. Little Alexei's cough is much better."

"Nie za shta," Natasha Borisovna answered. "I am glad he is doing well. No, no," she said, waving her hands in refusal as Nadezhda Ivanovna extended her hand with payment for the medicines. "You keep it. But perhaps the next time you are making your *fruktovnii* soup, Nadezhda Ivanovna, you might send me a jar. No one makes fruit soup like you."

The younger woman smiled and blushed at the compliment. "I'll send Misha over with some this evening. Thank you again."

Natasha Borisovna watched her leave and envied the rosy cheeks and glowing skin, only slightly marred by concern for her son, that Nadezhda Ivanovna had. Once her own face and body had been that resilient. All the men had thought so.

The giggling gaggle of window-shoppers bursting into her shop brought Natasha Borisovna out of her memories. With colorful sweatshirts sporting college names and mascots emblazoned across their chests, and happy, healthy, pearl-white smiles and burning wallets, they meandered around Natasha Borisovna's little store, calling to one another over some oddity or find. Natasha Borisovna could already hear their vapid thoughts and misplaced amusement at her shop and its contents.

Any minute now they will expect me to perform a magic trick, Natasha Borisovna thought churlishly. Fools always want what they do not need, and more than they have.

"Hey, old woman," called the leader of the group. "Do you have any charms to bring more money?" He laughed with his companions in smug assurance that her answer would be no or that even if she claimed to have such a device, it would not work. Her shop did not boast wealth, and Natasha Borisovna knew people would expect one who could make wealth to have it on display for all to see.

Natasha Borisovna's dark eyes narrowed. "You have it on your person even now. I believe you have some change, no?"

The blond man looked at her skeptically, perceiving a hoax. "Sure," he said, going along with the game. He dug into his front pocket with a large, calloused hand and thrust out his palm full of coins of various denominations for Natasha Borisovna to inspect.

She made a show of searching through the coins for the one that would carry her bidding. She found a shiny new penny. Her lips curled into a humorless grin as she plucked it from his hand. A copper coin could carry a great deal of mischief and pain, and could cling to its owner with a perniciousness unrivaled by any other coin. Natasha Borisovna held the penny in her cupped hands and breathed upon it. She felt the smirks on the young faces but showed none of her own feelings as she concentrated on bending the metal to her wishes. She turned and considered the glass vials lined neatly on her back shelf. Their only labels were colorful bits of ribbon tied around their delicate necks, but Natasha Borisovna knew their contents. She had collected each drop of their essence over the years, and used them judiciously. She took one with a bit of greenish-gold ribbon down and unstoppered it. A thick wisp of green gas twisted upward like a cobra and then sank back into the bottle. Natasha Borisovna carefully placed one oily green drop on the coin's face before closing the vial and putting it back in its place. Rubbing the oil into the coin, Natasha Borisovna muttered in a low, guttural voice.

"Bozha moy, daite etomu cheloveku to shto on poprosit. Daite yemu diengii i bolshe." Natasha Borisovna smiled and offered the coin back to the young man, who took it, looked it over a couple of times, and then shrugged his heavy shoulders.

"Whatever," he grumbled, dropping the coin back into his pocket before turning and leaving with his friends.

Natasha Borisovna watched them leave. "Be careful of what you wish for," she warned under her breath. They didn't hear her, and wouldn't have heeded her if they had.

Jack sat quietly in his hotel room and watched the sun go down while the news rambled on about world events. He didn't pay it any attention. As the light dimmed, he felt the need to kill sharpen in his belly like a serrated knife sawing back and forth on his innards. The glass window felt cool against his naked skin, which burned hotter and hotter with every moment. He had cracked the window open slightly to let in the congealing air. It brought the smells of the city and the night with it.

Was that a whiff of perfume? his feverish mind asked. *No,* was the disappointed answer. His tense body slumped against the cool pane until anticipation stretched it taut against the chilling window again. His steamy breath clung to the glass. The rubber band twisted tighter in his gut.

Across the street the shop windows darkened, metal gates rattled closed in front of them, and their keepers left. Except one. The gypsy woman had not closed her store yet. Jack watched a man hurry in with something under his arm and then leave empty-handed moments later. He quickly dissolved into the brewing mist. The old woman lowered her shades, locked her door, and turned out the light. Hers was the only shop on the street not heavily guarded by security devices. The rumors were enough to keep robbers and vandals away.

Now they will come.

Eagerly, Jack's eyes scanned the darkening street. The fog billowed in, creeping around the edges of buildings. It swallowed cars and landmarks, diminishing his view, but he could smell them . . . feel them . . . hear them. They would come, and Jack could choose his prey from among the evil sinners plying their soul-corrupting trade. Pointed heels, short skirts, low tops, big breasts, long hair, short hair, color didn't matter; pretty eyes of all hues made to lure a man in; sweet smells of rose, lily, and musk; red lips, open arms, warm bodies, and black souls. Jack inhaled deeply. Yes, they were coming. Their calls to the passing cars rang in his ears and hummed through his blood. He stood and went over to the bed. With great care he put on his meticulously laid-out clothes. He chose his glossy instruments with purpose. He polished a smudged scalpel with the warmth of his breath and the fine texture of a silk scarf. His hands twitched and curled around his shining tools as he admired their sheen. A proud smile warmed his young face, but not his eyes.

Perfect.

They would feed him and make the Ripper stay with him. Their lives were his food, their blood his nectar, and their souls his ambrosia.

Natasha Borisovna sat quietly at her kitchen table and drank the soup Nadezhda Ivanovna had sent over. She had felt the chill crawling up the street when she locked up her shop. It hid the evil soul out hunting for those weaker than itself to feed on and to nourish its evil. He was out there, and there would be another murder. That was life. It did not bother Natasha Borisovna. Everyone thought that evil only fed on the innocents, but only evil could sustain evil. A smart hunter knew to prey on those no one would miss. The boy was a poor chooser of victims, killing women who did not have enough darkness within their souls to feed his master for long. He had killed too often in too short a time to go unnoticed by the authorities. He was a nuisance.

Natasha Borisovna finished her soup and cleared the table. In a few moments she had the small kitchen tidied up and a pot of black tea steeping. She wondered if the blond man had wished upon his coin yet, She smiled. He would get what he wished for, but with a price. Everything had a price. The big fish would eat the little fish, and the sharks would eat them all.

Leaving the lights off, she strolled into her shop. She knew every item by heart, but she gazed into a crystal or polished a silver medallion or straightened some books as she toured her little store in search of something to focus her attention on. Her thoughts kept straying to the killer. How he had connected with the other, darker soul he fed and cherished, she did not know. She would not name him even in her mind, for that would bring him to her doorstep.

Was that what she wanted?

Of course not. She was an old woman, whose life, though unexciting, held much to do. Even contemplating the blond man's fate and the trick she had pulled on him did not amuse her. It held no weight.

Maybe a trip would do me good. But where would I go?

She had no family to visit. All had long since died, including her many grandchildren. Their children would not know or welcome her.

She cracked open the door and smelled the air deeply. The thick fog caught in her nostrils. To it clung the smells of life and death and hunger. Her blood quickened slightly with the small pulse of energy she felt from a few blocks away.

The deed is done. He feeds. Natasha Borisovna's eyes tried to penetrate the fog to see him feast on his victim, but age and darkness prohibited her. Disappointment and fatigue slumped her shoulders and weighed her body down. She closed the door again and stepped back into the shadows of her shop. Time had long passed since she had hunted in the darkness. *Babushka* had taught her all the tricks she would need to survive. They had served her well over the years. More than once they had saved her life from those who would destroy her for what she was, and from those who would have fed on her soul to empower their own. But it had been some time since she had been the hunter rather than the hunted. She looked over at the glass vials, which twinkled in their own eerie glow upon the shelves.

Out of the corner of her eye, Natasha Borisovna saw a dark figure take form as it emerged from the dense fog. Anger filled his steps. His body glowed with the power he had collected, but Natasha Borisovna sensed his kill had not yielded the energy he had desired. He stopped near the entrance to his hotel and looked across the street at her store. Natasha Borisovna held her breath and wondered if she dared.

Jack.

Anger roiled in Jack's stomach like rotten milk. The blonde had not been as corrupted by her life as he'd thought. Her youth still held too much naïveté to suit his needs.

Should have taken the older one with the suspicious eyes. She knew well enough to wonder about us. She has been around, but the girl had no fire. The condemnation scraped hard against his earlier sense of pleasure and dimmed it. It was already late, too late to clean up and hunt another. He'd have to wait until tomorrow.

I need more power now, Jack, the Ripper barked in his head.

Like a whisper brushing against the fine hairs of his ear, Jack heard someone call his name from somewhere in the empty night. With uncanny certainty, Jack homed in on its source. His eyes narrowed as he tried to cut through the dense mist hanging in the still air and see into the dark shop across the street.

The old woman has more than those women, the Ripper hissed. *She knows evil in her heart, and would sate our hunger for a long time. She's old. Her soul's corruption has aged. It will taste wonderful, like an aged wine, warm and smooth, but full of vibrancy.*

Jack debated. There were the rumors. Many said the gypsy was older than she looked, and that she could work more than simple charms. Some said she used black magic to perform her spells. Stories about what had happened to a gang leader who tried to rob her store made people very careful of what they said about the Russian woman. Even her own people spoke of her in reverent, even fearful, tones. A person like that would have more evil stored up in her than a few prostitutes walking the streets. Besides, the women with enough dark power to interest and benefit Jack had sought other ways of finding new customers and servicing their regulars. They would stay out of the Ripper's hunting grounds until it was safer. His prey had grown scarce, and the recent pickings less desirable. Maybe the old woman would do the trick.

There's still time.

Jack, came the call again.

Jack peered into the darkness but saw no movement coming from within the tiny store. He felt a presence. He felt her there, watching him in the darkness.

Get on with it. It will be morning soon.

Tomorrow, Jack thought. Tomorrow night, when she was not waiting for him, he would go in and do it. Jack felt the Ripper's disgust and anger at his disobedience, but instinct told him to wait. With resolute steps, Jack turned and entered the shadowy doorway of his hotel and made his way up to his room without anyone the wiser. From his darkened room he watched the gypsy's store for movement but saw none. Only when dawn approached with flares of light and chased away the fog did he sleep.

He had not come when she called, but he would. Natasha Borisovna knew he would come. He had to. She felt his hunger growing. It gnawed in her belly and fired her blood. She had long forgotten the excitement that accompanied the hunt. Her mind seemed to work faster than the day before. Her heart beat with more vigor. Spells and charms she had not used in decades came readily to mind. *Babushka* had taken her on her first hunt when she was a child. Those glorious days seemed more clear and vivid in her memory now.

Natasha Borisovna kept her shop closed for the day to

give her time to prepare. She ignored the passersby who peered into her windows as she collected items from around the store that would aid her in her quest. She paused in front of an ancient hand-carved oak mirror and took in her appearance. In her mind's eye the bags and wrinkles faded away, leaving her almond-shaped eyes bright and mysterious in their exotic slant. She saw her hair as it had been, raven black with a high-polished gloss. The breasts that now hung to above her thick, sagging waist had firmed and lifted to a more provocative posture, and her waist had dwindled to a delicate diameter. Her skin glowed with a fire that erupted from inside her heart, and looked as supple as fine silk. This would not bring him, but this was what she would have when she had finished with him.

A man tapped his finger on her glass door, and she turned to shake her head no, the store was closed. She knew he saw only a dowdy old woman staring bemused at herself in the mirror, but the ignorant had no eyes. She watched him go on to another shop down the row, and felt the confidence and pride that had once been her weapons regain their strength. Her shoulders pulled back squarely, and, her step lighter and more daring, Natasha Borisovna went back to her preparations.

Jack awoke, not that he had slept much. The Ripper had killed often over the centuries since his own body died, but he had always left his carrier to suffer the legal consequences when he could no longer hunt. Not this time. Jack knew all the Ripper's victims. He knew all the tricks to hunting them down and exacting their souls. He would not fail as the others had. He would kill the old woman and make the Ripper stay with him always. The power the Ripper brought with him was like none Jack had ever tasted before, and he would not relinquish it. They would be one. But first to kill the old gypsy.

The older the soul, the more power it wielded. Jack would have the advantage since the Ripper had lived for centuries, while the gypsy had lived only decades. Rested and less biased by the emotion of a disappointing kill, Jack discounted the rumors about the woman. All the things they said could not hold any truth. She was an old woman who would die soon anyway. Killing her would not prove difficult.

Jack smoothly sat up in bed and dropped his feet to the floor. He walked over to the edge of the window and looked down. The woman's store was closed. That puzzled him.

What could she be doing? It wasn't quite evening yet, and none of the other shop owners had closed their doors to the public. Jack didn't like it.

Do not trust her appearance, the Ripper advised. *She will not die easily, but her soul will compensate the effort.*

Jack thought that over. Her soul would bind them together for eternity. He was sure of it. He looked toward the west, where the sun sank lower in the sky with every moment. Soon darkness would enshroud the city, and the fog would hold it in its smothering grasp. Jack needed to prepare for this evening. More thought would go into the planning of this hunt than the others. More rested on this one night.

Natasha Borisovna carefully spread the cloth out on the table and smoothed each crease from the fabric. It followed her instructions and draped elegantly over the table's face and brushed the floor with a butterfly's kiss. Dyed a deep vermilion, the material appeared black. Gold symbols of ancient power woven into the dark threads centuries before circled the edge of the table's top. The pillar candles burned deep within themselves from around the room and threw flickering shapes upon the walls and the ceiling. Their delicate smoke gently wafted through the chamber, carrying powerful perfumes that calmed and focused Natasha Borisovna's eager mind. Her hands trembled slightly with anticipation as she placed a heavy carved goblet in the middle of the table. Around the chalice Natasha Borisovna arranged with infinite care white candles, one for each symbol on the dark cloth. Now the cup sat within two circles of power, the white candles and the gold emblems.

Using only the pillar candles for light as the shadows outside darkened and lengthened, Natasha Borisovna removed a long chain, which hung around her neck, from inside her blouse. At its end hung two keys. The heavy brass key was three inches in length and dwarfed the smaller, more delicate gold key that was its mate. Natasha Borisovna took the brass key in her strong fingers and inserted it in the lock for the heavy oak chest behind her store counter. With a twist and a whispered word, the tumblers in the lock fell into place with a loud click, and the lock cracked open. Taking a breath to steady herself, Natasha Borisovna took hold of the lid and forced the hinges to give way. After many years of disuse, they complained quite audibly, but the lid lifted, revealing the chest's interior. No dust coated the inner lining of velvet, nor had moths riddled it with holes. Although it had not been cleaned or inspected for decades, the fabric remained as pristine as when it had first covered the inside of the box. Natasha Borisovna reached into the chest. Her hands drew out a simple wood box without any closure and placed it on the floor next to where she crouched. Another box, heavily padded this time, was lifted out of the chest and opened, yielding crystal vials of all sizes and shapes. This, too, she placed on the floor next to her. A bead of perspiration wetted her cheek as it sank down the side of her face and dissolved in the fabric of her blouse. Her hands shook violently, so violently she had to clasp them together a moment before she could continue, when the enormity of what she planned enveloped her in its smothering grasp. Taking yet another deep breath, Natasha Borisovna reached into the oak chest and withdrew a beautifully ornate, hand-painted lacquer box from her homeland. She held her breath as she forced her stiff body to stand and cross the room to the side table that stood against the wall dividing her shop from her home. Another ring of white candles sat upon this table. Natasha Borisovna placed the ornate box within the circle.

"Zagoraitess," Natasha Borisovna commanded. The white candles burst into flame and encircled the lacquer box with a ring of light.

She then returned to the chest to collect the other two boxes, which she placed on the counter to inspect. Out of the padded box's compartments she withdrew three crystal vials, which appealed to her. She set them on the counter, lifting them one by one to see how the candlelight flickered through their glass facets. One caught the light and consumed it, turning it to a dark vermilion that cast a bloody glow.

"Yes," Natasha Borisovna crooned. "Yes, that is good. *Ochen horosho.*"

She carefully placed the flask on the counter and returned the others to their protective cells. She then lifted the lid on the wooden box, which had no carved symbols or writing on its surface for all to read. Its simplicity gave it more power and protected the contents stored inside. Strands of colorful ribbon, all precisely cut long ago, lay in a rainbow of hues. Natasha Borisovna's fingers twitched over them as she sought the perfect pair for her task. They had to match the soul they would identify.

"Red," she muttered under her breath. "It must contain red." Her fingers danced through the threads, then halted on a pair that caught her breath in her dry throat. Deep blood red throbbed and rushed down the lengths, growing darker and darker with every millimeter, until the very ends dripped ebony ink. "Yesss," she hissed. "These are the ones I need." She plucked the thin fibers from the box and laid them gently across her open palm. Her other hand closed the box while Natasha Borisovna gazed rapturously at the delicate ribbons of color that lay in her hand like a pair of open wounds. She picked up the vial and carried it and the threads over to where the goblet awaited them on the table. Once she had placed them in their proper order within the circle of unlit candles, Natasha Borisovna went to the oak chest and extracted a bottle of wine. She scrutinized its half-full contents and wondered if it still contained the potency it once had. She expertly uncorked the bottle with a loud pop, and let it breathe a moment before sniffing at the bottle's mouth. The wine had mellowed over the years, but the rich aroma that emanated from its heart brought back memories of Russia in the summer, when the hot sun had baked the grapes until they yielded their sweet, sugary juice when lightly squeezed. She smelled the rich earth, full of life, full of secrets. Wine was the boiled-down essence of the grapes and the earth and the sun into one pure liquid that could purify or distill one's self. Its powers, known only to a few, could bring a man to his knees in blessing or in damnation. Natasha Borisovna resealed the bottle to let none of its strength evaporate before she needed it, and placed the bottle on the table next to the goblet.

One item remained in the chest. Natasha Borisovna turned to remove that item when she noticed how dark it had become while she made her preparations. She would need to hurry. He would come soon, and she had to be ready for him or all would fail. She hurried over to the door and looked up at the top window where she knew he stayed. The light from his room spilled out into the night to keep away the fog prowling outside. Her breath snagged in her throat when the light went out.

Jack finished buttoning the last button on his shirt and put on his jacket. The night air had an added chill in it. It seemed to reach through the small space he had left the window open and tickled his spine with ghostly fingers. More than once he had fumbled while getting dressed, and he had unconsciously wrinkled his shirt while trying to put on his tie. He refused to look out the window again to see if the gypsy's shop had changed in any way.

With the meticulous skill he had always prided himself on, he arranged the assortment of implements on the smooth surface of his bed. They glittered wickedly in the lamplight and begged to be touched. Scalpels and knives of various sizes lay next to pincers and forceps. Jack examined each instrument down to the finest detail, looking for a flaw. He had lovingly sharpened each point, taking great pains to imbue their deadly edges with an ardent need to kill. They had tasted blood many times before. He could feel their hunger for more.

As he placed each instrument in the bag he carried with him on his rounds, Jack thought about the order in which he would use them. He could see the whole evening unraveled before him in his mind's eye. Pleasure and anticipation thrummed through him in hot waves of energy, while his blood throbbed and whooshed in his ears. His lungs ached for more air as he tried to contain the exhilaration of the hunt. Without glancing at the window, Jack turned and left the room, turning the light off just before he closed the door.

Natasha Borisovna smoothed the folds of her black dress down over her body. Her gnarled hands ushered the wrinkles out of the material and pleaded with the seams to give her ample body more room. She tore the scarf off her gray head and quickly unbound her long hair. With long, sharp strokes of her brush, Natasha Borisovna attacked her tresses until they crackled in long waves. He would come soon, and she had not finished her preparations. She glanced at her appearance in her bedroom mirror and saw the long chain and keys hanging down her front. She fed the keys down her bodice, and their weight carried the chain with them.

Back in her shop, she looked around to make sure everything was in its place.

"The knife! Where is the knife?" she asked herself. She could hear the minutes ticking past inside her head for an answer. "The chest." Natasha Borisovna's body moved rapidly to the chest to grab the last weapon. As her fingers closed around the carved hilt, she heard the doorknob twist and the catch give way. She hid the knife in the folds of her skirt when she saw the man's dark figure fill her doorway. The fog's icy fingers crawled in around him to invade her shop and poke its mischievous nose into her possessions. It sniffed at the incense and potpourri. It blew out some of the candles when it didn't like their odor. It pooled upon her floor like an evil quagmire and softened its master's steps so that he seemed to float across the room toward her with sickening speed.

"Good evening, Ms. Klimova," he said. His rich, melodic voice pronounced her name with a deceptive hint of respect. "I see you were expecting me." He looked about the room at the candles and the table. "Was this meant to keep me away?" he asked, amused.

"No," Natasha Borisovna answered. For the first time in all the years she could remember, she felt unsure of her ability to complete her task. She silently berated herself for challenging such a powerful opponent when she had not hunted in decades. *Nonsense. Remember who you are. You are Natasha Borisovna Klimova, direct descendant of the most powerful gypsy kings and queens who traveled across Europe. This upstart has no skill, and only the power his parasitic master gives him.* Natasha Borisovna stood straighter, pulling her shoulders back and lifting her chin in a fierce stance. "I thought to make you an offer," she purred with self-assurance. She could see the smirk of arrogant amusement that twisted his lips, and vowed to beat him.

"An offer? Perhaps a potion for a toothache or dry cough?" he mocked. "Sorry, not interested. What I want is more valuable and more costly . . . to you."

With calm purpose, Natasha Borisovna strolled over to the table. "You wish to bind Jack the Ripper's soul to your own for eternity, and make his power your own. Correct?" she asked with a haughty lift to her head and one eyebrow. That took him aback a moment, but he soon regained his impudence.

"The rumors about you don't do you justice, Ms. Klimova. I've never given the fearful ramblings of a bunch of uneducated peasants much credence, but it seems they may have had it right. My luck grows." He came to stand across the table from Natasha Borisovna with insolent abandon— a cat prepared to toy with its mouse.

"Killing me will only temporarily sate you both, but I know a way to turn the master into the slave, and the slave into the master." She watched him absorb her claim and examine it for truth.

"All right, I'll bite. How could you do that?" He threw his weight onto one hip and rested his long, artistic hands on the black bag he had set on her table.

"The people around here only think they know my true age, but I have performed spells since before their great-great-grandparents took their first breath. The magic needed to bind two souls together in one body is old but simple. I have performed it many times, as have my ancestors. My offer to you is this. Allow me to work my spell, and if it works, you let me live. You walk out of here and do as you please with your newfound power. You will have more power once it is done," she promised. "I will tell no one. However, if my magic does not work, and the Ripper still requires my life energy to feed on, I will not try to escape, and my life will be yours to take."

Natasha Borisovna watched him mull over her offer. Inside, her intestines twisted in on themselves, and her heart hammered wildly in her breast and in her ears. If he heard that, he would strike. She could not let him sense the bluff in her statements. His young, virile body could easily overpower her much older, stiffer figure. She could feel the fog reach under the table and wrap around her naked ankles like icy leg irons. Her palm began to cramp from squeezing the knife hilt so tightly. He still did not know about that. Should he attack, she might have a chance. *Keep your wits about you, Natasha.*

"How do I know this is not a trick?" His words snapped her attention fully to him once again. "I have heard about the tricks gypsies play on the unsuspecting." His scrutiny pinned her, clamping her jaw down on her tongue so at first she couldn't speak.

"I give you my word," she swore.

"Not good enough."

"I swear on my dead grandmother's soul that I will bind your soul and his together for all eternity, or you may kill me."

"I can kill you anyway, old woman. You should remember that."

Natasha Borisovna tried another tactic. "You are afraid to try my spell," she goaded in a questioning tone. "Maybe you are not strong enough to hold on to one as powerful as he is. Maybe he will leave you anyway once you have killed me, and the police will kill you for murdering all those women." She saw indecision and anger enter his eyes. "How much power can an old woman have in her body to feed a master of death such as that one? I am nearly dead even as we speak. Not much of a victim, not for a man who has hunted hundreds of young, strong women, who were full of life and energy," she jeered. "Maybe you should run along now and seek out a young prostitute to feed your master, boy." Her emphasis on the word *master* had brought fire to his narrowing eyes.

"All right, old woman. I'll let you try your spell, but if it fails, you will not die slowly. We have all night, after all," he growled.

Natasha Borisovna relaxed. Air entered her aching lungs with a crispness that burned. She tasted the evil chill of the fog and felt it sucking away at her warmth as it wound its way sinuously up her bare legs. The blood quieted in her ears, and her heart didn't beat against the walls of her chest like an inmate rattling a cage. Her mind quickly went to work dredging up the ancient spells of protection and confinement she would need.

"Zagoraitess," she commanded, lighting the ring of candles that separated her from her opponent. She saw him jump at the small show of power, and smiled. Sweet calm flowed through her veins. Her hands steadied. She placed the knife on the table so she could uncork the bottle.

"Why the knife, old woman? You weren't planning on using that on me, now, were you?" His voice slithered across the air and carried with it a threat of danger.

"We will need it for the spell," she calmly explained. Carefully avoiding the small flames, Natasha Borisovna lifted the bottle of wine and removed its cork. She gave it a second to breathe before pouring a small amount into the goblet. The powders she had sprinkled in the bottom of the cup quickly dissolved in the wine, unseen by the man. She lifted the goblet and swirled the contents around three times, all the time whispering the spells of protection under her breath. She looked across at the man and saw that he watched her, entranced. *Good. It is working.*

"Here. Drink," she ordered, offering him the chalice. He took it and stared uncertainly into its midst. She sensed the Ripper was canceling her instructions, and saw her fears coming true as he raised his head to look at her, and his eyes cleared of their earlier mists.

"Poison?" he asked. "Not very original, old woman." He placed the goblet back on the table and opened his bag. "I think we should just get on with the second part of this evening's entertainment. Don't you?"

Natasha Borisovna grabbed the bottle of wine and drank greedily from its contents. She slammed the bottle back down on the table and angrily wiped her wine-stained mouth with the back of her hand. Defiantly she dared him with her eyes and posture. "If it were poison, would I drink so readily from it? You are a fool if you listen to his lies," she sneered. "He prods you on to hunt for him again and again, leaving you to take the risks. Do you really think he wants to reside in your body for all time? Of course not. He is using you as he has used the others over the years since his own body died. He knows I will imprison him within you, so he poisons your mind against me."

Her words had stopped him. She watched him consider them. The struggle within him for control drew his brows into an angry frown, while his facial muscles twitched and his hands clenched and unclenched. Again, he looked at her with narrowed, suspicious eyes that searched for any failing in her health. She met his gaze with a haughty one of her own that told him she thought he was a weak-minded fool and unable to control the demon within him. His hand grasped the goblet once again and lifted it to his lips. He paused and watched her face, looking for the lie. She kept her thoughts to herself and let him stew on that while his lips hovered at the cup's edge. She nearly fainted when he sipped from the wine and handed the chalice back to her. She had to force steel into her arm and her fingers to keep them from shaking as she reclaimed her goblet and returned it to the center of the circle.

"Give me your hand," she commanded. He looked at her outstretched hand a long moment while the fog continued to search out the secrets of her shop. It found the side table with the lacquer box, but the lock kept it from discovering the contents. Its icy breath extinguished a couple more pillar candles, dimming the room to an eerie gloom. The white candles burned, uncaring of the fog's presence.

"Your hand, please," Natasha Borisovna urged. "We must complete the spell before the first light, or you will never possess him."

His hand slowly stretched across the table to lie in hers. The smooth white skin felt cold in her warm, callused palm. The clean, manicured nails reflected the glow of the candles. She turned it over so she could see the palm. His life line did not extend across his hand very far, and his heart line made the slightest of impressions in his skin. Natasha Borisovna smiled to herself.

"Do not move," she said as her other hand picked up the knife and slashed across his palm with lightning speed. He pulled on his hand and gasped in shock, but Natasha Borisovna would not let go now. She held his hand over the chalice and turned it sideways. The blood quickly bubbled up within the wound and poured into the chalice to mix with the wine. She massaged his wrist and the flesh at the base of his thumb to pump more of his life's essence into the cup. She heard his sounds of pain, and now fear tinged his tones, but she didn't stop until he yanked his injured hand from her grasp.

"What are you trying to do? Bleed me dry?" he accused, holding his bloody hand clutched protectively against his chest. He reached into his bag with his healthy hand and withdrew a white handkerchief with which he bound his hand to stop the bleeding.

"I am merely strengthening the spell by using your blood to restrain his presence within you," Natasha Borisovna calmly explained. "I do not want him to break free later. Do you?"

He appeared to consider her words, then shook his head no.

"Good. Then shall we proceed?" She left the decision up to him.

He nodded, but reluctantly, and with apprehension.

"Good. Now I need a lock of your hair." When he started

to protest, she said, "Quickly, while the blood is still fresh in the wine."

He debated, but nodded his head. Natasha Borisovna slowly circled the table until she stood next to him. She clasped the bloody knife in her hand and raised it slowly. If he spooked now, all would be lost. A tremor passed up her arm—part fear, part excitement. He grabbed her wrist with a cruel jerk, and wrenched her hand and the knife away from his head.

"No funny business, old woman. I'm warning you." To emphasize his words, he pressed a lethal-looking knife against her heart. Small and delicate in appearance, it would slide between her ribs with ease and reach her heart within a second of his thought. She looked at it and reconsidered her plan. This game was proving to be more deadly than she had remembered. She tried to breathe normally, but she couldn't take in enough air with that knife pressing against her breast. She felt a warm dew of perspiration coat her scalp as hot adrenaline pounded in her veins. The knot in her belly grew with every heavy heartbeat, and bile crawled up her throat to gag her. She had to force her eyes to rise calmly and match his.

"I am merely going to cut a lock of your hair. It is vital for the spell to work."

He loosened his grip on her wrist, but his eyes didn't leave her. If she even thought about diving the deadly blade into his neck at the carotid artery, she would drop into death as quickly as he. Instead, she measured her breaths to keep them all the same length. Her heart slowed, but her blood still sounded loudly in her sensitive ears. She could hear the fog sniffing about her chest. Out of the corner of her eye, she could see it rise up along the wall and reach for her first shelf of vials. She had to hurry.

The sharp edge of the knife quickly separated the hunk of hair from his dark head, leaving the smooth strands in her nervous hand. With haste, Natasha Borisovna returned to her spot on the other side of the table and put the knife down. She picked up one of the red ribbons and carefully bound the lock together. Then, plucking a few strands from the lock, she tossed them into the wine, which eagerly consumed the black fibers. The heat from the candles had raised the wine's temperature so that it began to stir on its own.

Natasha Borisovna choked on the first words of her spell when she saw the thick tendrils the fog had extended upward had reached the bottom shelf and were examining the vials resting there.

"Bozhe moi, daite etomu cheloveku to shto on poprocit. Pust fcegda budut eti dva duxi bmectie," she beseeched. "God, give this man what he asks for. Let these two spirits forever be together," she translated, hoping to appease the man, who now was looking at what the fog had discovered. Natasha Borisovna swallowed hard and glanced nervously from the fog's evil interference to the man to the chalice, which had begun to bubble. *"Bozhe moi, sdelaite etomu cheloveku to shto on sdelal. Daite mne evo dux i sushiest-vovanie,"* she commanded. She concentrated on the bubbling wine and urged it to complete its task.

"What's going on?" Jack asked. Anger had crept into his voice and replaced any fear he might have felt. "What are those?" He pointed at the rows of glowing vials that lined the wall. The fog had crept up to the second level.

"They are nothing," Natasha Borisovna answered. "Just some of the potions I use in my spells. Really, they are nothing." She stepped back from the table as he leaned toward her menacingly. The wine had not boiled long enough yet. She hoped she had gotten enough of his blood in the chalice before he stopped her. If not . . .

"Nothing, huh?" he asked. He stalked her around the table with slow, deliberate steps. "You wouldn't lie to me, now, would you?" he purred. "Remember, you swore on your grandmother's soul. That's an awfully big promise to break."

Natasha Borisovna kept pace with his steps. She hoped to buy enough time for the spell to take effect. His deadly knife glittered viciously in the candlelight as he waved it back and forth in front of him. She watched his eyes. They would show the first signs that her plan was working. And they did.

As he closed the distance between them, his sure steps became a stagger, and his eyes began to glass over into a blind stupor. *The powders are working.* Her heart leaped.

"What the hell . . ." He stopped and wiped his face with one hand. Perspiration misted his skin. "You witch. You poisoned me!" he shouted. His hand swept across the table and knocked over the chalice.

Natasha Borisovna gasped and jumped to rescue the goblet and its contents, but the side of the cup hit the table with a resounding thunk, and rocked to and fro on the tabletop. Nothing spilled out across the clean tablecloth. The contents had boiled down to nothing. Natasha Borisovna clutched her chest with relief. His fist sent her body reeling on the cold, fog-swept floor in a dazed heap. Her reflexes had dulled since her last hunt.

"I'll kill you, old woman!" he shouted like an enraged bull. "I swear I will." He weaved toward her on drunken legs, his knife outstretched before him. Natasha Borisovna's head still swam from the punch he gave her, but she managed to stay out of his reach and used the growing blindness overcoming him to keep herself alive until he succumbed. She opened the door that separated the shop from her kitchen, but the fog welled up and slammed it shut again. Its icy breath clung to her and slowed her down. She turned and fell back against the closed door to avoid Jack's hungry knife, but she felt the painful sting of its cruel bite as it sliced down her arm from her elbow to her hand. She pushed off from the door and put the table between them again. The white candles now burned with a deep crimson flame. Natasha Borisovna looked over at the side table and saw that those candles had also begun to burn a deep blood red. She resettled the chalice in an upright position in the center of the circle and watched it refill with a thick, oily fluid that clung to its sides and glowed in the light of the candles.

The man's screams jerked her eyes up to watch him.

Jack kept waving his knife about him to ward off his unseen foe, but the fire consuming him kept growing hotter and hotter. His vision had filled with an angry red glow that sucked out his insides and drew the energy he had collected from his grasp. He couldn't see the old woman, but he knew she was there. He could hear her laughing, at first in a slow, satisfied chuckle that grew into a soul-shattering guffaw that rang in his ears. His hand dropped the knife—not because it let go of the weapon but because it ceased to exist. He heard the Ripper and felt him struggle to break free of Jack's body, but to no avail. The two were intertwined in a tight mass of writhing energy and power that coursed from their darkest depths. They clawed at each other as they struggled to get out of the whirling vortex sucking them in deeper and deeper until, like a drowning victim in an undertow, they didn't know which way was up or out. Jack's last conscious thought was that the gypsy had delivered on her promise.

Natasha Borisovna collected a glass funnel from one of the drawers behind the counter and fit it gently into the neck of the glass vial with a smooth, steady hand. Her long, slim fingers clasped the heavy chalice and carefully lifted it. She did not wish to spill its precious contents. She was glad she had chosen this vial, which was a little larger than the rest. The added substance extracted from Jack and the Ripper would have plenty of room within their glass tomb. With painstaking care, Natasha Borisovna poured the oily fluid from the chalice through the funnel into the vial, which glowed merrily as it filled. Its reddish glow darkened at the bottom and emitted no light. The neck of the vial filled with the dense mist of the Ripper's fog and pressed against the stopper with which she closed the bottle. She then took one ribbon and began tying it in an ornate bow around the flask's delicate neck. She had to shove her thick black hair behind her ears a couple of times to complete the task because the dark mass kept obscuring her vision when it swung forward over her full breasts and delicate shoulders. As she made the final knot, Natasha Borisovna gently bit into her plump, red lip. She then carried the throbbing, glowing vial across the room and placed it on the top shelf where only a few vials resided. It would need to age awhile before she could use it in a spell. One must never use a spirit's essence before it was ready.

Returning to the table, Natasha Borisovna picked up the dark lock of hair, still bound by the red ribbon. She looked it over a moment before walking over to the side table, where she laid it down. She pulled the long chain hanging around her neck out between her pale, smooth breasts and plucked the golden key between two slim fingers. Leaning down so the chain would reach, Natasha Borisovna fit the key into the lacquer box's tiny lock and turned it. When she opened the lid, she found her collection still safely nestled in their places. She picked up Jack's lock again and placed him next to the last lock collected.

"Jack the Ripper, meet Adolf Hitler," she said in a sweet, dulcet voice as she brushed a fingernail against a dark black lock wrapped with a black and red and white ribbon. Her dark, rich laughter filled the tiny room with evil glee. "Two souls for the price of one."

POINT OF INTERSECTION

Dominick Cancilla

IT WAS NEARLY ELEVEN BEFORE THE MAN APPEARED BESIDE Cathy's bed. She had been lying covered in sweat under a single sheet, staring into the darkness, waiting. One moment there was nothing but the faint glow of her blinds backlit by streetlight, and the next there was a shape, and a voice.

"Cathy," he said, and nothing more.

She didn't cry out. She didn't do anything at all.

He grinned—Cathy could dimly see the white streak of his teeth through a gash in his shadowed face—and spoke again. "You're brave tonight," he said. "No running, no screams, no scrambling to get away. I'm impressed."

The man leaned forward, and Cathy saw the bright flash of a blade in his hand. Her eyes opened wide as she pressed herself back into the bed, as if a few centimeters could make any difference at all. Cold metal kissed her throat.

He laughed. "It's going to be easy tonight, so easy. Don't resist, and I promise that I'll let you die quickly." A gloved hand found its way into her hair and balled into a fist.

The pain startled Cathy. She shrieked and pulled away, but that reflex was stayed by the bite of the blade in her neck.

"Don't be a fool, Cathy," said the man, strengthening his grip on her hair. "You'll only make it worse."

Keeping the knife at her throat, he released her hair and climbed onto the bed, onto her. She could feel the press of his legs against her hips as he kneeled over her.

"I'm not going to rape you," he said, but the words offered little comfort. His left hand touched her neck, wandered across her shoulder, came to rest on her breast with only the sheet saving her from the touch of his glove. She shuddered.

The man leaned back a bit, resting himself on her pelvis. "I'm going to kill you in a bit." His hand kneaded her breast. "But there's no need to rush things." He turned his head a bit, twisted his mouth into a wry smile, and looked at her from the corner of his eye. "Does that scare you? The thought of death?"

She didn't answer. He turned his gaze to her neck and then lower; he pulled the sheet down, uncovering her chest and stomach. Cathy felt leather against her skin.

"You never do answer that one," he said, half whispering, although he was not worried about being interrupted. "It's funny, really. You'd think that a person would never die the same way twice, but you . . . you're always the same." His hand returned to her breast. "You always scream when I start to cut you, but it always sounds more defiant than scared. You fight until the last minute and then just collapse. I can never quite get you to beg for death, no matter how much I beat you, and I can never get you to just lie there and take it when I force myself on you. Not that I mind, really."

They sat in silence. He squeezed her breast hard, and then harder still, but lost interest when that elicited no response.

"Aren't you going to ask who I am? You usually do by now. 'What are you talking about?' or some such thing." The knife began to slide back and forth across her neck, almost gently, as if he were caressing her with it. "Tell me, what's gotten into you tonight?"

A car passed outside, throwing its headlights against the blinds, and Cathy could see a quizzical look on the man's face in the stripes of light. Had he looked down, the man would have seen young flesh patterned with dozens of thin scars.

"Well, I'll answer your question even if you aren't going to ask it." He leaned back until he was sitting almost upright on her and pulled the knife away from her throat, only to rest its point at the base of her neck a moment later.

He grinned. "I'm from the future."

His grin faded in her silence, and the knife began to trace a slow path down her chest, between her breasts, toward her stomach.

"We were colleagues, once. Actually, I was your assistant, if you want to get technical about it. We built a time machine, you stole it from me, and I'm here for a little revenge."

At her stomach, the knife changed course and began to trace the outline of her ribs.

"I stole the prototype from the lab after you ruined me with your lies, and I've been coming back in time to kill you ever since." He waited for a response and got none. "I started out by killing you the day before I stole the device, and then the day before that, and the day before that, and the day before that. Sometimes I'd kill you a dozen times in one of my days, each a day earlier in your time. You never saw it coming because it was in your future. Pretty clever, huh?"

Still she was silent.

The man's lips tightened, and he scratched the knife down her side. When she cried out, he grinned. "Much better, much better. Did you think you could pretend that I wasn't here?" He slapped her hard across the face. *"Did you?"*

"No," she answered, her voice tight and high. "No."

"Good." He relaxed again. "I like you at this age. You understand that you get younger every time I do it, don't you? I wish that I had realized what an attractive woman you were while we were still on friendly terms."

A glove wandered down her side, traced the curve of her hip. "You're a virgin now. I know that because I killed you while you were in the arms of your first lover, and that was, oh, maybe a hundred times ago. You would have lost it to the guy you're dating now. Clark something, I think his name was. Does it hurt you to know that you'll never get to that day now?

"Well, don't worry. You lost it the last time, and you'll lose it the next time. To me, of course. If I hadn't raped you an hour ago, I'd do it now, too, but you lucked out. I guess my lust for blood just outweighs the other kind, huh?"

The knife began to circle her left breast. "Maybe I'll cut it off. Or both of them. Then again, that usually makes you faint, and I want you awake for it this time."

The circles became wider, lazier, and stopped in their tracks when Cathy spoke.

"This isn't possible," she said softly. "If you kill me now, then I'll never build the time machine, and you'll never be able to come back and kill me."

"I don't understand it, either," he said without hesitation, pleased that he had finally gotten her talking. "We were never able to figure out how paradoxes would be resolved, and as far as I can tell, they just aren't. I remember helping you complete the machine, just as I remember killing you the day after, and the day after that. I can remember stabbing you in the bath, slicing you to pieces on a public subway, raping you in your parents' living room on Thanksgiving, driving my knife . . ."

As he drifted into nostalgia, the man let the knife drift away from Cathy's flesh. That gave her the opening she had been waiting for. Her left arm grabbed his wrist, twisting the knife away from her flesh, while her right shot out toward his nose.

She had been preparing for this night, and every night like it, since she was eight and her father had caught a prowler trying to strangle her in her bed. The police had found no sign of forced entry, and they had been unable to identify the body.

On the next night, the prowler had come again, and again Cathy's father cut short his attack with a shotgun blast. This time, the police assumed that the men were twins and tailored their investigation accordingly. After the third night, Cathy's father didn't even bother calling the police.

The mystery of how the same man could come after his daughter every night was lost on both Cathy and her father, but when the newly dug graves in the backyard began to number more than a hundred and Cathy began to report that the man had begun stalking her during the daylight hours, her father had known that unless he guarded her every second of the day, the madman would eventually succeed. There was no way that Cathy's father could protect her from such a foe, so he sought a more permanent solution.

Aikido was first—private lessons, every day. Then tai kwon do, then judo. Every night before bed, she completed two hours of calisthenics and weight training; every weekend she attended classes at a survivalist camp. By the time she was fourteen, Cathy could kill a man of any size in a dozen ways, but her father—not wanting to put his daughter to the test—still insisted on killing the attacker himself each night.

Cathy's father died at the stranger's hand when Cathy was seventeen. The killer had appeared behind him and driven a long, curved knife through his spine, grinning all the while. Cathy had broken the man's neck no more than thirty seconds later. From that night on, the man was her problem alone.

When Cathy moved away to college, she had hoped that the killer would be unable to find her. She was wrong. On her first night in her new apartment, he was there. Although the man had found her before when she and her father had stayed away from the house, there was something about being attacked in her apartment that drove home the point that she might never be free of him. So she decided to find out what she could about him in the hope that the information would lead her toward a more permanent solution.

Because the man never seemed to remember the previous attacks—and how could he when Cathy or her father had killed him after each one?—he was easily taken in when she acted coy and afraid. She got him to relax, to revel in her helplessness, and in that state he invariably began to talk. Cathy found out about the time travel story and learned that each night, before he killed her in the future, he tortured her into revealing where he could find her the day before.

The story both confused and upset her. She couldn't imagine ever doing something that could make a man hate her enough to kill her a thousand times over. But the man was a fact of her life, and whatever it was that she was to do to him in the future would have to wait for her to reach it.

After a lifetime of worrying about day-do-day survival, Cathy had begun to take it for granted. She'd made sure that nothing that could be used as a weapon was near her bed, she always slept in the nude so that she wouldn't be encumbered by clothing, and she'd chosen an apartment building that still had a working furnace in the basement. The basement furnace had burned well for the past three months with a steady supply of corpses. With everything taken care of and her combat skills far outstripping her opponent's, Cathy had almost begun to feel secure again. Only the exact time of his arrival each day was a variable.

That was why his ability to defend himself on this night came as such a surprise to her.

Before Cathy's blow even came close to connecting, the man was in motion. He moved like Cathy had never seen him move before; even with all her years of training, she could just barely keep track of his hands. Before she could react, he had deflected the blow, released the hold on his wrist, and pinned her own wrists to the bed.

His grip was incredibly strong, causing tears to well up in Cathy's eyes.

"Ha!" he screamed at her. "I surprised you, didn't I? You didn't think I had it in me! What a treat!"

Cathy could see his eyes wide and glowing, burning with reflected light. His grin was so tight that she would not have been surprised if his lip had split.

"Did you think you were the only one who could learn

from experience? Huh?" His hand released her wrist, slapped her across the face, and was back at her wrist in the blink of an eye.

Blood welled up in Cathy's mouth, but compared to the hundreds of injuries she had suffered at this man's hands over the years, it was not even worth noticing. What bothered her was the way he made her feel. For the first time in a long time, she was afraid.

"Two months from now—Christmas, actually—you really screwed up." He was almost laughing now, his voice rising to fill the room. "You taunted me, played with me. I was crying. Me! Crying! You were going to kill me slow and make me suffer. You broke my arm, then my leg, and then, behold! My time ran out, and I was pulled back to my present!" He laughed in short bursts, unable to control himself. "Do you think I can stay in the past forever? The later you, the one who invented the machine, would never have made such a stupid mistake, but you, you're not even through your general ed classes! You don't know physics from your own ass!

"You put the fear of God in me that time, I'll tell you. I guess the trained you coming from the past met me coming from the future and taught me quite a lesson. Well, the first thing I did was clock myself a few years into the future and get myself a self-defense implant and muscular enhancements. All your training and ten times your strength in just under two hours! The future's grand, I'll tell you that. Not that you're going to see it."

He looked down at her, laughed, and bent toward her neck. Cathy writhed but couldn't break his grip. When she tried to butt his head with her own, he avoided her easily.

Finally, when his lips were so near to her ear that she could feel their motion, he whispered, "You know, it's quite a bit more exciting this way. You're always so surprised, and your level of tension is much higher than it used to be. I adore the sight of you with fear in your eyes.

"And you know what? I think that I will rape you after all."

That was when the lights turned on.

The man sat up immediately, smiling, anticipating a new playmate. Was it a boyfriend? A roommate? Any nuance, any variation would be welcome, or so he thought.

At first, all he saw was the barrel of the gun. Then he saw a flash. Then nothing.

A shudder passed through the man's body, his grip relaxed, his eyes glazed.

Cathy threw the body off her and onto the floor, causing her liberator to take a step backward.

The figure holding the weapon was covered in a black, shiny skin, as if she had been sprayed with a coating of rubber. The weapon—its similarity to any handgun that Cathy had ever seen was superficial at best—melted into the woman's glove and was gone.

From the featureless black face came the voice of a tired old woman. It was filtered by fabric and by the years, but Cathy recognized it as her own. "His name is Martin Santino." She said it automatically, as Cathy had once said the Pledge of Allegiance each morning in grade school. "You will meet him during graduate school and write off his self-centeredness and eccentricity when you discover how well his interests and talents mesh with your own. Over the next ten years, with funding from both private and military sources, you will perfect a practical time travel device together. When the machine is completed, he will use it for his own gain, carrying out petty acts of vengeance and looting the past. You will expose him to the press. He will be sentenced to death but escape prison. The rest, by now, you know."

Another device emerged from the woman's glove, and she touched it to the corpse at her feet. The body glowed gold and became a pile of dust.

"Don't get involved with him when you meet him, Cathy. Don't listen to what he says. Don't try to change his ways. Don't invent the machine. Maybe, if you can do that, we can find some peace."

And then she was gone.

Cathy fell back into bed, weak, trembling.

In all the years, she had never gotten used to the ritual,

and these new wrinkles didn't make it any easier to take. With his new skill, there was more risk, but knowledge that there was hope, that it all might end someday, helped to ease her nerves somewhat.

Cathy knew that she would have a few hours of peace, and she intended to make good use of them.

As she reached for the lamp beside her bed, Cathy caught sight of the dust on her floor. *At least,* she thought, *there will be no more bodies to dispose of.* And she was asleep before her head hit the pillow.

DOCTOR, LAWYER, KANSAS CITY CHIEF

Brent Monahan

VINCE MARTELLI STOOD STOCK STILL IN FRONT OF THE OAK door, leaning well out over his Gucci loafers, right hand extended in midair, like a plastic figure on a model railroad layout. What had paralyzed him was not the name on the door's bronze plaque but the initials etched below the name. "M.D." "Fritz Nussbaum/M.D." Medical doctor. The person you went to when you were sick. Except that Fritz Nussbaum was a psychiatrist. A doctor of the mind. Walking through this door signified an official admission to himself that Vince no longer had any doubts. Once he crossed this door's threshold, he acknowledged at least partial responsibility for the nightmare that had muscled its way into his waking existence.

Vince drew in a deep breath. "Hut one; hut two," he said, softly but with the same kind of diaphragmatic kicks he had used to be heard at the line of scrimmage over stadiums filled with roaring fans. He wrapped his bear paw hand around the knob and rotated his wrist. It was locked.

With a twist of his other wrist, Vince exposed his solid gold Rolex. Six after six. Damn! Could the doctor have left already? It had taken every ounce of nerve Vince possessed to call Nussbaum's receptionist this noon and make the appointment. She had said "Doctor" preferred seeing patients during the daytime, especially on a first visit, but there was no way he could afford to walk into such an office while other people were there. Not Vince Martelli. He had capitalized on both his professional vocal presence and the genuine panic he could hear in his voice to convince the receptionist that Dr. Nussbaum could indeed see him the same evening, at six o'clock.

So, where was the son of a bitch? Vince wondered as he snatched a handkerchief from his coat pocket and wiped away the beads of sweat that had accumulated on his forehead. Parking his four-by-four, walking across the lot into the commercial building's lobby, and taking the only elevator (mercifully meeting no one the whole way) had consumed four of the six minutes. Nussbaum would have to have left near the stroke of six to have avoided him.

Vince balled his huge hand into a fist and slammed it against the door. And then it occurred to him that maybe Nussbaum hadn't had a five o'clock appointment. Maybe he had taken a seventh-inning stretch to catch a bite at a restaurant over on Route 1. Or to hoist a beer at a nearby bar. Sure as shit was where *he'd* be this time of day, at least if he was on the road. Growling, Vince pushed off the door and pivoted toward the elevator.

The door opened behind him.

"Mr. Smith?"

Vince spun around. Even though the man stood squarely in the center of the doorway, there was loads of room, both around him and above. He couldn't have stood more than five-foot-seven, which was half a foot shorter than Vince. A thick head of teased hair might have given him some stature, but the guy was as bald as the proverbial billiard ball. Bald, bespectacled, bowtied, and bowlegged. Vince imagined Nussbaum stripped of the armor of his expensive three-piece suit, standing on some Jersey beach wearing only a pair of swim trunks. Bullies from neighboring states would be trucking in to kick sand in his face. But aside from being bald, bespectacled, bowtied, and bowlegged, he had a reputation for big brains, and that was all Vince required of him.

Vince braced himself for the inevitable look of recognition, but it didn't happen.

"Mr. Smith?" the man repeated.

"Yeah. That's me."

The man took a couple steps backward. "Come in."

As Vince walked into the waiting room, he noticed for the first time the security peephole in the door. Nussbaum had probably been watching him for the past minute, trying to figure out why a big-time celebrity was standing at his door instead of Jack Smith. And then the shrink had figured it out, realized the need for a pseudonym. He was merely playing along. That had to be it. Weirdness in a psychiatrist's office was the last thing Vince needed right now. Vince relaxed enough to note that the receptionist's desk was empty. Just him and the doctor.

"Please, take a seat," Nussbaum bid, gesturing to one of the spindly, Bauhaus-type chairs to Vince's left. He closed the outer door behind him and crossed with a rolling gait to the receptionist's desk, off which he plucked a clipboard and pen. He presented them to Vince.

"I'll need you to fill this out," Nussbaum said. Before Vince could reply, he was moving to the inner door. "I'm on the telephone with a patient," he explained. "Try to relax." His slender figure slipped through the doorway.

Try to relax. Yeah, sure. Easier said than done. He must have seen the sweat pouring off Vince's head. Vince set the clipboard on the desk and moved toward the large mirror on the wall behind the chairs. For sure. Plenty of perspiration. His focus lowered, to the skin under his lake-blue eyes. Then to the angle of his well-chiseled chin. He thrust his jaw forward, forcing the skin taut. He held the unnatural position for several moments, then let go, shooting himself a grim expression.

Nussbaum had not shut the inner door completely. For a few moments, Vince had been oblivious to the psychiatrist's half of the conversation drifting out. But it started to sound too interesting not to eavesdrop.

"Lorelei, we have been over this a hundred times."

Vince sidled toward the door.

"No, in fact, that does *not* count for anything. The situation is still fundamentally the same. You're in a destructive, dangerous relationship, and you must leave him."

In the following silence, Vince returned to the clipboard and took it in hand, as if he actually intended to fill it out.

"Don't start that old game, Lorelei. I told you how. You have the telephone number, but if you need it again, I . . . Just by doing it. Lots of women have gone through this before you, and with much less resources. You're more afraid of your inability to survive on your own than you are of him, but that's irrational."

Vince circled the desk and approached the half dozen diplomas and certificates under glass that hung on the wall. Impressive as hell. Yale. Penn. Diplomate of this. Board member of that.

The woman must have interrupted again, but Nussbaum's patience was clearly wearing thin. "Listen to me . . . *listen!* When does he return? All right, that gives you another day. Come in tomorrow at ten, and we'll make the arrangements together. You can. Yes, you can. No more excuses. Tomorrow at ten. Good night."

Vince glanced again at his Rolex. Sounded like a battered wife. Probably close to what Cindy had told her shrink, even though he'd never laid a hand on her. Fists through walls, plenty of psychological warfare on both their parts, but never any marks on her. He was too smart for that. Not with all his hard-earned worldly possessions riding on the outcome. Never let himself get that out of control. Until now. Twelve damned minutes after. The clock had better not start until he got into that office. He heard the telephone receiver meeting its cradle. He thought about moving but realized he'd boxed himself in.

Nussbaum came through the door and found Vince reading the diplomas.

"Expensive paper," the psychiatrist remarked. "If you have some intelligence, enough time and money, they give you those as prizes."

"You're being modest, Doc," Vince said.

"Not entirely," Nussbaum countered, moving to the clipboard. "I don't want you to think my discipline is like a dermatologist's. I can't prescribe you some tetracycline and promise your inner blemishes will clear up in a week."

"I'm not here for—"

"You haven't filled out this form, Mr. Smith."

Vince cocked his head, unbelieving. "You *are* kidding, aren't you?"

"What do you mean?"

"I mean, we can both dispense with the deception." The doctor's face remained blank. "You *do* watch television, don't you?"

"Not very much. PBS. The Discovery Channel."

It wasn't the first time in his adult life that someone failed to recognize him, but Vince could count the incidents on one hand. If the guy had said he was a rabid football fan, the situation would have been mortifying, but he was, after all, just a shrink.

"I'm Vince Martelli."

Nussbaum's eyes semi-brightened. "You're the sportscaster."

"Right. And I didn't fill out your sheet there for two reasons. First, I'm not gonna be a long-term patient, and second, I'm paying for this session with cash. I can't have it on my health insurance record."

Nussbaum stepped to the side of the door. "We can talk about that later. Come in, Mr. Martelli."

"Vince."

Vince strode into the office. It was large and contained its expected huge desk, decorated with a banker's lamp and several matching mahogany frames, turned so he couldn't see the photos they held. In front of the desk was a pair of curve-backed chairs. A bookcase filled with heavy-duty textbooks and journals covered the wall to his left, and, to his right, three good Matisse reproductions under nonreflective glass hung above a leather divan.

"The classic couch," Vince exclaimed. "I thought it was such a cliché by now . . ." He let the remark trail off.

Nussbaum snatched several tissues from a box sitting on a wooden tea trolley near the door. "Perhaps you'd like to wipe your forehead?"

"Thanks," Vince said. "I'm more nervous than the time I faced Alabama for the SEC title. I was a Heisman Trophy candidate, y'know."

"No, I didn't." Nussbaum had reached for something else on the trolley. When he turned, Vince saw that it was a circular brown plastic bottle. He was opening it and tapping out part of its contents.

"What's that?" Vince asked.

"A beta blocker. Mild chemistry, to help you relax and get more out of our talk."

"Mild? Then you'd better give me two. I'm pretty big."

"That you are," Nussbaum said, offering two of the tiny white pills. "I imagine you got used to pills if you played big-time football."

"Not as much as most," Vince answered proudly. "I stayed as healthy as anybody in the NFL. The only bad time I had was when my leg got broken in the 'seventy-six playoffs." His eyes continued to roam the room, past the desk to the wall of glass that looked down on the building's parking lot and the landscape-divided professional complexes of Metro Park, New Jersey. His eyes widened at the sight of a brass telescope, mounted on a wooden tripod. It was apparently not enough for this guy to get his jollies prying into people's minds; between sessions he spied on the activities inside other offices.

Nussbaum had taken a pony-sized bottle of Perrier from the cart and was twisting off the cap.

"Don't bother dirtying a glass," Vince offered. "I can drink from the bottle."

"How big are you, Vince?"

"Six-three. Two twenty-six. Only gained twelve pounds since my pro days." Vince swallowed the pills and washed them down with a prodigious chug.

"Admirable. Would you prefer to sit or lie down?"

"I'll take the couch," Vince elected, handing the physician the empty bottle. He lowered himself onto the cool leather, completely covering its upper surface.

"What's bothering you, Vince?" Nussbaum asked, once he had crossed the line, defined by the back end of his desk, that separated his inviolate half of the office from that available to the patient.

Vince sucked in a substantial breath. "First, I want to be sure about something: psychiatrists are like priests and lawyers, right? I mean, whatever I tell you, you can't bring to the police . . . or they can't make you talk later on."

Nussbaum looked out the window. "That's correct. Whatever you have to say here is totally confidential. Please, try to relax."

"Okay. It started with a piece of mail I got at my condo. It wasn't junk mail . . . y'know, not addressed to 'Occupant.' This was expensive stationery. My name and address were handwritten. But it was still an ad. It called itself a confidential letter, from Dr. Milton Kronenberg. You know the name?"

"Should I?"

"No, I guess not. He's a plastic surgeon. Park Avenue. Very high-priced, very exclusive. The letter talked about the importance of looks and youth, in society and the business world. It assured that 'body enhancement' . . . his phrase . . . had become commonplace, and nobody thought of it as vanity anymore."

"How did you feel when you read the letter?"

Vince rubbed his hand along the line of his jaw. "I was teed off. The nerve of the s.o.b. I mean, this wasn't some form letter sent out to every house in my zip code."

"How old are you, Vince?"

"Forty-eight. But a pretty fantastic forty-eight, don't you think?" When Nussbaum failed to respond, Vince persisted. "Right?"

"What *I* think doesn't matter," Nussbaum said, still staring out the window. "What's important is the depth of *your* reaction."

Vince's hand strayed to his forehead. At least he had

stopped sweating. "Maybe I didn't make myself clear. I was pissed at this guy's nerve in contacting me unsolicited. I mean, that's still unethical in the medical profession, isn't it?"

"Public advertising is. A private solicitation is shady ground. Did you do anything about the letter?"

"I tore it into a hundred pieces and tossed it in the garbage." The Perrier's carbonation erupted suddenly from Vince's open mouth. "Excuse me."

"Certainly." Nussbaum swung around and headed toward his high-backed, tufted-leather chair. "But you continued to think about it?"

"No way. Life is too short to waste on petty annoyances. But then the bastard calls me!"

"Really?"

"Oh, yeah. Let me give you the conversation verbatim, okay?"

"Please."

"He goes: 'Vincent Martelli?' I go: 'Who is this?' He goes: 'I'm surprised you haven't responded to my letter.' Instantly, I know who it is. And I'm doubly teed off, because I have an unlisted number. I go: 'How did you get this number?' He goes: 'I was given it by the same friend of yours who's so concerned about your career. I had to agree with him, Mr. Martelli: the liquor and the years are starting to show around your eyes and your chin.'" Vince lowered his shoulder and craned his neck around to appeal to the psychiatrist with his eyes as well as his voice. "Can you believe it?"

"And how did you reply?"

"I told him I was gonna report him to the AMA and that if the day ever came when I did want plastic surgery, he'd be the last one to know. Then I slammed down the phone."

"And . . . ?"

"Five minutes later, the asshole calls again. Calm as anything, he says, 'I've done Don Meredith and Frank Gifford, y'know. I can keep my mouth shut, if that's what's bothering you.' To that I replied that if he ever called my home again, I'd personally and permanently shut his mouth for him."

"You threatened his life."

Vince's jaw worked up and down. "Not really." The vehemence in his voice was gone, dissipated by the psychiatrist's question. "It was just the kind of thing that automatically comes out when you're attacked."

"Was it an attack?"

Vince sat up. "Shit. I knew I'd have to be careful what I said in front of you. You shrinks assume whoever walks through your door has the problem."

"I assure you, I'm assuming nothing. Go on, please."

"My answer was just a knee-jerk reaction, okay? Like guys shout at each other across the line of scrimmage. Punch/counterpunch."

"This comment of his about liquor . . . do you drink heavily, Vince?"

Vince changed his focus from the psychiatrist to the bookcase. "Depends on what you mean by heavily."

"What do *you* mean when you say it?"

"More than a six-pack a night. Or . . . more than three double bourbons. I talk in terms of my size."

"Do you ever indulge in more than three double bourbons?"

The psychiatrist's monotone voice, coupled with an insistence on focusing everything back on Vince, was beginning to truly irritate Vince. "What's your point?"

"I agree that you were being attacked when this caller mentioned liquor. The sharpness of the attack, however, hinges upon the actual level of your normal consumption."

Finally, the shrink had ceded him a point. Vince felt suddenly as if he needed to get more peaceful, to press his back fully into the couch. He reclined again.

"Right, right."

"I take it this was not your last incident with Dr. Kronenberg?"

"Absolutely. But first, I've got to tell you about something else that happened to me, because I'm sure it's important."

"Go on."

"About a week after those phone calls, I was home . . . it's off season for football, y'know. I live in an exclusive condo community over in Short Hills. I'm watching ice hockey on the tube, drinking a second bourbon, and suddenly I'm asleep. One minute it's the second period, the next it's morning. I figure I was just bushed. But when I went down to the parking yard, my truck wasn't in my private space. I thought it had been stolen. Then I spotted it at the end of the lot. Nothing was missing, but . . . ."

"Who else has the keys to your truck?"

"No one. I drive a loaded Toyota Land Cruiser. That thing's my pride and joy. I'm sure you can see it out your window. Nobody but me ever drives it."

"I see."

Vince let in a long, slow breath. Despite having to relive the harrowing tale that had driven him to this couch, he was feeling calm. Really calm, for the first time in days. Bless better living through chemistry.

"So, I immediately go out to the golf course to play a round, and everything's fine. But that afternoon, when I walk into my kitchen, I find a bag on the counter, from a pharmacy I never deal with. Inside the bag are three different tubes of those new wrinkle-removing creams."

"How do you think they got there?"

Vince flung up his hands in frustration. "I must have gone out in my truck the night before and bought them. Like sleepwalking."

"Did you go to the pharmacy and ask if anyone recognized you from the night before?"

"Are you kidding? No." Vince curled up the corner of his mouth and shook his head slightly. As if Vince Martelli could afford to stroll into a pharmacy and ask if he'd been acting like an amnesiac. "What I did was cut back on the sauce. I knew Kronenberg was full of shit about my face, but it couldn't hurt to give my liver a rest."

"Sounds reasonable to me."

Vince grimaced. From here on, it was rough sailing. "But I started having this recurring dream about my skin. In the dream, I'd go into my bathroom to shave. I'd shoot lather into my hand and put it to my chin. Then I'd look in the mirror, and my skin was like an elephant's. Gray. Thick. Incredibly wrinkled."

"Dr. Kronenberg had gotten to you."

"Clearly. And still I pushed it all aside. Give it time to fade, I told myself. But then, about a week later, I was up with my lawyer and agent at Fox TV headquarters, to hammer out the next season's contract. You probably can't appreciate it, but these negotiations are a bear, no matter how many times you go through them."

"I would assume it actually gets more difficult every year," Nussbaum replied.

Maybe Nussbaum did appreciate the process, Vince reconsidered. The doctor knew his age and, therefore, knew approximately how long it had been since the name Martelli had been a thing of idolatry for football fans. His value as a sportscaster was rapidly reducing to his voice, his color commentary, and his looks alone.

"It's always difficult," Vince said evenly. "What made this intolerable was one of Fox's weaselly little lawyers beginning the negotiations by smiling and saying, 'What have you been doing in the off season to annoy the fans, Vince?' Seeing he's got me off balance, he says Fox has gotten a stack of letters commenting on my 'alky looks.' I refuse to open negotiations until this 'stack of letters' is rounded up. It turns out to be a total of three. One posted in Boston; one in New York City; one in Saddle River. They're all dated after Kronenberg's phone call. Each is on different paper. One's from an old ribbon typewriter, one from a laser printer, one handwritten, but as if the writer used his opposite hand. I demand photocopies of the three letters. They tell me I'm acting crazy, and that's strictly against company policy. The negotiations are over for the day. It doesn't take much checking to learn that Kronenberg lives in Upper Saddle River. The zip code on the letter mailed from New York City is the same one as his office's. Probably had a conference in Boston and mailed the third one from there."

"What did you do about this?"

"I march right up to his fancy office, push my way past his receptionist, and catch him at his desk reading Dow Jones quotes. He recognizes me right off, jumps up, and sticks out his hand. I wasn't expecting that. It took a little wind out of my sails . . . enough so I didn't punch him out. Thank God. But I let him know I was on to his letter-writing campaign, and if he did one more thing to me I was gonna sue him into the poorhouse." Vince listened to his voice as he spoke. It was incredibly calm, as if he were speaking of an incident whose emotionality had been dulled by a passage of decades. Those little pills had really kicked in.

"Let me guess," Nussbaum said, from his power position behind the desk. "He denied the whole thing."

"Hey! You're good, Doc. That's absolutely what he did. A cigar store Indian couldn't have played it more deadpan. When I told him I didn't appreciate the act, he said I should see a psychiatrist . . . that I'd been overcome by delusions."

"And you took his advice?"

Vince blinked several times. His eyelids were becoming heavy. "No, of course not. I figured he was using a classic offensive defense, but that was all right with me, as long as he knew I meant business. That was three days ago. I went straight home. Worked out in my private gym for an hour or so to blow off steam. Felt better. Put on the highlights tape of me QBing the Chiefs in the 'seventy-four season, and knocked down a few bourbons. Next thing I know, it's morning again. Another fourteen hours unaccounted for. I go down to check on my truck. It's in my reserved space, but I swear it looks like it's been moved. Parked farther to the left than I normally steer it in. I check my apartment, top to bottom. Nothing seems out of place. My golf bag's already in the back of the truck, so I head out to the club. Join a twosome. Second hole, I need my five wood. Take off the cover. There's blood all over the head. My buddy, Walt, sees it first and asks me who I killed. The other guy, Teddy, is laughing so hard it gives me a second to recover. I say it must have been the maid. A rat's been working over the garbage out back, and she must have used the club to nail it. I wash the head off in a water trap nearby and do my best to concentrate on the game. But I'm really rattled." Vince raked his splayed fingers through his thick hair. "When I get into the clubhouse, I call Dr. Kronenberg's office, give them a phony name, and say I'm from the AMA and need to speak to him. The receptionist tells me he hasn't come in. Her voice is edgy. I keep probing until she admits he was supposed to be there, but no one . . . including his wife . . . knows where he is. Later, I checked my truck and found a couple more drops of blood. In the bottom of my golf bag, I found a handkerchief with Kronenberg's initials on it." Vince tried to sit up, to be able to look at the psychiatrist when he delivered his next sentence, but the effort was too great. "I . . . I think I musta killed him while I was in a blackout. I've tried to remember, and I can't. Nothing. The reason I'm here is to ask you about these blackouts. Can you do any kind of test to prove I get them?"

"I'm sorry to say there is no such test, Mr. Martelli. Perhaps if you were to drink heavily in front of licensed physicians and they could monitor you . . . but you only blacked out twice, correct?"

"Yes."

"Then the blackouts probably had to do with your mental state and not the alcohol. I doubt seriously that they could be re-created."

"Shit. You understand that the police will be knocking on my door any minute now? I hear they don't do much the first twenty-four hours someone's missing, unless it looks like a crime's been committed. But then, even if they don't find him, they're gonna start asking questions. His receptionist recognized me. She musta heard me yelling . . . even if Kronenberg didn't talk about me afterward."

"I understand. And you were completely alone during the second blackout?"

"Of course. Christ! If I'd had someone with me, I wouldn't be here."

"All right. Can you sit up?" Nussbaum asked, rising from his chair.

"I don't . . ." Vince made an effort. "Do I have to right now?"

"No. Mr. Martelli, at any time since your first blackout, did you check your house for signs of entry, for listening devices and the like?"

"No," Vince said, confused by the man's bizarre change of tack. "What do you mean?"

"I mean that both you and Dr. Kronenberg could have been set up. Someone wanted both of you punished and cleverly arranged to make it look like one killed the other."

Vince laughed at the absurdity of such comic relief being offered by a top-flight psychiatrist. "I thought I was the crazy one, Doc! Why would anyone do that?"

"Perhaps you both share some common negative quality."

Vince raised his wrist lethargically to consult his Rolex. Plenty of time left in the hour. He could tell that this much-dreaded confession he had disgorged would have to be repeated . . . to another shrink or the police. Because Nussbaum's specialty was obviously paranoia. And fantasies. Might as well hear the guy out, since he was paying for the full hour.

"What negative quality would that be?" Vince asked.

"Heavy drinking, of course. Dr. Kronenberg is also a heavy drinker."

At this news, Vince managed to heave his bulk over onto his right side, so that he could see Nussbaum's face. "I thought you said you didn't know him!"

"No. I asked you why I *should* know him. I was less than honest, I'll admit, but I didn't want that piece of news to muddy your story. I've come to know him quite intimately, in fact. He not only drinks, but he also believes firmly that he is in complete control of his drinking. As you do. Which makes you both dangerous to society in general, because you both drive."

"Hey, I didn't come here to be lectured about my drinking habits!" Vince tried to bark. The words came out slurred, and with less than potent force.

"I'm sure you didn't. Dr. Kronenberg was also a cocky, self-important, aggressive man, who got more aggressive as he drank. It showed clearly when he got behind the wheel of his Mercedes. A gigantic silver 400SE. Which is how he came to dent the driver's door of a car he wanted out of his way. Stove the door in and zoomed past."

A warning bell went off in Vince's head. This lecture was going somewhere he knew he wouldn't like. Damn the rest of the hour. He wanted out. He tried to push himself off the couch, got halfway up, and collapsed back.

"Amazing what a couple little pills can accomplish," the man seated at the desk said. "I'm so glad you insisted on taking two. You're mighty big, Vince." He pushed himself off the desk and moved his bowlegged body swiftly to the trolley, grabbing an unopened bottle of Perrier in his right hand.

Vince struggled again, aided by the adrenaline squirting into his bloodstream from a million little pockets. This time he made it to his feet. A moment later, he was down flat on the carpet, felled by a crisply delivered whack of the Perrier bottle against his forehead.

"Kronenberg hit my door; you took off my bumper, with the ridiculous steel cage on the front of that tank you call a truck. Ripped it off and kept right on going. Hit and run."

"I remember," Vince said, trying to master his rage at being attacked, the bump on his head, and the drugs and panic in his veins. "You pulled ten feet past the stop sign. Right into the street. It was *your* fault."

"My fault?"

"It was! There was no way I was gonna stop, though. Nearly midnight. Nobody else at that intersection as a witness. The media would have had a field day with me."

"Because you were drinking, Vince," the little man said calmly. Then, in a nearly unintelligible shriek that made the veins pop out on both sides of his scrawny neck, "And I was not ten feet past the stop sign! I am an excellent driver! Excellent!" He spun around, rushed to the far side of the desk, and yanked open the top drawer. From it, he pulled a tire iron and a child's jump rope, capped on either side by red-enameled wooden handles. He labored to regain control, swallowing several times, as if to consume his agitation. "The same damned thing with Kronenberg. He sees me signaling to pull into the fast lane, but he's already made up his mind to pass me. Big man, in his big car. Get out of his way. Lays on the horn and the gas pedal at the same time. Never mind I'm in front of him. Bam! And then he flies on past. But not before I get his license. Just like I got yours."

Vince set both his knees on the carpet, aligning himself with the inner door. He knew it would take every bit of his concentration to overcome the drugs, but once he got going, his size and strength should be enough to get him to the outer door. Then it would depend on whether or not this madman had locked them in. He had to keep the guy answering questions, give his body time to pump out lots more adrenaline.

"So, you got into my house. Drugged my bourbon."

"That's right. Had to get into your house *several* times. First, I bugged every room. You picked a bad victim to fuck with, Vince. I make my living in the commercial security business. Locks. Closed-circuit cameras. Recently branched into the high-tech stuff. Build computer firewalls and so forth. Got access to every computer record in the world on you."

"And did you find a string of DUIs with the Division of Motor Vehicles?"

"No. Of course not. You're a hit-and-run expert. You make sure you're not arrested. That's why I have to take the law into my own hands, Mr. Football Hero. Just like I did with Kronenberg. I hope you appreciate all the time and care I took. Had to break into Kronenberg's office and get his stationery. Had to call the receptionist here today and cancel your appointment, a few minutes after you made the call. Then break in at five-thirty and be all set up by six."

"How did you disguise your voice to sound like Kronenberg's?"

"Computer. They have these wonderful wave generators now that can make anybody sound like a woman, a pansy, even a macho man like you."

Vince glanced back at his would-be killer. From where the madman stood, he couldn't see Vince wrapping the little

Perrier bottle in his huge grip. "What did you do with Kronenberg?"

"He's fertilizing a woods, about a mile from his ritzy mansion. Ran him off the road. And can I tell you how pissed he got when the tables were turned on him? Not for long, though."

Vince's output signals were definitely being scrambled, but his hearing was perfect. The stereo sense of his ears told him that the man was standing directly behind him and not more than a couple feet back. Vince grappled with his memory for those half dozen karate lessons he had taken in the seventies, to be able to endorse that academy. He rocked his weight onto his hands, drew up his right leg, and kicked upward and back, to the limit of his diminished powers.

Air whooshed from the man's lungs as Vince's foot connected with his groin. He doubled over so quickly that his glasses popped off the bridge of his nose. The tire iron and jump rope fell from his hands as he clutched at his testicles.

As soon as Vince lurched to his feet, he tottered around and threw the Perrier bottle at the man's face. It was a bullet, sailing in a tight spiral, but it was not delivered on the numbers. Instead, it struck the desk and exploded in a blossom of natural carbonation. Vince reoriented himself and staggered past the tea trolley, to the doorway, and into the outer office, where he collided with the receptionist's desk, rebounded, and fought for several seconds to maintain his balance. He found the blurred rectangle of the outer door and lumbered toward it. His hand found the doorknob.

The tire iron drove into the side of Vince's left knee, the force of the blow shattering bone and cartilage. Vince toppled like a mighty oak, his arms thrust out in barely enough time to shield his face from the door. He had never felt such agony, and only the dulling of the drug kept him from passing out.

"Now you know what Namath felt like. You shoulda finished me off in the other room, Vince," the little man gasped in a voice choked with both pain and rage. "Just like you shoulda finished off the Forty-niners in that playoff game, even though you were two touchdowns ahead. You don't have the killer instinct. Neither do I. But you're a killer anyway. Sooner or later, you'd run some child over with that big toy of yours. So I have to make myself into a killer, to protect society. The police don't protect us anymore; the goddamned judges sure as hell don't. Even MADD can't. It's up to decent citizens like me. I thought about just leaving you to face Kronenberg's murder, but you'd beat it. Thanks to the soulless lawyers, you rich people always win. And then you'd be out on the highway again."

The tire iron fell to the carpet. The jump rope came over Vince's head, looped once around his neck, and tightened. It would have been easier simply to have crushed his skull, as he had with Kronenberg, but he didn't want blood all over an innocent psychiatrist's office. So he pulled with all his might. Eventually, the clawing fingers lost their strength, the whipping back and forth subsided. He held tight for three full minutes after Martelli ceased struggling. Then he let go, collapsed into one of the Bauhaus chairs, and surveyed his work through squinting eyes. There was no joy left in his expression. He had tortured Martelli precisely as much as he thought he was owed for his own pain and suffering. The sportscaster's death was merely preventive justice, nothing to gloat over. Now all that remained was cleaning up the offices and wrestling the huge body out of the building unseen.

He returned to the inner office and groped around the carpet until he found his spectacles. Once they were back on his face, he felt much more in control. He turned out the inner office lights, not wanting any witness outside the building to register that the space was being used. More than enough light poured in from the reception area and from the tall floodlights in the parking lot. From his jacket pocket he pulled a handkerchief, preparing to wipe the office clean of prints from back to front. He walked to the picture window, to see how many cars remained in the parking lot.

Two stories below, the eighty asphalt spaces held just three vehicles: a late-model Lincoln Continental, Vince's prized Land Cruiser, and a white panel van with "Dave's Total Security Systems" neatly stenciled on its side. As he scanned the lot, Dave saw the taillights of the Lincoln come on, then glow bright red as the car backed up. And backed up. And backed up. Directly into the corner of Dave's van. Smashing out both the tail and parking lights.

As Dave watched in speechless shock, the Lincoln pulled forward five feet. A fat man in a dark suit waddled back to survey the damage. He looked first at his car, then at the van, then at the deserted parking lot, and finally at the office building. Satisfied that no one had seen the accident, he climbed back into his car.

"Son of a bitch!" Dave screamed. He rushed to the telescope and trained it down on the Lincoln, which had already begun to turn. The rear plate came clearly visible in the telescope's focus. "ARBITR8." On his way in, Dave had noted the law office on the first floor.

"Not again!" Dave wailed. And this time by a lawyer. His shoulders slumped. He had not even finished cleaning up after his latest administration of justice, and another bastard had steered his way into line.

Dave slowly straightened up. He looked at the handkerchief in his hand. Well, there was nothing to do but go on. It was God's will, and he was God's avenging angel. Tomorrow morning, he'd have to cancel the vacation to Cancún and begin the tedious process of learning every detail about Mr. ARBITR8. Dave shook his hand, sighed, and began dusting.

GRANDPA'S HEAD

Lawrence Watt-Evans

MY GRANDFATHER WAS BEING PACKED OFF TO THE NURSING home to die—he knew it, I knew it, we all knew it.

I was doing the packing—most of it, anyway. My friend Susie was helping out with the kitchen stuff and the old man's clothes, and Grandpa packed a few things himself, but I got to take care of about fifty years of accumulated clutter.

It wasn't much fun, but it had to be done if we weren't just going to throw everything away, and it wasn't really all that bad. I was grateful he hadn't had a bigger house and hadn't been much of a packrat.

A lot of it was just going to go into one of those rent-a-shed storage places and sit there until Grandpa died, when we'd sell it or give it away, and we all knew *that,* too, though we didn't say so, any more than we said aloud that he was going off to die.

There wasn't any point in storing more than we had to, though, so I was sorting through it all, seeing what we could just haul out to the curb with the trash.

I'd finished with most of it, boxing up the newer drapes, trashing the old ones, hauling the broken-down paisley couch to the curb for some poverty-stricken college student to steal for his dorm room, and so on, and had reached the attic, where I found a dozen cardboard boxes and a couple of footlockers.

I figured I'd start with the footlockers, so I found the keys in the collection Grandpa had given me and opened the first one.

And there it was.

There were scrapbooks and newspapers and some old clothes packed around it, so at first all I saw was the lid, which looked like tin or something. I didn't know what it was, but it looked moderately interesting, so I slid my hands down either side of the jar and lifted it up where I could get a good look at it.

I knelt there, staring at it, for a few seconds. Those seconds seemed like an hour—I know that's a cliché, but it really did seem a hell of a lot longer than it was.

I didn't scream or drop it or anything, which is a damn good thing, because it would have been a hell of a mess. I just held it, and stared at it, and turned it slightly to get a better look, and then when my hands started to tremble, I put it down, very gently, and stared at it some more.

You might think I'd have been confused, that I'd wonder what it was doing there, that I'd want to know *why* my grandfather had a woman's head in a jar in the attic, but I wasn't doing any of that.

I *knew,* right away, what it was doing there.

I could have tried to rationalize it, tried to explain it away, made up theories about medical specimens, all of that, but I didn't bother. What was the point in lying to myself?

Maybe if I hadn't recognized her—but I *did* recognize her, immediately. Even though I'd only seen her face before in old black-and-white photos, I'd looked at it enough that I knew it was the same face.

This was Constance Happerson's head.

And Constance Happerson was the family scandal, the woman Grandpa had been dating who had disappeared in 1945, and whose family had always suspected that Grandpa was somehow involved in her disappearance.

And sitting there in Grandpa's attic with that jar, I knew that her family had been right all along.

What's more, it looked as if it hadn't been some sort of desperate impulse or unfortunate accident. You don't keep a woman's head as a souvenir if you've been overcome by temporary insanity or are trying to cover up a botched abortion—the abortion theory had been the most popular at the time, as I understood it.

If you're a normal man with a dead body on your hands, you don't stick a piece of it in a big jar in the attic.

I'd known for years that Grandpa wasn't exactly a wholesome specimen—I mean, an old man's supposed to have stories about his wild youth, but Grandpa had more than his share of unsavory ones—but it was still a shock to realize that he was apparently a cold-blooded murderer.

And I had some decisions to make. There's no statute of limitations on murder, and I didn't particularly want to be an accessory after the fact, and that's exactly what I would be if I just ignored that jar.

But still, he was my *grandfather,* and he was a sick old man, and what good would it do to turn him in now, after all these years?

I couldn't ignore it, and I couldn't just call the cops, and that left just one thing to do.

Grandpa was downstairs, talking to Susie, having a little tea. He wasn't in any hurry to leave the house he'd lived in for so long and rush off to the nursing home, and he always enjoyed a chance to chat.

I went down the steps, brushing off the attic dust, and on down to the kitchen. The cupboards and cabinets were all standing open and empty, and a few boxes were stacked by the door; one box was open on the floor, waiting for the kettle and cups and the box of tea.

Grandpa and Susie were sitting at the table; she was laughing, and I guessed he was telling her one of his obscene war stories.

"Hi," I said. "Susie, could you do me a favor?"

She looked up, smiling.

"Take the car down to the corner and get it gassed up,

okay? We don't want to get stuck anywhere with all Grandpa's stuff."

"Can't we do that on the way?" she asked.

"I'd rather get it out of the way now."

She looked at Grandpa, and he said, "Oh, go on. The boy probably wants to talk some boring family business in private."

Grandpa was always pretty sharp.

Susie looked back at me, then stood up. "Gimme the money, then," she said.

I gave her a twenty and waited until I heard the car start before I sat down across from Grandpa.

He was looking at me expectantly.

"I found the jar in the footlocker," I said.

"Ah," he said with a nod. "I thought that might be it. Proves I *am* getting old, that I didn't think of it sooner and keep it away from you—wasn't until I saw the look on your face when you came in here that I remembered I'd left it there."

I was glad I was already sitting down. I'd known it must have been him, there wasn't really any other explanation, but to see him sitting there, calmly admitting it . . .

"You killed Constance Happerson," I said.

He nodded. "Sure did," he said.

I thought I was going to faint. "Why?" I asked.

"For fun," he said.

And that was absolutely the worst of it. My mouth dropped open, and I stared at him.

"Shut your face, boy, you'll catch flies," he said.

I closed my mouth, but I went right on staring.

He nodded. "Sure, I killed Constance. With a steak knife. Gutted her. Had a fine time doing it, too."

I was beyond shock; I couldn't react anymore.

"It was kind of careless, I guess, doing a girl I'd been seen with so much," he said, "but I just couldn't resist. I was young and reckless, and there'd never been any trouble about the others, so I chanced it. And she was such a pretty thing, I couldn't bear to just dump everything when I was done, so I got that jar, and some preservative stuff . . ." He shrugged. "I used to take her out and look at her sometimes, but I guess it's been fifteen, twenty years since I opened that trunk."

"Others?" I said.

"Sure." He smiled, and for a moment I almost wanted to throw up. "I was . . . well, nowadays you call 'em serial killers; in my day we were sex maniacs, or thrill killers. I was one."

"I thought . . . I didn't know there *were* serial killers back then . . ."

"Oh, crap, boy, don't give me that. Every generation thinks it invented sex, or at least some kind of sex, and there isn't a thing a person can do in that department that wasn't tried back in the caves. You never heard of Jack the Ripper, fer chrissakes?"

"Well . . ."

He wasn't listening, though; he was on a roll.

"And H. H. Holmes, only his real name was Herman Mudgett—he built himself a house with his own private glass-topped gas chamber so he could watch pretty young women die. Albert Fish used to torture kids to death for fun—mostly black slum kids, and nobody cared till he killed and ate a white girl. Been going on forever, Jim—there've always been men with a twist in the sex drive somewhere, and I happened to be one of 'em. Nowadays they figure maybe it's some kind of brain damage from being walloped too hard as a kid, and maybe it is, because there's no denying my ma used to whale on me pretty good, but whatever it is, I've got it—isn't anything that gives me a bigger kick than killing a girl."

"But it's *murder,*" I said.

He shrugged. "Sure it is. But it's fun."

I sat there and stared at him and wondered if I was just having some especially realistic nightmare.

"Who else?" I asked. "How many?"

He leaned back and considered that.

"Well, I got started in Italy, during the war," he said. "I was on leave in Rome, and one of the whores tried to steal my wallet, and I decided to teach the little bitch a lesson, and I got a bit carried away. I figured I'd catch hell, that somebody would report the whole thing and I'd be court-martialed and sit out the rest of the war in Leavenworth—but no one did. No one noticed, near as I could tell. After all, there was a war on—people turned up dead all the time, all over the place. So as time passed I got less and less worried about getting caught, and I remembered more and more how much fun it was, and then I began planning how to do it again. At first it was just sort of an intellectual exercise, y'know, a daydream, but then I got more and more serious about it, and eventually . . . well, I think there were about half a dozen in Italy, and then the war ended and I was sent home, and I figured that was the end of it."

"Except for Constance Happerson."

Grandpa nodded. "Her, and plenty of others. I said I *figured* that was the end, I didn't say it *was* the end."

"There were others?"

"Sure. The first one back stateside was this girl I picked up in a bar in New York—I dumped her in the alley behind my hotel, and far as I saw, it never even made the papers. I guess that was why I figured I could get away with killing Constance."

"Jesus." I just stared at him, trying to make this make sense. He didn't look any different; he didn't look like a monster. He was a smiling old man with thinning white hair and liver spots.

But he admitted killing almost a dozen women, just for fun.

"After all the fuss over Connie, though, I stuck to strangers from then on."

"Jesus," I said again.

"It was especially easy in the late sixties and early seventies, with all those hippies hitchhiking all over the place, but there were always hookers—as long as I never picked 'em up the same place more than twice, no one ever noticed. So I'd go to New York one time, and the next I'd drive out to Pittsburgh, or whatever."

"How many?"

He shrugged. "Don't know," he said. "I didn't count.

Maybe three or four a year, most years; I slowed down in the nineteen-eighties, when my health started to go."

"That'd be more than a hundred!"

"Could be, yeah. Probably more than a hundred. Old Herman Mudgett killed maybe two hundred, they say."

I just stared at him for a moment, trying to absorb that. He looked calmly back at me.

"So what are you going to do about it, now that you know?" he asked.

"I don't know," I said.

"If you turn me in, I'll be dead anyway before they finish all the appeals and crap, and you'll have to live the rest of your life with it."

"What, I should feel *guilty* for turning in a mass murderer?" I burst out. "I mean, you may be family, Grandpa, but my *God* . . ."

He held up a hand. "No, no, Jim boy, I don't mean that. Christ, give me a *little* credit!"

I subsided.

"I mean," he said, "you'll have to live with the notoriety of having me as your grandfather. Think Susie would like that? Think any woman would?"

I thought immediately that yeah, some women *would* like it—the sort of women who wrote to convicted killers in prison.

I didn't think I *wanted* those women interested in me.

He could see what I was thinking; he smiled.

"So it's off to the nursing home after all, then? Hey, you can send me off to jail anytime, if you change your mind—have you looked at the rest of the stuff in that footlocker yet?"

"No."

"Souvenirs. All the books on serial killers tell you, we like to take souvenirs. Clippings, photos, locks of hair, all kinds of things."

"Like Constance Happerson's head."

"Yeah. I only did that once, though."

"Why did you do it?"

He shrugged. "Why does anyone keep souvenirs? To help

144

me remember, of course—to remind me how good it felt."
He blinked, then sighed. "I'd let too much slip away lately;
I'd almost forgotten some of it. Haven't looked in that trunk
in ages."

I sat there, not saying anything, again, just staring at him,
with his bifocals and dentures and crooked nose, that
familiar face I'd seen leaning over my crib when I was a
baby, that face that had been there watching at my Little
League games, that face that had been so proud when I
graduated from college—that face that had been the last
thing those women ever saw.

Finally, he shifted in his seat and said, "Go ahead and
ask. I know you want to."

I didn't pretend not to know what he meant. I asked.
"What *did* it feel like?"

And he told me. He told me details that would never be in
any of the books; he told me about doing things I couldn't
imagine thinking of doing. Cutting off Constance Happerson's head and keeping it in a jar was just the beginning;
he'd done unspeakable things to women, alive, dead, or
dying. He'd violated every opening, and then made his own
and violated those. He'd used knives, saws, ropes, whips,
needles, and his bare hands.

Some of the women had lived for days.

"Did you ever kill a man?" I asked.

He nodded. "A couple," he said, "as experiments, but
that just wasn't as good."

That didn't stop him from describing the experiments,
though.

He'd gone back to women, reminiscing happily about
torture and mutilation, sounding more cheerful than he had
in months, when we heard the car pull up. He stopped
abruptly—he had been talking about skinning a hooker on
a rooftop in Newark. We both turned and watched the door,
waiting for Susie to walk back in.

I realized, when I shifted, that I had an erection.

I felt sick, that I could react like that.

Susie didn't notice, or at least didn't say anything.

We finished cleaning out the house and got Grandpa

safely installed at the nursing home. I took the trunk of souvenirs home and stashed it safely away, securely locked.

When we left Grandpa at the home, he gave Susie a hug, then shook my hand.

And as he did, he gripped my hand with those bony fingers and winked at me, and said, "Bet she'd be a *lot* of fun."

I snatched my hand away. I wanted to punch the old man in the face for that, but I resisted.

No one would understand—not unless I told them the whole thing.

I wondered again whether maybe I *should* turn Grandpa in—but he was a dying old man, and I'd never escape the stigma. What good would it do now, so long after the fact? He didn't remember most of the names, if he'd ever known them; it wouldn't clear up any mysteries that still mattered.

Let it die with him, I thought.

But I knew it wouldn't, because I remembered every word he'd said, and I had the trunk of souvenirs. I knew that memory wasn't going away.

And that night, in bed with Susie, I couldn't help thinking what it would feel like if, while we were making love, I were to slip a knife under her ribs. I imagined the convulsive shock, the thrashing under me . . .

The next day, while Susie was out, I looked through the trunk. I found Grandpa's pictures and his diary. I read it; I couldn't resist.

I've never been good at resisting temptation.

And every time since then, when I touch Susie, when I embrace her, I imagine her dying struggles, her gasping for air, her blood spilling out. I imagine her limp and lifeless on the bed.

And every time, I wonder all over again whether I should turn Grandpa in, quickly, before he dies—it'll only be days now.

And every time, the idea of a scandal seems better and better.

Because my life's ruined anyway, one way or another—

the temptation, the curiosity, grows stronger all the time. At least, if I turn him in, I probably won't ever dare to act on those horrible imaginings he's left me. I'd be too obvious a suspect. If I turned him in, I wouldn't dare to give in.

At least . . .

Well, not with Susie.

LONELYHEARTS

Esther M. Friesner

THIS TIME I'M GOING TO GET IT RIGHT.

No more mistakes. I really can't afford them. I know I'm not the most precise or punctilious of men, but really, there's no excuse for adding one more error to an already imposing list of foul-ups. It doesn't matter that half—no, more than half my errors weren't really mine. In business as in your domestic scene, it never pays to shunt culpability onto your partner; not in the long run. Still, in the long alones of many cold four-in-the-mornings, it's difficult not to recall how Jessie screamed or Lida tried to run after strict and generous forewarnings and forbiddings or how Elaine just lay there and refused to see reason.

Excuses. Excuses are no excuse. This time I'm going to get it right.

This time I won't rush things. I thought I'd spent enough time observing Jessie and Lida and Elaine—analyzing the case, if you will. In retrospect I realize that I allowed an unforgivable excess of joyful anticipation to push me into action far too soon. I have no one to blame but myself for so much childish eagerness overwhelming what is—this is fact, not self-flattery—my ordinarily sound judgment. I will pretend that this time she is Christmas and I am old enough to know that all the gifts, even the most wonderful, will still be waiting under the tree for me whether I tear them open at six or at eleven.

Yes, that's a good image. If I keep that in mind, I will be able to wait. Christmas.

Even her name reminds me of the festive season: Holly. When I counsel my clients about their investments, I prefer to leave instinct and intuition out of it, though many of my equally successful Wall Street colleagues admit to playing the omens instead of the past-performance data from time to time. I am no voodoo economist. This time, though, I am almost ready to believe in some supernatural force drawing her and me closer together, making our romance as inevitable a thing as moonrise. Christmas and Holly, Holly and Christmas.

I saw a seven-page glossy spread about how she makes Christmas. It was pure luck. Normally I don't bother with women's magazines, even the upscale ones. If I do pick up a copy, I am too quickly appalled by the way the articles pull the poor ladies to pieces: items exhorting them to keep their marriages exciting by not letting themselves run to fat and frump followed by pages and *pages* crammed with a thousand and one new ways to bake family-pleasing desserts. How can they do it, publish such tug-o'-war tripe and still look themselves in the mirror? The money, I suppose. A confused woman is a vulnerable woman, and a vulnerable woman will always come back for more. That's the theory.

I honor and respect women far too much to subject them to such stress. I am an honest, forthright man. I say what I want, I state my expectations from the start, I don't play games. I am serious. Never doubt that.

And I am not afraid of commitment. I always follow through on promises. My mother taught me that, and my father enforced it. So in a way, I suppose I could blame them if this time turns out to be like all the others. But no; it won't. As I said, passing the blame doesn't forgive me my shortcomings. And besides, this time I am definitely going to get it right. No more practices, no more do-overs. This time is for real.

Christmas . . . Christmas . . .

By Christmas I will have a wonderful surprise for my parents. Can you just imagine their faces when I drive up to the front door and come sweeping into the house with Holly Windsor on my arm? *The* Holly Windsor. Mother will recognize her face—she watches her show on television whenever she can and praises her skills with fondant icing and ruching and dadoes (whatever they are) to the skies. Father will recognize her name. Just let them try to tell me I can do better than this! At last, at fucking last, I will have found the woman presentable enough for their expectations.

Gosh. Did I say that? Pardon me.

I can't wait to see how she'll wrap the presents we'll bring. I think that must be the reason I fell so hopelessly in love with her: the gift wrapping. That was what first caught my eye in the magazine spread, you know. I was waiting for Mother to have her hair done for the Halloween dance at the club, and I just happened to pick up the magazine that promised to teach women how to make it a perfect Christmas. How do they dare? Halloween not even over and done with, and already they're hyping Christmas! Hurry, hurry, rush, rush, don't take a spare moment for yourselves, ladies. No sooner have you given your family that flawless Fourth of July with sparkler-studded red-white-and-blue sheet cake than you've got back-to-school ("Make That Brown Bag Lunch *Exciting!*") staring you in the face. Get over Christmas and there's Valentine's Day waiting in the wings, Easter just around the corner. Survive preparing a romantic champagne brunch for two, get past making three dozen Ukrainian Easter eggs, and you can begin worrying about digging the best fucking veggie garden in the neighborhood.

Pardon my French.

How can anyone do such things to the ladies? So much extra work for them to do, as if all there is to running a successful home isn't enough already. No wonder so many of them have forgotten what their real roles are. I'm not at all surprised by all their whining for us to do half the chores. The poor dears. I tell you, it makes me want to cry.

She won't mind the work, though. I don't think she'll ever panic or try to sidestep her responsibilities or give me a second's worry about the housework or the garden or our social calendar. She'll remember all the family birthdays. I won't have to do a thing. I work hard enough for a living. I have a degree from Yale and an MBA from Harvard. I may not know which side to cheer for during the game, but I bring home a substantial salary, plus benefits. Any woman would be glad to have me.

Honored to have me. That's what Mother says. Father just shakes his head and doubts aloud that there are any *real* women left out there, since all this libber nonsense got stirred up. He is too much the gentleman of the old school to say so to their faces, but whenever I would bring home a girl in high school or college, he would ask her a few short, to-the-point questions about her attitude toward the things that really count in a woman's life. Then he would give me the same sort of look he reserved for the times when I brought home a report card with a B on it.

This is why training is so important. Father says you can't teach a young bitch new tricks once the libbers have gotten at her, but I am an optimist. You can teach people all sorts of things if you really try. It's all a question of motivation. Father would understand, if I'd let him in on my plans—past failures included—but I'd rather surprise him with the pièce de résistance when I get it right. Father is a great source of motivation.

Did I mention that she makes her own gift wrap? She does. She's quite famous for it. She takes potatoes—just common, ordinary, garden variety spuds—and she slices them right in half. Then she takes a smaller knife and carefully gouges out a festive pattern in the flesh. In the magazine, she did snowflakes. Red ink and green on lovely pure white cloth. *Cloth!* No prepackaged paper for her, oh no! No silly apple-cheeked Santas or fat teddy bears dressed up like sugarplum soldiers. And the ribbons were gold, with gilded pine cones attached to the bows, and sprays of real holly snipped from her garden tucked in just so.

Just so.

She'll do.

I realize that there is not a lot of time left until Christmas. I mustn't rush things, but I don't dare to dawdle, either. I do so want to surprise my parents this year! The one good thing about mistakes is that if you learn from them, they lose a little of their sting. Do you like Kipling? "The things that I learned from the yellow and brown have helped me a lot with the white!" That's from Kipling, or as close as I can come to recalling the line without going to the bother of looking it up. I know I really should do my research, but I feel I ought to be allowed a *teensy* bit of imprecision just at the moment. Time wasted looking up the exact citation is far more profitably spent on my plans. I need time.

I already know where she lives. That was easy to learn. Her house has been the subject of enough feature articles for the town to be named in print over half a dozen times. She lives in Connecticut, in one of those darling little towns in Litchfield County. So do we. Oh, I maintain a city address, but it would devastate Mother if she heard me refer to my apartment as "home." Home is where they know you better than you know yourself.

So Holly and I were close even before I took notice of her life. Another omen? I know she didn't plan it this way, but isn't it convenient? Almost considerate. I'll take that as a gentle wink from fate. I'm sure that she and I will laugh about it someday.

There is no mistaking her house from the pictures. I am very good at divining location from photographs. There are plenty of clues, if you have the desire to ferret them out. I have had both the desire and the need.

Elaine's place was the first one I had to locate through photographs. She said in all her interviews how she never gave out her address or phone number except through her agent. He vetted callers so thoroughly it left CIA security checks looking like those "Hi! My name is . . ." badges they make us wear at company parties. That was understandable. All sorts of strange types will try to call up beautiful women, but when you are not only beautiful but an up-and-coming name model into the bargain, well then—!

But in one interview she granted, she was at home in her Manhattan pied-à-terre, the view from the window plain to see. Once I examined it under a magnifying glass to read the name of the florist across the street, all I really needed was a telephone book. Oh, and a dog! The ASPCA does such admirable work. Did you know how many lovely older dogs are up for adoption? Some of them can even pass for purebreds once they've been properly groomed. Proper grooming is everything. I thought she would understand that much.

She loved dogs. She posed with her little dog in her lap for that photograph. My dog and I made the dawn commute from Central Park West to Bloomingdale's every Saturday and Sunday morning for a month. Bloomingdale's is on Lexington and 59th, her place several blocks farther east and uptown, in the high sixties. Why not have the cab drop us at the florist across the street?

Because any woman should be honored to have me. I will never do anything that might seem desperate. That would be one mistake from which a healthy relationship could never hope to recover. I've read the magazines.

A month. It took a literal month of Sundays before my dog and I just happened to cross paths with Elaine and her pet. After that it became easier. I noted the time of our meetings. I took steps to repeat the coincidence. I took pains to locate a nice little bistro nearby, properly public, so that my initial invitation to coffee had small chance of being refused.

Things matured to my liking after that. Another two weeks, and I no longer needed the dog. Elaine was very sympathetic. She didn't think it at all odd when I materialized on our Sunday walk route unaccompanied, the tears still brimming in my eyes. Only she could understand my loss. That day we had our coffee in her apartment.

I wish she would have been as eloquent and well informed on subjects of world import as she was when speaking about dogs.

You have to understand, I was working under a deadline. My parents were expecting us for Christmas, but it was nearly Thanksgiving before we could meet. She had to be made presentable. Oh, not as to her appearance! That could not have been more impeccable. But Father says that a woman's looks don't last and she'd better have some intelligent conversation to offer when she loses them.

You would have thought she'd have at least enough brains to be grateful. I was offering to improve her. In retrospect, I suppose my timing might have been better, but, as I said, I was working under a deadline. I did rush things a bit. Not even the most news-hungry paparazzo had a glimmer that I was seeing this lovely woman, every man's midnight fantasy. And if she'd dropped a casual mention of me in her Argus-eyed agent's ear, it wasn't tagged with my real name. I was going to make her a gift of that for Christmas, along with the engagement ring.

I do love Christmas.

It was almost comical: We finished making love for the first time, and I tried to strike up a conversation about foreign policy! Elaine was not amused. I urged her to speak her mind on the really vital subjects of the day. Not only was she singularly ill informed about world politics, economics, even basic geography (I blame the public school system), but she had the nerve to keep dragging the conversation back to our recent encounter.

She had a list of quibbles and complaints that were tiresome as well as insulting. I did not attend the best of the best Ivy League schools to have some skinny little piece of meat tell me about how much better her other lovers were. A man is more than the sum of his parts, *definitely* more than the measure of one part alone. I told her so. She laughed.

I excused myself from her bed with some dignity. I knew then that she wasn't going to do. I suppose I should have been a gentleman and made my retreat with no further comment, but after I was dressed I overheard her cooing over that repulsive little dog of hers, showering it with more true affection than she had even bothered to feign for me.

I disposed of the dog afterward. Of the two of them, it was the less likely to raise the sort of fuss that would bring the neighbors. As a matter of fact, it didn't so much as yip when I slid my hands around its throat. It was like crumpling a cardboard tube. I'd had more difficulty handling my own dog, who was bigger and put up more of a fight. It might have felt different without my gloves on, but it was November. I have delicate skin, for a man. Women have often remarked about it with envy.

A woman really ought to cultivate her mind.

I hope Holly won't want a dog.

Mind *and* body. By body I mean more than surfaces. Mother often grizzles on and on about how poor Uncle George, her youngest brother, is saddled with a sickly wife. Of what use are all his accomplishments, social and financial? Aunt Valerie has made a life of dying by inches without the good taste to get it over with. Mother has always been loud in voicing her hopes that I won't be led astray by a pretty shell concealing a bad case of dry rot.

I think Mother will be pleased this Christmas. This time I've chosen well. Holly *jogs,* did you know that? So much time and effort invested in keeping a perfect house, setting a perfect table, serving foods not only delectable but exquisitely presented, and she *still* finds time to jog!

That's how I have it planned for us to meet. Once I have the photographs of her house to go by, once I gather up as many clues as I can, I'll take it upon myself to observe the comings and goings at her gate. And what a wonderful, wonderful reward for my patience I'll eventually have! To see her come crunching down the gravel drive alone, in shorts and a light nylon jacket, terry-cloth bands on her wrists, keeping the perspiration out of her eyes, holding back her hair. I think it will have to be a Sunday morning. Everyone jogs on Sunday mornings. Sunday mornings have always been good to me.

Out the gate and off to the right, following the line of the high, weathered brick wall that bounds her property. I'll watch her go. I know her sort of neighborhood. People who can afford it pay to put woodland around them, distance between them and their neighbors. But the roads are public property.

I'll follow her.

No, wait; I made that mistake with Jessie. We hardly even got to know each other before she began to scream. Even after I told her how very much I already knew about her, how fascinating I found her life as an aspiring actress, how I'd watched every single episode of that short-lived sitcom of hers, and taped them so I could watch them again and again at my leisure. Why, the silly woman, she screamed and screamed.

I don't even want to try remembering the foul names she used against me. I am not a *stalker*. Ugh. Can't a man admire a worthy lady from afar without being lumped in with those degenerates, those losers? To think she'd call *me*—! I shudder. I shudder, and I weep. The age of the true romantic is dead. People like Jessie killed it willingly, but I refused to let her turn my threatened humiliation into the final nail in its coffin.

Thank God there aren't that many people running through that part of Central Park at that hour.

I won't follow Holly.

Instead, I'll study the streets, pick my own route to intercept hers, come running past her in the opposite direction. Loose laces, yes. I can trip. I can fall so that it looks painful. She'll stop to ask if there's anything she can do to help me, and I'll be grateful. Women love to take care of men; it's what they were born for. From that point on, it shouldn't be hard to strike up a casual conversation.

Better to make your first impression with charm rather than appearance, although I do look rather dashing in a running suit. Ha ha.

If Lida would have jogged, the resulting shortness of breath might have helped persuade her to give up that filthy habit.

To smoke in this day and age, with all the evidence, all the social pressures against it! No wonder I didn't take her seriously when she lit up that first cigarette. I suggested that perhaps it might be best for her health if she quit. She laughed and said she'd rather die if she couldn't have her nicotine fix. I thought it was just her flamboyant way of making a rebellious gesture that she didn't really mean.

I have never again made the mistake of not taking a woman at her word. Lida taught me that.

Lida also taught me the perils of courting a lady who refuses to act her age. I grant you, one could quite reasonably blame the atmosphere of her workplace for both her attitude and her unhealthy habits. Surrounded by rock stars steeped in drugs, in careless sex, in the infantile world of immediate demands immediately gratified, could she have been otherwise?

Well, yes. Given the chance, urged to make the effort, inspired by the desire to please a man whose only wish was to help her live her life the right way.

I don't know what it is about Christmas. No matter how loudly I decry the magazines' unseemly headlong rush into the season, no matter how annoyed I feel when I notice evergreen wreaths going up in stores while Styrofoam jack-o'-lanterns are still on display, I still find myself swept up by the urgency of the season. That year there was the added pressure of Cousin Gwendolyn's wedding. Why the girl needed to have it in January! The bleakest of months, and she decides no other will do for her bridal. She wasn't even pregnant.

That was small of me. But still, I can't help feeling that if I would have been allowed more time with Lida, I could have brought her around. Instead, there was the specter of Gwen's wedding leering at me, and Mother leaning over the Sunday afternoon roast beef to ask me for the thousandth time whether I was going to be bringing a young lady friend with me, Gwennie's mama needed to know *soon*. The seating plans, you know.

At first I said no. Why borrow trouble? It was only October, and Lida still didn't know I was alive. She would, though. I had it all planned. I wasn't going to make the same mistakes I'd made with Elaine and Jessie.

But then I felt Father's eye on me. "You haven't brought home a nice young woman since you got out of grad school," he said. "What's the matter with you?"

"Nothing," I replied.

"Don't give me that. Look, you're a healthy young man, aren't you? You should be dating. You live in New York City, for God's sake! Don't tell me you can't find *one* decent girl there." He took a bite of roast beef. "Not like the kind you used to bring home. Pieces of meat with eyes, every one of them."

"Please, dear, he's grown up since then," Mother said. "He'll find a nice girl. He can bring her here for Christmas."

"If that's what he's looking for," Father rapped out. "A nice *girl?* We hope. The way things are going these days, half the young people don't know if they're Martha or Arthur."

"Darling! What a thing to say!" Mother sounded hurt on principle, but the way she was looking at me . . .

So I said that I knew that I was Arthur right enough, thank you, and that I had been seeing a very nice young lady. And I had been *seeing* her; it wasn't an outright lie. Anyone with cable TV could see her if they tuned in to the *Rock Hot!* news. I'd been seeing her elsewhere as well. It doesn't take much inquiry to find out when certain shows are taped, when certain on-air personalities head for home. Lida scorned cabs and feared subways. I saw a lot of her in the evenings when she left the studio and walked the three blocks to her bus stop.

Father's mouth grew small. He's not a man to voice his doubts about his only child—not at the dinner table—but he has his little ways.

"It's just that we're not seeing each other *seriously* yet," I said. "Bringing her home for Christmas, taking her to Cousin Gwen's wedding, that's a major step."

Father snorted. "Either she's yours or she's not." He ate another piece of meat, and the topic was closed.

At the time, I was positive she was going to be mine.

Beautiful, famous, well informed, worthy. Even if she only reported music news, she still had a legitimate degree in journalism. She had to. You didn't just waltz into the studio and get a major network job without solid credentials. I know. I looked it up. Computers are wonderful. I couldn't accomplish half as much without them.

Always carry a briefcase. Attachés are best. It gives you an air of solidity, even stodginess. This is not always a bad thing. You can overdo it, though. If a man with a briefcase who is also wearing a suit asks a woman like Lida whether this is the right stop for the M11 bus, you can bet the bank that she'll turn away with a sneer. Anyone dressed that well in the environs of her studio would be hailing a cab or ducking into a private car. But pair the proper attaché with something black and rumpled, collarless but clearly expensive, and you're of the tribe. I prefer Mark Cross.

Now that I think of it, the clip-on ponytail might have been a bit much.

She did laugh at it when she found out it was a fake. She didn't mind. When she called me pathetic, I knew she didn't mean it the way Elaine did, or Jessie. She had the most wonderful sense of humor. I hope Holly does. I'd hate for it to have to end like—

No, no. You get nowhere with negative thinking. Holly's the one for me. We were meant for each other. Lida and Jessie and Elaine only *seemed* to be right. They looked good on paper. Sometimes you get a company like that—bright and shiny and full of promise in print between the covers of their prospectus, dead in the water when the trading starts.

If only Lida hadn't smoked. If only I'd have known how strongly the habit had ahold of her. They say you can never really hope to displace a woman's first true love from her heart. With Lida, I made the mistake of thinking that was me.

It wasn't supposed to take long to break her free of the habit. I know they say it takes weeks, months, even years, but that's without love there to inspire you and lend you strength. Willpower. It was nearly Christmas, and I'd as good as promised my parents that I'd be coming to see them with a proper guest. Lida would have to be presentable by then.

She adored the idea of a weekend together, just the two of us. She didn't know until I got her alone with me in the car that my family had a little place near Stowe. She was enchanted by the chance to "do the whole fuckin' preppie thing," even if she didn't ski. (Pardon *her* French!) I asked her to watch her language when we went home for Christmas, and she complied so readily—I never heard her utter another scrap of foul language in my presence—that I had only the highest of hopes that tobacco would go the way of profanity.

For my sake. Because she loved me.

Mother used to say that no one can ever love you as much as your parents. I didn't like to believe that, but I'm afraid I must confess that she was right, at least as far as Lida went. She could stop the foulness that came out of her mouth but not the foulness that went into it. She exercised both nasty habits to the fullest when she saw our weekend accommodations.

"I thought you had more money than God," she accused the instant after she stepped over the threshold of our modest family home-away-from-home. I grant you, it was rustic, simple, off the beaten path. But Father said that you either went north to ski or not. It was good enough to provide shelter between runs. I know it couldn't hope to live up to the image most people have of winter vacation homes at resorts like Stowe. It wasn't even *at* Stowe; but I hadn't said it was. *Near* Stowe, yes; quite near, if you knew the back roads as well as I did. Father always did hate crowds.

Things went from bad to worse after that. She entered the cabin with an unproductive attitude and kept adding layers of sulkiness and black mood throughout the weekend. And the smoke! The whole purpose of our weekend together was to break her of the habit, but it just seemed to aggravate the situation.

I asked her not to. What was a day or two without sticking

one of those smelly things between her lips? For my sake. We'd had early snow that year. Mother had said how much she was looking forward to using the cabin. If my parents decided to take a ski weekend of their own anytime that season, Mother would know what had been going on the instant she opened the cabin door. You can never get cigarette smoke out of curtains.

I fail to see why Lida felt compelled to take out her disappointment in the accommodations on me. It was as if she set out to provoke me on purpose. She refused to give up her cigarettes, she refused to take them outside, she refused my offer to take her back down the mountain and home again. I gave her every chance. I think she wanted to make me suffer. What can you do with a person like that?

Now that I think it over, I might have done well to take her to one of the better Stowe resorts. But the whole reason for our trip was to have time enough alone with her to make her drop the habit. I did it all for her. Good heavens, do you think I *like* that bourgeois shack of ours? I'm as fond of the amenities as the next man. I will gladly trade a week of roughing it for a day in a slick hotel with the proper number of tiny little shampoo/conditioner/body lotion bottles in the bathroom. I have *never* liked the cabin; something about it gives me bad dreams.

The last straw came when I woke up on Sunday morning. My dreams that weekend had been haunted by images of my parents' faces, hanging over the dinner table and demanding to know what I'd done with the nice young lady I'd promised to bring home for Christmas. Father had the carving knife and fork in his hands. He leaned over the roast, steam rising from its crisp brown outer layer of fat, and as the knife descended he asked me, "Well? Where is she? You said you'd bring her. Or was this one just another figment of your imagination, too?" The knife sliced into the side of the roast slowly, a shiny trail of liquid oozing out, following the bite of the blade.

And before I could force my mouth open to reply, the knife passed over the eyes.

I sat up in bed with a cry of terror, my hands to my face. My cheeks were streaked with fat tears, hot, searing streaks of burning agony across my palms.

And Lida? She grunted like a sow, rolled over, sat up, gave me a cold stare, and reached for her cigarettes. Not a word of sympathy.

"I wish you wouldn't do that," I said, reaching across her and laying my hand over hers on the cellophane-covered pack.

She said, "Fuck you."

It wasn't French, and I don't think she deserved to be pardoned for it.

It all would have turned out so much nicer for everyone concerned if she had only apologized and cooperated with me from then on. I tried to make her see that. She refused, spitting blood, waving her silly little lighter at me as if it were a villager's torch from one of those old *Frankenstein* movies. It was a little hard to catch her every word—her lip swelled up so fast!—but I got the gist: *now* she was going to walk out on me, not earlier, when I'd given her permission to leave, but now, when *she* said. So you see, the cigarettes were only a symptom. We could never have hoped to be truly happy together, not with her attitude.

I have no idea how I managed it, but I *did* get the smell of cigarettes out of the curtains afterward. At least I never heard about the matter from Mother, and she never was one to let something like that pass by without comment. It took me most of the rest of Sunday and two cans of Lysol Spray Disinfectant (Original Scent). I know it works, but I never expected it to work so well. I guess I just lead the right sort of life.

None of the others worked out, either, not even the girl Cousin Gwen introduced me to at her wedding. No matter how pretty or smart or well bred, each seemed to lack *something* to remove her from the running. One wanted to keep her job after we married, one didn't see the point to what she called "that phony country club-society-debutante thing," one turned positively green at the thought of bearing legitimate children. I don't know where they get their ideas, honestly I don't. No matter how ready Father is to blame it all on the libbers, I think it goes deeper than that. These ladies need help, serious help, but I never set myself up as a therapist. The only life I'm qualified to save is my own. Who really knows what—or *if*—they're thinking? Pieces of meat with eyes, every one. Pretty meat, tasty meat, but what can you do? You can't marry meat. Well, you can if you want, but I deserve better.

Holly Windsor is much better. And this time . . . *this* time . . .

December 22

Dear Louise,

Thank you so much for agreeing to come in and feed my cats while I'm away. I agree, something like this doesn't really harm our professional relationship.

You'll be pleased to know that things have taken a definitely serious turn with that Special Someone I first mentioned to you this past fall. In fact, that's the reason I'm going away in the first place. A man who's not afraid of commitment in *this* day and age, what a find! I don't have to tell you how much it means to me, especially after some of the nightmare relationships I've survived.

We are going to his parents' house for Christmas. He says he even *thinks* of me as Christmas personified; isn't that sweet? And in a way, I think of him as my Christmas, too, giving me absolutely everything I ask for, all that I deserve. Maybe it's part of your job to say such things to me, but no, I do *not* think I am being anal-retentive about Christmas. (Why you have to use words like *anal* never ceases to bemuse me.) It is simply a very special time of year for me, I like it to be perfect, and I'm prepared to do whatever it takes to keep it that way.

Yes, you don't have to tell me: a Christmas visit to the old folks means that it's the Official Inspection. Been there, done that. Flunked it a time or two. Passed it with my George's people, but I was younger then.

The young put up with so much nonsense in the name of love! All that scrutiny, a wedding that cost the earth, and in the end . . .

Poor George. So critical, such a hawkeye when it came to watching me for every possible flaw, no wonder he couldn't watch his own footsteps. Well, live and learn. Since that terrible accident, I've been very careful about the amount of floor wax we use on the grand staircase.

I've packed so many goodies, you'd think I was Little Red Riding Hood en route to Grandma's house! I don't think he's allergic to anything, but some of my recipes do use such exotic ingredients, especially the spices.

I'll just have to remember to find out, won't I? Allergies can be nasty. I will never forgive myself for not asking Paolo whether or not he was allowed to eat peanut butter cookies. He was so busy blustering about how he was going back to Milan, and nothing I could say or do would change his mind, that I forgot the Italian word for *peanut butter*. I know, I know! You and I have already worked through my misplaced sense of guilt, and I am *not* to bring it up again. The wonderful way you and the rest of my team rallied around, handling the media, doing whatever it took to keep things polite. How can I thank you enough? (Yes, dear heart, I know: On the "Pay To" line of your check. Jokey-jokey!) As you said, if no one took the trouble to press charges, it's emotionally counterproductive for me to harp on it. I've got to get up in the morning, look in the mirror, and tell myself, "Bury the past where you bury your daffodil bulbs, and get on with your life, my girl!"

Wish me luck. If it works out, you'll be invited to the wedding. (You *know* you're dying to see how I'd plan it!) If it turns out like the others, well, we'll just pretend he vanished off the face of the earth, too, won't we? Out of sight, out of mind. Life today is hard enough for a single woman without having to carry around the memories of a lot of unsuitable men.

But don't worry, darling. Patient to therapist, let me let you in on a little secret:

This time I'm going to get it right.

Love,
Holly

P.S. The can opener with the red handle is the *only* one to be used for opening the cat food cans. Touch the electric opener, and you're a dead woman.
Merry Christmas!

LIGHTING THE CORPSES

Del Stone Jr.

SEARCHING, SEARCHING, ZEKE ROARED ACROSS THE NIGHT, pausing only to burn a man and watch him die.

So easy, now, in the focus of his rage. So viciously fun. But he couldn't linger too long. He had others to burn. And one, a very special man Zeke called Father Baptist, a man who could not await Zeke's tenuous grasp on this world, would burn cell by cell, molecule by molecule, down to the ash of his soul.

Once Zeke found him.

Like this man, who was dying slowly and horribly as Zeke watched him, on the sidewalk outside Zeke's old apartment. Zeke had come here hoping to find Father Baptist gloating over his crime, but the apartment had been empty. Instead, he'd seen this man. A fifty-three-year-old CPA, divorced a year and a half, who was slowly losing touch with his life for the want of companionship. The man was loitering on the sidewalk, two doors down from his own unit, hoping the woman in 3F would open her door and step outside. If she did, he'd talk to her a moment, just a moment, and not ask her for a date—he wanted to do this thing gradually—and build on the innocence of another encounter tomorrow. He wanted to believe he was an attractive and witty and intelligent man, and he wanted to believe she would recognize those qualities in him, and he wanted to believe she would be the solution to his loneliness.

Zeke could see it. He could see it all, as if it had been printed in careful block letters on a third-grader's blue-ruled writing pad. He could see into the man's heart.

And this is how Zeke burned the man:

You are a fat, over-the-hill, dumb bastard, and you're gonna be alone until you finally get sick of it and ram the business end of a 9mm up your trap and pull the trigger.

Zeke chuckled as the man suddenly frowned, unsure of himself, and turned, shuffling unsteadily to his apartment, one hand lightly brushing the wall and dragging a little, as if he were about to faint and wanted to catch himself. The man saw himself differently now. Gone was the hope he might have a chance at this woman, or any other woman. His hair seemed to bleach gray as Zeke watched, his stomach sagged over his belt, his spine softened, and he aged to death in an instant, the flesh sliding from his bones in slippery, wet clumps of despair.

The man went back into his apartment. Six months from now, on a night that would have no end, the man would load three hollow-tipped bullets into the clip of a Ruger . . .

Zeke smiled. So easy, now, in the focus of his rage.

So easy, now that Zeke was dead.

Fire.

Fire was the great reducer, making everything simple, a brief rage of combustion and then a satisfied ash that could be reduced further to a mere black mark, a scar of carbon that said nothing more than something was burned by somebody.

Zeke likes fire.

He likes his fires.

A pile of leaves raked into the gutter. A candle made from melted crayons. His sister's Barbie Beauty Salon, spirited out of the house and into a weedy lot down the street as she and Mom sit in the pediatrician's waiting room to have a fake pearl tweezered out of her ear, stupid brat.

Zeke likes his fires. They say to him: Something was burned by Zeke. A nightmare, scorched from memory.

If Father knew, if Father knew, if Father knew . . . oh God, if Father knew.

And Zeke likes that, too.

Zeke roared across the night, stopping at a convenience store he'd stopped at weeks ago, hoping Father Baptist would be there, reliving his own torment or renewing his hatred. The store was closed and vacant and dark. A large patch of floor tiles by the counter had been scraped up. Zeke remembered why.

Zeke had always wanted to put the match to somebody. Sidle next to them, unnoticed, as they picked through undercooked scrambled eggs and grease-soaked fingers of sausage at a Shoney's breakfast bar, for instance, and scrape the business end of a kitchen match against the zipper of his Levi's and touch the flame to the trailing edge of their shirt sleeve and watch the whole works go up in a cough of combustion, their sudden intake of breath and their screams tickling that part of his brain no other act of pleasure ever touched.

Zeke chuckled and did not hear himself. He never heard sounds now—the crack of a jalousie window as he worked the pane from its frame, the breaking-bone sound of a doorjamb being chiseled away from a deadbolt. He could no longer taste the bitter highball of perfume and sweat; he could not feel a woman's fingernails digging trails of fire across his cheek, the vibrating spasms of her throat shaking loose with a scream as he ripped her panties from her thighs.

But he could *see,* the living people around him and the fears about themselves that secretly ate out the center of their lives. The deadness in them. They were corpses of hope and self-delusion and fantasy. Touch a flame to those things, and you burned off the good parts about themselves people so desperately needed to believe, and you uncovered the real person hiding inside, a tight little cinder of terror.

But there would be no second burning at the convenience

store. Nobody was home, not even a security guard to keep away the curious from the scene of Zeke's final crime.

Certainly not Father Baptist.

It is time to burn something again.

Mom and his sister are gone somewhere. They're gone a lot after Father gets home from work. Funny, how they're gone so much after Father gets home from work.

Now Zeke is going somewhere, too. The weedy lot. To burn something. He has one of Father's empty Falstaff beer cans, filled with charcoal starter, and a book of matches. Maybe he will burn the lot, or write his name in flames.

Maybe he will make an effigy of Father in twigs and leaves and burn that.

But he will burn something.

He is walking away from the house, the beer can hidden in front of his thigh, when he hears the front door bang open and a deep voice boom across the yard. "Where are you going?"

Instantly, his heart becomes a slab of meat in his chest.

"Just down the street," he squeaks out.

"Come here," his father commands.

He pivots to the left and sets down the beer can behind the bole of a pine tree.

"And bring that with you," Father says.

The slab of meat in his chest rots in a way he can feel throughout his body. He trudges back to the house, feeling as though he is walking to his execution.

Zeke roared. He dipped briefly at the hospital to see if Father Baptist had burned himself. While there, he paused to show a nine-year-old girl that she would not beat the cancer spreading through her rickety bones, and for good measure he showed the girl's mother that yes, it was true, she really was to blame for what had happened to her daughter. The girl became a skeleton before Zeke's eyes. The mother grew fangs and began to eat herself, ripping chunks of flesh from her arms, her calves, and swallowing them in bloody lumps.

Zeke crossed the interstate and torched a truck driver with the realization that he'd failed as a medical student and there was never, ever any chance he'd pass his GRE for that master's in counseling. The trucker became a cloud of flyblown ash.

He torched a waitress who had dreams of becoming a model. He torched a would-be jet jockey. And the pale little man who looked like a boy and rocked himself to sleep with idiotic visions of becoming a golf pro—Zeke lit him up with a bolt of self-doubt, and the man-boy popped like a hundred-watt bulb.

They were all dead. Burned out and dead.

Except Father Baptist.

Father sniffs the can. His nose wrinkles.

"There's something in there," Zeke offers meekly, "but I wasn't going to drink it."

"Empty your pockets," Father whispers. Zeke's stomach drops a couple of notches, because the matches are in his pocket, and Father is not stupid.

And because he knows his father will search his pockets anyway, no matter what Zeke does to satisfy him or please him, Father will search his pockets because he is speaking in the doctor whisper he uses to search Zeke for cancer the way every good father searches his son, or the policeman whisper he uses to search Zeke for concealed drugs, or the coach whisper when he must check to make sure Zeke is still a boy and didn't change into a girl overnight, so Father will search his pockets and then search beneath his T-shirt and then into his Fruit of the Looms and then . . .

The whisper is strangely hoarse, coming from deep within the voice box, and it is all rattly and trembly as if Father were afraid of something.

"What's this?" Father says, producing the matches as if he had just performed a magic trick. "Let's see now . . . lighter fluid and matches. Were you planning to have a barbecue?"

Zeke stares at the floor, not saying anything.

So Father says, "Let's see what else you're hiding."

* * *

Dead.

It was a stupid thing, really. After being so careful for so many months, Zeke had screwed up. Once. Just once.

The cops had given him a name, the Backroads Killer, because he worked the rural roads, the isolated house trailers, the yuppie castles in the woods with satellite dishes aimed through gaps in the trees and BMWs parked beneath enclosed patios. The Backroads Killer. A joke to Zeke. Cops always named criminals they couldn't catch, as if a name implied mystical abilities. The cops hadn't caught Zeke.

But Father Baptist had.

Zeke had been careful. Pantyhose over his head, the car parked off in the distance, that sort of thing. But he'd screwed up with the girl at the convenience store at that intersection between two state roads, the intersection giving a reason, he guessed, for the convenience store and a boarded-up John Deere distributorship. That and a traffic light that blinked yellow for one direction and red for the other, and you had what passed for a town.

Zeke could have continued on to the farmhouses and shanties he knew were hidden in the woods downroad, or he could have turned left or right. But he'd stopped, there where the roads intersected like the crosshairs in the scope of some celestial hunting rifle.

The girl behind the counter was pretty and nervous, and he liked them that way, and he liked her, and he liked dragging her by the hair of the head to the storage room at the back of the building, her screaming and crying and the way she knocked over the stacked six-packs of Evian only inflaming his lust. She begged him not to hurt her, and she told him her father was a minister at the Klamath Briggs Baptist Church and how could he do this to a minister's daughter, but it was afterward, as he was wiping off his dick on her shredded blouse, that she turned mean and said she'd have the law on him and there were a hundred men in the community, her father included, who would track him down and cut off his balls, and that she hoped the video camera had gotten a good picture of him.

Video camera.

God, that had pissed him off. A video camera, a fucking video camera. How could he have been so stupid?

He stalked out into the store and found the camera, hidden above the coolers so that it filmed anybody who came through the door. Jesus Christ! Stupid! He ripped the camera from its mount and smashed it against the floor, and at that moment the girl made a dash for the front door. A spike of anger shot through him, from his stomach into his throat, and he hurled himself at her, knocking her into the counter. He grabbed her by the side of the head and slammed her skull against the floor and bellowed at her to tell him where the recorder was, but all she did was whimper, the spittle bubbling between her lips like beer foam, so he pounded her head against the floor, again and again, then one more time.

Finally, he stopped. She was out. Her body was limp. Her hair had created Rorschach dragons and thalidomide bats in an orange-red smear of blood on the dingy floor tiles.

He yanked a set of keys from her belt and went behind the counter, where the safe was hidden. The recorder was inside another locked box. When he popped the cassette, the breath rushed out of him in a relieved gush. For a moment, he considered simply taking the cassette with him, but as he went around the counter, past the magazine racks, he paused by the neat rows of Zippo lighter fluid cans. The idea alone suffused him with a kind of energy that transcended sexual pleasure.

He torched her. He left the cassette on her chest and doused her with three cans of lighter fluid and then set her off like a Fourth of July barbecue.

And as he shifted his car from reverse into drive and headed off down the yellow-light-blinking road, his heart pulling in a multitude of directions, a white Ford turned into the parking lot.

A white Ford.

He'd forgotten about the white Ford as the days, then weeks went by after he'd burned up the clerk and then watched as his handiwork played on the six o'clock news and the local newspapers. He felt the secret swell of potency crest as the cops and state agents fumbled about, clueless as usual, and all the delicious details of those murderous minutes began to fall out of memory.

Zeke would have to do it all again.

But he never had the chance.

A knock on the door. A nervous peek through the venetian blinds. A white Ford parked in the guest space in front of his apartment, too battered and rusted for a government car or a cop's. Zeke opened the door. A man in a red-and-blue flannel shirt, blue jeans, hiking boots— nothing special about him. Except his eyes. His eyes were so old, so filled with some emotion that had gone beyond hate, that Zeke actually felt a tittering thrill of terror squiggle up his spine.

Then Zeke saw that the man was holding a gun.

The man said, "You *do* understand," and pulled the trigger.

Zeke felt something—the bullet, a force, something so elemental that it couldn't be resisted—slam him into the wall, and then the joints in his knees came unpinned and he slumped to the floor, waves of pain crashing over him and threatening to send him under.

The man loomed above him. He looked as big as God, but he looked meaner, crazier than any brimstone-preaching backwoods Baptist's version of God. He'd put away the gun. Now he had a gallon can of gasoline. He was unscrewing the lid.

"I've been looking for you," he said, his voice barely above a whisper. "All these weeks. I saw your car. After you, you—" His voice split into a sob. "Killed my—my— daughter—"

He splashed gasoline, and Zeke's terror rose convulsively above the pain and he tried to crawl away, a hitching groan gurgling out of his throat. The man spilled a trail of gasoline to the door, tossed the can aside, and fumbled a Bic butane lighter out of his jeans pocket.

"You force me to do this," he said with a wistful smile. "But I want you to understand something."

He spun the flint wheel.

"As a servant of God, I love you."
Zeke roared.

*Father is searching and mumbling in his sweaty voice,
"You could have something here or maybe something in
here, and it's my responsibility to find out what's going on,
and if punishment is required, then punishment it will be,
because it's my job to raise you right; you know that, don't
you? Don't you? You've put me in this position—you've
forced me to do this, and I'm only doing what every good
father should do . . ."*

*Zeke is half sitting, half lying in the bathtub, his clothes
tossed hurriedly onto the bathroom floor, and Father is
searching him, and Zeke's mind is a blood blister hidden
somewhere beneath a callus of fear and shame as he waits for
Father to groan suddenly and twitch as if he were having a
seizure and then finish his search. His father's words sink
into Zeke's thoughts like thunder muffled by distance, and
with some kind of fevered half-awareness Zeke knows a
storm is out there and he must seek refuge, so he imagines a
wall of fire rising all around him, a protective ceiling of flame
that evaporates the rain and absorbs the lightning and scours
clean the dirty, nasty things falling from the sky of Father's
eyes.*

Zeke roared across the night. Dead. Burned and dead and
revived by his rage, a force of hatred now. He blew into the
Klamath Briggs Baptist Church and burned each and every
person there, from the matronly choir director who knew
she would hear the angels sing when she went to her sweet
bye-and-bye, to the church softball coach who lived alone
and gave teenage boys rides to games and someday planned
to have a private session in the dugout with his fifteen-year-
old star pitcher.

He torched them all, moving silently and invisibly
through the pews, the back rooms, the musty basement
stacks of hymnals and cheap Bibles that were passed out to
the homeless. And as he drifted back upstairs and swept
down the aisle, his rage gathered about him like a cassock,

he encountered an elderly couple who had just arrived, who had come looking for news after hearing the terrible story about Reverend Lockwood, and did the county jail allow visitors because they wanted to see him, to talk to him, to hear it from his own lips that he'd murdered that man because they just *couldn't* believe it, they *couldn't*.

The county jail. Zeke smiled. Then roared.

The fire flickers and dies.
The search is over.
Father is saying, "This is your doing. You know that, don't you? You were sneaking off to start a fire. Fires are bad things, and you should know that. I thought I'd taught you better than that, but apparently I haven't. It's my responsibility as your father to raise you right, to make sure you know the difference between good and bad. Fires are bad things, and you were going to do a bad thing, and now I have to make sure you never do such a thing again. Until you demonstrate to me that I can trust you, I'll have to search you every day. Do you understand? And I want you to realize that this is your doing, that you are forcing me to do this. If I were you, I'd be ashamed. I'd be very, very ashamed. I'd be so ashamed that I'd never breathe a word of this to anyone, because if you do, everybody will make fun of you, or worse, they'll think you're crazy and send you off to reform school or jail or the insane asylum. So if I were you, I'd just keep my mouth shut, and as long as you keep your mouth shut, I'll keep my mouth shut. Do you understand?"

Zeke nods. His thoughts are consumed by a single idea.

"I want you to understand something else, too," Father says in a firm voice. "I want you to understand that I'm doing this because I love you. I really do.

"I love you."

Zeke's thoughts are consumed by a vision of fire.

He burned them. Stupid wads of people, eaten alive with fear. He left a trail of fire across the land, and when he arrived at the jail it was like a hot breath of desert wind, stirring papers and swinging open doors shut and setting the overhead lamps to pendulumming, so that surly deputies looked up with frowns and inmates tossed in their bunks or cut loose with inexplicable snarls. A deeper shade of gloom seemed to fall over the place.

Zeke drifted down the corridors. An embezzler was here, and a man who had grabbed a money bag from a restaurant manager, and a man who'd beaten his wife, and a car thief, and even a couple of drunks.

He passed them by.

It was in the final cell, in the deepest recess of the building, that Zeke found his prize. Lying on a bunk, his hands behind his head, his eyes closed but his mind deliciously open, notions of God and sin and the frailty of human spirituality spinning in his absurd circle of thoughts. Zeke became a shadow beneath the bunk and listened to Father Baptist, the former father, the former emissary of piety and forgiveness, dance around the rotten core of doubt that lurked beneath everything he was telling himself.

Zeke sent inquiring tendrils of himself snaking up the bunk posts, pouring through the wire mesh that supported the mattress and curling beneath the sweat-soaked, olive drab blanket that covered Father Baptist, and he took his time doing this because, like the man he'd torched back at his old apartment, he wanted it to be a gradual thing, a search across the night and now a slow, stealthy approach, building the anticipation to a climax that would surpass the hatred he felt for this man. He went patiently, parts of him sliding up the wall like a curtain being raised, flowing into then out of cracks and cemented joints between cinderblocks, and parts of him drooping from the ceiling in leechlike, squirming gobbets that slipped silently beneath Father Baptist's flesh.

There.

Zeke could see it clearly. All the things this man had done to cover it up, and still Zeke could see it, could touch it, could burn away the deeds and convictions this man had formed over his lifetime to bring the terror squirming to the surface, into the light of what passed for truth, everything else withering in the heat of awareness.

This is what Zeke told him: *What you fear about yourself is true. You are your devil.*

Zeke backed away.

The man's eyelids snapped open. His muscles cinched into rigid cords, the way an epileptic's body galvanizes during a seizure, and the humanity flowed out of his face, a cold shock of terror freezing his expression into a stare so blank, so devoid of any human quality, that Zeke actually moved back another step, fascinated but at the same time a little apprehensive, the way he'd felt when he torched Father Baptist's daughter and the fire began to spread to the counter and the surrounding racks of candy bars and potato chips.

Father Baptist's hands crawled beetlelike to his chest, where his heart slammed against the walls of his ribs like a diesel engine torn loose from its mounts. Flames that only Zeke could see began to consume Father Baptist's body, whipping higher, through the ceiling, wrapping into a funnel of heat that scoured the flesh from his bones and the bones from his soul and transformed the tiny room into a smelter from which a lifetime of pain began to melt and run. Zeke retreated to the opposite wall. The heat was too intense, the light too bright, and he looked away. But still, he loved it. He loved it more than the look on a woman's face when he broke down her door, more than watching flames ripple across the prone body of the girl at the convenience store, more than any of the dumb bastards he'd torched tonight. This is what he'd waited for, the depths of this man's convictions fueling the pyre of his doubt, and it was beyond anything he could call satisfaction to watch the need that had given purpose to this strange afterlife flame up with such cataclysmic agony. He settled into the pits in the cinderblock wall and shouted gleefully into the inferno, *How does it feel, you son of a bitch? How does it feel for a man like you, a goddamned minister, to know the devil inside you?*

How does it feel to burn?

The room winked black, and a voice that sounded like a doctor's voice as he searches a patient for cancer, a policeman's voice as he frisks a suspect for drugs . . . or a father's voice as he searches his son for matches: *It feels pretty good, Zeke.*

Visions of fire.

Zeke liked his fires.

Something was moving on the bunk. Something he couldn't quite make out. Something plated over with snake scales and bristling with stingers, and it skewered Zeke with a ray's tail that sent pulses of raw pain scalding through him, jerking him aloft, an acid tendril slithering into a hangman's noose around his neck.

I want you to understand something, it whispered. It had Father Baptist's eyes, but that was all, and when Zeke's rabbiting gaze darted into them, he saw fire that only a minister could imagine.

You force me to do this, it whispered again, wrapping him with more tendrils and pulling him closer.

Then closer still.

But I'm doing this because I love you, it said.

Yes, Zeke whispered, understanding again the ragged agony of this peculiar love as it licked over him in a smear of pain, reducing everything to its most simple form, a black ash that said nothing more than: Something was burned here.

Zeke roared.

ECHOES

Cindie Geddes

OFFICER RICHARD PERISH NEARLY TRIPPED OVER THE BODY AS he went into the bathroom to listen to the cassette recorder found at the scene. The officers trying to do their job at the same time as they tried to keep the press out were all yelling and giving orders, unloading and loading equipment, banging around and ruffling papers. The air was thick with noise and the familiar scent of blood and decomposition, and the bathroom was the only quiet place in the house. Leaning back on the toilet below the little window, Officer Perish took a deep breath and turned the tiny cassette player over and over in his hand. Found as it was, so near the body, it had to be important. Yet he hesitated. He felt childish and vaguely frightened, which made him angry. With adult resolution, he sat up, swore under his breath, and pushed Play.

The voice, when it came, was strong and familiar. It started in on the story abruptly, making him abruptly uncomfortable with hearing such personal disclosure. So much for his training.

"My trust was stolen when I was ten, along with my virginity, by the father of a close friend in Carson City, Nevada. Mr. Trask. A pedophile, I suppose, because it wasn't just me. His advances, his rape, continued for almost a year until I moved across town and had an excuse to stay away. I'm okay with all that now, though, and yes, I know it wasn't my fault. I thought it was for a long time, but that all changed on a windy summer night three years later. It's all still very clear in my mind. An epiphany of sorts.

"My best friend, Cory, woke from a nightmare that scared me almost as much as it scared her. She was crying and trying to be very still and then began to struggle. Tears streaked her face and wet the hair at the side of her face, turning it to spun gold in the pale glow of the moon through my open window. 'Stop! You're hurting me!' she gasped, and suddenly it was so familiar. For a few minutes I couldn't move, not even to wake her and deliver her from her terrors, which I knew I could do because I knew those terrors intimately. It was a strange revelation for me when she told me how she had been molested by an uncle for two years when she was eight. All of a sudden I realized I wasn't the only one. But she was still having nightmares about it; I wasn't.

"That night, lying on opposite ends of my bed, we both cried and shared our stories and our innermost feelings of betrayal and distrust. It was a long night that drained us both so much that we slept most of the following day. We vowed then and there never to tell anyone about each other's secrets. We also vowed never to be victims again. Both are easy when you're fourteen.

"So why am I telling you this? Some sick cry for attention to get my career back on track? No. That only works when you make it up. If it really happened, it makes people uncomfortable. No fantasy in reality. Besides, my career's going to be coming to an abrupt end as soon as I find the courage to follow through with my plan. No, I'm telling you this because I want people to know why I did what I'm going to do. I don't want anyone to misunderstand. I've always been like that. It's very important to me to have people understand my motivations. Drove my ex-husband crazy that way. He hated the way I was always explaining everything. Of course, he thought he knew everything already, especially about me. I hate people like that.

"He never wanted me to be an actress, either. Wouldn't even let me model. I think he liked the idea of having me all to himself. Something pretty to decorate his life with. Y'know, I don't even remember why I married him anymore. But I was only eighteen then, and everyone's entitled to a few mistakes. At least I learn from mine. Besides, good things do come out of bad situations. Like Traci. I have custody now, and we get along very well. She's almost eleven and the smartest little girl I know. And I don't say that because I'm her mom. I'm more objective than that. And she really is remarkable.

"It's been ten years since the divorce, twelve since the wedding. But that's not important.

"What *is* important is the fact that my nemesis, Mr. Trask, is out of jail. No, I didn't put him there. Like I said, I never told anyone until I was fourteen. But I guess I wasn't the only one he played with, because a six-year-old girl came forward a year after I told Cory. The little girl's mother had him arrested. It made all the papers because it brought seven other little girls forward. And one boy. The oldest was nine. Except me. Like I said, I was ten.

"So, with all these firsthand witnesses, the trial went smoothly, and Mr. Trask was put away for life. Life doesn't mean the same thing it used to, does it? I mean, if life was only sixteen years, then Mr. Trask would have been dead of old age long before he had a chance to ruin the lives of little children.

"Mr. Trask. I don't know why he made us call him Mister. All the other dads let us use their first names. Maybe it was a power thing. Or maybe it made us seem subservient to him. Who knows? When you're as fucked-up as he is, do you really need a reason? I doubt it.

"Y'know, it's funny that back then, with Cory, *she* was the one having nightmares. They scared her so bad, I kept expecting to see her with gray hairs at school in the morning. I didn't really understand then how a dream could scare a person so terribly. But tonight, lying alone in this big bed, in my big house in this big, ugly city, I tell ya, I sure don't feel like Katrina Tyler, Star of Daytime's Hottest Soap. No, tonight, knowing he's out there, free, I feel like little Katie Tulomy again, Catch of the Day on the Monster Menu.

"Mama used to laugh when I told her that there was a monster trying to get me at night. I guess most adults respond that way. Not me. I never laugh when Traci's scared. I'll stay up all night with her if I have to, but I'll never tell her she's being a baby or imagining things. How can I? I can't convince myself, sometimes, that it's over and no one's gonna come take me out of my bed. We tell ourselves and our children that there's nothing to be afraid of in the dark, but we know it's a lie. Because at night we remember."

Richard Perish looked at the cassette recorder again as he pushed the Off button. It was hard to listen to this, made even harder by the fact that he knew who Katrina Tyler was. His wife, Patty, never missed an episode of that soap, and Katrina Tyler was a sort of idol of hers. A lot of the guys at the station watched the show, too. Mostly they just watched her because she was easily one of the most perfect women God ever created. Richard had seen her himself in this month's *Playboy*. Just an interview and a few at-home shots, but even with her clothes on, she put the centerfold to shame. Of course, Richard only read it for the articles. Really.

"I'm doing a scene today the housewives and college girls supposedly dream about, but I hate them. It's one of those Giving It Up scenes. Y'know, the kind where the girl is mean to the boy, but the boy knows she wants him, so he grabs her and kisses her. She slaps him, he grabs her again, she struggles at first and then succumbs. If a guy did that to me now, especially now, I'd have him up on charges so quick it'd make his head spin. What kind of shit is that to be teaching boys? Oh hell, there's not many boys watching anyway, right?

"I don't know why I let these things get to me. It's just a stupid TV show. And I do mean stupid. Do you believe I've been kidnapped four times, I've found out about two illegitimate children, killed one man, and been dead three times now? Of course, I wasn't really dead. No one ever is on the soaps. So real life's at least got that one up on the soaps: when you kill someone in reality, they stay dead.

"Did I tell you Cory's dead? Yeah. Four years now. Suicide. Found out her daughter was being molested by her husband. That'll do a number on you, all right. Last time I saw her was my wedding. Unless you count her funeral. It was open casket. The Irish are a weird bunch, aren't they?" There was a double click from the cassette recorder, and then the monologue continued. Richard felt like a twisted audio voyeur, if there was such a thing, but reminded himself that this was part of the job.

"Well, that's done. I was brilliant as usual, but Kirk was a little grabby. Sometimes he has a hard time distinguishing reality from TV. All this publicity's going to his head, I think. I'll have to have a talk with him after the show.

"Did I tell you how I found out about Mr. Trask being released? I don't think I did. Anyway, it wasn't on the news or in the papers. With the elections less than a month away, I guess they don't have time to report such little things. But I *did* find out. I almost wish I hadn't. But I did. I saw him outside the studio a little over three weeks ago. I don't know what he's doing here, he was in prison in Carson City, y'know. How does an ex-con get the money to come to LA? Maybe he got a job first. Maybe he's been out longer than I think. God, I hope not.

"Anyway, he was outside the studio and he was *old*. I remember him as huge, like a bear, and taller than the ceilings. His hair was the color of tar, and he had a beard like Grizzly Adams (to this day, I can't stand beards). He used to look huggable and friendly and laughed like a giant. Now he looks like a shriveled Salvation Army Santa after a three-day bender. He's so small, shorter than me, and probably the same weight. I came out the side entrance and I saw him, asleep against the wall, in filthy clothes, with a cup beside him that read 'second chance.' There were two quarters in the cup. I almost added a third before I recognized him.

"There were people waiting in the parking lot for my autograph, just as there are every night, and I signed every one of the little scraps of paper before getting into my car and bursting into tears. I'm not really the type who's normally apt to be hysterical, but I think I was then. My hands shook so bad I couldn't get the key in the ignition. That's probably a good thing. I might have killed myself or someone else if I had tried to drive in that condition.

"When I finally did get home, Traci was asleep. Thank God. Like I said, she's a smart kid and she can always tell when something's wrong with me. How could I explain all this to her? Mrs. Wilson, on the other hand, she's my sitter, she could care less what goes on in my daily life. I mean, if I came home and told her I witnessed a murder or something, she'd just say, 'That's nice,' grab her sweater, and head on out just as she does every night. It's a good thing, too, I guess. I've got enough people who want to know the details of my life without getting it from my sitter. You know, I found a reporter going through my garbage last month? *My garbage!* Jeez, you'd think people would have better things to do.

"Anyway, I was pretty shook up having seen Trask and all, so all I wanted was to just crawl into bed and try and dream it away. But I knew I'd only have nightmares, and that would just be too much. So instead, I went up to Traci's room and just watched her. Sometimes, most of the time, actually, just being around her makes me feel so much better. I watched her sleep, watched the way she dreamed with a little smile on her face, and once again swore that she would never go through anything like I did. I guess that was when I decided I would have to kill him.'"

Officer Perish ran a shaky hand over his forehead as he listened to the pause and click that told him something new was coming up. He thought of his own daughter, Maria, only six, and how he hadn't spent more than four hours with her all week. That would have to be remedied this weekend. Maybe they could go to the museum together. Maria loved those dinosaurs.

"Perish!" a loud voice bellowed in his ear.

"Jesus Christ, Ray!" he yelled as he dropped the recorder onto the floor, where it spewed its batteries onto the ceramic tiles.

"Christ, sorry. A little jumpy, huh?" Ray, his partner of a little over four months, tried to smile but didn't quite succeed.

"Yeah, go figure. You ever seen anything like this before?"

"Close, but not this sad. Anything on that tape?" he said as he propped his butt on the edge of the tub.

"Yeah. Everything. The whole damn story, it sounds like. At least it was before you made me drop the goddamned thing."

"Sorry," Ray said, picking the recorder up and popping the batteries back in. "It doesn't look broken. These things are supposed to be made pretty good."

"Yeah, well, let me see it." He took it and pushed Play.

"I'm not sure how I'm going to do it yet," the melodic voice began again, as if oblivious to its recent collision. "I mean, of course I don't want to get caught. That's the hardest part: planning the perfect crime. I used to read mysteries like they were going out of style when I was in high school, but after a while they became predictable. But they've turned out to be pretty good background material.

"Now, like I said before, I've dealt with all the shit surrounding Mr. Trask. I want that clear. He doesn't have any control over my life, and I don't have any weird hangups about men or anything like that. But that doesn't change the fact that he *is* back and that he *is* showing up in some weird places. Usually when I'm with Traci.

"That first time I saw him, outside the studio, I was alone. And a few days later, when I was at the dry cleaner's and he was there, I was with Kirk (he needed a ride). The third time, I was getting Traci from school, and he was there again. This time he was all cleaned up, wearing a sweater vest and corduroys. Like a teacher! Christ, I hope no one actually hired him to work with children! He smiled and waved as if we were old pals. I almost wet my pants.

"So that's probably how he found out I have a daughter. It's been two weeks since I saw him at the school, and I've seen him at least four times since. I'm not sure how he's doing it. But he was bagging groceries when Traci and I went to the grocery store, he was leaning against a lamppost and reading a paper when I took her to her dance lesson, and yesterday, when we went to the movies, he was sitting two rows behind us. Today, he was driving a cab that picked up my neighbor as Traci got into the car so I could take her to school.

"Traci's an awfully perceptive little girl, and she knows something's wrong with me. I told her I'm having bad dreams, and she believes it. It's true, too. I think she can tell when I lie. She's very smart.

"The nightmares started, what? Two or three days after I saw Mr. Trask again? Somewhere in that time frame. And they're bad, really awful. I never had nightmares about Mr. Trask before. I think I told you that. But now, every time I close my eyes, he's there. It's like I'm reliving the whole goddamned thing again. Maybe my unconscious is trying to remind me so I'll be more careful with Traci's safety. It shouldn't worry, I'm very careful. She is not allowed to stay overnight at anyone's house, and I don't let her visit her friends except during the hours I know the mother's home. It took a while to figure out the schedules, but I've got it now and it works well. Traci doesn't seem to mind. She's pretty much a homebody by nature."

Richard hit the Stop button and looked at Ray, who was rubbing his bald head. "Shit. Sounds like a confession."

"I know."

Ray looked at his watch. "You know, it's past seven. You should go home. You can listen to that thing there better than here. Less distractions. I'm going to see what I can find out about this Mr. Trask. I'll call if I find anything interesting."

"Sounds good. I'm starving anyway. You wanna come by for dinner? Patty's a great cook."

"I'd love to, but I'm not really hungry yet. Rain check?"

"Sure thing. Tomorrow."

"Tomorrow it is."

At home, belly full, head heavy, and ready for a nap, Officer Richard Perish went to his room, closed the door, and set the cassette recorder on the nightstand next to him. Maria was asleep, and Patty was content watching a romance she'd gotten at the corner video shop. She'd heard about the case, at least a little, from the news and had hounded him for details all through dinner. He couldn't tell her, even if he had wanted to, and he certainly didn't want to. It was the worst case he'd ever worked on, and he felt he'd be lucky if he got off without a few bad dreams of his own.

Patty had been understanding, if a little frustrated, and had granted him the time alone he needed to finish listening to the tape. By the looks of it, he was well over halfway through with the story of Katrina Tyler.

"In my nightmares," she said over the soft hum of the recorder's machinations, "I'm ten again. I know as soon as the dream begins, because I feel small and afraid. It's dark, like it always was, and Sara Trask is asleep in the bed next to me. There's a night table between us. I always thought it was so neat that she had two beds like that. It seemed so fun to go to her house and share her room just like I was her sister. Of course, that changed. After it was all over, I never stayed the night at anyone's house again. And I hate hotels with double beds. I always demand a single or a queen. Even if it's me and Traci. She's still young enough not to mind sleeping with her mommy.

"So I'm in Sara's spare bed and something wakes me up. Maybe it's his footsteps or his breathing or just the smell of his cologne. Maybe little girls can just sense these things. But something wakes me up, and I'm instantly afraid because this isn't the first time. The first time it happened, I wasn't scared until he took my clothes off.

187

"I know I'm dreaming, but that doesn't make me any less frightened, it doesn't make the sensations feel any less real. He picks me up, carefully so as not to make any noise. But I know to be quiet, like a little mouse, so I don't wake Sara up. Sara's got asthma and needs her sleep.

"He takes me past his bedroom where his wife mumbles in her Valium dreams, to the den, where he puts me down on the big green couch. He starts his game the way he always does, like I won't notice what he's doing. All I can think is that I hope he hurries this time because I'm tired and it's cold in his big, wooden office. His hands are cold, too, but I don't complain. He's told me before that if it weren't for me, he'd have to do this to Sara. And with Sara's asthma, it might kill her.

"I did cry the first time. I screamed even. But with his hand over my face, no one heard. I didn't mean to. I tried to be quiet, but it hurt so bad I thought I was going to die. And when he was done and I saw all the blood, I almost passed out. But Mr. Trask slapped my face and explained why all men did this. He explained how the blood makes a girl a woman and how it only hurts the first time. I asked why men had to do this, and he told me that if they didn't, it hurt them very bad and could even kill them. Mrs. Trask didn't know about the pain, so I could never tell her. We wouldn't want her to worry about Mr. Trask.

"So as he undresses me and counts my fingers and my toes, his hands cold and a little shaky, I shiver in the chilly room and remind myself about Sara's asthma and Mrs. Trask's fears and squeeze my eyes tight so maybe he'll think I'm sleeping and go away. It never works.

"When he's done, he lets me leave on my own. I go to the bathroom, clean myself up, and try not to cry. He lies. It hurts every time. But I don't bleed anymore.

"I go back to bed and huddle as deep under the covers as I can. I peek out at Sara and think about her asthma. I desperately wish I had it, too.

"So that's my nightmare. The same every time I close my eyes. It always takes me a while when I wake up to remember it was only a dream; it's all over. Then I remember he's back and I have to go check on Traci. She's just next door, but I know that doesn't protect her.

"You know, I always wondered if Sara knew. Did he molest her, too? She didn't come forward at the trial, but I still wonder. I think it would be much worse if it was your own father. How could you get over that? How could your mind ever deal with such a thing? I also wonder if Mrs. Trask knew. I think she did. Maybe she didn't *think* she did, but the way she looked at me, especially on those mornings after, I think she knew. Deep down in her heart, she knew what he did to me and all those other children. She just didn't know how to stop it.

"But I do."

Another click told Richard that that was the end of what Katrina had to say that night. When the tape began again, time had passed, but there was no way to know how much.

"I saw Traci talking to him today." The voice from the tiny speaker of the recorder was shaky and a little raspy, like that of a longtime smoker. "Outside the school again. He looked very different this time, dressed in overalls, like a groundskeeper. They were standing together by a flower bed. All the flowers were dead; I guess he was explaining why.

"It was everything I could do to keep from killing him with my bare hands. All I could think about was the nightmares, except now I saw Traci in them. And then there they were, standing together like best buddies. Had he so much as touched my daughter or had we just been alone, I would have. So help me God, I would have ripped his dick off and shoved it down his throat until he choked to death." She took a deep, shaky breath before continuing.

"He actually introduced himself as Terry Turner. Traci smiled and told me he was teaching her botany. I couldn't say anything. There were people around. So I took Traci's hand and nearly ran to the car. She won't be going back to that school, I can tell you that much.

"On the way home, she asked me again what was wrong. I told her I wasn't feeling well. I don't think she believes me anymore."

Another set of clicks, and the voice came back, this time quiet, a near whisper. "Can't sleep. Nothing new. I took a leave of absence from the show so I could get this over with. It wasn't very hard, the writers had been dying to have me kidnapped again anyway. So I have ten days. Ten days, and this will all be done.

"Traci hasn't been back to school in, I guess, four days now. It hasn't helped much, though. Somehow he must have found out where we live. Probably that day in the cab. He was helping Truman, our neighbors' gardener, reseed his lawn. Truman introduced me to him as I walked up my drive. He said Mr. Trask was his cousin from Florida, down to help with the business for a while. I ignored them.

"The nightmares are worse. They've changed. As if they weren't bad enough already. Now it all happens to Traci. Every time. And I'm the one asleep in the bedroom Mr. Trask passes on his way to the den. I hear them, but I can't wake up, I can't stop them, my body won't move, and I can't even yell for help. And Traci always screams like it's the first time. Sara still doesn't wake up.

"I bought a gun Tuesday. One of the makeup girls had a friend who had a friend who had a gun to get rid of. I gave the money to her, she gave it to the friend, who gave it to the friend, who gave it to me. Not even the original owner knows who has it now. It feels good in my hands. Solid, strong, and cool.

"It has to be this week. I can't keep Traci out of school much longer, and I can't stand the nightmares anymore.

"I'm so tired."

"I talked to Truman today and found out where his 'cousin' lives. It's all the way across town, over by the studio. I can make it there, do the job, and get back in under two hours. I don't think I'll even have to break in. The way he keeps following me, I'm sure Mr. Trask will just let me in. It wouldn't even occur to him that I'm all grown up now and can stand up to him. No, he's too used to helpless little girls. He won't even know what hit him. But some people will. All those little boys and girls will know one of us got even when they find him dead and castrated. And they'll cheer.

"I go tomorrow."

Richard Perish waited for the clicks and hit the Stop button. He wiped a heavy hand across his forehead and was surprised to find sweat. Sitting here, listening to the confession of a killer, was unlike any other experience of his life. He knew what was going to happen next; he'd seen the results himself. Still, to hear the words . . . he wasn't sure he was ready for it. But it was his job, so with one less-than-steady finger, he set the reels rolling again and listened to the end of Katrina Tyler's story.

At first there were no words. Her voice hitched and cracked in heart-wrenching sobs. After a full minute, Officer Perish was ready to turn the player off again and save any more of this until morning. But then she regained control.

"The best-laid plans, huh?" She laughed miserably. "It was all so clear to me. I didn't expect him to make this move." There were intermittent metallic sounds in the background, metal lightly tapping metal. "It wasn't supposed to happen like this. Traci . . . oh God, Traci." The words turned to sobs again, but they didn't last.

"I guess I should explain. I've told you everything else. Yesterday, I vowed to go after him tomorrow. Right? Remember? Well, I won't. He's already here. It was about midnight when Traci woke me up. She was standing by my bed, shaking. Said she heard something. I asked her what, but she didn't know. Like footsteps, she told me, maybe. Then I heard it myself, and I knew. It was Mr. Trask, and he was going through all the downstairs rooms. Looking for my daughter. But he didn't know where to find her because this wasn't his house, and Traci wasn't in Sara's room.

" 'Mommy?' she asked. 'Is someone here?'

"I told her yes. I couldn't lie. I told her it was a very bad man, a bad man who used to hurt Mommy. She started to whimper, and I told her to be very quiet, like a little mouse. I pulled her onto the bed, where she curled up against me like an infant.

"I heard Mr. Trask on the stairs.

"Traci began to cry. I told her we needed to pretend we were asleep and maybe he would go away. She tried, I think, but still she couldn't help crying. So I put my hand over her face, gently, so that he wouldn't hear us.

"I squeezed my eyes shut. He was still coming up the stairs. I tried not to breathe.

"I held Traci still even when she struggled. I know what it's like to be so scared. I only wanted to help, help her not be a victim, keep her safe from the horrible Mr. Trask.

"Traci didn't struggle long, but it wasn't until she stopped that I started to worry. I . . ." The voice broke again. Katrina Tyler cleared her throat and took another shaky breath. "I killed her. She's dead. Here on my bed. I can see the mark of my hand in the moonlight. I suffocated her. I didn't mean to. I swear, I was trying to save her. Oh God, it wasn't supposed to be like this. It was never supposed to be like this."

There was a long pause, in which the tape kept running. Two minutes passed, then three. Richard pushed Fast Forward until he heard her voice again. "Traci's gone. She's in heaven because she was innocent. When I was ten, I would have rather been dead than his victim. Maybe I did save her. Maybe it's better this way. Now she'll never be hurt, never be abused or destroyed. Now she'll always be safe.

"He's in her room now. Been there for a good fifteen minutes. I think he got there just as Traci was dying, but I can't be sure. It doesn't matter now. What *does* matter is that I don't become a victim, too. He'll be here any minute now. I can feel him like a cold spot. But it's okay. I've got the gun. I'll leave the tape running for you."

The next came in a series of one-sided conversations.

"How did you know?" Katrina said.

Silence.

"Well, it's my turn now."

The swishing of fabric.

"What do you mean? Of course I can. You don't . . ."

The thud of someone sitting heavily on the floor.

A metallic click.

"I didn't kill her, you did. And she's safe now. Safer than I ever was." She sighed deeply.

"I know. I want to be safe, but . . ." She moved closer to the recorder.

"Yes, I can! I *can* be safe! And I will! Try and stop me!" She laughed loudly, her mouth no more than inches from the recorder's tiny mike. But it was cut short by the deafening discharge of the gun.

The tape ran out in silence.

The phone rang, but Richard didn't hear it. His mind was still held captive by the sound of the gunshot on that tiny tape recorder. Seeing Katrina Tyler's bloody body, the gun still gripped tight in her hand, the top of her head gone, was not as bad as hearing that tiny frightened voice followed by the roar of the gun. The sight of the blue, lifeless body of her ten-year-old child was not as chilling as the words she spoke into her empty room. These were sounds he would never forget. Sounds that would not only haunt his dreams but every silence of the waking world as well.

"Hon?" Patty knocked tentatively on the bedroom door. "It's Ray. He says he has news."

Richard took the call but didn't listen. The sound of that one lone gunshot had already told him all he needed to know. It was no surprise to him when Ray told him that Mr. Trask was still in jail, not even up for parole for another year.

Later that night, Patty and Richard Perish were awakened by the cries of their only daughter. "Mommy!" she yelled. Obviously having a nightmare of her own.

"I'll get it," Richard told his wife. "My turn."

"Thanks, hon," Patty said, rolling over and going back to sleep.

Richard went to his daughter's room and sat on the edge

of her bed. Maria wrapped her thin arms tightly around her daddy's waist. "Oh, Daddy, Daddy," she whimpered, with only the residual tears used strictly to garner affection. "Somebody's in my room."

Richard smiled, knowing, as only a father knows, that the house was safe and secure. "No, honey, there's no one . . ." He stopped, heard the echo of Katrina's gun. This time, he did not tell her it was her imagination, did not tell her to go back to sleep. He held her close and stroked her hair, whispering words of love and comfort, hoping they were true.

LIFELINE

Yvonne Navarro

"I KNOW YOU'RE AWAKE, GRANDMOTHER."

Eir Garvey opened her eyes reluctantly at the sound of her granddaughter's honeyed voice. Oletta sat by the side of her bed, so beautiful, staring at her with eyes that were like deep, black pools, devoid of everything. Sunlight leaked through the blinds and stripped her smooth, dusky skin, threw midnight-blue highlights into her black hair before it fell into her eyes and disappeared. No shine there or glint of moisture on colored irises. Just the darkness of a dangerous soul.

"What do you want?" Eir's voice was a croak, the best her damaged lungs could offer. Too many years of nervous smoking, but what did it matter now? She was old, ninety-one last week. She hardly talked anymore, and she wore diapers because she could no longer walk to the bathroom twelve feet away. Her blood pressure was low, and the doctors had shoved a double plastic prong up her nose to pump oxygen into her, lessen the burden of breathing on her tired body. There was nothing wrong with her mind, and they said she would live on for years.

"Just to visit." Oletta didn't move or try to touch her. "I missed your birthday."

"I'd . . . hoped you wouldn't come," Eir wheezed.

The young woman cocked her head to one side, reminding Eir of a vicious dog that contemplates its victim before attacking. "You've never liked me," Oletta said. There was no regret in her voice. "Why?"

The bed suddenly felt too small, the linens beneath Eir insidiously confining, as if they had come to life and twisted around her lower body. She started to panic, then relaxed; it wasn't as if she could run anyway. Too little air or the wrong answer—these questions could kill her either way. She wanted to die . . . or did she? She took a long time to answer, but Oletta didn't leave or look away, just waited.

"You're . . . dirty," Eir finally whispered. "Inside." It was too late in her life for deception.

Oletta's smile was wide and lovely, showing brilliantly white teeth beyond the rich, red lips. The incisors were slightly pointed but fit neatly into her bottom teeth; their shape gave her speech a slight lisp that most people found endearing. "Such a thing to say to your only granddaughter," she admonished. "What would Mother and Father say?"

"They don't know you like I do." The struggle to get the words out was nearly more than Eir could take. "They can't . . . , *see.*"

"No," Oletta agreed. "They can't." She turned her face toward the window and studied the closed blinds without comment.

She's giving me time to regain my strength, Eir realized in despair, and then she's going to keep on. She's not going to leave me in peace, not now or ever. The old woman wished she could sit upright, then get dressed, pick up her purse, and leave the nursing home and its death-shrouded rooms behind. First she would go into the bathroom and take off this clammy, disgusting diaper. All impossible; she had no choice but to lie there and let her body replenish its pitiful strength, try and build reserves to speak the difficult words that were yet to come.

Finally, she had the air to do it.

"Why don't you just kill me?" Although the question came out in broken syllables, it was not hard to understand. "It's what you want." Eir's fingers stroked the sheets as she waited for Oletta's response, felt the nubbiness of the cheap fabric. Everything was cheap in this place—the sheets, the toilet tissue and generic baby powder, the lives of the forgotten old people left here. She jerked when her granddaughter's breathy answer came from only an inch or so away from her left ear. She hadn't seen Oletta rise from the chair.

"I don't kill old women."

Waiting for the pathetic remains of the heart muscle in her chest to slow its jarring beat, Eir couldn't answer for a full minute. She waited for it to give up entirely, just stop, and wondered what dying would feel like. She wanted to die. She wanted to live. She couldn't make up her mind anymore.

"Then *who?*"

Oletta's gaze slid over her grandmother's face, those black eyes like dull oil, emotionless and filthy. "Who said I've ever killed anyone at all?" she asked softly. "Maybe I haven't."

"Liar," Eir hissed. "I can *see*—"

"You *see* too much," Oletta interrupted. She stepped to the window and fingered the string for the blinds. Her nails were long and expensively manicured, exquisite, each a polished bloody red with a tiny, glittering lightning bolt on its center. Oletta's face turned back toward the bed with excruciating slowness, but this time she didn't smile. "I'm the same as you."

"No—"

"Now who's the liar?" The black eyes had taken on a strange, burning intensity, like oily smoke. She hadn't watched television in months, but her granddaughter's gaze made Eir think of when she had, of the films on the news programs that showed the oil fires raging in Kuwait, killing plumes of mist rising in the air above the ruins of a destroyed country. Oletta's thoughts were inside Eir's head,

and that's what they were like. "I can see inside you, too,"
Oletta continued. "You've done the same . . . *questionable*
things that I have."

It had been a long time since the frail old lady had
laughed, and the sound was more like a bark, loud only
because of the harsh cough that pushed it from her chest.
"Not as bad." Eir coughed again, remembered where she
was, and looked fearfully across the room at the bed on the
other side of the chair in which her granddaughter had been
sitting. Her roommate was there, yes, but asleep. Or pretending. She looked back at the young woman standing by
the window. "Not as many."

Oletta shrugged. "Killing is killing," she said softly. "Not
quantity."

"But I stopped," Eir managed. "Years ago." She didn't
want the memories that swept through her mind, had
thought they'd faded to nothingness three quarters of a
century ago. She should have known better; there are some
things you never forget.

"And so shall I."

Silence as the two women, one young and vibrant, one so
very ancient and ill used, examined their own thoughts. To
Eir the rush of old times was like having a forgotten and
mildewed box topple from the attic and crash inside her
head, its unwanted contents exploding and spreading debris
from which she only wished to hide. Oletta's were different,
Eir knew. No doubt she flipped through them like neatly
organized file folders, those sharp and lovely fingernails
poking and prodding amid the mental notes and photographs while she savored the contents.

"They'll catch you."

"They already have. They just haven't come for me yet.
That's . . ." That tilting of the head again, careful contem-
plation of her own impending destruction. "Tomorrow, I
think. The day after, at the latest." Oletta sighed. "My life
has been good."

Eir glanced at her in surprise. "You have many years left,"
she rasped. "In prison."

Oletta chuckled, and the sound was beautiful but fragmented, like broken church bells. "I don't kill old women," she repeated in a low voice. "And I don't go to prison." She twisted the string to the blinds around the first two fingers of one hand and began a slow pull; the blinds began to rise, casting a golden square on the floor that bled away at its bottom edge as it got larger. "It's so sad that you are trapped here, in your bed and in this dingy room. You must wonder what my life is like."

"No," Eir said sharply. The emphasis cost her tremendously, and she almost couldn't get the next words out. "I don't *want* to know."

"I think you do." The blinds were halfway up now, and Oletta's head and shoulders were a dark shadow above the wash of bright light that had climbed to her collarbone. "It's very stressful, you know. My lifestyle is costly. I work a lot of hours and have to answer to a lot of people to support it." A small frown flickered across her forehead and was gone. "I don't care for it very much anymore. I suppose I've gotten . . . tired." She looked at the floor for a moment. "I don't think anyone really appreciates what I go through on a day-to-day basis. You, in particular, have always disappointed me. Of all the people in this family, in the *world,* you should empathize with me. But you don't."

Eir's voice was a strained whisper. "You're mad," she choked out. "At least I *healed."*

"Yes, you did," Oletta agreed calmly. "I do envy the way you were able to change yourself, to *stop* what you were and become someone else." She let go of the blind's cord at the halfway point, leaving her face in shadow as she stretched her hands into the sunshine, turned them palm up and studied them. "I can do that, too, you know, although in a slightly different way. It's taken some practice, but I can . . . *become* someone else."

"You . . . can?" Eir asked faintly.

"Yes." That smoky look again, its effect washing across the room like a wind from hell. Oletta twined her fingers together briefly, then walked to the side of the bed and began straightening the covers, tucking them carefully around her grandmother's tiny body. Eir wanted to cringe away from that tainted touch, but she didn't have the strength. "It's not so hard," Oletta continued. "Not much beyond seeing inside someone's mind—you know how that is—but just not *stopping*. Sliding all the way in and leaving only the tiniest thread of yourself behind to find your way back—assuming you want to, of course. It does require tremendous will and mental strength. It took me ten years to finally do it successfully." Standing at the side of the bed, Oletta shrugged daintily and looked at her grandmother from beneath half-closed eyelids. "Now I've done it so much it's second nature."

"Go away." Eir dropped her hand over the edge of the bed and fumbled along its side, trying to find the call button for the nurse.

"Looking for this?" Oletta held up the beige piece of equipment in one hand. Its cord, extra long so Eir could take it with her to the chair or dresser back in the days when she'd still been able to walk, trailed somewhere on the floor as Oletta turned and placed it carefully on the windowsill. There was no way Eir could reach it now. "But I was telling you about my life," Oletta said evenly. "I'm so terrible at describing things, aren't I?" She smiled at Eir. "Better I should simply *show* you." She snatched up Eir's cold hand before the elderly woman could pull away.

"No—"

And suddenly Oletta was *there,* inside Eir's mind, and doing the incredible by pushing the old woman's essence out. Never would Eir have guessed Oletta had this kind of ability, the massive mental mastery it took to actually *transfer* consciousness with someone else, to force someone else to see the things Eir was seeing now.

Dear God, Eir thought crazily. *Please just let me die right now!*

The first one: an impulse thing, a sudden fit of temper because she didn't like his tone of voice. Naked in the kitchen of his uptown apartment, the two of them fixing a drunken four A.M. breakfast following the ecstasy of steamy, one-night sex. He'd said something snide about women, about her, and suddenly she was more than furious, she was practically rabid *with rage. Whatever his words, they were unimportant now, so trivial she couldn't or didn't care to remember them except to recall her wrath that this man, who had joined with her only a half hour before and spilled himself inside her body, had mouthed such a careless, ugly insult. In any event, the forgotten words faded in the shadow of the HUGE thing she'd done to him as retribution, and standing over his body with the carving knife in her hand, she'd felt no regrets at all. He'd deserved to die, just as she deserved to feel the warmth of his blood against her bare skin, her breasts, her belly, like the spray of perfectly temperatured bathwater as it burst from the cavernous split she'd made along the curve of his neck. Five minutes before, he'd been a handsome, well-built man with fine green eyes and soft, longish hair the color of summer hay. Now he was twisted and ugly, covered in sticky red streaks drying to brown. The healthy pink glow of his skin had bled away to the gray of industrial walls.*

So long ago, and so simple to deal with. She'd wiped the blood from her feet with paper towels, gone into the bathroom and taken a shower with the cleaver still in her hand, then flushed the bits of ripped paper towels down the toilet. She'd dried herself with his towel, dried the cleaver and put it away, then carefully eliminated every trace of herself from his apartment—fingerprints, hairs on the bedsheets, even checked his clothes. In his pocket she found a matchbook with the name of the bar in which he'd picked her up, and, just to confuse things, she stripped his wallet of cash and credit cards. Back at her place, she systematically cut his credit cards into pieces so small they couldn't be identified, and that night she divided the debris among Dumpsters in three different locations . . . on her way to treating herself to a lobster dinner she bought with his cash.

Since then, so many others that she literally lost count, nameless men, a few women taken as experimental lovers solely to be disposed of, others actually forgotten with the passage of time. Dozens of stolen lives, half a hundred or more, until the numbers simply didn't matter anymore. The only ones of importance were the last three or four because of her unaccustomed carelessness, foolish slip-ups that built a *path straight to her door. Too tired to run, too much work to start over, she'd done it all anyway, and what was left in life but exhaustion? All that spilled blood, but she could not spill her own, could not bring herself to end her own existence in pain and blood, or even with a mouthful of sleeping pills. Her mind's eye obliged her with an alternative future, unfolding a picture of herself surrounded by cold and mildewy gray, the stone walls of a women's prison for as long as she continued to draw breath. Die or go to prison, two choices, but she could do neither.*

Cornered like a dog, until the spark of the idea that had brought her to the nursing home today. A third option, and a chance for a fine-tuned revenge on the withered old woman who had worried her all her life.

Grandmother.

Eir choked and felt balance try to slip away, reached out blindly until her hand found something, the chairback, cool vinyl under her fingers, and she grasped it and held on for dear life. She felt oddly lightheaded and . . . *tall* somehow, wobbly. When she opened her eyes, she was looking at the bed and her own dried-up, ancient body beneath the sheets, except the eyes that met her gaze were crafty and black as tar instead of faded hazel. Her new body felt smooth and sensuous, too decadent to be controllable. No wonder Oletta had been doomed; this body would be a beacon for the unspeakable in a women's prison, and capital punishment still wasn't used in this state. Eir had never tried the sort of mental somersault that Oletta had mastered, but desperation could be the catalyst for stranger things. She would have herself back or die trying.

"No." Eir's head snapped up at the raspy voice. It was downright obscene to hear her own voice but be trapped in another woman's murdering body. "You can't switch again. You don't have the strength—or the time."

"What are you talking about?" she hissed. Eir moved toward the bed and her true body, already preparing for her first attempt. There was a good chance it would kill her, but it was worth the risk—as long as she was in the right body when it died.

Oletta swallowed and the chest on her stolen body heaved as she struggled to pull in enough breath to keep talking. "Foolish old woman—you always were," she croaked. "You could see my victims, but little else. I . . . lied about the police."

"What do you mean?" Eir's fists balled at her sides as a feeling of doom dropped onto her. "What did you lie about this time?"

Her face smiled, mouth stretched hideously beyond what had been a normal smile for Eir a lifeline ago. "I lied about the *tomorrow* part." Oletta managed another wheezing breath, smiled again as her newly aged gaze flicked to something over Eir's shoulder.

"It's *now.*"

Eir whirled to face the door of her room and had to clap a hand over her mouth to keep from screaming at the sight of the four uniformed police officers filing through the door. Two men, two women, their eyes all cold and hard, fingers twitching eagerly above deadly revolvers.

"Oletta Garvey," the lead one said. It wasn't a question but an emotionless statement of fact. "You're under arrest."

BLAMELESS

David Niall Wilson

SUSAN POURED THE LAST OF THE GIN OVER HER ALREADY diluted orange juice and took a big gulp. In the background, loud and insistent, little Bobby continued to wail. She could almost imagine that the sounds were meant as penance, that the stabbing pain of the headache they brought was for atonement, not accusation. Almost.

Retrieving the bottle of formula she'd been heating on the stove, she threw her own empty bottle into the trash and moved slowly into the hall, heading for the baby's room. Her baby's room. Hers and . . .

She felt the chilling touch of iced gin on her wrist as her hand began shaking violently. She had to get a grip on this, a tighter grip even than she had on the baby bottle in her hand, which was threatening to collapse from the pressure. There was no reason for this to ruin her life—their life.

She tried once more to soothe herself with a quick gulp of her drink. At least she could lower the level in the glass to where she wouldn't be spilling it. God knew that she and John had enough to worry about without her greeting him at the door in gin-soaked clothes.

The baby's door was slightly ajar, leaking a small wedge of light into the gloomy hall. Susan had not yet bothered to turn on any of the home's other lights, feeling that the dim, colorless atmosphere was more fitted to her own mood. Now Bobby's wailing cries, emanating from the same spot as the only light in the house, had an almost hypnotic, focusing effect. She felt as if she was being drawn forward, no choices remaining, drawn forward and back at the same time.

John had been gone so many times over the last few years. Sometimes just a day, other times nearly a month. Business. Paying the bills. Building for their future. All these were fine reasons for his absence. They made sense, and they made money, and through it all he was as straight and reliable as the proverbial arrow. Blameless. But, damn it, he was always gone, and she had been weak.

Susan had considered herself fortunate, unemployed and twenty-six, still living at home with her aging parents, when John had asked her to marry him. He was kind, gentle, very successful . . . and the only one to offer. Of course, she hadn't exactly been out and available. In fact, if it hadn't been for fate, her flat tire, and almost phenomenal persistence on John's part thereafter, she never would have gone out with him, either. She had been comfortable, if not exceptionally happy, living at home and sharing all of her deep emotional moments with an endless series of romance novels.

Now they were a family, living together in their own small home: she, John, and Bobby. The baby. She still couldn't bring the words *their baby* to her lips. Not when she couldn't be sure. Not when her one moment of weakness had drawn tight the strings of her destiny. She brought her drink there instead, crossing the room's threshold with a sudden, jerky step.

It seemed preternaturally bright in the room. Everything was bright yellow and blue. Stuffed creatures great and small fixed her with lifeless, leering stares. She went to the side of the crib and looked down at her crying child. Chubby fingers groped for the bottle in her hand, tiny feet moving in tandem. So innocent. Blameless.

She gently placed the bottle in his hands and watched—

almost tenderly—as he eagerly brought the nipple to his mouth. Then his eyes rose to hers, locking with them. Green eyes. Sea green, dancing eyes. Just like his father's.

She bit off a cry of surprise at the intensity of the memory that one quick glance had sent shivering through her. Collapsing into the chair beside the crib, she rolled into a ball—into herself—swallowing the last of her gin as the room began to fade, as her sight grew dull.

The air swirled, solidified by the smoke of a dozen different brands of tobacco. The lights, dim and hazy, filtered through stale, cloudy air to tease at her senses with colored fluorescent rainbows. Unknown challenges seemed to hover on all sides, untested waters.

Heads turned as she entered, tentative steps and wide eyes announcing her naïveté to the world. Fascinated, she moved inside, committing herself. The doors slid shut behind her with quiet finality.

The stool she chose lay in a shadowed, isolated corner of the bar by the pool table. She sank into the cool plastic of its cushion and placed her purse on the bar, bringing her eyes up to meet those of the large, curly-haired bartender.

"Gin and tonic," she managed, her tongue seemingly reluctant to form the words. It was as if the words, once spoken, would cement her to this strange, frightening new place . . . as if silence might shield her.

The man disappeared without a word, swiping his white towel across the bar where previous patrons had left traces of bottles, glasses, and slowed reflexes.

She nearly jumped off her stool when she felt the man's hand come to rest on her shoulder.

Somehow he was just there . . . tall, imposing, dark hair waving back over his shoulders. The first thing she saw, as her heart struggled to flutter back to earth, was his eyes. They were a deep sea green, compelling and warm. She wanted to get up . . . to run, to escape back to her lonely home and her empty bed. Then he spoke.

His voice was as warm as his eyes. "Hey, pretty lady, mind if I join you?"

She wanted to scream, "Yes! Yes, I mind." She wanted this dark stranger with the powerful eyes to disappear . . . wanted his hand to release her shoulder from the growing glow of warmth it was pulsing into her traitorous body. She shook her head, almost imperceptibly. Whether he noticed or not, she never knew. He sat down.

She managed to tear her eyes from his—why was it so damned hard? His arm rested on the bar, one large, slender hand firmly planted atop her own. She stared—fascinated. On his forearm, almost mystical in the odd, glowing haze of smoke and neon light, was a tattoo of a dragon. It was green and gold, curling around his wrist and snaking back up to slavering jaws and glittering eyes that seemed to peer back at her from just below his elbow. She had never been so close to a tattoo—the thought almost amused her. It added to the surreality of the moment; she felt a strange detachment. How many times had she read about people feeling they were outside reality looking in?

"You don't look like a regular," he was saying. "New in town? Slumming? How about a hint?"

His words seemed like some off-kilter script, a not-quite-real-time overdub from another planet. His eyes were still dancing. Wildly, her mind fought for control of the situation. An image from her childhood surfaced: that snake in *The Jungle Book*, what had its name been? Kaa? She felt the way the boy must have, as if she was being hypnotized. At the same time, her rational side told her it was only her own fear, her guilt over being out with John away, that had robbed her of her wits. That and the damned gin. The drink she'd ordered would not be the evening's first—not by a long shot.

Somehow, once she had stepped through the doors of this place, a commitment had been made. She could still hear Father Simon intoning, "To commit the sin in your mind is to commit the sin." She knew that whatever happened next, she was guilty. It was like an inevitable chain of events had grabbed her and was rushing her along, helpless. No escape.

"I . . . I have to go," she managed, feebly moving to rise. "I'm sorry."

His eyes flickered from amusement to curiosity, somehow managing to do so while snaking up and down the length of her body. She cursed whatever stupid impulse had led her to wear such a short skirt.

"You haven't finished your drink," he observed, nodding toward the glass that now sat before her. Reaching for his wallet, he threw a five on the bar. "On me, friend," he said. The bartender shrugged and took the bill. Susan was far too slow to protest.

There had been more. More meaningless words. More drinks. Her mind drifted through scattered images—stumbling from the barstool, strong arms supporting her, soothing words. Heat. There had been such heat wherever he had touched her. And he had touched her over and over, lingering in places and ways that John never would have dreamed of, especially in public. They had been in his car before she even realized she would not be going home that night, her thigh pressed so tightly against him that he had trouble manipulating the gear shift—or had the lingering tangles of his arms and her legs been intentional? More heat . . .

The room slowly focused . . . becoming one with the final glimpse of her dream/memory. The house had seemed so surreal the morning after. He'd dropped her at her car, the reality of the day seeping insidiously between them. Somehow his eyes seemed less bright—the tattoo more threatening, less mysterious. She didn't even know his name. And the sunlight had shone through the tinted glass of the car's windows, bright and hot, like a spotlight.

There she is. Adulteress. The guilt had erased the final remnants of the night before, leaving her with the realization that her life—everything about it—was irreversibly changed. Something was lost. The fuzzy, pounding pain of the headache would pass. The hangover would fade. The guilt would grow. She had been raised a strict Catholic. Guilt was a built-in reflex, familiar and relentless.

Now she lived in an alcohol-warped dream state. Everyday chores passed by in meaningless drudgery. Every conversation, everything she and John did, was like some stilted, pseudo-life play. Each moment seemed hinged on that coming confrontation, that one ruinous second in time when her sins would be laid bare. The realization that there was no reason to believe John would ever know did nothing to change things. She knew. Somehow, she thought, the baby did, too.

It was in his eyes—Bobby's—when he looked up at John. He smiled, curious as any other child, but it did not seem to have that bond, that natural recognition a child has for his parent. It was the same look Bobby would give one of their friends or her parents. When looking at her, those eyes were much more expressive. Possessive, even.

John had been so happy. "Pregnant?" he'd exclaimed, his face almost comical, as though he'd never even considered the possibility. "We're going to have a baby? Our baby?"

It had been all she could do not to break down into hysterical sobs. She had smiled shyly, the tears somehow passing for happiness, while her heart screamed, *I don't know! I don't know!*

Bobby continued to suck down the formula, tiny feet kicking contented circles in the air. She tried to smile down at him, to find that bond that was expected of her. There was a bond, but it was built on guilt, pain, and self-recrimination. His vacant baby smile seemed more like an accusatory leer, her living, breathing, and unforgiving conscience. She feared she would never love her child, would never know the joy that she and her own mother had shared.

She reached out, brushing a straying lock of feather-thin hair from Bobby's forehead. He batted at her with one tiny fist, and she jerked her hand back as though she'd been bitten. Sucking in a deep breath, she could only stare as her skin grew clammy. The empty gin glass fell from her nerveless fingers, bouncing once off the arm of her chair as it tumbled to the floor.

On the baby's arm, curling and twisting in an intricate swirl of green and gold, was a tiny dragon. Its eyes were pinpricks of emerald, glittering and evil.

She nearly fell. Only a supreme effort and a gulping spasm of tortured breath enabled her to reach out, catching herself on the side of the crib. Even so, she found herself kneeling, head hung and eyes closed, on the carpeted floor. Kneeling in repentance. Kneeling in trembling fear. After long moments of concentrated effort, she managed to still her pounding heart enough to rise.

It was a hallucination. It was a figment of imagination and guilt combined—a cruel trick of her mind upon her heart. That was reality, and she grasped at it. Babies aren't born with tattoos, no matter who the father. Tiny children do not have snaking, serpentine lizards wrapped around their forearms; and she wasn't crazy.

She rose slowly, keeping her eyes carefully directed at the floor beneath her. It was one thing to convince herself of what she would not see, another to force her eyes to cooperate. One quick peek. One short flash of her eyes over the arm of her child, and things would right themselves again—as right as they could ever be. She tilted her head, brought her sight in line with Bobby's flailing toes . . . traced the chubby line of his belly, which rose and fell as he fed . . . reached his arm.

She screamed then, and this time she fell—hard. The eyes still stared up at her from Bobby's arm, leering. That vision, Bobby, the crib, the dragon, all of it blurred before her eyes in a surreal panorama of fear and nausea. Blackness yawned invitingly, and she dove inside. From far away she felt her head striking the floor, sending small sparks of light to dance in the void. Then there was nothing.

"Honey? Susan?" The words slipped sinuously through the darkness to drag at her, pulling her to the surface. She fought, struggled for the peace and the solitude, but the voice was insistent. John.

At first, she couldn't recall what had happened. She lay on the floor in Bobby's room, her head cradled in the arms of a large teddy bear John had used as an improvised pillow. She blinked her eyes, afraid of the pain that moving would bring. There was a dull throb in the back of her head, pulsing along with her heart. John. Bobby. "Oh my God," she whispered.

Whirling, she staggered to her feet, nearly falling back to the floor as vertigo took control. She grasped the edge of the crib, hands digging into the wooden railing and rocking the small bed violently, nearly toppling it.

"What the hell are you doing?" John said, worry and anger now battling in his eyes, which strayed down to the baby. He grabbed her under her arms, steadying her. She paid no attention, shaking her head and looking into the crib. Bobby lay, wide-eyed and on the verge of frightened tears. His arm was covered by a tiny blanket. Hidden. Momentary relief flooded her as she fought to regain her senses, but just as soon, it was gone. John, having decided she was now steady on her feet, had released her and was reaching for Bobby.

"No!" she cried, regretting the outburst instantly and the explanation it would require. Without taking time to think, she stumbled away from the crib, letting her knees buckle beneath her again. Falling. John's hands hovered for a moment over the blanket, about to wipe out years of happiness with a single gesture . . . without a chance. Then he pulled back, rushing to her side and breaking her fall, all signs of anger gone.

"Honey," he asked urgently, "what's wrong? Are you . . . drunk?"

Her own anger flared momentarily, until she caught sight of the empty glass lying beneath the crib. What the hell else was he supposed to think?

"No," she managed. "I . . . I was sitting there in the chair, watching Bobby sleep. I think maybe I just stood up too fast. I passed out, and I think I hit my head."

"You've got quite a knot on it," John commented, brushing his fingers across her scalp gingerly and pulling her a little closer. "You've got to be more careful. What if you'd fallen on the crib?"

Her anger almost returned. Was that it? Was he concerned only for the damage she might have done to the damned baby? The baby that wasn't even . . . she took a deep breath. That line of thought led only to trouble. She needed to get her wits back and figure out what to do before John saw.

"Would you get me a glass of water, honey?" she asked, sitting up slightly. "My mouth is kind of dry."

"Of course," he said, rising quickly. As soon as he was out of sight, she stumbled across the room and dug out one of Bobby's sleepers. One with long sleeves. Working frantically, she pulled off the shorts the baby was wearing and stuffed him hurriedly into the heavier outfit. She was just zipping the front as John walked back in.

"What are you doing?" he asked, puzzled. "Isn't it a bit hot for that?"

"I felt a chill," she said, drawing Bobby up to rest against her chest. "You can never be too careful, you know."

John shook his head, but he did not argue the point. "Here's your water," he said, holding out the glass and reaching for the baby. Reluctantly, she handed him over, fearing each moment that John would get some wild urge to unzip the sleeper. He did not.

Somehow she managed to cook supper. Soon after that, Bobby was asleep, sweating slightly in the heavy sleeper, but safely tucked in. Her heart racing, she led John off to their own bed as quickly as she could. She did not really want to make love—not now—but she needed the closeness, the comfort of him. Besides, the more tightly she was wrapped around him, the more totally they were bonded, the less chance that he might grow restless, might go in to check on the baby. It was several hours before he fell asleep in her arms, and another hour beyond that when she allowed herself to drop into a restless, fitful pit of darkness and nightmares. Dragons filled her dreams, dragons and dancing, sea-green eyes.

"It's only a three-day trip this time, honey," John was saying, gulping down the last drops of his third cup of coffee and reaching for his briefcase. "After this, I promise, I'll take some time off—time for you and Bobby."

She just smiled, her face a mask of false, plastic complacency. Her mind was whirling—making her dizzy and nauseous. John took her in his arms, giving her one last hug, and started down the hall to the baby's room. Her heart froze, then began pulsing so heavily that the sound deafened her. What if he saw? Was this the moment? The end? Her knees began to tremble, and she fell heavily into one of the dining-room chairs, eyes riveted to the hall—to that door.

She saw John come out through a milky haze. He was smiling, calling some sort of childish farewell over his shoulder to the doorway, to the baby. She rose, numb and cold, allowing him to hug her a last time but unable to return any pressure.

"Honey?" he said. "Is something wrong? You look pale . . ."

"I . . . I'll be all right," she answered, shaking her head slowly back and forth. "I just didn't sleep well last night. I think I'll lie down for a little while."

"Well," he said, obviously not convinced, "I'll be at the office for a couple of hours before I take off. If you need me, call, okay?"

"I will," she said softly. "Have a good trip."

Then he was gone.

She hesitated, not wanting to do what she knew she had to, but in the end she had no choice. She felt almost as if she were floating as she moved slowly down the hallway to the baby's room. Bobby was awake, gurgling and spitting, tiny arms windmilling in pointless baby circles. His eyes followed her as she approached—he seemed to understand. Surely, when he was grown and she could share this with him, he would understand. She reached down gently and unzipped the sleeper, sliding it back off his shoulders. His diaper was wet, but she paid no attention to it. In a few moments, it wouldn't matter. The bath would cleanse it all away. The bath could purify him.

Steam rose in heavy, aromatic clouds from the tub. The water was hot—very hot. Beside the tub, she had laid out the items she would need—bandages, Vaseline, and a ball of gray, fluffy steel wool.

Bobby lay on a towel on the floor beside the tub, gazing up

at her in curiosity. She returned the gaze as lovingly as she could, but the dragon, that damnable tattooed monstrosity on his arm, seemed to writhe and twist, mocking her.

"It's okay, baby," she explained softly, picking the child up and holding him above the water in the tub. "Mommy's going to fix everything. Don't you worry. Daddy will never see it."

Bobby went into the water with a hiss of steam and a scream. She ignored him, grabbing the steel wool in one hand and holding him tightly with the other.

"Don't fight me, honey," she chided, eyes glazed. Bobby's eyes were rolling back in his head, his breath stolen by the blistering heat and the shock of the pain on his tiny arm as she rubbed frantically. It took only a few short moments, though they stretched in her mind to an eternity of red, bloody water that swirled and steamed, and racking sobs of pain that shook her son mercilessly.

Then it was over. The arm was a mass of red, bleeding and raw, but there was no sign of the dragon. She was safe— everything would be fine. Tears of happiness welled in her eyes, and she lifted Bobby carefully from the water, pulling him close, mindless of the blood.

Just as his breath returned, bringing with it the outraged screams of pain that would go on and on, he opened his eyes. It was only for a second—one long, accusing second— but it was enough. Her heart almost stopped. Then she remembered the eyes. The sea-green eyes. Not her eyes, not like John's, either. His eyes.

Someone would notice. Someone would mention it to John, maybe a friend at work, when she wasn't even around. He would wonder—how could he not? Tests would follow. Blood tests didn't lie. She had to finish. She had to make sure.

The house was dark and silent when John returned three days later. There was no light on the porch, but the front door was unlocked.

"Susan?" he called out, setting his things by the door and

looking around the room, trying to adjust his sight to the darkness. "Susan, are you here?"

There was no answer, but he could hear a sound coming from down the hall, from Bobby's room. It was a steady creaking noise. He headed down the hall, flicking on the lights as he went. Somehow the sudden brilliant illumination did nothing to comfort him. An icy claw was gripping at his heart, unreasoning fear hurrying his steps.

"Susan?" he repeated as he entered the baby's room. She was sitting in the rocker, her back to him, rocking slowly up and back. The curtains were open, and she seemed to be staring out into the darkness beyond.

As though only just becoming aware of his presence, she rose, still not speaking. Bobby was cradled in her arms, wrapped tightly in a soft blue blanket that covered him so completely that he wondered if the child wouldn't be too warm, and as she slowly turned, he could see that her face, though a trifle gaunt, was alight with a beaming smile. He loved the way her eyes glittered when she was happy, beautiful, deep brown eyes, just like Bobby's. Maybe she was feeling better, after all.

Returning her smile, he walked closer, and she turned slightly, letting the blanket that covered his son's face slip aside. Bobby's head lolled to the side, and he could see that the baby's breathing was rough and very weak. A tiny arm slid out from beneath the blanket, covered in crusty bandages. He felt the scream building, rising from so deep inside that he was afraid he'd be trapped within it, that it would never break free.

Susan was not paying any attention. Turned fully toward him now, she smiled at him vacantly, perhaps staring right through him. It was impossible to tell through the blood-stained bandages he could now see covering the upper half of her face.

"Don't you see?" she asked impatiently. "Everything's going to be all right now, honey." Her voice sounded unnaturally tight—strained.

"My eyes wouldn't see, but I've fixed them. They won't be

able to lie to me, not anymore. I'll be much better now, better to Bobby and better to you."

He saw her quiver, as if she were crying, but there was no way to tell.

"I know he's our son, now, our brown-eyed baby boy, yours and mine, honey. Welcome home."

DEEP DOWN THERE

Clark Perry

I

LATE IN THE AFTERNOON THEY FIND DAVID KEMPLER IN THE cemetery, up on the hill where his wife is buried. In one hand he holds a near-empty bottle of whiskey, in the other a shovel. He stands as silent and motionless as the cold stones around him, a slumped silhouette against the deep orange sky. Two policemen have parked their patrol car at the cemetery gate, and they stand leaning against the hood, waiting for me. By the time I arrive, Harlin Adderly, a burly fireplug of a man, has popped open his holster snap, and his fingers twitch absently against the butt of his gun. "Brother Harlin," I say warmly.

"Brother Bud." A thick wad of tobacco bulges his lower lip out as if he's been punched. "Caretaker called us nearly an hour ago. Tried talking to him. Looks at me, but he don't hear me. Knowed you was sorta taking care of him as best you could, Brother Bud, so I called you up."

I nod grimly and clap him on the back. "Appreciate that, Brother Harlin. He's been through a lot."

The other officer—Simms, I read from his badge, someone I don't know—says, "I don't care what the Sam Hill he's been through. If anybody was to come here today, we'd have to turn 'em away. Him up there with that gun and all."

217

He means the hunting rifle on the rear window rack in David's truck. "You don't have to worry about that," I say. "He's not the type to use it."

Simms turns on me, his long face chapped red by the brisk winter wind. "Like I can guess that from just lookin'."

Adderly watches David closely, the way he probably watches suspects just before he moves on them. "Now we'll go up there and get him down for you, you want us to."

"No," I say firmly. "I know you mean well, Brother Harlin, but please let me do it. He listens to me. But he's probably too drunk to drive. Can we leave his truck up there?"

They look at each other, and Adderly shakes his head. Simms says, "Can't have no vehicles in there after the gates is locked up. They'll get towed away."

"Well, I'll just leave my car. It's outside the gates."

They look at each other again, then they look at my car, in the slow, seemingly mindless manner cops look at things like cars. And each other. They practically shrug at the same time. With a final nod, I start up the narrow paved road.

"If you need us . . ." Simms calls after me. I keep walking, pretend not to hear him over the harsh wind that rises with the approaching night.

David's eyes are closed when I reach him, and for a moment I think about horses and how they can sleep upright with their legs locked. Then he hears my footsteps and looks at me with bleary, sunken eyes. He regards me quietly for a moment, then holds out the bottle. "Care for a shot?" he asks in a surprisingly unslurred voice.

I take the bottle from him. "Not here," I say sharply. "You shouldn't be up here, David. Remember? You promised me."

He sneers. "I didn't promise you I'd never come up here."

"You promised me you'd never come up here *alone*. Like this. Look at you. Think how you look to those two cops down there."

David glances down the road at them and sighs. "How long they been there?"

Blackouts again. "About an hour. They tried talking to

you, David. Did you even hear them? They called me at school."

David chuckles. "Oh. Like, I hope you wasn't praying with the quarterback or nothing."

"Actually, I was ministering to the prom queen, who's pregnant with his kid."

David looks at me, and for a moment his glassy eyes clear up, and, as we have done so many times since his wife's death, we make contact. We laugh. It comes deep out of our chests, the sudden hilarity of the situation we're in. Not the situation itself, which of course is bad, but the appearance of it, how it must look to the cops below. I worry that laughing might further frighten the already edgy policemen, and somehow the thought of *that* makes me laugh even harder. David crouches and sits heavily on the wet grass, the shovel falling away from him. I kneel beside him and, after a moment, catch my breath.

"David, let's get out of here. Go hole up at my house. You don't need to be here. Not now. Not like this."

He keeps shuddering with laughter, only I can't hear him laughing. I lean in closer and realize that he is crying, the kind of silent, open-mouthed, shoulder-racking sobs that only the deepest grief can cause. His pale, pained features compress into a sad grimace I've seen many, many times in the bleak months since his wife died. David hugs himself as if to squeeze away all the pain, but it doesn't work. It never works. So I reach out and hug him, too, and we sit there like that for a long time.

He stops sobbing, out of pure exhaustion more than anything else, and after a while clutches my shoulder. "M'okay, m'okay," he mumbles through the snotty mucus that covers his face from nose to chin. "M'okay."

"I know," I say soothingly. "I know you are. Let's get out of here. Lord willing, I oughta have a sixer or two in the fridge."

He nods, and together we rise. He rubs his eyes clear and drags a plaid shirt sleeve across his face. I pick up the shovel and slide it into the bed of the truck, and then I wedge the whiskey inside David's heavy tool box.

I look up. David stands there on his wife's grave, hands on her marker, rough fingers tracing the name chiseled into the smooth marble. I chose the marker for him, two days before the funeral.

I stand a few feet behind him and wait for him to tell her good-bye, as he often does. That is probably one of the few truly therapeutic suggestions I have given him. "Go to her," I told him. "Go to her and talk to her, tell her that you miss her, you still love her. Stay with her awhile, then leave. Leave, David, and tell her good-bye."

David looks at me, and I realize I have spoken that out loud. His eyes search mine, and he shakes his head slowly. "No," he says flatly. "No. I can't. Can't do that."

I tense. "Why not?"

"Because," he says, pulling the keys from his pocket and tossing them to me. I follow him back to the truck, and when we get in I start the engine. As we ease down the narrow road, just before we pass the cops, he stares intently at the small marker for Jerry Devlin, just inside the gate. "I can't say good-bye, Buddy, because she's not there."

David and I never talked about what happened to us in high school. Not while his wife was alive.

Poor, sweet Patricia was not the problem. If anything, she had steadied and strengthened David against his own fears and nightmares. They'd met a decade ago, just after high school, and married immediately. I returned from Bible college to find them living a picture-book dream of upper-lower-class domesticity and family values.

David went to work for the utility department and later became an electrician. She cut hair and spread gossip at a strip mall beauty parlor. They got drunk on Friday nights and repented at church on Sunday mornings. They planned to have children.

Though we attended the same church, David and I grew distant during these years. I do not blame Patricia; though she regarded me with some disdain, I recognized that she now filled the role I once held in David's life, that of a stabilizing presence. And this was fine, even if it meant watching a longtime friend become merely an acquaintance.

But when Patricia died beneath a truck hauling bottled water, I reached out to help my childhood friend. David was falling again, and I had to catch him.

II

High school was uneventful until we met Jerry Devlin, and that's when everything changed.

Jerry was a bookworm, acne-scarred and reed-thin, with a voice not many people liked—not even teachers, who were sympathetic because Jerry was poor and lonely and made good grades.

Not many people liked him. To me, Jerry was an angel.

David and I met Jerry the year he moved to Sheffield. Sophomore year, the freshman frights having calmed now. Not yet seniors, almost juniors, a social position that offered safety in its blandness.

I played second-chair saxophone in the marching band. David played the cornet and played it badly, and thus occupied a chair position far lower than mine. Jerry played the drums with a devout concentration our school hadn't seen before. During football season, he wore the tri-toms and beat powerful, precise rhythms with a vengeance. During concert season, he was hunched behind the copper timpani like a wizard casting careful spells over a boiling cauldron.

Jerry's smiles were shy and downcast, even when he trusted you. His father was dead, and his mother spent their welfare checks on liquor. The stigma of being on the free lunch program, coupled with his threadbare and often pitiful appearance, led him to devise his only defense: he expected rejection and met laughter with laughter until the situation proved otherwise. In my dreams, I can still see his soft brown eyes come alive with the promise of friendship that I offered.

We became fast friends, Jerry and I. David came along for the ride.

Jerry read so much that we let him do book reports for us. The only problem was that Jerry loved horror. We prodded him to vary his tastes so our reports wouldn't all sound the same; this was no problem. He had time to read everything. One day he'd be seen purchasing a shiny new paperback, the next he'd be swapping it, dog-eared with a rolled spine, at a used-books store. The newer the novel, the faster he read it.

The classics, however, he savored slowly with a self-control I admired. These ancient and musty books from the local library were penned by strange unknown authors whose names begged to be spoken: Lovecraft, Machen, Blackwood, Dunsany, Tarchetti. They fell from Jerry's tongue like exotic incantations.

He loved this stuff and was amazed to find such a selection in our north Alabama public library. David and I never read these; their narrative seemed too stiff for our young, impatient souls, though our interest could be piqued when Jerry told us the basics of the plot or described the monsters. I liked the new horror, with its hallucinatory, almost surreal violence; when this began to appear fully formed and visualized in the movies, I abandoned books altogether. David, even harder to please, eventually moved on to true crime books, but only the ones with photographs.

Once, while wasting an afternoon in David's father's car, Jerry announced: "I found out where all these old books came from."

"Me, too," David said, slouching at the wheel. "People wrote 'em."

"No, look here." I turned, and from the backseat Jerry held up a hardcover book, its threadbare cover slightly warped. He'd opened it to the front flap, where a brass bookplate had been affixed. Through the tarnish I could make out, in curly script: "From the private library of GEROME ANTHONY HOLCOMBE." Jerry sucked the inside of his cheek. "Now where have you heard that name before?"

I recalled the public library downtown, an imposing old house whose ground floors were lined with metal shelves. In the foyer hung a great oil portrait of a thin-faced, balding man standing purposefully on the banks of a river, one foot propped on the bow of a rowboat resting in the shallows. "The Holcombe House?"

"Bravo," Jerry said. "The public library!"

"You mean, it used to be his house?"

"Says so in the phone book," Jerry said. "That little history of the town in the front part?"

David cackled and gleefully beat a few blasts on the horn. "Jesus, you read *everything!*"

"So who was he?" I asked.

"Really rich guy," Jerry said. "Inherited tons of money from his dad, who owned a steel mill in Birmingham. Basically he spent his whole life spending it. Traveled a lot, bought a lot of books. No family, so when he died sometime in the nineteen-sixties, he left everything to the city. Made them promise to turn his house into a library and keep all his books."

Jerry, of course, taught us much, much more about the man.

III

Midnight finds us slumped on a couch in my study. David drains his seventh beer and disappears to the kitchen for the eighth. I let him fetch me more orange juice. His drinking I don't approve of, but at least he's talking. At least I know what's going on in there.

Guilt is the link here, I try to explain to him. Simple guilt. He had not been there to save his wife, and he had not been there to save our friend Jerry Devlin in high school. Plain and simple, I argue.

"But I *was* there with Jerry," David says. The more he drinks, the more lucid he seems. "So were you. Can you ever forget that?"

"No," I say, though I've tried. I have tried.

"I thought I could," he says. "And for a while, I think I did. What happened down there, Bud?"

Carefully: "We don't know."

"Are we sure?"

Stronger, slower: "No. One. Knows."

Then David starts in. Starts the story again, as he's done so many times. And it assumes shape and substance in my mind, blossoming like a dark flower. Against my wishes, I go with him down into the dark earth and stone, crawling through narrow cracks and crevasses. Mud-slick and ice-cold. There in the safety of my own comfortable study, my whole frame aches and throbs, and I tremble so badly I have to hold my mug with two hands.

My telltale symptoms go unnoticed by David as he relives our nightmare.

Small Southern towns don't breed the various psychoses found in large metropolitan areas. Here the weaknesses of the mind manifest shadows far different from the city. Things are different here, closer to the bone, more personal. One is *known* in these places; there is no anonymity. If only by the proximity of others, you are more attuned to sickness, pain, and the everyday edge of sanity that all of us walk, some of us acknowledge, and few of us, sometimes, have the grave misfortune to slip from.

This was a hard, strange truth I encountered while pursuing my studies at North Alabama Bible College. Psychology was to be my career, but after a disturbing internship at a mental health clinic, where I observed doctors dealing paltry cures to the amazingly complex problems to which people fell prey, either psychology abandoned me or I abandoned it. I came home with a degree I had earned but could not fully use, and the hard certainty that the mechanics of the mind can never fully be explained.

An incident from my childhood is a testament to this.

At the age of four, I was trapped for more than an hour in a discarded refrigerator outside the rusted, sagging trailer where my Uncle Bob lived. When my mother, terrified and angered by my prolonged absence, by chance pulled open the door of that airtight coffin, I fell out, gasping in the dirt, clawing myself away from that evil, hot darkness with tiny fingers bruised and bloodied from beating the inside of the door.

I barely remember crawling inside. Uncle Bob and I were playing a game, and I did not want him to tag me, because I would have to do whatever he wanted, so while he counted I ran for the refrigerator. I recall the door closing, one upraised hand silhouetted against the disappearing daylight. Everything after that is lost to me, and my mind did not record anything until the door opened, the daylight returned, and I tumbled forward to land at my mother's feet. She was yelling at my uncle, saying that he shouldn't ever touch me again, but I know I was trapped inside the refrigerator with no one to help me. How could my uncle have been touching me in there?

But of my time spent inside that dark, mildewy space, I remember nothing. It exists as a blank shard in my head—a space with some substance, though its particulars have been forever lost to me. I was not allowed to see my uncle again, and he died soon after. My mother never spoke of the incident, although she apologized repeatedly from her deathbed, her mind gripped in a delirium that made her repeat, "I'm sorry he did that to you," over and over.

I have blocked the memory, pure and simple, the actions of an infantile mind seeking to protect itself.

This is how I explained David's blackout to him, the blank period of time in which Jerry Devlin was pulled down that narrow, jagged passage to his death. And after the grief and the shock had passed, David came to accept my explanation. Within weeks of the accident, he was back in school, and though he had counseling for some time after that, I was confident that he had recovered from the trauma and could continue his life.

Then, years later, his wife was killed. But even that in itself wasn't quite enough to set David off. Not until he stood graveside at the service and watched his wife's coffin being lowered into the ground did David snap. Just as the reverend blessed her soul on its journey, David's face went white. He fell to his knees and reached for her. When she passed from his view, he fainted.

After the funeral, when we were alone, David told me that Jerry had come for his wife, and soon after would come for us.

Later David is sick, so I steer him to the bathroom, pull off his sweaty clothes, and run a hot shower. Afterward I put him in the guest bedroom. His house is a mess, has been ever since Patricia died, in spite of the efforts of a few nearby relatives. At my insistence, he's moved in with me, an unlikely marriage of sorts. For better or worse. Sickness and health.

I rinse out the coffee pot, fill the machine with water and some stale Maxwell House. David will need coffee later this next morning. It's Monday, and so will I. I set the timer for six A.M.

The sink is filled with dirty dishes, and in the moonlight through the kitchen window I see a fuzzy green mold growing on them. Mostly plates and glasses for pizza and beer, David's meals of choice lately. Looking for dishwashing soap, I open the curtains of the window above the sink and gasp. Outside in the sharp moonlight, I see what David has done to my backyard.

Holes. At least a dozen of them. Thank God for the wooden fence. What would the neighbors think? That I owned a dog who has a lot to hide?

David digging holes in my backyard. How deep they go I do not care to discover. Judging from the piles of dirt beside each one, about six feet.

Deep enough.

When sleep comes for me, it is like a dark hole against the black of my eyelids. Blacker than that which surrounds it, the hole grows, angles up toward me, not to swallow me whole but supinely, as if to offer entrance.

When I do not go gently—which is rare—I am seized with a cold fright that brings me fully awake. Sweating into the pillow, I lay there helplessly, knowing I must try again or face the horrible morning sunlight soon to come through my window.

I turn down the thermostat, and the air, now chilled, helps quell my fear of going deep down there, beyond sleep, where things are cold and silent.

IV

Leaping from the jagged edge of the bluff, heart clutched cold, arms back-spinning in small tight circles, I screamed.

The brown river rushed up at me with alarming velocity, its surface rippling with undercurrents and eddies, hidden forces that had taken the lives of so many swimmers over the years. I punched through the water, ears and nose flooding. Tickling bubbles cascaded past my face, and all was black around me. I kicked and swam upward, praying that up was indeed up, and the darkness grew brighter, and I broke the surface with a gasp, then wiped my eyes and paddled for the nearby shore.

Soon my toes found purchase on mossy pebbles and rocks, and I sat on the beach between Jerry and David. Earlier, Jerry had lowered his backpack with a long piece of twine procured from shop class at school. David had been the first to jump, and had mustered the additional courage to curl into a cannonball just before impact. Then Jerry had fallen like a knife, arms at his sides, barely making a splash. Now they smoked cigarettes and grinned like daredevils. "That's a *long* way down." David chuckled.

Jerry grinned. "Holcombe came here in a boat—this is the setting of that portrait. I doubt he had the guts to do what we just did."

"So let's see what he saw," I said. "Where's this cave, now?"

"Right behind you, Bud."

Above us the bluff towered like a castle wall, its rough face covered with a thick blanket of kudzu. The cave was almost hidden behind a tall oak that had been consumed entirely by the leafy green cancer.

Beneath this canopy, the cave's vaulted ceiling stretched away like the roof of an open mouth. At the base of the tree—whose backside was mysteriously free of the clinging kudzu—Jerry pointed out the collapsed skeleton of a dog, its few remaining ribs jutting up from the soft earth like brittle white knives.

The cave corkscrewed back several yards and disappeared around a bend. Jerry withdrew a red pocket flashlight, one I remembered seeing in David's cluttered glove compartment. "That thing work okay?" David asked.

Jerry flicked it on. The beam seemed pale and weak, but maybe it was just the sunlight, filtered through the greenery. Jerry grinned. "What's the matter? Afraid of the dark?"

The world at our backs, we entered the cave.

Twenty meters in, the cave shrank suddenly, forcing us to our hands and knees. The air was cool on our clammy skin, and I felt the onset of a slight headache. The stone floor was smooth and slick, and before long I realized it was not rock but mud, dirt on its way to becoming rock, packed and hardened by the water and cool air that found passage here.

In the feeble slash of light thrown forward by the flashlight, the cave narrowed around us like a swallowing throat. We clambered forward in short peristaltic bursts of energy, surrounded by echoes of our labored breathing.

"It seems farther than it really is," Jerry said. "It gets narrower, too, just up ahead. We have to lie down and crawl."

The tunnel shrank and flattened into a thin, flat crevasse that stretched in all directions as far as the light would shine. We stepped up and slid forward, the ceiling only inches from our heads. Several times I fought back the urge to stand up, to press my body against the living rock through whose capillaries we moved. I concentrated on the soles of Jerry's sneakers just ahead of me and pulled myself toward them as they receded.

Soon we reached the chamber, a circular space roughly ten feet in diameter, worn into the stone by the spiraling waters of a long-dry underground stream. The walls were grayish with streaks of burnt orange, the roof smooth with concentric ledges forming the lower half of the chamber. Jerry propped the flashlight so it shone upward, and we sat shivering, smoking bent cigarettes in the yellow light.

"See the walls," Jerry said, but we had already noticed the graffiti, some of it etched by people we knew from school. Crude hearts drawn with crosses at their centers that supported the initials of young lovers. The cartoonish bust of a woman, broken curves across rippled rock. Profanities, accusations, promises, and assorted bravado, silly scrawl more suited to the margins of yearbooks.

And he pointed at a narrow, jagged hole we had not seen, as it was hidden by some trick of shadow. Directly across from the crevasse by which we had entered this chamber, there was another opening from whose lip issued forth a thin rivulet of water that slid down the ledges into the center of the floor, where it pooled and presumably continued on through some underground conduit.

Jerry slid to the hole, ran his hand beneath the water, and wiped his face. "There's more in there. I read about it in Holcombe's book." He patted the waterproof book bag sitting at his feet.

Holcombe's books accounted for nearly one fifth of all the books at the library. His reading interests were wide. Conversely, his writing interests were narrow, and here was where Jerry found his treasure.

Inspired by the more ghoulish elements of his preferred fictions, Holcombe had tried his hand at writing. The book, titled *The Subterranean Ones,* was short and simple, a fictional "true document" concerning the wealthy and eccentric narrator's discovery of a race of underground beings who live as the dim mirror images of those above the earth. Wispy and pale, more liquid than solid so as to afford greater movement through the earth, they feed on our dreams and fears and, when we get too close, our flesh.

The narrator sets forth this improbable scenario in a straight and utterly convincing tone. It is fiction disguised as nonfiction, and therein lay its hold on Jerry, who was always willing to believe the unbelievable. When he read passages aloud—and over a few weeks, he did read the entire text to us—his lips quivered like those of an awe-struck altar boy delivering a prayer.

In 1956, Holcombe published the book himself after unsuccessfully shopping it around to various publishers. There is no record of how many books were printed or sold, and only one copy was included in the man's donation to the library. No one had ever checked it out until Jerry, and the title vanished soon after.

At the back of the book, surely a cheap but effective ploy to heighten verisimilitude, was a crude map showing the location of the cave in which our humble narrator encountered this supernatural race. Jerry immediately recognized the high bluffs and shoreline of the Tennessee River, just below our high school.

V

Over coffee, I order David not to visit Patricia's grave unless I'm with him. He nods, bleary-eyed, and shuffles out to his truck, looking twenty years older than he is.

Sheffield High School, my alma mater, is white and smooth, like a clinic or museum. I slide through the students fumbling at lockers, chatting in groups, waiting for the first bell to ring; I feel like an imposter, no longer a student and yet not part of the institution. I function in my own capacity here, separate from teaching and administration. Inside my office, it's quiet and warm, so I open the window wide. I spend an hour reviewing for that week's appointments with juniors and seniors, during which I will outline the usual options of college, trade school, or, in most cases, immediate entry into the working class.

Between second and third periods, I wander to the boys' bathroom on the first floor, pausing throughtfully at the door to the band room where I spent so much time with Jerry. Behind the large wooden door, I can hear someone practicing lessons on the snare drum, a roll of sharp *rat-a-tats,* then a series of such attacks, but the rhythm isn't steady, and the drummer can't sustain what the music asks. Jerry could fire off more complex rolls with two pencils on a lunch table.

Sadly, I push on to the bathroom, where beneath the sharp industrial cleanser I catch the faint tinge of cigarette smoke. In the stall, I remember what is was like to smoke, the cool draw of a freshly lit Marlboro. I quit after Jerry died because the smell reminded me too much of him.

Back in my office, the phone is ringing. The principal asks me to see Howard Clemmons, a troubled sophomore with a rather thick disciplinary record. "This young fellow needs some honest counseling, Brother Bud," the principal suggests quietly. "You know what I mean."

Five minutes later, there's a knock at my door. I open it and usher Howard inside. He studies me gloomily from beneath thick red bangs, then sits heavily in the chair next to my desk, clutching a tattered spiral notebook. His cherubic face is pale and dotted with freckles except for the right cheek, which sports a wide purple bruise. "That's one nasty knock you took, Howard."

"I fell." He shrugs deeper into his black leather jacket and won't meet my eyes.

"Principal says you got in another fight. What about?"

"Nothing."

I open his file on my desk and make a show of sorting through all the papers. "Lot of fights over nothing, Howard."

"Look," he says, suddenly angry. "I just want out of here. In two months I'm sixteen and I'm *gone,* understand? Until then, I'm not taking shit off nobody."

"Watch your language, Howard."

"Watch yours, preacher boy. Look, why don't you just gimme the standard sermon and get it over with, okay?"

"Where are you living now? Principal says you've left home."

"Me and my parents don't get along. I'm staying with a cousin, so don't even think about calling some damn social worker or anything."

"What's this cousin like?"

"None of your business."

He clutches his notebook tighter. Beneath his dirty fingers I see a decal on its cover, a pink triangle. Suddenly, the air shifts and I can smell him—sour, stale, and sweaty—and it sickens me, so I rest my face in my hands and breathe through my mouth. "Did you ever hear the story of Sodom, Howard?"

He grins, eyes full of hatred. "Sounds X-rated, Preach."

"I'm not a preacher, but I'll tell you the story because I doubt you'll ever read it yourself."

"Oh, I know all about it. My dad was screaming that crap at me when he threw me out."

Howard's father, Brother Howard Senior, is a deacon in our church, and I have counseled him and his wife many times concerning their son. "Then you know what happened."

"I know Lot's wife got turned into a salt shaker all because she looked over her shoulder."

"Before that," I say. "Why were they driven out and told not to look back? Because the place was full of *sin*, Howard, that's why. Because two angels came into town, and Lot took them into his house. He wanted to protect them, you see, because they were such beautiful creatures and he knew what would happen to them."

Howard stares out the window, the bruise turned toward me, and it looks like a huge black teardrop spilling out of his angry eye.

"And sure enough, that night a group of men came to Lot's house. And they said they wanted to see the angels, and Lot said no. And they said they would tear the house down to get them because they wanted to *know* them. They wanted to *know* them, Howard, and that's a sin."

"What isn't, these days?"

"And the angels heard these filthy men, and they were angry and filled with the wrath of the Lord, and they came out of the ground and struck them again and again until their words and desires were no more."

Howard stares at me curiously, as if he hears something outside the room. "They did what?"

"They hit them. They hit them hard, Howard, a lot harder than the blow that caused your bruise there. Great is the Lord's vengeance over those—"

"No, wait a second. They came out of the *ground?* Thought they were in the house."

I draw in a breath, and suddenly I can taste Howard in my mouth, wet and earthy like something spoiled. Coughing harshly, I slide my chair to the open window to take in a fresh gulp of air. "You can't go on like you're doing, Howard. It's the cause of all your problems."

"These aren't my problems. They're everyone else's. I'm the way I am, and that's it. I can't do anything about that, and I'm sure as hell not going to be made to feel bad about that, not by you or my dad or anyone else."

Outside, students in gym class are heading for the football stadium. The crisp spring air calms me, and I chuckle deeply. "I'm praying for you, Howard. I truly am."

When he whips out his chair and storms out of the office, I am rooted to the spot, helplessly watching the kids running track, the cars on the street beyond, the sunshine fluttering through the trees. Although Howard's footsteps echo down the hall, I am afraid to look back.

When I get home from work, David is slumped over the steering wheel of his truck, his shirt covered with blood.

"Oh, Jesus." I'm whipping the door open, examining him, frantic to find the wound.

His eyes flutter open. "Hurt myself," he says slowly. "At the house."

The house. Where he works, a construction site across town, once acres of empty pasture, now cleared for a new housing subdivision. David is working on some electrical wiring there. The smell of dried vomit fills the cab. I unbutton his wet shirt and peer carefully at his blood-slicked chest but can't see anything. "Where are you hurt?"

He holds up his right hand. There is a deep gash along the underside of his forearm. He grins. "Flesh wound."

Half angry, half relieved, I manage to get him out of the truck and into my kitchen, where I pull off his shirt and throw it in the trash. He starts to protest but is drunk and can barely sit up straight. I lightly sponge off the gash, clean it with hydrogen peroxide, and smear it with disinfectant cream. Then I wrap it in thick gauze and tape it snugly. "Wanna be the first to sign my cast?" he asks, holding up his wounded arm.

"What happened? How'd you do this?"

"I fell," he says. "Up on some second-floor scaffolding. I lost my balance and fell. Caught a nail on the way down."

"Listen, let me fix you some coffee. You need to see a doctor."

"Hell, you'll do." He snickers, rubbing the bandage. "You done a right fine job with me here, Doc."

"No," I say softly. "No, I haven't."

"I got fired, too," he says. The boss had smelled his breath and fired David on the spot. He'd been climbing up to retrieve some of his gear when he fell. "That's why no doctor," he explains. "I was fired. I ain't covered by their insurance no more." He chuckles, shifting restlessly in the kitchen chair. "If I just coulda fallen earlier in the day . . ."

Fifteen minutes later, I return from the convenience store with a case of beer. I shove it into the empty fridge and tear off a lukewarm can. David is in my study, looking at my yearbook. I open his beer and place it in front of him. He seems not to notice.

He is looking at Jerry Devlin's class photo.

"We left him down there," David says quietly. "He's come back."

"No," I say. "No, we didn't. And no, he hasn't."

David smiles weakly and reaches for the beer. "Right," he says in a patronizing tone. Then he holds up the other book, *The Subterranean Ones*. "You don't know how many times

I've been to the library, trying to find this," he says with a sad, scared grin. "Shoulda known you'd have it."

Trembling, I kneel beside him and take the slim volume. "David, I haven't seen this in years, ever since Jerry—where did you get it?"

"Tucked back behind the yearbooks. Why're you hiding it all this time?"

I flip through the yellowed pages, then stop at the end and stare at that horrid map again. I blink and cock my head to one side, and the ragged shoreline suddenly becomes the vague shape of a boy's profile, mouth open in a scream. I slam it shut and drop it into his lap. "I don't remember anything about this, David. I thought we left this thing down there."

He turns back to the yearbook, to Jerry. "It's all coming back," he says.

VI

The darkness stole my voice. My heart hammered so loudly I felt that if I opened my mouth they'd hear it.

In the receding light, I watched Jerry and David crawl into the smaller hole. They beckoned me to follow. The hole smelled of earth, of decay. I pulled myself after them, anxious to catch up with the fading light Jerry held before him.

This passage was different. Jagged rocks protruded from all angles. Our bodies did not fit here. Our bodies did not want to be doing this. We had to bend and stretch because this place was not meant for us.

A few yards in, Jerry stopped us.

"Check this out," he said. "Nobody move. Nobody make any noise."

And he turned off the light.

Around me, the stones waited, grew colder. And then, they breathed, soft and pliant against my body, rolling me gently as they blew out the cool breath of stone. And then, to my horror, they inhaled, pulling at me like a slight and subtle current an unsuspecting swimmer will ignore, a horribly patient force that will, without warning, yank and snatch whatever lies within its evil range.

And my voice was freed, and I screamed, and then I was gone.

They dragged me the few remaining yards into the next chamber. Jerry kept shining the light in my eyes. Someone had lit a cigarette, and that familiar smell helped me come around. "He's waking up," said Jerry.

The light left my eyes. Jerry propped the flashlight so it shone upward, and I saw where I was. A smaller, tighter chamber than the first. Where the other was rounded out of the rock, this one seemed *bitten* somehow, a huge chunk simply torn away, and we had filed in to fill its absence. I could barely see another, even smaller opening that extended deeper into the earth. There was not much room. I felt Jerry and David against me.

Jerry watched me carefully. David was smoking and staring at our surroundings. "You okay, Bud?"

"Yeah. What . . . happened?"

"You just screamed," Jerry said, tugging David's cigarette from his fingers. "We thought you were kidding, but then you didn't move. You were breathing funny. We pulled you in here to splash some water on your face. You better?"

"No," I answered. "I don't think I should be in here."

"Okay," said Jerry kindly. "Let's just check out the walls a second, and then we'll leave."

"We're not going any further," I said shakily.

"No, we won't. We'll look at the walls and go."

The walls. Covered with spidery scrawls that glowed faintly in the dimness of the flashlight. At first I thought of some rare mineral, its veins coursing around us. Then I discerned shapes and figures. Strange hieroglyphs. My eyes watered, and I could not focus on what was before me.

Jerry was pointing the shapes out to David. "Now this one Holcombe put in his book, that page before the map where he drew—damn, where is it?"

The book bag was missing.

"Guess I dropped it back in that first chamber when Bud passed out," David said. "Gimme the light, I'll go back after it."

"No, please. Please don't." I trembled.

David nudged my shoulder with a light fist. "It's cool, okay? You keep the flashlight here, I've got my lighter. Okay?"

I thought I would feel better if I nodded, stayed agreeable. David flicked a flame on his lighter, and I listened to him clamber back the way we had come.

Jerry slid closer beside me. "Hey, it's okay. You don't have to be scared."

I shook my head to show him I wasn't scared, but I started crying. He gave me the flashlight, and I clutched it like a talisman. He made shushing noises and gently slid an arm around me.

And then there was no light.

The darkness was so sudden that I thought I had passed out, but by blinking I could see the ghostly after-image of Jerry, his face near mine, flickering closer and closer. Through him I could see things moving and my speech was again stolen, my lungs squeezed empty. I was a child again, the refrigerator tight around me, like arms that would not let go, and the air wet and hot, taking me in, clamping down hard on what it could get. And before I passed out, one clear thought surfaced from the terror that gripped me: if I do not beat this back, I will die this time. I know I will die.

From the darkness, things moved toward me, and I struck them, each blow filling my eyes with light. Then I screamed. I remember that much.

VII

While David showers, I order pizza and sit on my back porch steps, staring in amazement at the holes he dug. When did he do this? My mind ponders possibilities. When I was at work, perhaps. Or maybe out searching the nightclubs, trying to find him. The timing here is no great mystery. There are explanations. I curtain off the rear windows of the house so David will not see the holes; I want to see how long he will avoid the subject.

Wrapped in an old blue terry-cloth robe, David goes to his truck, retrieves a box of cigars, and joins me in the study. Stole them from his ex-boss, he proudly tells me as he yanks off the cellophane, flips up the lid, and tosses one into my lap. "Have a Tampa, son."

Smoke circles the ceiling of my study like storm clouds. We say little. The pizza arrives, but we're not hungry. A tension exists between us, and I break it with an obvious question. "You were going to dig her up, weren't you? The other day."

"I was gonna make sure she was still there."

"Where would she be?"

"Down there, with him. With all of them."

I slide over to where he sits, cross-legged and strangely peaceful, gazing contentedly into the night beyond the window. "Jerry's down there. We know that much. But he's not coming back for us. Please stop thinking that."

"Me?" He turns to look into my eyes. "Oh, that's a joke, right?"

"What do you mean?"

He snorts, a sick little chuckle. "God damn, Bud. I mean, *God damn.* You're blacking out on me or something."

I back away from him. There is something in his eyes I've never seen before. Sadness has shone its ugly light there many times; so have anger and desperation. I have seen all those in David's droopy, burned-black eyes and reached out in the only way I know how, to help a friend. To make sure that he isn't alone.

"You," David says carefully. "You're the one who told me that, Bud. The day of the funeral, after you fainted."

Stunned, I shake my head. "You need to stop this right now. For your own good."

"Right there in front of everybody. We hadn't talked about Jerry in years. As soon as they lowered her coffin into the hole, you fainted. You don't remember."

"David, think about what you're saying. Please."

"When you came to, you waited till we were alone, and then you warned me not to crack, not to tell anyone about Jerry or those—those *things*—or he'd come back. He'd come back and get her."

"That was you," I protest calmly. "That was you."

David considers this for a long moment, takes a deep drink. Then, "Are you sure?"

I clasp my hands to keep them from shaking, and think of the prayers I have sent aloft through them. For many nights I have prayed that David not be alone in his pain and suffering. These prayers have been answered, and my hands will not stop shaking.

Later we are outside, and the watchful pale eye of the moon is hidden by thick black clouds. David holds the bottle to his lips as if to sip, then lets it thump against his chest and clutches it like a prized toy. "Okay. We gotta stop this. Now."

"I want to," I say gently. "I want you to, David. There's nothing stopping you."

"There's *her!*" he shouts, mouth webbed with spittle. "What have they done with her?"

"Nothing."

"I need to see her! To be sure."

"If you do that, you'll be arrested. They'll ask you questions, and they won't let up until they've pried the truth out of you."

"Then we need to tell them about it!"

"We can't do that. They won't believe us."

"I don't care!"

"But I do, David—"

"Wait, we've got the book! See? We'll show them the book. We couldn't do that until now because you'd lost it."

"No. They just won't understand. I know you need to see her, David. I know it's the only way."

He lowers his head as if to sleep. I raise his face to mine and take the bottle as it falls from his limp hands. His bleary eyes take me into focus after a few moments, and he moans, brow drawn up like a fist, and I can see his pain. "Here, here," I say. "It's fine, David. Just fine. We'll get her. Now take this."

And with the bottle I nurse him. Like an infant.

Rain patters around us, and soon the dry hole becomes slick with mud.

VIII

I found David there, deep in the dark, whimpering and lost, searching for the lighter he'd dropped when he heard my scream. I was covered with mud, but he thought it was blood. I told him that they came for Jerry, they came and took him. And if we didn't leave, they would take us as well.

Tears streamed down David's face. He clutched the book bag and made no sound, shivering close to me. I held him, cooing softly, and soon he relaxed, safe in my hands.

It was nightfall when we emerged. Clouds obscured the moon and stars, and the blackness hung so heavy that David believed us still to be inside the stone. I eased him by taking him to the river's edge and lowering him into the water. I washed him clean, then myself, and we climbed the winding trail to the bluff, alone in the darkness except for each other, with not even the stars to guide us.

They never found Jerry Devlin because he was not there.

The rescue crews and volunteers all donned yellow helmets and took flashlights and flares and ropes and first-aid kits and disappeared around the bend of the cave and into the crevasse. Some of them even found the chamber. They shone their lights down the smaller tunnel that produced the tiny rivulet.

They searched for three days, in teams, but Jerry Devlin did not arise from the dead. His spirit was now freed to swim through stone. His empty body lay there, curled in a distant pocket of rock they could not see, mud stuffed in his mouth, ears, and nostrils. Smeared across his eyes. A corpse embedded in its own tombstone.

* * *

Late in the afternoon, they find me in the cemetery, up on the hill where David's wife is buried. As they approach, I drop the shovel, the bottle. I have no gun, but they search me anyway. Adderly stands nearby, watching with hooded eyes.

The handcuffs bite into my wrists as I struggle, and someone locks his arms through mine, pulls me away. I cease and go limp so they will not throw me in the back of the patrol car.

They take turns with the shovel, cutting through the loose dirt with grimaces and grunts, rubbing gingerly at blood blisters after they pass the tool to the next in line. Adderly asks me questions, but I am very tired and can only answer with the voice of stone.

They hit bottom, the coffin lid, and work its edges free to pry it open. They stare with slack faces, and soon their eyes turn toward me.

Adderly slides his face in front of mine, threatens me. *Where is he? Where is she? What have you done with them?* I stare at him, through him, to the hole beyond. He slaps me once, twice, maybe more, and then the others pull him away, pressing close to protect me.

Down there, I am saying in the voice of stone. *Down there.* The words erupt from my heart like gusts of wind, are sharpened as they pass through my constricted throat, then hammer against the inside of my skull. And Adderly finally understands. I see his eyes go wide with fright and anger, and he lets loose a shout. They whirl on him, afraid he is coming after me, but he runs to the hole and points and shouts some more.

With great effort, they uncover the whole of the coffin and manage to slide a length of rope around and behind one end. They pull until the coffin tilts and stands upright in the hole. When they see what they have uncovered, they drop to their knees.

There, clutched in sweet mud, lies David, forever silent, curled like a sleeping infant in the arms of his wife.

KNACKER MAN

Richard Parks

"HOW MUCH FER A COW?" THE FARM WIFE KEPT WIPING HER hands on the stained apron. The part of the Knacker Man that was still Jack Litton, educated in the finest public schools and exposed—if that was the right of it—to higher education at King's College, could only think of Lady Macbeth from the Scottish play. The Knacker Man knew no more of plays than he did of the signs on the pubs in Whitechapel, no more to do with him than the trees along Abbotsford Lane. The Knacker Man was all business.

"Dead how long, Mum?"

"Two days and a bit. See for yourself."

He followed her out to the paddock behind the house, eyes idly following the slow roll of her hips as she walked, still drying her reddened hands. She paused only long enough to open the gate and let him in.

The cow was down on its left side maybe ten feet from the water trough, its right fore and hind legs already swept out to the three o'clock position from the bloat. More than a bit past two days, he figured, but no less than he expected. It had been a fat one even before the bloat, big-boned and heavy.

"I can give a shilling for her, Mum. Two, if one of your lads gives me a hand."

"Done for two, then."

He heard her calling out toward the fields while he went back to the road to fetch his wagon. He guided his mare with a sure touch as it backed the wain through the open gate. He freed the lever pole from its lashings and swung the counterweight free. It was a rather clever arrangement, and he was proud of it, the lever pole mounted near the front of the wagon acting as a small derrick. He probably could have managed the carcass himself, but the help was worth a shilling. The farm wife's son arrived then, and the Knacker Man gave him a professional glance up and down. He was big-boned and heavy, too, with a glisten of sweat from the haying.

The Knacker Man pulled a loop at the end of the rope attached to the long end of the lever and forced the dead cow's four legs close enough to gather with the rope. "Lend us a hand, then." With him on one end of the lever and the boy guiding the carcass, they lifted it onto the wagon bed between a carrion goat and a late foal that did not live. It nestled securely between them, four legs pointed generally to heaven. He thought of using the tarp, decided there wasn't much point. He thanked the boy warmly and counted out the coins into the woman's palm.

"Next round in a fortnight. Good day to you."

He tipped his hat and climbed into the wagon bench. One shake of the reins, and the stolid mare started off, hesitating only a moment as it adjusted to the change in weight. The Knacker Man turned off onto the wagon road, waved once to the boy closing the gate, and continued on his rounds. Late summer was no time to be dawdling in his line of work.

Hedgerow-bound fields spread out on either side of him, broken by copses of old trees lining the road here and there, guardians of freshwater springs or simply spared the axe to make a place for the stones pulled from the fields, or for reasons no one remembered. The Knacker Man appreciated the shade of them over the cart road, looking out as he did into the fields as the farmers gathered the hay into their wagons while the sun pressed down. Once two small boys broke away from the haying to toss clods of dirt at the wagon, but their aim was bad, and their father, angry as much for the lost work as at the discourtesy, called them back. The Knacker Man smiled and kept on going, humming the tune of a very old song over and over till the words spilled out:

> *Bossie's gone, Dobbin, too.*
> *Knacker Man takes them for his brew.*
> *Sack of bone meal, pot of glue.*
> *Knacker Man brings them home to you.*

More child's rhyme than song, but he rather liked it. The same way he liked his work. Simple, not glamorous—certainly never that!—but useful. As the song passed the time, he passed his own time in review. Thirty years, come winter. Useful. New use for old carrion, that was the Knacker Man. All things die, but not all things need be buried. He didn't even mind the smell; it was familiar, almost soothing in a way that didn't need questioning. The flies were another matter, but they kept mostly to the goat.

"Mr. Knacker Man!"

A child's voice called to him from the side of the road by one of the smaller crofts along his route. He looked down at a little girl with blond hair and large green eyes. Her smock was patched more times than even Lowland practicality required, but it was clean. She held a box half as large as herself with the lid tightly closed.

"Well, now, Miss. What can I do for you?"

She had a grave expression on her face as she lifted the lid just enough for him to see.

"Oh, dear . . ."

The kitten had been black and white; it was hard to tell that now with its little body caked with dirt, the neck turned at an angle that was not possible for a living thing, which of course it was not.

"A horrid motor car." Her eyes watered just the slightest

bit as she pushed the words out. "Mum says they're not supposed to be on this road."

"Indeed not," the Knacker Man agreed, equally grave as the situation required. "Horrid newfangled knickknack. I'm sorry for your loss, Miss, but your kitten really should be buried."

The girl nodded. "Mum told me to. I had a funeral and everything. But I was thinking . . . well, I wondered . . ." She looked at him.

"If I would take her, Miss?"

She nodded, blushing fiercely. "We've not got much money. And the motor car wasn't supposed to be there, and Merry didn't know about them, and now I've lost her and it's just not *fair,*" she said, her child's sense of justice clearly outraged.

Life isn't fair.

Be still, Jack. She'll learn that lesson soon enough, and not from us. We've enough to answer for.

The Knacker Man looked down at the girl. "Of course I'll take her, Miss." He considered. "The market for kittens is not so much as it was, you understand, but I think I can go as high as three pence. Will that do?"

She nodded, still grave. "It's not just for me, Mr. Knacker Man. Mum could use a bit of help. I—I don't think Merry would mind."

The Knacker Man looked at the ramshackle cottage. "I'm sure of it," he said. He fumbled in his pocket, found the coins and counted them out to her, and carefully took the box. She started toward the cottage but hesitated.

"It won't hurt her, will it?"

He smiled and shook his head. "On my word, Miss."

The Knacker Man watched her go, then out of a very old habit glanced around to see if anyone had noticed them together. He put the box up on the wagon bench and continued down the road. When he was well out of sight of the house, he found a shaded spot on the side of the road and buried the kitten with the shovel he always carried among the tools of his trade.

Almost there. She's just two farms down.

Leave it to Jack to point that out. Jack had been restless, for the first time in years. The Knacker Man had almost forgotten Jack Litton, failed medical student, failed everything. Buried deep for thirty years with no place in the Knacker Man's ordered life, but now here he was like a bad tooth when you never wanted and least expected.

You don't understand.

That was truth. No matter. Jack stirred, but he could not command. They were on the short path now to the rendering plant, where the vats and the grinding stones waited to create new life of a sort from his carefully gathered wares.

Sack of bone meal, pot of glue . . . just a few more stops along the way, then another day done, no different from any other.

She'll be wanting us today, Knacker Man.

"Tell you that, did she?" Knacker Man put the words on the air, though there was no one to hear but the mare.

Same as a fortnight ago. And two before that.

He didn't have to ask who Jack boyo meant; the Maccam farmstead, empty since the last of them died three years before, now taken over by someone else. Lathams, from somewhere in the Midlands, the neighbors said. The name meant nothing to the Knacker Man, but *she* did. Standing alone in the doorway of the house. A still-handsome woman, for all her years. Hair might have been red once, but it was hard to tell now. She had watched the Knacker Man drive by that first time; he had seen the recognition in her eyes, but he did not know what it meant. So he had tipped his hat, and she had not called for him, and that had been that. But on all his rounds since, she had been at the door to watch him. That was the day Jack had come to stir again.

I know her.

"You're mistaken, Jack. Go back to sleep."

A grumbling submission followed, as it always did when it came to the nut of it. *I know her . . .*

"Shhh . . ."

Silence.

The Knacker Man looked down at his reins, ahead at the road, anything but the farmhouse coming steadily closer on his left. Maybe she wouldn't be there today, maybe if she was, she would not call—

"Knacker Man!"

He pulled on the reins on instinct and habit, no chance now to plod along, pretend not to hear. The mare was stopping, switching her tail a bit as a few stray flies lit on her rump. The woman had stepped free of the door and stood now halfway down the slate walkway, waiting for him.

Nothing for it . . . As he approached, the woman extended her hand, and he took it briefly and tipped his hat.

"I'm Maggie Latham," she said. "I don't think we've met yet."

He smiled. "Thank you for the courtesy, Mum, but I'm just the Knacker Man. Have you got something for me?"

"You'll have to decide that for yourself," she said, friendly enough but not smiling, no, not a bit. The Knacker Man shrugged, then climbed down from the wagon and followed her out to one of the lambing sheds behind the house. A hedgerow nestled close by the back lot; beyond and barely visible through the trees was the green and tan mottle of the hayfields. The shouts of the workers were faint in the distance.

"In here." She stood aside and let him enter the dim shed first.

The lamb lay on a pile of blood-soaked straw. Its throat was neatly cut, the blood now darkening but still very fresh. The Knacker Man put a hand on the little corpse. Still warm, even.

"Why did you call me, Mum?" he asked.

"For the lamb. That is what you do, is it not?" She had her hands clasped behind her back like a headmaster lecturing a dim child.

The Knacker Man looked back over his shoulder at her. "I'm a corbie, Mum. I clean up carrion. This lamb is fresh meat, slaughtered not yet an hour past."

"Yes," she said. "By me."

"Why, Mum?"

"To bring you here, Jack." There was a tremor in her voice, rising now. She took her hands from behind her back,

She held a large revolver in her right hand. It shook only a little bit. The barrel was pointed squarely at his back.

I told you.

"My name is not Jack, Mum. You've mistaken me."

She shook her head. "No, I haven't. Whatever you call yourself now, it is you. Jaunty Jack, Saucy Jack. Jack the Ripper."

"No one's heard or seen of that foul creature in nearly thirty years. Whoever he was, he's long dead."

"Not yet," she said. Her hands were very white on the pistol grip. "Don't you know me, Jack?"

The Knacker Man did not know her. He listened to the quiet voice of someone who did. *On the last day. The day I killed Marie Kelly.*

Jack shared a memory with him. The Knacker Man shuddered, feeling himself walk out a door, closing it behind him on a scene so horrible his mind could not contain it. He shut down the image Jack fed to him, waited till that part of it was past. Then he stepped away from the door, the smell of blood as fresh as that of the lamb. There she stood at the head of the stairway at the end of the corridor, far enough away to be out of reach, close enough to see, to *know.* The Knacker Man remembered Jack putting on his best magic smile, starting forward with the cozening greeting already formed, the chance to confuse, to delay just enough . . .

Too late.

She turned and was down the first stair, then silence. But Jack, smile faded, panic rising, following down, could not see her, could not hear her run. It was as if she had disappeared off the face of the earth, taking Jack's magic with her.

"Where did you hide?" The words came out, and the Knacker Man didn't know if it was himself or Jack speaking then.

She smiled grimly. "Under the stair. You walked no more than three paces from me. My heart almost stopped. But it didn't, Jack. And then you left."

"Why didn't you go to the police?"

That was Knacker Man asking the sensible question. Jack was still there; the Knacker Man could feel him hovering just out of consciousness, as if finding the memories had exhausted him.

"And die like Marie?" she asked. "All the girls around Whitechapel knew by then—the coppers didn't *want* to catch you. And then my name bandied about as the one poor girl who could put the finger on Saucy Jack? No. My mother's family had farms in the Midlands, and I stayed with them long enough to find a man who didn't know or care what I'd been. I got away, or thought I had till I saw you last month driving your carrion wagon for all the blind world to see."

Jack showed a little interest then; he'd always told the Knacker Man a different version, his likeness on every street corner, the hounds of the law snapping at his heels. But of course he'd assumed she'd gone to the police.

Poor Jack died for naught.

The Knacker Man dismissed that. *Poor Jack lived for naught.* Knacker Man understood the woman's fear; that silly rumor about the royal family's connection to Jack the Ripper was already on the streets, and many high and low believed it. Much amusement for Jack, sure enough. But the question the woman answered was not the one he'd asked. "I meant now. Today. Or last month, if you knew who I was."

"And have it all come out now how I'd run away? They'd arrest me, too. And if you hadn't recognized me yet, you would sooner or later. Don't talk nonsense."

"I'd ask the same of you, Mum. At most you'd get a lecture. Being where you were would be proof of nothing, and if your husband knows as little as you think, I'd be confounded. And if I'd recognized you last month, then I'd figure you'd known *me,* and would I keep to my rounds and give you all the time you needed to unmask the man you thought I was? If it's for your own revenge for your friend, then say so and have done. *Be* done. But you've killed Jack once already, and twice seems a tad greedy if you don't mind my saying."

"You're Jack. And you be damned, but you're alive!"

The Knacker Man shook his head slowly. "He's dead, Mum. For all that, his ghost stirs now and again in the place where he lived. Jaunty Jack died when you saw him square in the face and got away. No one understood that about him—Jack thought he was on a mission from God Almighty himself. He thought he was *magic!* But there was no magic in him. No divine mission. And for all his brave talk, he was just a poor fevered wretch about to be caught and hanged for the monster he was. That was the blow, Mum. Headsman's axe and hangman's noose all rolled into one."

"So?" she asked, her thumb on the hammer.

He shrugged. "So Jack ran away into the fields and forest like a gutshot hind, and he *died*. I'm all that's left of him, cleaning up after death, new use for old carrion. Kill me for revenge if you will, men have died for less, but know what you're doing. I'm the Knacker Man."

"Revenge?" The barrel of the gun drifted downward just the slightest bit. She looked as if she wanted to laugh. "I thought you knew," she said.

"Who you were? Jack knew, I think, but he's nothing real now. I don't give tuppence. You're in no danger from me."

She shook her head. "Marie," she said. "Marie Kelly. The last poor girl the Ripper took, they say. Only it wasn't Jack, it was me. I killed her." The Knacker Man just stared at her, but she went on. "Marie was pregnant. Did you know that?"

"Jack knew. I doubt it made any difference."

"It did to me. She was my friend, and she was pregnant with my beau's child." She smiled then. "Yes. A harlot can have a beau. A harlot can have someone promise to take her away from her awful life, and talk so sweetly that she does him for free. Only he was doing the same to Marie."

"You blamed Marie?"

"I blamed him, too, but Marie most of all. Shall I tell you how much I blamed her? Shall I tell you what was in my purse that day as I came up the stairs and found Jack already there? It was a scalpel. Just like the ones you . . . he . . . used. There was cold murder in my heart, and before I was done they wouldn't have known the difference."

"You didn't, Maggie," he said gently. "Jack did."

She did laugh, then. "No difference. I wanted Marie dead, and she was really, horribly dead. I killed her, and for thirty years now her poor face is the demon of my dreams."

For a moment, then, Jack was awake again, seeing through the Knacker Man's eyes into those of Maggie Latham. One mad ghost recognizing another. Then he was gone again, but not before one last whisper.

Why do you think she called you here? She died, too; somewhere deep down she knows it. Be kind to her, Knacker Man.

The Knacker Man thought of little girls and dead kittens, and he looked at Maggie Latham and did not see much difference. The revolver was still trained on him, but that didn't seem so important.

"What are you waiting for, Maggie?"

She blinked. "Waiting?"

"Why am I here, then?"

Maggie pulled back the hammer. There was a distinct click as it settled in position. "I thought I'd made that clear enough. I'll say that you tried to attack me. I'm a respectable woman now; they'll believe me."

"Certainly." The Knacker Man waited.

She blinked again. "Why aren't you afraid? Why don't you try to take the gun?"

"With you a good seven paces clear and the pistol lined on me all the time? If you want me, you have me; there's no question of it."

"I don't know much about guns," she said.

"You clearly know as much as needs knowing."

"I could say it's not loaded."

"That you could. But the open cylinders I see would call you a liar." He smiled a rueful smile. "It's such a little weight on your soul, Maggie. Barely a fig as such things go in the measure of the world. Is it really so hard to bear?"

"You haven't much time," she said, and her eyes told the Knacker Man that she did not hear him.

Are you dim, man? Jack managed a little interest. *She didn't bring you here to kill you. Quite the opposite.*

I know, Jack. But I'm not you. Be still.

Be kind to her . . .

I said be still, Jack. And Jack was still. When the Knacker Man finally stood and took the gun from Maggie's nerveless fingers, it was none of Jack. Just the Knacker Man, doing what was needful.

He left Maggie's clothes in the barn draped over a rafter near the dead lamb and the revolver, and from there to the open door the straw was raked enough to cover the sign. Now the Knacker Man drove his wagon with the tarp in place, his wares respectfully covered.

I am truly sorry, Knacker Man.

Reason enough to be sorry. There would be questions, and of course he was there about the lamb if anyone asked. Maybe they would believe him, maybe not. Nothing for it. Stolid as the mare who pulled his cart, the Knacker Man worried no more than he had to. New use for old carrion, and the bone meal didn't much care whose bone was used.

Sorry . . .

That was Jack, nattering on again. But there was no place for Jack now. Jack was of Whitechapel and the fogs of London. The Knacker Man was of the quiet countryside, doing his work, serving the need he found there. Cleaning up the dead. That was what he did, what he was, and all he need remember. *Shut up, Jack. Your past caught and then spared you. In heaven's sight, I don't know why, but there's no one to disturb you now.*

Tired . . .

Rest, then.

The Knacker Man listened to the new silence until it grew less a comfort and more a burden, then he sought for the rhyme again.

Sack of bone meal, pot of glue . . .

In a little time, in the quiet reigning over the long country road, the Knacker Man sang Jack's ghost back to sleep.

SO YOU WANNA BE A HITMAN

Gary Jonas

TRAFFIC PISSES ME OFF. I CAN'T UNDERSTAND HOW ALL THESE morons get their driver's licenses. Check this out. I'm driving along, and I see that traffic is all messed up a block ahead. I whip over to the righthand lane because I'm gonna hop on the expressway, right? Well, needless to say, there's a truck in the right lane who's trying to get over because the driver's an illiterate fuck who can't read the sign that says "Right Lane Must Turn Right."

So I have to stop and wait. Gets on my last nerve. But it almost turns out okay because I get to rubberneck at the accident that has traffic all screwed up. This Toyota Camry tried to run over a Buick Regal. The Regal won. So I'm watching them pull this bitch out of the Toyota. She's got on this stupid-looking pink outfit that just goes to show that people will wear damn near anything. I wonder if she'd have chosen that ratty old thing if she'd known she'd get killed in it.

I'm watching the paramedics try to revive the old bat when I hear the screech of tires, and my eyes lock onto my rearview mirror. This blue Audi almost hits me. Long-haired hippie at the wheel is flipping me off. I look ahead and wave back at him, 'cause I gotta admit that it was my fault. Someone had let the truck squeeze in while I was gawking.

I drive on, thinking about how cool it is to see the bodies up close and personal rather than watch *Faces of Death*. I mean, you're there, and the bodies are there, and you can smell the death and be thankful that it wasn't you decked out in a pink jumpsuit with your brains splattering on the concrete. Only two drawbacks. One: there's no pause button. Two: there's no rewind.

So I get on the expressway, and I'm cruising along at seventy miles an hour when suddenly that Audi, which I'd forgotten about, cuts me off. The asshole swerves right into my lane and slams on his brakes. Bad idea. I've been dealing with morons who stop to turn right. Dolts who can't figure out that a continuous lane means you don't have to stop. Idiots who poke along like they're parking in the middle of the road. No one's gonna cut me off like this loser.

I swerve to avoid the collision, and I gun the engine. He won't be able to keep up. No way. I dart in and out of traffic. But the jerk follows me. I glance back and see that his passenger, this stupid-looking bitch with a mohawk, is hanging out the passenger window. She hurls a beer bottle at my car. The bottle smashes into the trunk with a loud thunk. One more dent to add to my collection. I cut across three lanes of traffic and slip off the exit ramp that takes me to work. I make a note of the license plate—personalized to say "2-CUTE."

It would have ended right there. I mean, traffic pisses me off, but I don't hold a grudge for more than a couple of minutes tops.

I say it would have ended.

See, I work at this place called We Cash Checks. I deal with all these lowlifes who come in with their thousand-dollar two-party personal checks. The folks who have huge handwritten payroll checks where you can tell they added an extra digit or two themselves. People who have no ID. And, of course, drug dealers who want money orders to get rid of all that cash. Launder it and all.

SO YOU WANNA BE A HITMAN

I get into work. My first customer is this dude who wants money orders. I'm thinking drug dealer, but he's kinda old and hasn't got the look. You deal with them long enough, you recognize who does what. This guy has some serious bucks, but I can't see him out there selling dime bags.

"What's your story?" I ask as the money orders are printing.

"I'm in town for a gun show." He slides a card under the gate that protects me from potential robbers. Like that grate will stop a bullet. Yeah, right.

I pick up his card and smile. "You sell MAC-10s and shit?"

"I sell anything."

"How much?"

"Depends on what you want."

"Say for an Uzi."

"Thousand bucks," he says.

"Too much for me. How about a Beretta 93R like that guy in them books uses?"

"Mack Bolan, the Executioner?"

"That's the guy," I say.

"The 93R is pretty rare, but I've got a Beretta 92S in the van. Sell it to you for two-fifty."

"What the hell," I say. I've been skimming a little extra every now and then from the company. The lowlifes aren't the only ones who can add a digit to a check. "I'll take it."

So he hooks me up. "Beretta 92S," he says. "One of the most reliable military pistols around. Made in Italy. Locked breech, double-action semiautomatic. Takes nine-millimeter Parabellums, box right here at no charge. Magazine capacity fifteen rounds."

I pick up the gun. It has a slide-mounted safety. It's heavier than I expected. "Fifteen rounds in a clip, eh?"

"It's not called a clip. It's a magazine."

"Whatever. Anything I need to know?"

He explains a couple more things, then takes off.

I hold that gun and feel safe. The rest of the world had better be nice, or I'll give them what for.

That night I drive home hoping for someone to piss me off. No one does. I go to bed disappointed.

The next day I show up for work, and I think about taking the Beretta inside with me, but I decide against it. I slip it into the glove box and go inside. My boss is there waiting for me.

"I want to show you something," he says.

I follow him into the back room, and he puts a tape in his VCR. "Watch closely," he tells me.

The tape is of me. It shows me altering a check, slipping it into the drawer and taking out a few bills. If you look real close, you can see me tuck the bills into my pocket.

He should have just fired me. But no, he has to be an asshole. He grabs me by the ear and pulls my head down onto his desk. He calls me all kinds of names and punctuates each with a slap or a punch to the face. He breaks my nose, blacks my eye, and damn near busts one of my ribs.

"Get the fuck out of here," he says.

So I go.

I think about the disgruntled postal employee in Edmond, Oklahoma, a few years back who went in, blew away his fellow employees, then killed himself. I think about the nut who shot twenty-two people at McDonald's. I think about the guy in Killean, Texas. They all had it wrong. I sit in my car and finger the trigger of my messenger of death.

Nobody fires me.

I don't go back inside. I leave like it's no big deal that he kicked my ass and all.

When he goes home, I'm there waiting at his house. He has a nice place. I'm in the backyard kicked back in the hot tub with my Beretta sitting on the side. My camcorder is set up on a tripod to catch all the action.

My ex-boss isn't married. He was, but his old lady wised up and blazed a trail after he hit her one too many times. He once told me that after a hard day cruising around to all his check-cashing outfits, he likes to soak in the hot tub and let it take away his aches and pains.

He comes out wearing his towel and sees me.

"I'm calling the cops," he says, and turns.

"Not so fast," I say. I stand up and grab a towel. The night air is chill, but it feels good after being in the tub for so long. Steam rises off my body.

My ex-boss turns toward me. His gut sticks out more than I would have guessed.

"Damn," I say. "You look like the Pillsbury Doughboy. You ever think about working out?"

"Listen here, you little punk," he says, and then he sees the gun.

"What was that?" I ask.

"Nothing."

"I hate that. If I didn't hear something and I ask you to repeat it, you always say 'nothing.' I believe you said something about a little punk."

"Put the gun away."

"Oh, okay. No problem. You want me to get rid of the gun, all you gotta do is say so."

"Put it away."

"Just say the word," I say, pointing the gun at him. I walk around so his back is to the hot tub.

"Whatever it is, I'll say it. You want your job back. Fine. No problem. Just put the gun down."

"Why is it that whenever someone points a gun at someone in a movie, the person not holding the gun tells them to put it down? I mean, do you really think that works? Has it ever worked in a movie?"

"Look, I'm sorry for hitting you," he says, backing up.

"You're sorry, all right. You're also dead." And I pull the trigger three times. My ex-boss flies backward and makes a hell of a splash in the tub.

"He shoots, he scores."

It's easy to kill someone. Much easier than I thought. I throw on my clothes and look at the neighbors' houses. No lights come on. I figure they aren't home. I've got some time. I move over to the body and pull it up a bit, then turn the face over to the camcorder. I hold up one of my ex-boss's beefy hands and wave it at the camera.

I hope it caught all the action. I want to be able to freeze-frame on his face as the bullets strike home. He looks even dopier in death than he did in life.

My first kill. I did it for free.

I'm at home that night watching the video I shot. It isn't very good. Most of the voices are totally lost. And most of the time the camera is focused on the fence. None of the good action is on film. I walk through the frame at one point, and so does my ex-boss. But the good stuff isn't there.

I erase the tape.

I really enjoyed killing him. It was a thrill. I figure that if I have a career, it ought to be as a hitman. I'm not Italian, but I've got an Italian gun. Still, not being Family might make it tough to get jobs. Hmm.

I could place an ad in *Soldier of Fortune,* but I read about some guys getting busted by hiring out as mercenaries. I decide I'll be a private hitman. I want to do one more free job, but it can wait. It'll be 2-CUTE and 2-GOOD to ponder.

So I sit in my apartment and try to think of ways to get clients. I decide my best bet is through work. The boss is dead, so no one knows I got fired.

First thing in the morning, the cops show up at my workplace. I act like I don't know why they're here.

"What's up?" I say. It's what I always say to the cops when they come in. Sometimes they want help finding someone they think plans on cashing a check or someone who uses us for money orders.

"Seen Mr. Paulsen today?" one cop asks.

"No, he doesn't come in 'til three or so."

"Did you see him last night?"

"I saw him yesterday afternoon when he relieved me," I say. "Why?"

The cop gets right in my face as if to judge my reaction. "He was murdered last night."

I give him confused. "Do what?"

"He was killed at his house last night. You know anything about that?"

"You're kidding me, right?"

"No."

"He's seriously dead?"

The cop nods.

"Shit," I say. "Now I gotta try and get ahold of Marion. See if she can work today." I hesitate, then look the cop in the eyes. "Who's gonna sign my paycheck?"

"A man was killed, and you're worried about your check and finding a work replacement?"

"Yeah."

"You're not too broken up about Mr. Paulsen's demise."

"He was an asshole."

"Any idea who might want to kill him?"

"You know how many death threats we get in here every day?" I ask. "Limp-dick asswipes come in here trying to cash all sorts of bogus checks, we turn them down, and they get pissed. Maybe he pissed off the wrong scumbag."

"Evidently. What happened to your face?"

"I got mugged yesterday outside my apartment. Where were you?"

"Cute. Got anything that might help us?"

"You know what? We got videotape security. Maybe we got the guy on camera. You could scan through and see if anyone gives him some major shit."

While we're talking, several lowlife bastards come in to cash their checks. A few of them don't come in 'cause they smell bacon, but some of the more legit jerkwads form a line and give us heavy sighs.

I get the tape for the cop, making sure it's not the one Paulsen showed me yesterday. The tapes—there are three of them—tape over each other every day. I grab the one that'll cover from five to closing, which won't have me on there anywhere. I give it to the cops and promise to call them if I think of anything else.

I'm, like, relieved, you know. It went pretty well. They probably suspect me, but not any more than anyone else in this lousy city.

I start cashing checks.

Two o'clock rolls around, and this hot-looking babe strolls in dressed to the T's. She's got an ass that won't quit, world-class tits, and long blond hair. She takes off her shades when she comes in. Her left eye is damn near swollen shut.

Right ahead of her is a welfare bitch. The welfare bitch is a po' white trash slutty-looking thing. She slides her check under the grate, and I shake my head.

"Can't cash this for you yet, lady."

"What do you mean?" she demands. The welfare bitches always cop attitudes. They don't work for nothing, so naturally they feel as if everyone owes them everything. Bitches.

"What I mean is that the check is postdated. Bring it in Monday, and I'll cash it."

"I don't get it. It's a check. It's to me. Cash it."

See how they are? "Look, lady, the check isn't good until Monday. It's dated for the first, see?"

"Well, why did they send it to me if I can't cash it yet?"

"Maybe they wanted to piss you off."

"You cocksucker! Give me my money!"

"I ain't givin' you shit, lady. I bust my ass, pay taxes, and all so that you can sit on your fat ass and draw a check."

"I'll have your job for that remark!"

"Yeah, right. You don't want a job, bitch. Every time you decide you want more money, you lie back, spread your legs, and fart out another kid. Now get the fuck outta here!"

She cusses some more but takes her check and leaves. The hot babe with the black eye approaches.

"Help you?" I say, not paying her injury any mind. We get all sorts in here, you know.

"I was wondering if you could cash my husband's check for me. He's signed it already, but the bank wants to put a ten-day hold on it, and we have to pay the rent."

"Let me see the check," I say.

She slides it over, and I look at it. She has his ID and hers, too. She slides them to me. I compare the signatures from the ol' boy's driver's license and the check, and it's clear to me that he ain't the one who signed it.

"This is forged," I say. "Can't help you."

"Forged? But he signed it, see?"

"Can't help you. Next?"

"Wait," she says.

"What?"

"Look, I'm in a bad way here. My husband raped me last night."

"Rape by your husband?"

"That's right. I said no, and he forced me. Even slapped me around. He hasn't done that in a long time. I thought he'd changed."

"Shows what you get for thinking."

"I'm trying to leave him," she whispers. "That's why I stole his check. He threatened to kill me. Help me. Please?"

"At least you didn't cut off his pecker like that psycho bitch back east. I gotta tell you, though. You leave him, he'll hunt you down. Don't go thinking you can hide. I know his type. You could get divorced and file restraining orders and all, but none of it will do you any good. If he's as bad as you make him out to be, your only option is to have him killed."

She stands there in stunned silence. "What?"

"Hire someone to knock him off."

"I wouldn't know where to look. I—"

"Tell you what," I say, and look at her driver's license to get her name. "Michelle." I look her in the eyes. "I'll go ahead and cash this. You give some thought to what I said. You want to go through with it, I know someone who'll take the job for five hundred bucks. Make it look like the ol' boy dissed a gang member." I scribble my number on a piece of paper and slide it to her, then give her the cash.

I'm thinking that if she tries to turn me in to the cops, I'll just say I gave her my number when I asked her out on a date. If I get a male cop, he'll nod and figure he'd have done the same. Get a lady cop, she'll figure I'm a male chauvinist and give me some lip about it, but she'd buy into it, too.

I go home that night hoping Michelle will call. I sit by the phone all night willing it to ring, but it doesn't.

Next day, I get to meet the new boss at We Cash Checks. He's an okay guy, hired on by the head company to run the show until a new manager can be found. I'm on my best behavior all day, and that stresses me out. I hate being nice to all the losers I gotta deal with.

It's damn near six o'clock when I finally get home. I grab my mail and toss it on the kitchen table, then glance at the answering machine. I have two messages. I press the Play button.

First message is a damn bill collector, so I press the Skip button. Next is Michelle. She wants me to call her, so I do. I get her on the line.

"You wanna go through with it?"

"Yes," she says. "But the price is too high."

"How much you got?"

"Fifty bucks."

"Fifty bucks?" I shout.

"It's all I have. If your friend can't help me for that, I understand."

"Maybe we can take the rest out in trade," I say.

"I won't fuck you or suck you," she says.

"Whoa! I know you won't believe this, but I hadn't even thought of that. Don't worry, I don't have problems getting laid. I was thinking more along the lines of having you there with a camcorder."

"You want me to tape it?"

"Yeah. You tape it, I'll only charge you fifty bucks."

She hesitates, obviously thinking about what a sick puppy I am. But then she says she'll do it. We set the time for tomorrow night. I jot down the address and tell her I'll be there with guns on.

She doesn't laugh.

I'm there at the appointed time, of course. I bring my camcorder and my Beretta. I didn't have to work today, so I spent a lot of time flipping through gun magazines at the supermarket. Trying to get a better feel for my profession.

Michelle lets me inside.

"He won't be here for thirty minutes or so," she says.

"Cool. You want me to do anything special here or just whack him?"

"What do you mean?"

"Do you want to party? Play with the scumbag before I waste his ugly ass?"

"I don't think that's such a good idea. He's a lot bigger than you, and if you don't kill him fast, he'll probably kill you."

"You think so, do ya? I saw your hubby's check. Scumbag works for the city. Probably sits on his ass all day."

"Just shoot him when he walks in, okay?"

"Okay, lady, but you make sure that camera is in focus. And don't turn away, or I'll kill you, too. Got it?"

"I won't turn away."

I hear her hubby's car pull into the drive. I stand to the side of the door and wait while Michelle starts filming. I can hear my next victim walking up the porch steps.

"Is it in focus?" I ask.

Michelle nods.

"Good," I say more to myself than to her.

The door opens, and her hubby walks in. He doesn't look to the side, so he doesn't see me. But I see him, and I don't squeeze off a shot. I hold myself back, knowing I'm up a creek.

"What are you doing with that camera?" her husband asks. He doesn't sound too mean right now. Just curious.

Michelle knows better than to look at me, which is good. I wish I could call this off. I know that this killing will be investigated. Her husband works for the city, all right. He's a damn cop!

"I'm filming," Michelle says.

"Filming me walking in the door?"

"Filming you getting killed," she says, "for all the awful things you've done to me."

"This is a dumb joke," he says.

I know I can't leave. I'm screwed. I want to shoot him, but cop killings get investigated to the max. I know I shouldn't have come.

He sees her look over at me.

Shit.

He turns.

Our eyes meet.

I raise the gun.

He opens his mouth and goes for his shoulder holster.

I pull the trigger and watch his blood, skull fragments, and brains spray the wall.

He falls.

Michelle stands there in shock. She knew it was gonna happen, but she lowers the camcorder and stares at the body of her husband, the cop, who she said beat and raped her.

"Give me my fifty bucks," I say.

"What?"

"My money. Pay up, lady."

She goes into the other room and returns with two twenties and a ten. I take the camcorder from her. "I got a question for you," I say.

"What?"

"You interested in running away with me? I do the killings, you tape them for me."

"No way," she says.

"Then we got a problem."

"We do?"

I nod. "You've seen me. You could identify me if I'm caught."

"Wait a minute," she says, taking a step back. "I hired you! If I talk, I'll go to jail, too."

"Pretty woman like you? I don't think so. You've probably got the crying routine down to an art form."

"Wait," she says. "We can work this out."

"Yeah," I say, and pop her in the forehead.

I go out the back way.

* * *

I gotta hand it to Michelle, she held that camera pretty damn steady. I kick back that night and watch the tape over and over. I pause and rewind. I advance the tape frame by frame to take in all the details. I get that killing burned into my memory so I can call it up whenever I want. Then, since I'm not stupid, I tape over it. I let the VCR record a John Wayne movie on top of my handiwork. Then I toss it onto the shelf with my other tapes.

I'm not gonna hang around here for too long. The heat will be too much. I won't run just yet, though. I won't make things easy. I didn't know that cop. I knew Mr. Paulsen, but they already asked me about him.

I think things through, see. I know that with ballistics and such, they might link the killings. I also know that the gun dealer won't talk. He's a shady type himself, and with him living in another state, I doubt they'll ever find him. So I go into work on Monday like everything's normal.

I put in my two weeks' notice, saying I'm gonna move out of state, and I fight back my natural urges while cashing welfare checks for lazy bitches and making money orders for the drug dealers.

All the while, I'm thinking of ways to make more than a lousy fifty bucks a shot as a hitman. Professional-like. I'm still coming up with ideas when I get in my car to go home. I won't take a job unless the pay is good and I can get a videotape.

Right as I'm thinking that, I see a blue Audi in the rearview. It's 2-CUTE. Mohawk is driving, and her hippie boyfriend is sitting shotgun. "Well, well," I say under my breath as I wait for them to catch up. "One more freebie, just for fun."

THE RUG

Edo van Belkom

EDNA DOWELL SWEPT THE FLOOR, RESTING ON THE END OF HER broom almost as often as she passed its bristles over the shiny wooden floorboards. She was an old woman on the downside of seventy and more than a little senile, but still sprightly enough to clean the house by herself. It took her longer to do the job than it used to, but by stringing together enough spurts of energy, she usually could get it all done in a day.

After a short break, she swept the remaining corners of the living room and then passed the broom around the legs of the couch and end table, bringing a small pile of dirt and dust toward the much larger pile in the middle of the floor. That done, she took another moment to catch her breath.

The house was run-down but clean. Old, mended, and recovered furniture was scattered about the room, as mismatched a collection as you might expect when someone did much of their shopping on garbage day. Each piece had a character all its own, from the chesterfield she'd picked up behind the bowling alley to the chairs in the hall that used to sit in the laundromat, from the pictures of other people's families hanging on the wall to the bookcases full of books she'd never read.

266

And then there was the big oval rug she'd found behind the funeral parlor two blocks over. The design on it was quite faded, but there wasn't a hole or worn spot to look at. A true wonder of a find, in more ways than one.

Edna's breathing finally eased into a regular rhythm, and she knelt down on the floor. Then, lifting up the edge of the rug, she swept the dirt underneath it. The dust swirled toward the rug as if being sucked in by an unseen wind, then settled onto the floorboards in a scattered pile. With a satisfied nod, Edna lowered the edge of the rug back onto the floor. There was a slight bulge in it now, but she paid it no mind. In a week or two, when she felt up to cleaning again, the bulge would be gone . . . as would the dirt beneath it.

The first time she'd swept the dirt under the rug was on the day she first brought the rug home two years ago. Just as she was finishing up her cleaning, there'd been a knock at the door. With nowhere else to sweep the dirt, she quickly swept it under the rug and tossed the broom in the closet.

Her guests that day had stayed for hours, and it was a whole week before she remembered what she'd done with the dirt. But when she pulled back the rug to sweep it up and take it out to the trash, she was surprised to find it gone. Not just spread around or absorbed by the rug's fibers but gone without a trace. After that, she swept dirt under different parts of the rug to see if it would happen again, and it did. In time, she learned to sweep everything under the rug, and it eventually became as much a part of her cleaning routine as Misters Murphy and Clean.

Unfortunately, not all of her little problems could be handled so easily. The current problem, or perhaps just the latest incarnation of a constant problem, had to do with money, or lack thereof.

Three years ago, her pension had been deindexed and no longer kept pace with the cost of living. Then, last year, her rent had gone up three percent, the maximum amount allowed by the government's rent control board. She'd made up the difference with what little savings she'd squirreled away over the years, but that was all but gone now. She wasn't sure if she was one month behind in her rent or two, but what did it matter? She only had enough money for groceries, and she'd be damned if she'd go hungry while giving that do-nothing slumlord another red cent.

He'll be coming around soon enough asking for his money, she thought. *He can ask all he wants, but I can't give him what I don't have. He can threaten to throw me out, too, but I won't move. He might own this house, but this is my home.*

She patted the bulge in the rug, and it shifted slightly under her touch.

The knock on the door didn't surprise her; she'd been expecting it for some time. She hadn't paid her rent in months, and her landlord was anything but patient. As if on cue, the knocking grew louder and more frantic as the man on the other side pounded harder on the old wooden door.

Edna slowly got up from her chair in the living room and began shuffling her way to the door. "I'm coming, I'm coming," she said in a voice that was barely a whisper.

"I know you're in there, Dowell," the man shouted. "I seen you pick up your mail."

When she reached the door, she paused for a moment's rest, then unlocked and pulled the door open.

Marty Genetti was a squat Italian man with a full head of black hair that was blow-dried straight back in the shape of a cycling helmet. He was probably in his fifties but still looked like the teenage hoodlum he'd been more than thirty years ago. "I come for the rent," he said.

"And a good morning to you, too, Mr. Genetti," said Edna.

"Yeah, it's a great morning, but it would be even better if you had the rent money you owe me."

"I haven't got it."

Marty just shook his head. "That's crap. I know for a fact that the pension checks went out today and you already took in your mail."

"Well, the check wasn't in the mail," she lied. She couldn't possibly turn over her pension check. There'd be nothing left for her to live on.

"Nice try, Dowell. But never bullshit a bullshitter. You got your check today, and you're going to give it to me or I'll boot you out. I got six families practically begging me to live here."

"I don't have it," she said, her voice beginning to crack.

"Fuck this," Marty muttered, barging his way into the house. "Where did you put the mail? In the living room?" He walked into the large room off the hallway, looking for envelopes. There were a few Christmas cards on the windowsills, but they'd been there for years. "What about the kitchen?"

"No!" Edna cried. She'd put the mail in the pantry, but it wasn't very well hidden, and he'd find it there as soon as he looked.

He went into the kitchen, Edna following as fast as her feet could take her.

"What's with all the cookie tins? That where you keep your stash?" He started taking the tins off the shelf and opening them one by one.

Edna did keep some bills and a few coins in a couple of the tins, but that was emergency money for doctor's visits and medicine. If he took that, she'd literally be without a penny to her name.

"Stop it!" she shouted. "Stop!"

"Oh, am I getting warm?" He laughed, almost as if he was enjoying his little act of terrorism.

"Please, stop!" she pleaded again, but her words only spurred him on.

He found a Christie's tin with some money in it. "All right," he said. "This is a start . . . let's see what else we can find."

Edna began trembling in frustration and anger. If he kept on like this, he was bound to find her pension check, and then she'd be left with nothing. She had to do something, but what?

"Hey-hey! Here's a twenty," he said, looking more and more like a neighborhood bully shaking down kids for candies.

Edna glanced at the kitchen counter. Her rolling pin was

there, a chipped and cracked rolling pin made out of marble she'd found years ago in a Dumpster behind the Commisso Brothers Italian bakery. She stared at the rolling pin for what seemed like forever, then finally picked it up . . .

"You gotta have a piggy bank here somewhere."

. . . raised it over her head . . .

"Or maybe a roll of pennies—"

. . . and let it fall.

Marty Genetti stared up at Edna, his green eyes bulging out of their sockets in a look of surprise, and one side of his head crumpled up like a squashed paper bag. His fingers were closed tight around the money—Edna's money—but that didn't stop her from cracking his fingers open and prying the bills from his fists. After she'd picked the loose change off the floor, she counted all the money and put it in neat little stacks on the kitchen table. It wasn't much, but it was more than she'd thought she had stashed away.

She looked down at the corpse in her kitchen and was struck by a thought. With some effort, she got down onto the floor, turned him on his side, and pulled the billfold from his back pocket. It was made of black leather, as soft as baby's skin. She opened it up, and a smile broke over her face. The wallet was stuffed with bills, the smallest of which were twenties. She took out the money and placed it on the table, marveling at how springy the stacks of paper were.

She replaced the wallet and patted his pockets for any loose change. She found a few more bills—mostly ones and fives—and a bunch of quarters. She considered taking his rings but figured they'd probably be more trouble than they were worth, and picked herself up off the floor. Then she sat down at the table and counted the money. There was more than a thousand dollars there, more than enough to pay the back rent *and* stock up on food.

As she sat there filled with joy over the windfall, she began to think about her situation. If the landlord was dead, whom would she pay the rent money to? Oh well, not to worry, somebody would be by asking for it sooner or later.

She was about to get up to put the money in a safe place

when her foot kicked against the dead body on the floor. "Oh dear," she said, realizing she had a bit of a problem on her hands. Killing Genetti had been easy—he was a nasty, dirty little man who'd gotten what he deserved. However, getting rid of his body, now that would be tricky.

Edna sat down and thought about it.

When it came to her, it was like a new day dawning in her life, as if somebody-up-there was telling her she'd done a good thing.

If Marty Genetti was dirt, the only place for him was under the rug with the rest of it.

Edna got up from the table and made herself tea. When she'd finished the cup of orange pekoe and was sufficiently rested, she began dragging the corpse into the living room. It wasn't an easy task, but by nightfall she'd pushed, pulled, kicked, and rolled the body into the middle of the living room. Then, with little ceremony, she raised the edge of the rug, gave the body one last roll, and lowered the rug over on top of it. The rug barely covered it, and the hands and feet stuck out from the corners, but at least the face, with those bulging eyes and lolling tongue, was hidden from view.

Out of sight, out of mind, she thought.

And went upstairs to bed.

In the morning, Edna came downstairs rested and chipper, having had the best night's sleep in ages. Outside the sun was shining, the air was fresh, and it was a beautiful, beautiful day.

As she entered the living room, the first thing she noticed was the bulge in the rug. It was quite lumpy but considerably smaller than it had been the night before. The second thing she noticed was the curled pair of hands lying just beyond the near edge of the rug and the pair of black shoes, soles up, on the floor at the other end. The hands ended at the wrists, and the exposed flesh and bone were smooth, as if they had melted away like candle wax rather than being cut by a knife. The feet were similarly disembodied—socks, skin, muscle, and bone melted away at a slight angle.

Unsightly mess, that, thought Edna, picking up the edge

of the rug and quickly kicking the hands underneath with a flick of her fluffy pink slippers. Then she walked around to the other end of the rug and swept the shoes underneath it, too.

"There," she said aloud, noticing there was a bit of color to the rug now. "Much better."

She went into the kitchen, humming a tune.

The lump in the rug took about a week to go away. Each day, Edna would come down the stairs to see it smaller by half. The last few days, she heard a sort of slurping sound coming from the rug, and every once in a while a crack, but then that eventually stopped and the rug lay flat again, not a lump to be seen.

Sipping her morning tea by the front window, Edna took a moment to look at the rug more closely. If she wasn't mistaken, it looked newer somehow, the design on it brighter and more colorful. It looked like two bright red pools surrounded by some darker colors, but other than that she couldn't make out what it was.

She finished her tea, went upstairs, and got dressed. She hadn't been shopping in weeks, and the cupboards were practically bare. Now that she had money in hand, it might be a good idea to stock up on groceries.

She was just about ready to leave the house when there was a knock on the door.

"Now, who could that be?" Edna said aloud.

She went to the door and opened it to find a middle-aged woman standing on her front porch. She had coal-black hair, dark tanned skin, and wore a large round pair of dark sunglasses. Although it was quite mild out, she had on a big fur coat made from dozens of tiny pelts. Edna thought of the poor hamsters that had died in the creation of that coat and disliked the woman immediately.

"Edna Dowell?"

"Yes!"

"I'm Maria Genetti. My father owns this building."

"Isn't that wonderful," she said warmly.

The woman took off her sunglasses, revealing small

brown eyes that were covered by far too much makeup. Her painted eyes narrowed into slits as she looked at Edna. "So, he left the house a week ago to collect overdue rent, and he hasn't been seen since. And since you're one of the two tenants of his that are overdue, I was wondering if he came here."

Edna was silent a moment, thinking what she should do. If she said he'd been there and then left, the police would surely come asking questions. If she said he'd never been there, then this woman—this evil, evil woman—might go away, but she'd end up leaving with all the overdue rent money. That would never do!

She looked up at the woman. "Maria?"

"Yes."

"He was here, Maria."

"Really? When?"

"This morning."

"That's wonderful," she said with a sigh of relief.

Edna nodded. "He came in here looking for rent money." She paused a moment, as if trying to remember. "And then he went into that closet over there and never came out."

The look on the woman's face soured. "What are you talking about?" But then, ever so slowly, a look of terror crept over her features as Edna's words preyed on her mind.

"Let me see!" she said, barging past Edna toward the closet at the end of the hall.

No manners, thought Edna. Just like her father.

The young woman opened the closet door and peered inside.

Edna went silently into the kitchen, knowing the woman would stand there in front of the closet for a few moments unable to see anything in its shadowy depths.

"There's nobody in here," she said, her head still buried deep in the darkness. "Where did he go?"

She pulled back from the closet and turned around.

Only to get a good look at the rolling pin . . .

"What happened to my—"

. . . up close.

* * *

Maria Genetti had had some money on her but not much. She certainly wasn't as well off as her father had been. After Edna had gone through her purse and pockets, she barely had two hundred dollars to show for it.

Oh well, she thought. *Better than nothing.* She put the money in her own purse, stepped over the body in the hallway, and left the house to do the shopping.

When she returned an hour later with her wheeled wire cart laden with groceries, she was surprised to find the dead woman's body lying facedown in the hallway. Standing over the corpse, she tried to recall what had happened, then began nodding.

"Yes, yes," she said. "Of course. Mustn't leave people lying around in hallways. What would the neighbors think?"

And with that, she took off her coat, brought the grocery bags into the kitchen, then dragged the body into the living room. As she moved the body closer to the rug, she noticed something strange about the floor covering. The edge of the rug was trembling slightly, like the upper lip of a starving man who'd just caught the scent of fresh-baked bread.

"Patience," she told the rug in a tone of voice more suited to house pets than home furnishings.

Then, with one last push, she managed to move the body into position. She raised the edge of the rug, gave the body a kick, and watched as the rug curled around the corpse, pulling it under.

"Thank you," she said to the rug. "Now, where was I?" She saw the empty wire cart standing at the front door. "Just about to go shopping."

She put her dirty tan coat back on and left the house, headed for the market.

The lump in the rug was gone in just under three days. Edna spent nights sitting in her rocker watching the rug slowly getting smaller, shrinking like a block of ice on a warm spring day. There were still the same slurping sounds coming from it, but only for a little while and only near the end.

After the lump was gone, things settled down, and Edna was at peace knowing she had more than enough money to live on and that any new problems that arose could be easily swept under the rug.

She was happy for the first time in years.

About a week later, there was another knock at the door. "Who is it?"

"Police, ma'am."

Edna glanced through the peephole and saw the uniformed policeman. "What do you want?"

"I'd like to ask you a few questions, Mrs. Dowell. We're looking for two missing persons, Marty Genetti and his daughter Maria."

Edna was silent. If she didn't let the policeman in, he might get suspicious, thinking she had something to hide. Better to let him in, answer his questions, and send him on his way. "Just a minute," she said, opening the door.

The police officer was young and handsome, with short blond hair, a bushy blond mustache, and pale blue eyes.

"Come in."

"Thank you, ma'am."

"Now, how can I help you?"

"Well, I've been going through the neighborhood asking everyone if they've seen either of the two people. Marty Genetti owned a lot of property on this block."

"Is that so?"

"Yes, and he was known to make visits around the first of each month to collect rent from problem tenants."

"Problem tenants?" she asked with a smile. "Well, that must be why I never saw much of him."

The police officer gave her a polite smile.

Edna looked shyly away and noticed the rug.

It was moving.

The policeman kept talking. "That might be so, but some of the people on the street said they saw him knocking at your door a few weeks ago."

Edna suddenly felt warm all over. From what the policeman had said, she couldn't deny Genetti had been there. Perhaps it would be better to play along. She took her eyes off the rug for a moment and looked up at the policeman. "Oh yes, that's right," she said, feigning recollection. "You'll have to excuse me, my memory isn't what it used to be."

"That's all right." The policeman nodded. "My mother's like that sometimes."

"He *was* here. Came to check on a leaky tap in the bathroom, but I'd fixed it the day before, so we sat and had tea in the kitchen. Ate two and a half of my biscuits, and then he left."

The policeman scribbled some notes in his book, asking Edna further questions about when Marty Genetti arrived and how long he had stayed.

"I can't recall such things very well. It might have been ten minutes, it might have been an hour."

As the policeman continued making notes, Edna took the opportunity to glance back at the rug. It was less than a foot away from the policeman's big black boot, inching closer.

"Perhaps you'd like to join me for tea as well?" she asked, walking across the living room and placing both feet on the edge of the rug to hold it in place. "I brew the best on the block."

"I'd love to, ma'am, but I've got fourteen more apartments to check out, and the captain doesn't like approving overtime."

"Another time, perhaps?"

"Maybe."

"Oh, that would be wonderful."

The policeman took a few tentative steps to the door, waiting for Edna to escort him out. When he finally realized she intended to remain standing in place on the edge of the rug, he said, "Well, good-bye."

"Good-bye," chimed Edna. "And good luck."

When the man was gone and the door closed, Edna stepped off the rug and pointed an admonishing finger at it. "Naughty rug!"

A ripple coursed over the edge of the rug, and then it was still.

* * *

Ten days later, there was yet another knock on the door. "Who is it?" Edna asked.

"Health Department."

Edna said nothing. Why would the Health Department be knocking on her door? "There's nothing wrong with my health," she said. "Thanks just the same."

"No, ma'am. Some people on the block have been complaining of a bad smell these last few days. I need to take a look around, see if it's coming from your apartment."

"I don't smell."

"No one's saying you do, ma'am. But there were several complaints, and I've got to check out the entire block."

Edna thought it over. If there was a smell (which there was not!), the man wouldn't be easily shooed away. Better to let him in to take a look around, satisfy his curiosity.

"All right," she said, at last opening the door.

He was a middle-aged man with a mustache and graying black hair. The name over his pocket read "Dave." As he stepped inside, he began sniffing. "Something die in here?"

Edna sniffed, too, smelling nothing. "You watch it, sonny. I might be old, but . . ."

He stepped further into the house, sniffing like a bloodhound.

It was obvious to Edna he was looking for something and wouldn't stop until he found it. Best to stop him first.

"Oh, I know," she said. "Maybe it has something to do with the hole in the wall inside the pantry."

Dave looked at her curiously. "What hole in the wall?"

"Come and I'll show you." She led him into the kitchen and opened the door to the large walk-in pantry filled with canned food, the steering wheel from a 1972 Maverick, and two department store mannequins. "See that hole there?" Edna pointed inside the pantry and stepped back to let the man by.

"I don't see anything."

"Maybe it's behind Dolly."

Dave shifted one of the mannequins, then tried the other. "Nope."

He began easing himself out of the pantry when the back of his head was bashed in by Edna's rolling pin. He let out a cry and slumped forward. After a moment, he put a hand over the back of his crushed skull and moaned in terrible pain. His foot slipped on the kitchen floor, and he fell backward, hitting his head again.

As blood pooled on the floor around his skull, he looked up at Edna, his eyes blinking as if to ask "Why?"

In answer to the question, the rolling pin came down again, sending his forehead deep into his brain.

It took Edna the rest of the day to drag the body into the living room, and the rest of the night to clean up the blood.

By the time Edna dragged herself upstairs to bed, the lump under the rug had shrunk by half and the rug itself was colored with deep black-and-purple swirls that circled the two crimson pools like hurricanes around an eye.

The next morning, the lump was gone.

It had been two days since Dave had visited, and Edna wondered why more Daves hadn't stopped by—or even a Bill or a Bob. But while it was a concern, future visits from the Health Department weren't what worried her most. It was the rug. It had started getting unruly.

Ever since the policeman's visit, the rug had begun to move. Not much at first, mind you, just a few inches here or there, but enough that Edna was forever setting it right. Over time, it began roaming the room, its bright red circles looking more like angry eyes with each passing day.

Now, every time she walked through the living room, it moved toward her, its edges rippling and undulating as if in a wave. At first, she thought it was cute that the rug followed her around like a cat wanting milk, but as the days wore on and there were no more visitors, the rug had gotten downright feisty.

This morning after breakfast, when she walked past it on her way upstairs, it had nipped at her feet, taking one of her pink slippers from her foot in the process.

"Bad rug," Edna scolded, kicking it with her other slippered foot. "Bad."

And then the rug lurched forward, pulling the second slipper off her foot, leaving her foot scratched and red with blood, as if it had been rubbed with sandpaper.

Edna ran from the living room and hurried up half a dozen steps before turning back around. The rug was there on the landing, trying to flow up the first step but unable to pull itself off the floor.

Edna sat there for a long time, catching her breath and watching the rug with a mix of fear and fascination. Finally, it glided back into its familiar spot in the middle of the living-room floor, where it lay still except for the wave that undulated around its edge every few minutes.

After watching the rug for a while, Edna took a few tentative steps toward the landing. With each step, the rug became more restless, almost like a dog growling at the approach of a stranger. As she set her foot on the landing, the rug slid across the floor, its leading edge curled back in a sneer.

Edna turned around, ran up the stairs into her room, and slammed the door behind her.

Edna spent the next day in her room. Twice she ventured out, trying the steps, only to find the rug waiting for her at the bottom of the stairs.

It had managed to curl over the first step and was inching up the second. Seeing that, she went back into her room and crawled back into bed.

But as the day wore on, the first pangs of hunger began to gnaw at her belly. It had been more than twenty-four hours since she'd had a bite to eat, and with each further hour that passed she grew more acutely aware of how hungry she really was.

It almost made her laugh. The kitchen was full of food, and her purse was full of money, but the thing that helped her to get those things was the same thing that was going to deny her their pleasures.

It was almost better to be penniless and starving.

Almost, but not quite.

She pondered her situation well into the evening and was finally struck by a thought, a way to satisfy both hungers—hers as well as the rug's.

She picked up the phone.

And ordered a pizza.

INTERVIEW WITH A PSYCHO

Billie Sue Mosiman

THE PLACE WAS ALABAMA, A HUNDRED MILES NORTH OF MOBILE, the village named after Paul, one of the apostles. It was 1965, and the young people hadn't deserted yet to make their marks on the world. More than three hundred souls inhabited the surrounding small farms and homesteads. In Paul stood two country stores, one with two gas pumps selling overpriced fuel, an ancient one-room unpainted house that served as the U.S. Post Office, and two churches, the Pentecostal Holiness and the more sedate Baptist.

Hank Borden lived two miles down one of the many dirt roads leading from the main blacktop that wove through Paul. He was going to be eighty-one in a few days. He had never lived anywhere but in the old gray plank house on ten acres of thick second-growth pine. He had never been married, and his family was all dead, parents and five siblings.

He spent most of his days sitting in a rocker on the tin-roofed porch that aproned the front of the house. He had many thoughts, some of them damnably confusing, and nothing but time to think them.

He knew the girl was coming. She had interviewed nearly all of Paul's elderly over the past six months, and she would not bypass him. They said she was putting together a book of the interviews, an oral record of the area that covered the years between the Depression and present times. She had arrangements, they said, for the publication, and was being paid a princely sum of money for an advance against royalties. Imagine a writer coming out of this place, this backward evil place, he thought, spitting a stream of tobacco juice into the bare yard.

Well, he had many things to tell her. Things no one else knew. It was time he let the truth out. He once thought he would never tell. Had he before now, the local sheriff would have come with his deputy and taken him away in handcuffs. But he was dying. He wanted to tell it now. He felt compelled to share it with someone.

He had already suffered two strokes, coming back from them without the aid of doctor or hospital. He still couldn't straighten out his right hand—it was deformed into a clawed thing, gnarled fingers pulled in toward the wrist—but he had learned to manage. What couldn't he do with just one capable hand? Nothing that mattered anymore. And his speech was slow and halting now, he had to take his time formulating thoughts into words, but he rarely spoke to people, so that did not significantly hamper him. He could speak well enough to communicate with the girl.

He watched the road and waited.

She would be along shortly.

On a sultry summer day with the air as dense as a chainmail suit, she drove into his yard and stepped out of a mint-green Ford Galaxie with dented and rusty fenders. He sat in the wooden rocker on the porch waiting, not even bothering to offer a greeting or a wave. His heart was fluttering so in his chest, he hoped not to keel over before he could tell his life story. He scowled through the blinding sunshine blinking from the chrome on her car. When she stepped from the vehicle, he was not surprised to see she was a pretty thing. She was the granddaughter of a woman he had always thought handsome, even as she aged. This one, this girl, looked a lot like her mama, too, having inherited a petite build and dark brown shiny hair and eyes so dark the irises appeared black. He was glad to see she was small. He had never cared much for heavy women.

His expression softened as she came toward the steps, and the dappled shadows of a mimosa near the porch threw her into shade. He could not smile, knowing what he was about to disclose, but he did say in a civil tone, "Hello there, young lady. They said you were coming."

"Hi, Mr. Borden. How are you doing today? I guess my mission has preceded me. You know about my book?"

He gestured with his good hand that she take the second rocker next to him. When she was comfortably seated, he said, "Everyone knows. You can't go into Potts' store without someone bringing it up. You're a regular sensation around Paul. Who would have thought we'd produce a talented girl like you?"

She smiled and brushed back a wisp of bangs from her forehead. "I love this place," she said. "That's why I wanted to tape all the stories about it so it could be preserved in print. Do you mind if I turn on my tape recorder while we talk?"

"Go ahead, won't bother me any."

She pressed a button on a recording machine that was about the size of a hardback book.

"Now," she said. "You know what I'm after, right? I want you to just talk to me as if we were having an afternoon chat about your past. We can talk like friends, you don't have to worry about how it sounds or anything. I'll be transcribing the tapes and typing them up in your own words. I have a release form here that I'd like you to sign, if you don't mind. It's just a formality the publisher asked me to have contributors put their John Hancocks on." She pawed through a fat leather shoulder bag, brought out a sheet written in small print, and handed it over with a ballpoint pen.

He held the paper on his knees with his damaged right hand and painstakingly signed his name with his left. It looked like hen scratchings on dry ground, but he knew that was of no consequence.

"You don't want to read it?" she asked.

He gave her a bemused look. "Nah, that's okay. I can't read much without my glasses anyway."

"I can read it to you . . ."

"Not necessary. Now, where should I start?" The fluttering was back in his chest. It was going to be difficult, the most troublesome event in his life, to confess to his crimes. Especially to this unsuspecting and innocent young woman. How did you make horror and depravity come out sounding like anything other than it was? He was not going to offer excuses. He had long ago realized there was no excuse under heaven for his sins.

She folded the paper and put it and the pen in her purse again. "Anywhere you'd like," she said. "When you were a boy? Or when you were grown and living through the Depression, that might even be better."

"Well, it started when I was just a boy. I had turned just thirteen . . ."

"The Depression started then? But . . ."

"No," he said. "I'm not going to tell you a story like you've gotten from the other old people around here. My story isn't about surviving the Depression or what it meant to go from horse and buggies to cars or from slaughtering our own animals to buying store-wrapped meat. I have an entirely different tale to tell you."

She gave him a perplexed stare, but her attention was rapt, open to whatever he wished to tell her. "Well, go on, then. Whatever you want to say is all right with me. What started when you were thirteen?"

"Murder." He must get that out into the open before he lost his courage. There was no point in wasting this young woman's time.

The girl was visibly shaken. Her eyes widened perceptibly, and she swallowed and blinked.

"I'm afraid this won't be pleasant for you," he said.

"Murder?" Her voice was small and shocked. A fly landed on her cheek, and she shook her head to make it leave.

"That's when it started. My first kill. I'd like to tell you how it happened . . ."

Then the fluttering of unease in his heart settled, and he stared out across the yard and across the dirt road to the deep green forest beyond. This was hard, but he could do it. He had done many arduous things in his life.

He told her how he came to have an unabiding hatred for the man who ran the sugar cane mill. The mill took in the cane from farmers in the county and put it through a press to get the succulent juice squeezed into a great vat, where it was made into syrup, and canned and shipped throughout the state. Hank's father grew a few acres of cane, and Hank was the one who took it by wagonload to the mill and sold it.

"His name was Rufus, the mill man," he said. "A more cruel individual you might never want to meet. He not only called me names, but he would reach out and slap me when I didn't unload the cane lengths quickly enough to suit him. My ears would ring half a day afterwards. I've always suspected I don't hear so well because of that.

"The thought of revenge haunted me day and night. It was like a tumor growing down in my gut. I didn't tell my daddy Rufus treated me so awful. Daddy needed the money from the cane. He'd just have told me I must be slow and quarrelsome and that Rufus had every right to slap me around for it.

"I'd lie in my bed at night and ponder how to do away with Rufus. I planned it all very carefully, every detail, and then when my chance came up, and there were no witnesses present, I rushed Rufus on the catwalk that ran around the perimeter of the huge syrup vat, and I knocked him into it.

"Oh, did he scream and curse me! Then he grew frightened because there was no way out of the vat, no ladders along the curving slick inside of it. It was at least six or eight feet to the top from the level of syrup where he slapped around, fierce and furious. He was going to drown in all that sweetness when he tired of dog-paddling and keeping his head up. When the thought got through to him, he began to beg me to throw him a rope.

"I just stood on the catwalk and grinned. It took some time, but Rufus started losing strength and began going under. His hair was slicked down on his scalp, and syrup had glued his eyelashes into clumps. He kept licking his lips and coughing. He flailed awhile. He even cried.

"But when I left for home, my cane unloaded and paid for, Rufus was drowned, his lungs full of sugar cane syrup. They found him the next day and thought it an accident. All I remember is feeling triumphant. It was a great victory, that first murder. I had rid myself of a burden that made me feel lighter and happier than I had ever been. It is *exhilarating* to kill, you know. There is absolutely no other adventure like it."

The girl sucked in her breath, and he glanced at her.

"Do you think I care if you tell people this?" he asked. "You can go straight to the sheriff when you leave here, if you want. That won't bother me. But first you might want to hear the rest."

She nodded, her lips pressed together in a tight line. She disapproved vehemently. So be it. He had not expected otherwise.

"After that, it was much easier," he said, continuing. "Anyone who crossed me or caused me pain, I found a way to send to the grave. I made them look like accidents, and no one questioned the deaths. There's an advantage to living in the country, and that is one of them. People don't expect violence, and the law doesn't look for an explanation." He paused before he said the rest. It was bad enough he admitted killing for revenge. Now came the part he hardly understood himself. He wondered if he could explain it so that it made any sense at all. He had contemplated these events for decades now, and he was still confounded.

"There were maybe six or seven murders like that, where someone did me wrong and paid for it. I had a high sense of justice—too refined, some might say—and there were just too many folks around here who treated me without respect. Then . . ."

He stayed silent so long, remembering, that she cleared her throat, and that prompted him.

"Then something happened to me. Inside. Here." He lifted his liver-spotted left hand and pointed to his head. "And here." He laid his hand against his heart and sighed audibly. "Maybe it was because I'd killed so many already. Maybe it was because I was hard now and cold and had stopped caring for the value of human life. It might have been because it was so *easy*. People are vulnerable, they don't watch out for themselves. They walk right into the most dangerous situations without proper consideration of the jeopardy.

"I've thought on it and am not sure what exactly made me change."

He gazed at her, his eyes reflecting bewilderment. He glanced away and leaned forward in the rocker to spit tobacco.

"In my thirty-second year of life, I killed for the first time without having a grudge against the person. I killed a woman. A stranger to these parts, someone passing through."

He saw the girl turn aside her head and close her eyes. *Yes,* he thought, *this is the worst. You must be strong to hear this.*

He continued, his voice removed and unemotional. "I flagged her down that night. I was walking outside of Paul, aimless, restless. I felt this *urge* tearing at me . . ."

It came back to him, that spring night with the crickets chirping in the ditches alongside the road, and the pines swaying and sighing with a sweet, gusty little breeze that cooled his face. The blacktop was still warm from a day in the sun, and he could feel the heat through the soles of his shoes.

He was in a state. He had been walking the floors of his old house in the dark before he felt compelled to leave it. His parents were dead, and he was alone, too alone. He was not a good-looking man, and women were not attracted to him. He was socially inept and couldn't start up conversations with women. He passed them on the streets in Evergreen when he went shopping there and was mystified at how tongue-tied he found himself.

But this night, he hadn't started feeling agitated over the lack of female companionship. Something had entered his mind, and it wouldn't leave. It was a raging thought process that came from deep down inside him, not a voice, not some demon or other personality, just his own mind turning in on itself and going crazy. Like a snake that swallows its tail, his mind was devouring itself whole.

He couldn't sit, couldn't be still. His hands clenched and unclenched as he paced back and forth, back and forth through the darkened rooms. The sound of his footsteps on the bare boards of the floor unnerved him. The breeze blew the window curtains in, billowing them, and he swatted at the ghostly whiteness of the muslin as he passed by. He wanted *something,* what did he *want?* He wanted to be anywhere but here in the old creaking house. He wanted to be anyone but himself. He wanted . . .

He wanted to kill *someone.*

When the realization came, was internally verbalized, he fairly sprinted through the hallway to the porch, leaped to the ground, and headed into Paul. He walked quickly, his breath coming in and out of his lungs, arms swinging to propel him even faster toward his destination. He didn't hate anyone. He didn't despise or fear anyone.

But someone must die, Jesus, yes. If he didn't kill, he knew he would explode into a million tiny pieces and be absorbed into the universe. If he did not find someone to murder, he would lose his mind, it was as simple as that. There was a *gnawing* going on, as if a hungry rat ate at his brain matter. He felt his control going, dissipating like smoke filtering out through his ears and thinning into the fragrant pine-scented night air. The only way to preserve his sanity was to commit murder.

Her car came along slowly, the headlights shining on his back and throwing his tall shadow onto the pavement before him. He turned, stepped into the blacktop's center line, and began waving his arms over his head.

She was in a 1950 DeSoto, dirt brown. She pulled over to the side of the road, and he came to her side of the car.

"What's the matter?"

He looked down at her face, a round, bland, doughy face, and he said, "Get out of the car."

His voice must have scared her. She drew back and began to put the transmission into first gear.

He reached inside the window and turned off the ignition, taking the keys. He punched in the light button, and dark swelled around them, wrapping the two of them and the car in an ebony cocoon. "Get out of the car." The rage he felt was a tidal wave rolling over him.

He couldn't see right. Her outline blurred for him as she stepped from the DeSoto. The car dimmed into nothingness at her back. He couldn't hear anything but his own fury screaming KILL, KILL, KILL, setting up a cacophony in his head. She was talking to him, he saw her mouth moving, but she might as well have been talking to a deaf man.

He reached out and took her arm, led her behind the car to the grassy embankment and down it into the ditch. He was heading for the woods, knowing even in his frenzy that he should be careful and not do anything out in the open where another car might drive by and its occupant see him.

In there, in that midnight wood, he threw her to the ground, straddled her body, and choked her to death. It was over in minutes, and as soon as it was, the storm in his mind released him. He hung over her, panting, dripping saliva, his heart beginning to slow to a normal pace.

This would not be thought an accident.

And that did not make any difference or deter him for a minute. He would take her body, and they would never find it.

"So she was the first I killed for no reason that I understood," he said, finishing his tale for the girl and her recorder. "But not the last."

"Oh, God."

The girl had her face covered with her hands. Hunched over that way, she reminded him of a little Raggedy Ann doll, bent into a pretzel shape. "Please don't tell me any more," she said. "I don't want to hear."

"But I have to," he said. "I've begun now, and we have to finish it."

He looked at the tape through the tiny window of the cassette recorder and said, "It's almost to the end. Why don't you get another? I have a lot to tell you."

While she found another tape in her big purse, he thought he should reassure her. He saw how her hands trembled. "I'm not going to do anything to you. I don't want you to be afraid. I'm too old, for one thing, with a bum hand. You could easily free yourself. But that's not why you needn't be scared of me. You see, a few years ago, it stopped."

She fumbled with the tape, loaded it, and hit the Record button again. Her head came up. "It stopped?"

"The urge. It just went away and never returned. I don't know how else to explain it. One day I woke, I'd overslept, it was almost noon, and when I sat up, I knew. It was as clear to me as if an angel had visited the room and spoken through a megaphone in my face. I wouldn't have to kill again. I was free of whatever madness had stalked me all those years of my life. It was like coming up from deep down in the depths of the Gulf of Mexico. I swam into the day and into a newfound life. I felt sorry for the first time. I felt so sorry that despite my jubilation at being loosed from the killing urge, I began to weep. I folded over my legs, and I cried like a baby. All those people. Those . . . corpses . . ."

The girl shuddered. Tears stood in her eyes.

"They're behind the house," he said sadly.

"Who?" she whispered, horrified.

"The ones who weren't accidents. The ones I killed to satisfy the rage."

He looked back out across the road to the forest wall. He spied two cardinals in flight, red flashes through the green. "There are plots for them that I couldn't even now lead you to. The woman from the DeSoto is there. She'd be a skeleton, nothing left of her. And there are many others, so . . . many others. I never counted them, it wasn't like I was tallying up a score or something. I only know I was on a hunt for years. All my waking hours were spent on the hunt."

"For your next victim?"

"Yes. When I worked for my paychecks as a foreman at the sewing factory, I was on the hunt. When I shopped for food, I was hunting. When I finally got a car and took little trips into the panhandle of Florida and down to Mobile and up to Montgomery and Huntsville, I was on a hunt.

"That's why I was never caught, I suppose. I took them from everywhere and brought them dead back here. Back *there.*" He meant the untamed acres behind his house where he had buried the bodies.

"Why didn't you turn yourself in when you . . . when you stopped?" she asked.

"I didn't want to go to the electric chair. That should be obvious. What happened to me was something unexplainable, something that I had unearthed by killing with my full faculties, a beast inside me that I called forth through vile hatred. I have lived with my guilt after the day I woke up knowing what I was and what I had done. That was not punishment enough, I know. But I was a coward. I knew what death was, I had caused so much of it. I feared my own death, what it held for me. It was not until this last year, when I knew I was going to die—my heart is failing—that I've faced it. When I heard of your project, I knew I had to tell. There are missing people, families bereaved and wondering where their loved ones disappeared. Now you can let them know. I've put things to rest finally."

"Do you know the names of the people you buried in the graves?"

"Yes," he said. "I kept their wallets and identification papers." He stood shakily from the rocker, spit tobacco onto the ground, then moved to the screen door. "You won't leave, will you?" he asked, holding the door open and looking to her. "Will you wait here for me to bring it all to you?"

She nodded. But he saw something waver in her eyes, and suddenly he knew she lied, that she would flee the moment he turned his back.

"Why don't you stop the recorder and come with me? It's a large box, and I might need help lifting it."

He saw how skittish she was and how unhappy at his suggestion. Nevertheless, she halted the recorder and stood to follow.

He smiled inwardly at the wonder of his persuasion. Hadn't he told her how vulnerable victims were, how they were led into danger without a qualm about their safety? Had she somehow missed that warning, deluged as it was with his rambling, detailed confessions?

In his bedroom, he held on to the polished maple bedpost to lower himself to his old knees. He reached under the bed frame into the dusty gloom there and pulled out a metal suitcase, an old tin contraption he had kept from the '40s. It was scratched and dented, and even the handle was missing. He struggled back to his feet.

"Could you lift it to the bed?"

He stepped away so that she could get a grip on the old suitcase. As she stooped, slipping her fingers beneath the heavy case, his good left hand felt along the dresser near him for the silver-plated letter opener he had bought in Evergreen one Christmas more than twenty years ago.

Just as the girl lifted, using her back, grunting, he closed his fist around the stiletto-sharp opener and plunged it with his remaining strength down into her back.

She screamed, dropping the suitcase with a clatter. She fell onto the quilt-covered bed, and the springs creaked in accompaniment. Her hands came behind her, feeling for the object sticking in her back.

He sat down on the bed to wait.

He talked to her as she died.

He said, "Don't worry, I'll make sure your things are back in your car, except for the two tapes, of course. I'll have to burn those. I can still drive, you know. I'm old, and it is true my heart is in terrible condition, but I can still drive your car into the river where they won't find it for ages. Not until long after I've departed this old earth. They will probably publish your book anyway. You had enough interviews to fill it already, didn't you? It was grand of you to care so much about this place. This wild, unrestrained, backwoods place."

"I thought . . . you . . . said . . ." She gurgled low in her throat, and a scarlet ribbon of blood slipped from the corner of her mouth. She had stopped trying to reach the letter opener in her back. She lay now with her arms at her sides like an obedient child taking a nap.

The light in her eyes was fading, flickering in, flickering out, a candle flame in the wind.

"You should never have taken the word of a murderer, young lady. I never did experience that day of reckoning, that day when the urge left. I wouldn't know what that might feel like and expect that never happens to people like me." He smiled beatifically. "I haven't killed anyone for a long time, though. I'm so old, and yes, I'm weak, and I can't go on the hunt the way I used to do.

"I have to wait for the prey to come to *me*."

She cried tears that wet his bed, she whispered a curse against him, and then she died.

After the tedious efforts of disposing of her car, catching a ride back to his house, and burying her in the woods behind his place, Hank Borden decided not to burn the tapes she had made of his life. He opened the tin suitcase and dropped them, along with a driver's license from her purse, onto the mounds of material he had collected over a long lifetime of carnage.

Someday someone would find all this.

After he was gone, after his pitiful old pump stopped pumping and he stepped into that void, they would come here and go through his things, and they would find out about his past. Only then would they know the real Hank Borden. The tapes would help them.

And all except for the profound remorse he said he had experienced, and the resultant change he claimed came over him, everything that he confessed on the tapes was God's gospel truth.

ICEWALL

William D. Gagliani

THE WIND.

Even through the thick Styrofoam padding and internal icewall, you could hear it. You couldn't escape its long, high-pitched wail. It drove ice particles like tiny projectiles, embedding them into the outer skin of the Jamesway hut with the sound of popping corn. The stretched canvas was pitted like that of an orange, and frozen solid.

After six months, the three things that defined my life broke down like this: the wind, the darkness, and the hut. And Frank. I guess that's four. Frank was certainly instrumental in my life, just as I was in his. Hell, in that little space we shared, there was no relief, from the elements or each other.

So why was I there at all? Adventure. Furthering the cause of science. Therapy. Take your pick or take 'em all. Even now I can't guess what went through my mind when I filled out the interminable paperwork that would eventually lead me to that Jamesway hut about two hundred miles "north" of the South Pole in the long winter darkness. I don't know why Antarctica seemed such a good way out of a lousy life. And I don't know why life was so lousy, not even now.

All I know is that after nearly six months on the Ice,

Frank changed. About the time he started complaining about those flickering lights out at the edge of the Icewall.

I never saw those lights, but he insisted they flickered there whenever he was alone. He'd drag me out into the near darkness and point, but there was never anything there. The Icewall's ridge always seemed as impenetrable and mysterious as ever to me, and as lonely. It drove him nuts that I couldn't see them, but I couldn't, and that was that. After weeks of this routine, we started ignoring each other more and more.

This particular day had dawned like the rest of them. No real light. No real difference in the temperature. No real difference in the instrument readings. No real difference in any damned thing. I had just finished checking the instruments in the dome fifty yards from the hut. Almost buried, the dome was an igloo. Or a white wart on dead skin. Take your pick. It's all in the perspective. Five steps led down into its interior, which was lined with shelves of instruments. There was the usual battery of thermometers and barometers, as well as a barograph to chart trends in air pressure. There were hygrometers and psychrometers to check and double-check humidity, which rarely changed, and a rack of electronic devices hooked up to the anemometer mounted on the metal tower outside. Snow gauges and ice crystal collectors sat outside, too. In the center stood our baby, the radio telescope. Banks of programmable listening and recording devices scanned the banded sky for movement. The dome also contained an easy chair and a small supply of food, in case one of us became isolated inside. A tiny stove provided inadequate heat. We used a lantern with a cable strung to the hut and hooked into our generator to provide lighting. There were candles, too, in case the cable were cut or ripped by wind or buried too deep.

This was the last winter for our little dome. After the thaw, after the relief plane came and whisked us away to the warmth of McMurdo and then Christchurch and home, another plane would bring a construction crew and a new dome. Twice as big and sparkling new, it would contain newer versions of all the instruments—in a third of the space—and a weather radar, or so they told us. Camp Ten would grow to include three more Jamesway huts and a big Robertson building, as well as the radar dome and a T-5 to house a larger generator.

Yessir, after Frank and I left, the place would turn into a regular dump, with a personnel roster of at least fifteen and a muddy Main Street. Our location had become big-time, even if we hadn't. That's why Frank and I took our twice-daily measurements with less and less enthusiasm, feeling replaced already. Whatever they'd do here wouldn't include us. After the hut, life was a blank to me. And I knew Frank didn't have much to look forward to, either.

I munched on a frozen chocolate bar from the emergency kit as I took the last of the readings and snapped down covers over the instruments and their dials. Breath clouded the air and blurred my vision slightly. I had stopped using the stove during readings, since it was barely worth the trouble. The measurements were mechanical, and I ignored the numbers—I just wrote them into the log with a damned pencil and forgot they existed. Pens were useless in the intense cold. The ink froze up and eventually burst the thin plastic cylinders. The new equipment would take readings and feed them into a computer, which would then store the data until a weekly satellite hookup requested transmission. It almost didn't need humans to work, and I felt obsolete with that fucking pencil stub grasped awkwardly in triple-gloved fist.

I closed down everything that needed to be and finished the chocolate bar, then climbed the steps and met the wind head on. Both hands wrapped around the nylon safety railing that led from the dome to the hut, I slowly made for home. I kept my head down to avoid the flying ice, which found the vents in the face mask with unerring accuracy. Even with heavy-duty goggles stretched over my eyes, visibility was impaired—not only by the ice but also by the tiny gouges the particles made. Goggles became useless after a few weeks of constant barrage, and these were almost new. I desperately wanted to keep them that way. I was attached to those goggles, as if they had become my eyes.

Fifty yards is a jaunt almost anywhere in the world, but it took me twenty minutes to negotiate against the wind. Every ten feet, the railing threaded through a flexible whiplike post, and I counted posts as I went along. I had once wondered why the dome was placed so far away. Long ago. The answer always gave me chills, even in fifty-below temperatures.

"In case of fire," a member of a long-gone winter's party had told me, while brushing loose locks of hair from his forehead with one hand and scratching a tangled beard with the other. "If a fire starts in the hut and you don't die in it, you want a place to retreat to. Get your ass sheltered, you know. If the fire starts in the dome, same thing. You don't want it to spread, and fifty yards is about right, just to make sure."

He had squinted a little then and drawn his features into a smirk, giving the impression of someone who knew better than to let these things get to him. Then he'd wandered off, scratching his groin. A real poster boy for the Antarctic project.

Fire. I remembered the lectures we'd had on fires.

"There's nothing worse than fire on the Ice," an overweight Major Kane had said with a frown. "If it doesn't kill you, you're almost as good as dead anyway. See, rescue is always days or weeks away, depending on the weather's cooperation. But you know about *that*, being weather buffs, right?" No one had laughed. "You can't put fires out on the Ice. Extinguishers freeze solid in hours. Those we've designed with antifreeze take a couple of days, but they freeze up, too. There's no such thing as running water, except the small amounts you melt for cooking and drinking. You get my point, I hope. Fire is death. No two ways about it. But if you can find shelter away from the fire—a decent shelter— you stand a chance. A remote chance, sure, but still better than nothing at all. So take care of your off-camp shelter. It might have to take care of you." He sat abruptly, as if he found his own words distasteful.

Somebody had laughed then, briefly. A nervous sort of laugh-bark that had echoed over our heads and died out.

Nobody looked to see who had laughed, because the same chill hung over all of us. The lecture had continued on a much lighter note, how to avoid sexual frustration while wintering in camp. Some wit had labeled that part of the sermon "Pulling the Penguin 101." We put fire out of our minds, but it lurked there all the same.

The Jamesway hut is shaped like a half-cylinder and covered with canvas. Inland stations sometimes use two— one slightly bigger—and piggyback them so that there's about a foot and a half of dead air space between the outer skin of one and the inner skin of the other. Inside that space they spray loose snow, which hardens to form a thick, frozen barrier—an icewall—and Styrofoam chips. Keeps most of the wind and cold out. But the newer buildings are much better, don't need the customized improvements, and the next party would get the two-story Robertson variation. I envied those guys. Frank and I were sick of the Jamesway.

I snapped open the outside door, and it flew out of my grip. There were flashes of light in the sky—the approaching polar morning—but it was still dark, about the same as late early evening, if you know what I mean. Take your pick, dark is dark. I pulled the outside door closed, unlatched the inside door, and I was home. The relative warmth caressed my face and began melting the blown snow on my parka and hood. I took off the garment and shook it in the doorway, then pulled off my fur-lined boots and slammed them against the door—snow melts, dampens the boots, and quickly freezes when you visit the dome later. Presto, no toes. Or even feet. We shook out boots and parkas diligently, you can bet on it. The fucking cold gets to you and the dark and so does everything else. Take your pick.

"Close the goddamn door," Frank growled at me. I was used to his mood shifts, so I ignored him. But I did shut and latch the door, as I would have in any case. He'd been nitpicky for a while now. I went to the stove and turned up the heat a little, even though it would still be a frosty fifty or so in the hut. It never gets very warm in there, because you're always trying to conserve fuel. Just in case.

"Trying to poison me?" he baited, but I wouldn't bite. I'd

been there way too long to care if he didn't like something I did. And the stove fumes weren't that bad. He was lying in his bunk—his usual position in the last few weeks—and looking up at the curved ceiling, a filthy pillow on his chest. He'd stopped taking readings, too. For a month, I'd been carefully forging his initials in the weather log every other reading, so no one would know that Frank had succumbed to the polar Bug. Lord knows I was close myself, but to see Frank acting like that was enough to drive me all the way to buggy if I let it get to me.

The radio was for emergencies only, and our tour wasn't up yet, so we couldn't very well call for a new deck of cards or something. And flights are almost impossible in winter—slots are liable to last less than an hour. Anyway, our old deck was good enough. Frank never played with me anymore, so I laid out hand after hand of solitaire for hours. The broken turntable sat silent on a bookshelf. Frank had smashed the useless records a month before, and pieces of vinyl still found their way underfoot. We had no such thing as CD technology at the Pole yet, and cassette tapes became brittle in the cold and snapped. So now we had no music. I bet the next guys would get a CD jukebox. Fuckers.

"Want to play some cards?" I asked offhandedly as I shuffled the deck. The cards were a little thin and crinkly but still did the job. I glanced at the female figures on the back. No regulation cards for us, no sir. I was holding "Brigitte," Frank's favorite. "Hey, Frank, it's Brigitte. She's callin' for you."

"Go fuck a penguin."

I shook my head. Not because there weren't any penguins within a hundred miles, and not because I wouldn't if given half the chance, but because his attitude was bugging me.

"Suit yourself," I mumbled, and made do with my own company, not for the first time. I arranged the cards so I could see all the girls. Brigitte, Renee, Michele, Dominique, Angela, and my favorite, Joconde. We had a good time together, and it was Frank's loss.

Later, I looked at my watch. It was going on midday, and my stomach was grumbling. "Look, let's eat. Okay?"

He was still staring up, that pillow on his chest. "Just leave me the hell alone." His voice was barely louder than a whisper, but I heard it. I heard it, all right.

As I said, he was changing. He'd been a nice guy for four months, and then he'd started acting strangely, since those lights he kept insisting he saw out by the Scott Icewall, fifty miles away. I wondered if the shrink at McMurdo could unravel the threads of his mind, but I knew it'd have to wait. And maybe I'd be better off keeping my mouth shut. Like with forging his initials in the book, I could probably cover for him if I tried.

"All right, my friend." I stood and scraped the chair on the plank flooring, trying for sarcasm. "I'll do the cooking. Once again." A corner of the Jamesway was set up as galley. I opened a few cans and mixed a couple freeze-dried things with water hundreds of years old and soon had what seemed like a reasonably pleasant smell drifting around the hut. At least it masked the stale odor we were forced to put up with all winter, which I had recently started to consider intolerable. You'd think old Frank would have shown some enthusiasm. For the effort, at least.

"First thing I'm gonna do when I get out of this place is get a haircut," I said, while I ate something labeled "Pork Chops and Applesauce." It had the look and consistency of puke, so it was better than the "Beef Stew with Vegetables." "What about you?"

Frank didn't answer.

"Well, anyway, I'll get my hair cut and my beard trimmed, and I'll go out to a real restaurant and order actual food. Not this crap they make us eat." I prodded the opened cans and foil packets. "A natural freezer here, and they don't even give us steak, like the boys at McMurdo get every goddamn day. Steak and fucking eggs for the boys, twice a day if they want it."

"You know damn well we ate all the steak," Frank hissed in that funny little whisper of his, like he's not getting any air in his lungs. "I told you not to eat it all so quickly, but you did anyway. Now we're stuck with this shit."

"Shut up, Frank."

"Now we're stuck with stuff that isn't even good laxative."

"Look," I said, "if you can't be nice, then just shut up."

"Sure, you wanted us to eat all the steak, and now we're out, and it's *my* fucking fault," he said.

"Shut up!" I screamed. I threw an empty can at him, but it bounced off a chair that was in the way. Frank didn't even bother to duck or move. He just lay in his bunk, hugging that pillow, and stared up at the ceiling.

Outside, the wind howled without letup. You can't escape that wind, you know, just like you can't escape each other. I suddenly wanted to hear that relief plane, that fucking great C-130 roaring overhead and setting down at the strip, and Frank and me waiting and waving.

Something dark rose up in me. I threw the hot food at him and missed. I wasn't hungry anymore. We had no words for each other—they'd all been said.

So life went on. Frank was different, there was no doubt about it. He barely talked to me, and when he did, it was with contempt that he'd somehow concealed for months. I continued to cook for us, but Frank never ate. I guess he must have been eating whenever I was out at the dome. I still took that walk twice daily, and I still forged his initials carefully, as if he were still doing his share for science. What shit! It was all me. I was doing it all in that godforsaken hut and in that dome. I took my readings carefully and recorded them in the log and then signed the entries, drawing either my own initials as I always had or, every other time, drawing Frank's—"FLG." No one would ever know he'd caught the Bug. I couldn't tell on a buddy, even if he *was* driving me apeshit.

About a week after our last fight, the one about the steak we didn't have, we made up. Or I made up with him, anyway. He was on his back in his bunk again and ignoring me.

"Man, I think this'll be the last tour, buddy," I said. I hoped we could talk. You know, bury the hatchet, as they say. I mean, we hadn't talked in days. "I just can't take this isolation anymore, and this darkness. And the fucking wind."

To be fair, the sky was getting lighter every day. But noon still seemed sort of like twilight, and the wind screeched through rips in the hut's canvas. Two days before, I'd fixed the cup anemometer—a gust of wind somewhere between sixty and seventy miles per hour had knocked the cups right off the damn thing, so I had to climb the bastard and put in one of the replacements. I had begged Frank to give me a hand, but he wouldn't budge. Wouldn't even look at me. So I'd gone out on the Ice and climbed the tower with a safety line that I had to unclip every few steps so I could clip it above me and take a few more steps. Two hours later, I had come crawling into the Jamesway and collapsed on the floor, all my limbs frozen and my face rubbed raw by the wind despite the mask.

"Why bother?" Frank had asked no one in particular from his bunk. While I had to admit that he was partly right, it also made me so angry that I could barely focus my eyes. I'd noticed that happening before, too, like the coming light was bothering my pupils or something.

Well, Frank had his version of the Bug. I might as well be entitled to mine. Take your pick.

"You know what I'm sayin' about the wind? It drives the breath right out of your lungs and digs at the inside of your stomach. Course, you been staying real cozy while I've busted my ass covering for you. So maybe the wind isn't getting to you anymore, eh, Frank?" I laughed.

Frank mumbled something that I couldn't catch.

"What?"

"I said why don't you just shut up and leave me alone."

"Okay, Frank. Have it your way. Just a couple more weeks of this, and we'll be out of each other's greasy hair. Right?" I asked the girls.

But they wouldn't answer. They were getting just like Frank.

So I cooked for both of us again and watched Frank's food

get cold across the table from me. Another peace offering wasted. Thank God we were going to see real daylight soon.

The next day, Frank tried to kill me.

It happened during the night reading. I took down numbers and ate a chocolate bar and forged his initials again. I'd been writing that the "day" readings were mine and the "night" ones his. I figured this system would do to cover his dereliction of duty. Frank was still a buddy, Bug or no Bug, and I wasn't going to let him get in trouble when we got back to McMurdo. Jesus, when were we going to get back? I shrugged, then checked my—his—initials and closed the logbook with a snap. It was about half filled with tiny penciled entries, all in my careful hand and with both our initials displayed near the dates.

Wait. I sat up straight. Feverishly, I riffled through the log's blank pages. A date was circled in red, a date that was coming up. I'd been damned careful with the *initials,* but I had neglected to disguise my own handwriting in the actual entries. What would they make of that? It was too late to change them, unless . . .

Unless I brought Frank the logbook and we went over it together. That was it. We'd go back, and he'd just write in the entries after I erased them. Simple. I unzipped my parka and shoved the logbook inside, between the heavy sweater and woolen shirt. Then I slid the face mask up and over my nose and mouth, and snapped the new goggles over my eyes. I could barely see, but I had little choice. The wind was gusting at sixty-five, and ice chips were digging into anything too soft to withstand the assault. The red paint had long since been flecked off the instrument tower, and every other surface was as pockmarked as my face.

So I doused the lantern and stepped up, into the ice storm. It wasn't a whiteout, since that condition occurs when there's hardly any wind at all, but it was close enough. A whiteout is reflection that turns everything to milk and blends horizon with sky until you might as well be swimming in a bath of the stuff. Right then the horizon didn't even exist, and the hut might as well have been perched on the dark side of the moon. The only thing linking me to that warm Jamesway was the nylon safety line railing, strung from hut to dome and flapping like a flag on its thin posts.

I took hold of the line with both mittened hands and began the trek. I tried to breathe through my nose, since drawing in breath could easily bruise a lung. I pulled myself along, warmed only by the thought of hot soup—okay, hot salted water some halfwit had once christened *soup* while delirious or drunk or both—and some chocolate and the girls. Step after difficult step, the crunch of the snow under my boots lost as soon as it was created, I counted posts and slowly reached the halfway mark—a three-foot stretch of line dyed brilliant red. It was almost as comforting to see as the door of the Jamesway would be.

With my arms doing the work and my mind trying to propel me forward to the hut, the stove on high, the hot soupy stuff and my hands warm as they cupped the mug, I suddenly found that the line was limp—*much more limp than it should have been between posts.*

I pulled faster and heard my breath rattling in my throat—or, rather, *felt* it rattling there—and my steps got longer and quicker and the ice drove into my open mouth and I almost didn't care because I could see something just barely but it was coming up and I was home, I was almost—

Frank had untied the nylon railing and somehow brought it back around and what was in front of me now wasn't the Jamesway but the dome. I had spent a half hour walking and was exactly where I had started from.

For the first time, I contemplated death. *I was at the dome.*

I looked back, toward where the hut would be, and saw for the first time that the line of posts did curve slightly to the right. There was no way I could find the hut in the storm, not without the railing to guide me.

Panting from exertion, the bruises in my lungs and nostrils throbbing, I straddled the railing and fell into the doorway and down the five steps. My face mask was gone, torn off sometime during the walk. My nose and lips were numb. My cheeks were slabs of marble.

Hands trembling, I flicked the switch on the lantern and watched a whole lot of nothing happen. I turned it a dozen times, the *click* of the switch loud even above the wind outside. I followed the cable out the door and started pulling, wrapping the thin wire around my hand and elbow. It was cold and stiff, but it came. It came all too easily. The snipped end reached my hands and I saw the metal poking through the clean cut. In a rush of anger, I threw the useless cable out the door and turned back into the dome. I lit the stove and forced myself to calm down and think—

Calm down and think.

It was obvious. Frank had tried to kill me. He hadn't actually failed yet, I realized as I tasted vomit at the back of my throat. I was alive, yes, but as long as he was there, in the Jamesway, and I was here, there wasn't much I could hope for beyond a cold resting place. The Bug had finally driven him to the edge, and now he was after me, and I was dead because there were still two weeks until the relief plane would come and it was still night and I started to cry.

Tears froze in my beard, pinching as they pulled the individual hairs away from my skin.

Maybe I could survive—wait out the storm—and make it back to the hut. It wasn't impossible.

But what if the weather continued like this for weeks?

Antarctic weather is characteristically unpredictable—hell, I knew that—and a weeklong storm was nothing new, especially during the tail end of winter. And a two-week storm didn't stretch the limits of my imagination much, if you know what I mean. Even then, the relief plane might have to wait another week for a long enough slot to bring up our replacements and the Camp Ten expansion materials. I might have to survive in the dome for three weeks or more.

Awed with the thought, I checked the supply cabinet. Fuel for at least a week, maybe two if I stretched it. Not bad, since I had rarely used the stove while taking readings. Food was another matter. I'd steadily nibbled on the emergency rations and chocolate until there was little left. The bottom of the storage locker peered at me emptily. There was a scattering of chocolate bars and protein supplements. A few days at most, especially at such temperature extremes, where the body requires some four times its normal caloric intake. I could hear that fucking fat major lecturing in my mind, and it wasn't pleasant. I wasn't in very good shape, foodwise. Water wasn't a problem, except that I'd use up fuel melting it out of the doorway ice.

I unpeeled and ate a candy bar.

Then I sat and tried to think clearly.

Take a new set of readings. See what the weather looks like. Pressure, same as before. Temperature, minus sixty-three Fahrenheit. Winds, fifty-eight, gusting to sixty-five. Hell, the standard charts don't even bother with wind speed over forty, and the coldest wind chill's at winds forty and minus sixty: an incredible minus one forty-eight.

Give or take a few worthless degrees, that's what I faced out on the Ice.

My only chance was to wait out the storm and hope that it wouldn't last much longer.

I glanced at the wooden floor and counted empty chocolate wrappers, the remains of dozens of visits. It seemed I'd had as much of a hand in my own death as Frank, that bastard. I turned the stove as far down as I could so it would still heat a small circumference and curled up in the shabby easy chair. Sometime later, I fell asleep.

Dreaming.

And saw flashes and scenes of my two winter tours on the ice and of what came before and saw too much and cried in my sleep. A mysterious figure repeatedly took my life in his hands and strung it around in a circle and led me to where I had started. Each time, I rushed out into the dark to stop him with hands numbed by the cold wind.

And each time, I watched as my fingers fell off, one by one, leaving raw white stumps with which I could no longer grasp the limp rope. And when I caught a glimpse of the figure, my own face peered back at me from inside the fur-lined hood.

I shuddered and moaned but let myself dream on and off, preferring the release of nightmares to the real cold inside the dome.

I occasionally awoke and remembered and the wail of the wind was one long sound outside as the ice drove itself in a frenzy and smashed into whatever obstacle man had so foolishly placed in its way. And I saw that man *was* foolish in thinking that any such place could be tamed, and, if anything, I sympathized with Frank for having felt that way just a few weeks sooner than me, that's all.

Frank had got the Bug, and I was going to die because of it. But maybe I deserved to die. Something was telling me that, too.

I drifted in and out of sleep for hours or days, I'm not sure. When I remembered, I ate chocolate and turned up the stove with trembling fingers that fumbled at the tiny notched wheel.

The wind. Always the fucking wind.

I wanted a haircut. I cried and the tears froze.

Like watching someone else wake up, I slowly opened my eyes and came to the realization that the wind—though it still screamed and hooted through the cracks of the dome—had lessened somewhat. It was downright quiet.

Hands I couldn't feel shook as I covered exposed skin and lifted myself out of the chair I'd considered my final resting place. Frost crackled and rained about my feet as my stiffened parka tore away from the chair fabric.

When I stepped through the doorway, I knew what I would find. The wind had indeed died sometime during the "night," and the new ice had settled. Two feet of hard, granular snow spilled into the dome, dribbling down the steps like water, and I ignored it. Leaving the door open, I stood on the Ice and saw that the nylon railing and posts were altogether gone, blown away after all. *Now there was no proof.*

The anemometer was cupless again. Wires that fed the dials inside the dome were flapping limply, their insulation ripped ragged. The snow gauges were buried. I couldn't have cared any less.

Now that the air was clear again, the hut was visible fifty yards away. A little lower on the brightening horizon, maybe, and more rounded on top than before, but certainly there. It hadn't blown away. By my reckoning, I had spent five days in the dome.

My boots crunched almost happily in the new icy snow as I made for home.

Off to my right, the polar morning peeked over the Scott Icewall. I stopped to watch as the thin rays painted the sky bands of pink and violet. I looked through the clouds of my breath, hoping to see the flickering Frank had seen for weeks, but there was nothing. Just ice and snow and wind, and the coming day.

There was no smoke coming from the pipe chimney. Breath streamed out in front of me, and for the first time I felt the spring that would soon taint the air with a near warmth. The relief plane might already have been a dot in the sky. I reached the hut and spent a few minutes clearing the doorway of new fall. Then I went in.

It was dark, darker than outside. There was no light, no lantern or candle. There was no heat. My breath came in ragged little gasps, and my vision blurred as I looked around. Where was Frank? Where could he have gone?

I felt around for the panel that led to the tiny alcove where the generator sat, silent. A flexible metal pipe led from the generator to a jagged opening carved into the wall, through the layers of ice and skin, and out. For the exhaust. *Check the fuel gauge. Empty.* Fuel gurgled as I poured, careful not to spill a drop or to give fumes time to gather. Then I started the generator and waited as the lights in the Jamesway flickered and gained intensity. I closed the panel and entered the main room.

Frank was on the bunk.

My first thought was that he was being pretty damned callous, lying there like that, not giving a damn about my life or death. My second thought was that I should kill him for it. My third thought was almost unthinkable, but I couldn't keep it out of my mind as I dripped water or fuel— *fuel*—all the way to the bunk.

He hadn't moved. Not since before the storm. Maybe not for weeks.

Maybe not for weeks.

The grease-stained pillow was on his chest. I touched his face. It was solid. The pillow was encrusted, had frozen solid, too. His eyes were open and staring.

A sound gurgled out of my lips. If he had sat up then, or winked, or moved a white hand, I would have run screaming from that hut and welcomed the slash of wind-driven ice particles down my throat. I turned away from Frank and went to the table, unzipping the parka and pulling out the logbook. The pages were frozen closed—nightmare sweat had frozen them together. I tore at the paper edges with clawing fingers and felt sharp pain as ice stabbed the soft skin under my nails. Forcing the covers open, I looked at the entries I had written, those with Frank's initials and mine. *Weeks.*

I half-turned to face the bunk, hoping to see—to understand—and Frank spoke.

"About goddamn time you got back. Get the stove lit, and make it fast. I'm sick of you, and I'm sick of this wind. And those lights out by the Icewall have been driving me nuts. Night after night, those damned lights flickerin' on and off like some sort of code."

Funny, for the first time in weeks I couldn't hear the wind at all.

I lit the stove and faced Frank.

"You drove me apeshit," I said.

"You always *were* apeshit," he retorted. It was a neat trick. His blue lips didn't move at all. My stomach tightened.

"I hate your frigging guts!" I shouted. "I hate you, and I hate this place."

He laughed and that was enough for me. I leaped on him and dragged him off the bunk. He made a solid *thunk* as he hit the planks. I pried the pillow from its perch on his chest and felt stiffened material tearing there. I threw the pillow across the room, into the galley. Then I went to the stove and turned it way up, watching the flames grow taller and taller.

I had to melt the ice off the pillow.

Flames licked upward. Suddenly, I felt a spark strike my beard and smacked out its little yellow tongue, and the smell of burnt hair filled my nostrils. I dropped the pillow and watched as more sparks jumped and ignited the woolen blankets on the nearby bunk, the wet planks.

"There is nothing worse than fire when you're on the ice."

"If you don't die in it, you're as good as dead anyway."

"Take care of your shelter, and it'll take care of you."

"There is nothing worse than fire."

"Frank!" I shouted. "Fire! Frank!"

There was no answer. His clothes had caught, and smoke was forming rapidly in the center of the room. There was a smell, sickly sweet and somehow revolting, that clung to my nostrils. The stink of burning polyester and Styrofoam gagged me.

"Carbon monoxide is probably already forming." It was fat Major Kane, sitting on my bunk. His face wore a bored look. The lecture was too much even for him.

"Take care of your shelter, and it'll take care of you."

I grabbed a box of rations from the galley and hefted it out the door. The fire glowed now, even from outside. I went back in to find gloves and a new face mask and to get Frank. But it was too late for him; he was on fire.

I felt liquid in my eyes.

"Frank!" I shouted one last time, and then the place was ablaze and I had no choice but to get out. I grabbed the box and felt it slip out of my clumsy grip, then managed to cradle it in my arms and stumble a few shaky steps toward the dome, following the line of recent footprints. My way was lit by the flames behind me, which were now licking through the roof and into the cold polar air. I watched for a moment, enthralled, then followed those quickly fading footprints to where they led. To the dome. Maybe later I'd head for the Scott Icewall.

In a week or so, if the weather held, the relief plane would come. Meantime, the dome would be shelter enough. Fifty yards was indeed the right distance. I wanted to thank the major, but he was gone. And the girls were gone. And Frank.

ICEWALL

I already missed Frank. He was a buddy. Even if he did complain too much about those lights I never saw.

I left him there, in the Jamesway hut. With the wind.

For John W. Campbell and Philip K. Dick.
And for my parents.

A SOUTHERN NIGHT

Jane Yolen

THE CAR EDGED UP TO THE RAMP, SLOWED, THEN MOVED forward in fits and starts. Finally, it stopped, and a woman got out. Her heartbeat was erratic, and she was weeping softly.

Two nighthawks swung lazily over the car, then looped off past the trees at the lake's edge. An owl cried its territory like the sound of a desperate child in the night. It moved closer on silent wings, then flew off beyond the highway.

The woman walked up and down the ramp three times, her hands wrangling with themselves. Then, as if the hands had come to an agreement, they fell to her sides, and she went back to the car. Opening the front door, driver's side, she reached in and—oddly—turned on the interior light. Next she released the handbrake, closed the door, and watched as the car headed slowly down the ramp and into the water. The tears continued to track down her cheeks; she did not wipe them away.

The car floated for a long time, rocking a little like some eccentric cradle, before sinking into the muddy water. The bubbles were what had first alerted us; they made the same heavy popping sound, like the old carts in St. Andrews that the witchhunters used to float the old hags into the North Sea.

The boys woke screaming as the dark water closed over the car. The little one thought it was a kind of game at first, and his screams were high and delighted. His brother managed to scramble out of the car seat and tried to open the door, first the back doors, then the front, but they were locked down, childproofed. It was when his fingers got all bloody from trying to pull up the locks that the little one understood something was terribly wrong and began screaming for real.

We ran the sequence three times to be sure we got it right, then we pulled them out of there. No use letting them get all dirty and wet with fright.

It spoils the meat.

THE FORGIVEN

Stephen M. Rainey

"SAY IT!"

Dyer's eyes were two smoking pistols, black and deep. His right hand, raised above his head, gripped a long, gleaming straight razor; his left clutched a strawlike tuft of his victim's hair, pulling the head back so the jaw hung slackly open. The man, eyes bulging in terror, could barely force air in and out of his lungs, much less comply with his captor's command.

"Say it!" Dyer cried again, tensing his right biceps in preparation to strike with his razor. "Go on."

Webber tried to speak but managed only a weak gurgle deep in his throat. A thin stream of saliva ran from his lower lip.

"I know you can do it," Dyer said, voice now soft, controlled. His tensed muscles relaxed slightly. "Say 'I love you. I forgive you.'"

At last, Webber found his voice. Weak and raspy. "I . . . can't."

Dyer shook his head in disgust. His victim was tied securely to a wooden armchair in the bedroom of the rented house, lit harshly by a single bare bulb in the pole lamp. Webber's sweat had formed a pool around the legs of the chair. The hemp rope binding his wrists to the armrests had chafed the flesh, now burning bright red and drenched with stinging perspiration.

"What . . . do you want from me?"

Dyer laughed unsteadily, lowering the razor for a moment. "I want you to forgive me. It's your Christian duty."

"Why are you doing this?"

"Because I must."

Dyer released Webber's hair, and the head drooped heavily forward. He leaned down to look directly into his victim's bloodshot eyes. "I want to know . . . how do you feel?"

Webber glared back for a moment, disbelieving, then his will faltered under the penetrating stare. "I'm . . . scared."

"You should be. Do you want to die?"

"No . . . of course not."

"Do you want to go to hell?"

"No."

"Then forgive me!" Dyer spat at him, and slapped him stiffly across the cheek. "Say it!"

Webber's cheek went crimson from the blow. His eyes dulled briefly in shock. Dyer's blood cooled again, and he leaned down.

"Say it into the machine." He pointed to the cassette recorder on the bed, its spindles revolving with a soft whir. "I want your family and friends to know how bravely you died. You're not a hypocrite, are you? You have faith?"

Webber stared at the younger, wild-eyed figure, voice again stolen by terror. A harsh breath managed to claw its way up from his lungs.

Dyer had randomly selected Webber as his quarry, watched him for weeks, determined that he was just the right man: a family man, middle forties, with a wife, two daughters—ages thirteen and nine—middle class. Churchgoing.

"You suffer the sin of pride," Dyer said. "Open yourself to the Lord, and turn the other cheek. Isn't that his commandment? You are a God-fearing man. I know this, for I've seen you go to church and I've seen you pray." He wiped his forehead, pulling back a strand of damp, sandy hair with the hand that held the razor. "Do you think you're not going to die?"

Webber gawked at him, his brown eyes drawn to Dyer's own opaque gray, his features twisted with every possible facet of fear. "Why?" he gasped. "What do you want?"

"What do you think I want? Tell me."

"I don't know what you want."

"All my life I've wanted to know . . . to see . . . how powerful is our Lord Jesus Christ. I must see His will overcome what would seem to be insurmountable odds. That's all. I *must* see."

Webber shook his head slightly.

"Do you think I'm a madman? A psychotic murderer? Is this what you think?"

"No, but I . . ."

"Liar!" Dyer's hand smacked Webber's face again with a loud *thwack*. "I *am* psychotic, you fucking fool. I'm as loony as a fucking goony bird. And I am going to kill you. But I want you to forgive me. You say to me, 'Richard, I love you and I forgive you.' A man of God would be able to do that. You are a hypocritical, lying man. Me . . . I'm as honest as a saint. I don't lie. I speak truth, Tim. Can you do that? Speak the truth?"

"If you're looking for a man of God, why don't you talk to a minister?"

"The Lord Jesus ate with sinners and common men. Men just like you. Thieves, liars, cheaters. I know you lie to your wife, you know. What's your secretary's name . . . Jean?"

"No!" Webber cried, straining vainly at his bonds. "You don't know anything about her! Or my wife!"

"I know a lot about *you*, Tim. I know how much it would tear you apart if I took your daughters. What if I were to bring them here, right here in front of you? I could tie them up. Slice off their little panties. And with this . . ." He flashed the razor. "Go inside of them."

"Shut up! Shut up! You bastard! You . . ."

"Forgive me, Tim, and I'll make it quick. Show me that the power of God is great. I know you're angry, and scared.

I understand that, believe me. But the Lord said, 'the things that are impossible with men are possible with God.' Surely you believe that. I saw you in church."

Webber could only groan. "Shut up. You *are* a liar. You bastard."

"Would you like to kill me?"

Webber's eyes grew bright. "I would. God forgive me, I would love to kill you."

"How do you expect to be forgiven if you don't forgive me? You don't love me, Tim, that's the problem here. You are commanded, 'Love thy neighbor as thyself.' My Lord, Tim, we're neighbors. I've practically been living with you for two months, and you never even knew it." Dyer's rented house lay only two blocks from his victim's. He'd staked out the house and appraised its resident family with intimate precision.

Webber grunted, anger and adrenaline bolstering his spirit. "You're nothing but trash. Walking garbage."

"I don't like that kind of talk, Tim," Dyer said softly. He lifted his razor, and Webber's face suddenly turned to chalk. "We grow by suffering. By the time we're finished here— and that time is entirely up to you—I expect you will have grown quite a lot. I sincerely believe I'm going to see the power of God show through in you. I have high hopes for you, Tim." Dyer then gently placed the gleaming blade of the razor over the little finger of Webber's right hand. The older man tried to curl the finger under his palm, but the binding rope prevented him lifting the hand more than a centimeter. His fingers could only helplessly grip the end of the chair arm, vitally exposed.

"Please," he whimpered. "Don't. I'm . . . sorry."

"Sorry?" Dyer cried, his composure spontaneously withering. "I'll show you sorry!" He brought his other hand up and placed it heavily atop the blade, then brought his weight down fully. The blade sliced cleanly through muscle and bone at the knuckle, and the pink digit shot three feet into the air, followed by a thin geyser of crimson.

Webber screamed shrilly, the cords in his neck nearly bursting through his flesh.

"Forgive me, Tim," Dyer said softly. He picked up a towel from the pile he'd left on the bed specifically for this purpose and gently wound it around the bleeding hand. Webber gasped brokenly, and his head slumped forward. His eyes had gone dull and vacant.

"No, no," Dyer said tenderly, taking a glass of water from the nightstand. "Here." He splashed it into Webber's face, who sputtered and gurgled and moaned in agony.

Dyer retrieved the severed finger and held it up for Webber to see. The older man seemed to wilt with a shuddering moan. Dyer tossed the finger into a corner. "Look, Tim, I'm sorry. I told you I'm going to kill you, right? It can be easy, or it can be hard. You still think you can get out of this, but you can't. Even if you could, you'd be damned, Tim. You'd go to hell. Sayeth the Lord, 'Whosoever will save his life shall lose it; but whosoever will lose his life for my sake, the same shall save it.' Really, Tim, your best bet is to profess your faith, admit you are a sinner, and forgive me. Come on. Admit you've been a hypocrite all this time. It'll do you good."

Webber could only sob softly, his body convulsed.

"Please . . . forgive me."

No response.

"Say it!"

Blood began to mix with the pool of sweat beneath the chair. The light burned harshly as outside the shaded window the sun began to drop slowly toward the horizon. Dyer heaved a deep sigh.

"We could be here until midnight at this rate." He harrumphed disgustedly. "Let's start again." He rose, glanced at the cassette deck to check his tape. "Halfway through side two. That means we've been here over an hour. Your family will have a lot to endure when they hear this, don't you think? I hope you'll show them that you're really a fine husband and father and you're no longer a hypocrite. Hey . . . would you like to say something to them?" He picked up the microphone and held it in front of Webber's face. "Tell them hello. Say, 'Hi, Nancy. How are you? It's me, Tim.' Come on, say it."

Webber weakly gazed back at him, drooling blood from a bitten lip. Dyer suddenly thrust the razor behind his right ear, applying just enough pressure to bring a grimace of pain to Webber's face.

"Say it or lose the ear. Right now."

Taking a slow breath, Webber whispered, "Hi . . . Nancy."

"See!" Dyer exclaimed exuberantly. "Now we're getting somewhere. Say 'How are you?' Come on."

"How . . . are . . . you."

"Say, 'It's me, Tim.'"

"It's . . . me . . . Tim," he repeated, dropping his head in shame.

"Say, 'I love you, Nancy.'"

Webber tried not to speak. The pressure behind his ear grew sharper. "I love you," he blurted. "Nancy."

"Now say, 'I love you, Richard. I forgive you.' Say it."

The razor pressed hard.

"I . . . I . . . no."

The razor swept forward. The lobe and lower half of the ear fell away, accompanied by a deluge of rich blood. Webber screamed again, his voice high as a tortured sow, his back arching almost to the point of breaking.

Dyer stood up and paced. "Dammit, Tim, you're prideful. You're so certain you can hold out and get out of this somehow. But you're alienating yourself from the love of Christ. With an ego like that, you'll never get past St. Peter. 'How hardly shall he that has riches enter into the Kingdom of God,' sayeth the Lord. Jesus wasn't referring only to money, my man, no sir. You are rich in pride, Tim. It's a tough obstacle. But don't you see I'm here to help you?"

"You're twisting the truth into lies," Webber cried amid his pained breathing. "It's you that's the liar!"

"I forgive you for that," Dyer said. "You're hurt and angry, and I'm sure you're confused. But if a self-professed lunatic can do it, then surely a Christian man like you, a normal, *sane* man, can humble himself before God and do the right thing." He sighed and paced again. "Well, I don't have a lot of pride, like you. But I like to think of myself as a creative man. And now, I think I'd like to go fetch your daughters. I'll start with Ellen—she's the older one, right? I'll fuck her here in front of you, then I'll slaughter her like a little pig. Then it'll be Jenny, the younger one."

"No!" Webber screamed. "Don't you dare touch them! Fuck you, you son of a bitch! Damn you to hell! Damn you!"

Dyer sighed patiently, raised his razor easily, and drew a slow, deep gash down his victim's cheek. Webber's voice rose an octave.

"You . . . son . . . of . . . a . . . bitch."

Dyer checked the tape, found it very near the end of the side. "Gotta change the tape," he said, shutting it off and popping the Eject button. He removed the full cassette and replaced it in its case, then took a new one from the stack on his shelf. He inserted the blank cassette into the machine and began recording again. "Maybe we can get through this before the end of side one this time. Personally, I'm getting hungry and would like to get this over with so I can have some dinner. But of course, if staying here all night is what it takes, I'm willing to make that sacrifice.

"But Tim . . . I *am* going to kill you," he said loudly, for the benefit of the recorder. "And before you die, you *are* going to forgive me."

Tim Webber had lasted one more hour. He had finally admitted he was a sinner and forgiven Dyer as his torturer had decided he'd get nowhere without Webber's daughter Ellen. As Dyer was putting on his jacket to leave the house, Webber had broken down, pleading for him not to harm the young girl.

Satisfied at last, Dyer had slowly cut Webber's throat, leaning close to watch the life leave his victim's eyes. Webber choked on his own blood, his face contorted with his final agony. But he'd died with an expression of rage that dampened Dyer's hope for him. The man had lied again. He had not accepted the Lord and forgiven his transgressor. He had died a liar and a coward.

Thinking back on that now, Dyer realized that one failure had been his ultimate undoing. Despite his best efforts, he had been unable to reach the man with God's word. And those men before him had been no better. In fact, they had died violently, full of hate, having grown so uncontrollable that he'd had to kill them prematurely.

The straps now around his own wrists immobilized his hands. The cold metal beneath them was slippery with his sweat. He hated to admit it to himself, but he was afraid.

"The court of the state, having duly and rightly acted in accordance with the law, has found Richard Dean Dyer guilty on three counts of murder in the first degree, and as such has sentenced the guilty to death by electrocution. Sentence to be hereby carried out." The bailiff gave Dyer a penetrating stare. Behind him stood a priest and two armed officers, each eyeing him coldly, but with faces pale. The bailiff said, "Do you have any final remarks for the record before execution?"

Dyer looked sorrowfully at the priest. "I think this is a mistake. I'm psychotic, I told you that. There must be a new trial. They disregarded my insanity plea. It's not right."

Two officers checked the straps around his wrists and ankles, tightened them a final time. Then one of them lifted a roll of gauze tape and pulled off a length to be fitted around his eyes. The second held a black hood at the ready.

Frantically, Dyer shook his head. "Dammit, Father, I did it for the likes of you. I tried to help those people. I was closer than you've ever been to saving those souls! Are you listening, Father?"

The priest sadly closed his eyes, cleared his throat, and opened them again. "Please . . . no more, my son. It is too late. I suggest you pray with me. There isn't much time left."

Do you think you're going to get out of this?

Dyer gaped at his assassins standing ready to prep him for death. He heard the rattle of the metal bowl over his head as it was lowered.

Do you think I'm not going to kill you?

"You're all wrong," Dyer whispered. "So wrong."

The bailiff looked to the priest and shook his head. "It's time, Father. I suggest you give him his last rites."

The priest genuflected, and softly began to mouth the words of absolution. "My son, are you sorry for having offended God with all the sins of your past life?"

Dyer shut his ears. He was going to die. He would forgive them. He *had* to forgive them. He nodded.

"Ego te absolvo . . ."

Gauze tape covered his eyes, then was pulled taut. The black hood draped over his face and the metal helmet lowered with a final clang. He felt hot leather straps pulled around his chin, and a rubber mouthpiece was pushed roughly between his teeth. Then he could not even squirm. The chair embraced him with rigid finality. He felt water dripping over his hands, improving contact.

In a muffled voice, he managed, "I forgive you . . . I forgive you . . . I forgive . . ."

His words were cut short as his lips drew back in a fierce rictus. The first charge of fifteen hundred volts caught him like a fist. He felt his eyes bulge and his muscles convulse. His back felt blistered by a gust of fiery wind.

The next charge, three thousand volts, enlarged his heart by half its size. Smoke curled from beneath his fingers. Every hair on his body stood rigidly at attention.

"Forgive . . ." trailed away in his blackened brain.

SAFE

Gary A. Braunbeck

1

VIOLENCE NEVER REALLY ENDS, NO MORE THAN A SYMPHONY
ceases to exist once the orchestra has stopped playing;
bloodstains and bullet holes, fragments of shattered glass,
knife wounds that never heal properly, nightmarish memories that thrash the heart . . . all fasten themselves like a
leech to a person's core and suck away the spirit bit by bit
until there's nothing left but a shell that looks like it might
once have been a human being.

My God, what do you suppose happened to that person?

*I heard it was something awful. I guess they never got over
it—hell, you can just look at 'em and know that.*

Drop a pebble in a pool of water, and the vibrations
ripple outward in concentric circles. Some physicists claim
that the ripples continue even after they can no longer be
seen.

Ripples continue.

A symphony does not cease.

And violence never really ends.

It took half my life to learn that.

2

Three days ago, a man named Bruce Dyson walked into an ice cream parlor in the town of Utica, Ohio, and opened fire with a semiautomatic rifle, killing nine people and wounding seven others before shooting himself in the head.

Some cry, others rage, many turn away, and life will go on until the next Bruce Dyson walks into the next ice cream parlor, or bank, or fast-food restaurant; then we'll shake our heads, wring our hands once again, and wonder aloud how something so terrible could happen.

Newscasts were quick to mention Cedar Hill and draw tenuous parallels between what took place there and what happened in Utica. When one of my students asked me if I was "around" for the Cedar Hill murders, I laughed—not raucously, mind you, but enough to solicit some worried glances.

"Yes, I was around. Excuse my laughing, it's just that no one has ever asked me that before."

At a special teachers' meeting held the previous evening, a psychologist had suggested that we try to get our students to talk about the killings; four of the dead and three of the wounded had attended this school.

"Do any of you want to discuss what happened in Utica?"

Listen to their silence after I asked this.

"Look, I don't want to make anyone feel uncomfortable, but odds are someone in this room knew at least one of the victims. I know from experience it's not a good idea to keep something like this to yourself. You have to let someone know what's going on inside you."

Still nothing—a nervous shrug, perhaps, a lot of downcast stares, even a quiet tear from someone in the last row of desks, but no one spoke.

I rubbed my eyes and looked toward the back wall where the ghosts of the Cedar Hill dead were assembling.

Go on, they whispered. *Remember us to them.*

"Sixteen people were shot. You have to feel something about that."

A girl in one of the middle rows slowly raised her hand. "How did you . . . how'd you deal with what happened in Cedar Hill?"

"In many ways I still *am* dealing with it. I went back there a while ago to find some of the survivors and talk with them. I needed to put certain things to rest and—wait a second."

The ghosts of the four dead students joined those from Cedar Hill. All of them smiled at one another like old friends.

I wished I could have known them.

Tell them everything.

Go on.

I nodded my head, then said to the class: "Let's make a deal. I'll tell you about Cedar Hill only if you agree to talk about Utica. Maybe getting things out in the open will make it easier to live with. How's that sound?"

Another student raised a hand and asked, "Why do you suppose somebody'd do something like that?"

Tell the tale, demanded the ghosts.

Remember us to them . . .

3

I've gotten a little ahead of myself.

My name is Geoff Conover. I am thirty-six years old and have been a high school history teacher for the last seven years. I am married to a wonderful woman named Yvonne who is about to give birth to our first child, a boy. She has a six-year-old girl from her previous marriage. Her name is Patricia, and I love her very much and she loves me, and we both love her mother and are looking forward to having a new member added to our family.

This story is not about me, though I am in it briefly under a different name. It's about a family that no longer exists, a house that no longer stands, and a way of life once called

Small Town America that bled to death long before I explained to my students how violence never really ends.

I did go back to Cedar Hill in hopes of answering some questions about the night of the killings. I interviewed witnesses and survivors over the telephone, at their jobs, in their houses, over lunches, and in nursing homes; I dug through dusty files buried in moldy boxes in the basements of various historical society offices; there were decades-old police reports to be found, then sorted through and deciphered; I tracked down more than two hundred hours' worth of videotape, then subjected my family to the foul moods that resulted from my watching them; dozens of old statements had to be located and copied; and on one occasion I had to bribe my way into a storage facility in order to examine several boxes of aged evidence. There were graves to visit, names to learn, individual histories lost among bureaucratic paper trails that I had to assemble, only to find they yielded nothing of use—and I would be lying if I said that I did not feel a palpable guilt in deciding that so-and-so's life didn't merit so much as a footnote.

I do not purport to have sorted everything out. In some instances the gaps between facts were too wide and I had to fill them with conjectures and suppositions that, to the best of my knowledge and abilities, provided a *rightness* to the story that nothing else could. Yvonne says I did it to forgive myself for having survived, to be free of the shame, anger, guilt, and confusion that have for so long threatened to diminish me. She may be right. No one asked me to do it; nonetheless, certain ghosts demanded it of me—and I say this as a man who'd never thought of himself as being particularly superstitious.

I cleared my throat, smiled at the ghosts in the back of the room, and said to my students, "In order for you to understand . . ."

4

. . . what took place in Cedar Hill, you first have to understand the place itself, for it shares some measure of responsibility.

If it is possible to characterize this place by melting down all of its inhabitants and pouring them into a mold so as to produce one definitive citizen, then you will see a person who is, more likely than not, a laborer who never made it past the eleventh grade but who has managed through hard work and good solid horse sense to build the foundation of a decent middle-class existence; who works to keep a roof over his family's head and sets aside a little extra money each month to fix up the house, maybe repair that old back-door screen or add a workroom; who has one or two children who aren't exactly gifted but do well enough in school that their parents don't go to bed at night worrying that they've sired morons.

Perhaps this person drinks a few beers on the weekend—not as much as some of his rowdier friends but enough to be social. He's got his eye on some property out past the county line. He hopes to buy a new color television set. He usually goes to church on Sundays, not because he wants to but because, well, you never know, do you?

This is the person you would be facing.

This is the person who would smile at you, shake your hand, and behave in a neighborly fashion.

But never ask him about anything that lies beyond the next paycheck. Take care not to discuss anything more than work or favorite television shows or an article from this morning's paper. Complain about the cost of living, yes; inquire about his family, by all means; ask if he's got time to grab a quick sandwich, sure; but never delve too far beneath the surface, for if you do, the smile will fade, that handshake will loosen, and his friendliness will become tinged with caution.

Because this is a person who feels inadequate and does

not want you to know it, who for a good long while now has suspected that his life will never be anything more than mediocre. He feels alone, abandoned, insufficient, foolish, and inept, and the only thing that keeps him going sometimes is a thought that makes him both smile and cringe: that maybe one of *his* children will decide, *Hey, Dad's life isn't so bad, this burg isn't such a hole in the ground, so, yeah, maybe I'll just stick around here and see what I can make of things.*

And what if they do? How long until they start to walk with a workman's stoop, until they're buying beer by the case and watching their skin turn into one big nicotine stain? How long until they start using the same excuses he's used on himself to justify a mediocre life?

Bills, you know. Not as young as I used to be. Too damn tired all the time. Work'll by God take it out of you.

Ah, well . . . at least there's that property out past the county line for him to keep his eye on, and there's still that new color television set he might just up and buy . . .

Then he'll blink, apologize for taking up so much of your time, wish you a good day, and head on home because the family will be waiting supper.

It was nice talking to you.

Meet Cedar Hill, Ohio.

Let us imagine that it is evening here, a little after ten P.M. on the seventh of July, and that a pair of vivid headlight beams have just drilled into the darkness on Merchant Street. The magnesium-bright strands make one silent, metronome-like sweep, then coalesce into a single lucent beacon that pulls at the vehicle trailing behind.

Imagine that although the houses along Merchant are dark, no one inside them is asleep.

The van, its white finish long faded to a dingy gray, glides toward its destination. It passes under the diffuse glow coming down from the sole streetlight, and the words "Davies' Janitorial Service" painted on its side can be easily read.

The gleam from the dashboard's gauges reveals the driver

to be a tense, sinewy man whose age appears to fall somewhere between a raggedy-ass forty-five and a gee-you-don't-look-it sixty. In his deeply lined face are both resignation and dread.

He was running late, and he was not alone.

A phantom, its face obscured by alternating knife slashes of light and shadow, sat on the passenger side.

Three others rode in the back.

None of them could summon enough nerve to look beyond the night at the end of his nose.

The van came to a stop, the lights were extinguished, and with the click of a turned key, Merchant Street was again swallowed by the baleful graveyard silence that had recently taken up residence there.

The driver reached down next to his seat and grabbed a large flashlight. He turned and looked at the phantoms, who saw his eyes and understood the wordless command.

The driver climbed out as the phantoms threw open the rear double doors and began unloading the items needed for this job.

Merchant Street began to flicker as neighbors turned on their lights and lifted small corners of their curtains to peek at what was going on, even though no one really wanted to look at the Leonard house, much less live on the same street.

The driver walked up onto the front porch of the Leonard house. His name was Jackson Davies, and he owned the small janitorial company that had been hired to scour away the aftermath of four nights earlier, when this more or less peaceful industrial community of forty-two thousand had been dragged—kicking, screaming, and bleeding—into the national spotlight.

Davies turned on his flashlight, gliding its beam over the shards of broken glass that littered the front porch. As the shards caught the beam, each glared at him defiantly: *Come on, tough guy, big macho Vietnam vet with your bucket and Windex, let's see you take us on.*

He moved the beam toward a bay window on the right.

Like all the first-floor windows of the house, this one was covered by a large sheet of particle board crisscrossed by two strips of yellow tape. A long, ugly stain covered most of the outside sill, dribbling over the edge in a few places down onto the porch in thin, jagged streaks. Tipping the beam, Davies followed the streaks to another stain, darker than the mess on the sill and wider by a good fifty percent. Just outside this stain was a series of receding smears that stretched across the length of the porch and disappeared in front of the railing next to the glider.

Footprints.

Davies shook his head in disgust. Someone had tried to pry loose the board and get inside the house. Judging by the prints, they'd left in one hell of a hurry, running across the porch and vaulting the rail—scared away, no doubt, by neighbors or a passing police cruiser. Probably a reporter eager to score a hefty bonus by snapping a few graphic photos of the scene.

Davies swallowed once, loud and hard, then swung the light over to the front door. Spiderwebbing the frame from every conceivable angle were more strips of yellow tape emblazoned with large, bold, black letters: "Keep Out by Order of the Cedar Hill Police Department." An intimidating, hand-sized padlock held the door securely closed.

As he looked at the padlock, a snippet of Rilke flashed across his mind: *Who dies now anywhere in the world, without cause dies in the world, looks at me—*

And Jackson Davies, dropout English Lit major, recent ex-husband, former Vietnam vet, packer of body bags into the cargo holds of planes at Tan Son Nhut, onetime cleaner-upper of the massacre at My Lai 4, hamlet of Son My, Quang Ngai Province, a man who thought there was no physical remnant of violent death he didn't have the stomach to handle, began muttering, "Goddamn, god*damn, goddamn,*" and felt a lump dislodge from his groin and bounce up into his throat and was damned if he knew why, but suddenly the thought of going into the Leonard house scared the living shit out of him.

Unseen by Davies, the ghosts of Irv and Miriam Leonard sat on the glider a few yards away from him. Irv had his arm around his wife and was good-naturedly scolding her for slipping that bit of poetry into Davies's head.

I can't help it, Miriam said. *And even if I could, I wouldn't. Jackson read that poem when he was in Vietnam. It was in a little paperback collection his wife gave to him. He lost that book somewhere over there, you know. He's been trying to remember that poem all these years. Besides, he's lonely for his wife, and maybe that poem'll make it seem like part of her's still with him.*

Could've just gone to a library, said Irv.

He did, but he couldn't remember Rilke's name.

Think he'll remember it now?

I sure do hope so. Look at him, poor guy. He's so lonely, God love 'im.

Seems antsy, don't he?

Wouldn't you be? asked Miriam.

That was really nice of you, hon, giving that poem back to him. You always were one for taking care of your friends.

Charmer.

What can I say? Seems my disposition's improved considerably since I died.

Oh, now, don't go bringing that up. There's not much we can do about it.

How come that doesn't make me feel any better?

Maybe this'll do the trick, said Miriam. *"Who laughs now anywhere in the night, without cause laughs in the night, laughs at me."*

Don't tell me, tell the sensitive poetry soldier over there.

I just did.

They watched Davies for a few more seconds: he rubbed his face, then lit a cigarette and leaned against the porch railing and looked out into the street.

It's not right, said Irv to his wife. *What happened to us wasn't fair.*

Nothing is, dear. But we're through with all of that, remember?

If you say so.

Worrier.

Yeah, but at least I'm a charming worrier.

Shhh. Did you hear that?

Hear what?

The children are playing in the backyard. Let's go watch.

A moment later, the wind came up, and the glider swung back, then forward, once and once only, with a thin-edged screech.

Jackson Davies dropped his cigarette and decided, screw this, he was going to go wait down by the van.

He turned and ran into a phantom, then recoiled. The phantom stepped from the scar of shadow and into the flashlight's beam, becoming Pete Cooper, one of Davies's crew managers.

Davies, through clenched teeth, said, "It's not a real good idea to sneak up on me like that. I have a tendency to hurt people when that happens."

"Shakin' in my shoes," said Cooper. "You gettin' the jungle jitters again? Smell that napalm in the air?"

"Yeah, right. Whacked-out Nam vet doing the flashback boogie, that's me. Was there a reason you came up here, or did you just miss my splendid company?"

"I just . . ." Cooper looked over at the van. "Why'd you bring the Brennert kid along?"

"Because he said yes."

"C'mon, fer chrissakes! He was *here,* you know? When it happened?"

Davies sighed and fished a fresh cigarette from his shirt pocket. "First of all, he wasn't here when it happened, he was here *before* it happened. Second, of my forty-eight loyal employees, not counting you, only three said they were willing to come out here tonight, and Russ was one of them. Do you find any of this confusing so far? I could start again and talk slower."

"What're you gonna do if he gets in there and sees . . . well . . . everything and freezes up or freaks or something?"

"I talked to him about that already. He says he won't lose

it, and I believe him. Besides, the plant's going to be laying his dad off in a couple of weeks and his family could use the money."

"Fine. I'll keep the other guys in line, but Brennert is *your* problem."

"Anything else? The suspense is killing me."

"Just that this seems like an odd hour to be starting."

Davies pointed at the street. "Look around. Tell me what you don't see."

"I'm too tired for your goddamn riddles."

"You never were any fun. What you don't see are any *reporters* or any trace of their nauseating three-ring circus that blew into this miserable burg a few nights back. The county is paying us, and the county decided that our chances of being accosted by reporters would be practically nil if we came out late in the evening. So here we are, and I'm no happier about it than you are. Despite what people say, I do have a life. Admittedly, it isn't much of one since my wife decided that we get along better living in separate states, but it's a life nonetheless. I just thank God she left me the cats and the Mitch Miller sing-along records, or I'd be a sorry specimen right about now. To top it all off, I seem to have developed a retroactive case of the willies."

A police cruiser pulled up behind the van.

"Ah," said Davies. "That would be the keys to the kingdom of the dead."

"You plan to keep up the joking?"

Davies's face turned into a slab of granite. "Bet your ass I do. And I'm going to keep on joking until we're finished with this job and loading things up to go home. The sicker and more tasteless I can make them, the better. Don't worry if I make jokes; worry when I stop."

They went to meet the police officers, unaware that as they came down from the porch and started across the lawn, they walked right through the ghost of Andy Leonard, who stood looking at the house where he'd spent his entire, sad, brief, and ultimately tragic life.

5

On July fourth of that year, Irv Leonard and his wife were hosting a family reunion at their home at 182 Merchant Street. All fifteen members of their immediate family were present, and several neighbors stopped by to visit, watch some football, enjoy a hearty lunch from the ample buffet Miriam had prepared, and see Irv's newly acquired pearl-handled antique Colt Army .45 revolvers.

Irv, a retired steelworker and lifelong gun enthusiast, had been collecting firearms since his early twenties and was purported to have one of the five most valuable collections in the state.

Neighbors later remarked that the atmosphere in the house was as pleasant as you could hope for, though a few did notice that Andy—the youngest of the four Leonard children and the only one still living at home—seemed a bit "distracted."

Around 8:45 that evening, Russell Brennert, a friend of Andy's from Cedar Hill High School, came by after getting off work from his part-time job. Witnesses described Andy as being "abrupt" with Russell, as if he didn't want him to be there. Some speculated that the two might have had an argument recently that Andy was still sore about. In any case, Andy excused himself and went upstairs to "check on something."

Russell started to leave, but Miriam insisted he fix himself a sandwich first. A few minutes later, Andy—apparently no longer upset—reappeared and asked if Russell would mind driving Mary Alice Hubert, Miriam's mother and Andy's grandmother, back to her house. The seventy-three-year-old Mrs. Hubert, a widow of ten years, was still recovering from a mild heart attack in December and had forgotten to bring her medication. Brennert offered to take Mary Alice's house key and drive over by himself for the medicine, but Andy insisted Mrs. Hubert go along.

"I thought it seemed kind of odd," said Bill Gardner, a neighbor who was present at the time, "Andy being so bound and determined to get the two of them out of there before the fireworks started. Poor Miriam didn't know what to make of it all. I mean, I didn't think it was any of my business, but somebody should've said something about it. Andy started getting outright rude. If he'd been my kid, I'd've snatched him bald-headed, acting that way. And after his mom'd gone to all that fuss to make everything so nice."

Mrs. Hubert prevented things from getting out of hand by saying it would be best if she went with Russell; after all, she was an "old broad," set in her ways, and everything in an old broad's house had to be *just so* . . . besides, there were so many medicine containers in her cabinet, Russell might just "bust his brain right open" trying to figure out which was the right one.

As the two were on their way out, Andy stopped them at the door to give Mrs. Hubert a hug.

According to her, Andy seemed "really sorry about something. He's a strong boy, an athlete, and I don't care what anyone says, he should've got that scholarship. Okay, maybe he wasn't as bright as some kids, but he was a fine athlete, and them college people should've let that count for something. It was terrible, listening to him talk about how he was maybe gonna have to go to work at the factory to earn his college money . . . everybody knows where that leads. I'm sorry, I got off the track, didn't I? You asked about him hugging me when we left that night . . . well, he was always real careful when he hugged me never to squeeze too hard—these old bones can't take it . . . but when he hugged me then, I thought he was going to break my ribs. I just figured it was on account he felt bad about the argument. I didn't mean to create such a bother, I thought I had the medicine with me, but I . . . forget things sometimes.

"He kissed me on the cheek and said ''Bye, Grandma. I love you.' It wasn't so much the words, he always said that same thing to me every time I left . . . it was the way he said them. I remember thinking he was going to cry, that's how those words sounded, so I said, 'Don't worry about it. Your mom knows you didn't mean to be so surly.' I told him that when I got back, we'd watch the rest of the fireworks and then make some popcorn and maybe see a movie on the TV. He used to like doing that with me when he was littler.

"He smiled and touched my cheek with two of his fingers—he'd never done that before—and he looked at Russ like maybe he wanted to give him a hug, too, but boys that age don't hug each other, they think it makes them look like queers or something, but I could see it in Andy's eyes that he *wanted* to hug Russ.

"Then he said the strangest thing. He looked at Russ and kind of . . . *slapped* the side of Russ's shoulder—friendly, you know, like men'll do with each other when they feel too silly to hug? Anyway, he, uh, did that shoulder thing, then looked at Russ and said, 'The end is courage.' I figured it was a line from some movie they'd seen together. They love their movies, those two, always quoting lines to each other like some kind of secret code—like in *Citizen Kane* with 'Rosebud.' That kind of thing.

"It wasn't until we were almost to my house that Russ asked me if I knew what the heck Andy meant when he said that.

"I knew right then that something was wrong, terribly wrong. Oh Lord, when I think of it now . . . the . . . the *pain* a soul would have to be in to do something . . . like that . . ."

Russell Brennert and Mary Alice Hubert left the Leonard house at 9:05. As soon as he saw Brennert's car turn the corner at the end of the street, Andy immediately went back upstairs and did not come down until the locally sponsored Kiwanis Club fireworks display began at 9:15.

Several factors contributed to the neighbors' initial failure to react to what happened. First, there was the thunderous noise of the fireworks themselves. Since White's Field, the site of the fireworks display, was less than one mile away, the resounding boom of the cannons was, as one person described, "damn near loud enough to rupture your eardrums."

Second, music from a pair of concert hall speakers that Bill Gardner had set up in his front yard compounded the glass-rattling noise and vibrations of the cannons. "Every Fourth of July," said Gardner, "WLCB [a local low-wattage FM radio station] plays music to go along with the fireworks. You know, 'America the Beautiful,' 'Stars and Stripes Forever,' Charlie Daniels's 'In America,' stuff like that, and every year I tune 'em in and set my speakers out and let fly. Folks on this street want me to do it, they all like it.

"How the fuck was I supposed to know Andy was gonna flip out?"

Third and last, there were innumerable firecrackers being set off by neighborhood children. This not only added to the general racket but also accounted for the neighbors' ignoring certain visual clues once Andy moved outside. "You have to understand," said one detective, "that everywhere around these people, up and down the street, kids were setting off all different kinds of things: firecrackers, sparklers, bottle rockets, M-80s, for God's sake! Is it any wonder it took them so long to tell the difference between an exploding firecracker and the muzzle flash from a gun?

"Andy Leonard had to've been planning this for a long time. He knew there'd be noise and explosions and lights and a hundred other things to distract everyone from what he was doing."

At exactly 9:15 P.M., Andy Leonard walked calmly downstairs carrying three semiautomatic pistols—a Walther P.38 9mm Perabellum, a Mauser Luger 7.65mm, and a Coonan .357 Magnum—as well as an HK53 5.56mm assault rifle, all of which he'd taken from his father's massive oak gun cabinet upstairs.

Of the thirteen other family members present at that time, five—including Irv Leonard, sixty-two, and his oldest son, Chet, twenty-five—were outside watching the fireworks. Andy's two older sisters Jessica, twenty-nine, and Elizabeth, thirty-four (both of whose husbands were also outside), were in the kitchen hurriedly helping their mother put away the buffet leftovers so they could join the men on the front lawn.

Jessica's three children—Randy, age seven; Theresa, four; and Joseph, nine and a half months—were in the living room. Randy and his sister had just finished changing their baby brother's diaper and were strapping him into his safety seat so they could hurry up and get outside. Joseph thought they were playing with him and so thrashed and giggled a lot.

They didn't notice their uncle.

Elizabeth's two children—Ian, twelve, and Lori, nine—were thought to be already outside but were upstairs in the "toy room," which contained, among other items, a pool table and a twenty-seven-inch color television for use with Andy's extensive video game collection.

By the time Andy walked downstairs at 9:15, Ian and Lori were already dead, their skulls crushed by repeated blows with, first, a gun butt, then a pool cue, and, at the last, billiard balls that were crammed into their mouths after their jaws were wrenched loose.

Laying the HK53 across the top of the dinner table, Andy stuffed the Mauser and blood-spattered Walther into the waist of his jeans, then walked into the kitchen, raised the .357, and shot his sister Jessica through the back of her head. She was standing with her back to him, in the process of putting some food into the refrigerator. The hollow-point bullet blew out most of her brain and sheared away half of her face. When she dropped, she pulled two refrigerator shelves and their contents down with her.

Andy then shot Elizabeth—once in the stomach, once in the center of her chest—then turned the gun on his mother, shooting at point-blank range through her right eye.

After that, things happened very quickly. Andy left the kitchen and collided with his niece who was running toward the front door. He caught her by the hair and swung her face-first into a fifty-inch-high cast-iron statue that sat against a wall in the foyer. The statue was a detailed reproduction of the famous photograph of the American flag being raised on Mt. Suribachi at Iwo Jima.

Theresa slammed against it with such force that her nose shattered, sending bone fragments shooting backward down her throat. Still gripping her long strawberry-blond hair in his fist, Andy lifted her off her feet and impaled her by the throat on the tip of the flagstaff. The blood patterns on the wall behind the statue indicated an erratic arterial spray, leading the on-scene medical examiner to speculate she must have struggled to get free at some point; this, along with the increase in serotonin and free histamine levels in the wound, indicated Theresa had lived at least three minutes after being impaled.

Seven-year-old Randy saw his uncle impale Theresa on the statue, then grabbed the carrying handle of Joseph's safety seat and ran toward the kitchen. Andy shot him in the back of his right leg. Randy went down, losing his grip on Joseph's safety seat, which skittered across the blood-sopped tile floor and came to a stop inches from Jessica's body. Little Joseph, frightened and helpless in the seat, began to cry.

Randy tried to stand, but his leg was useless, so he began moving toward Joseph by kicking out with his left leg and using his elbows and hands to pull himself forward.

Nine feet away, Andy stood in the kitchen entrance watching his nephew's valiant attempt to save the baby.

Then he shot Randy between the shoulders.

And the kid kept moving.

As Andy took aim to fire again, the front door swung open, and Keith Shannon, Elizabeth's husband, stuck his head in and shouted for everyone to hurry up and come on.

Keith saw Theresa's body dangling from the statue and screamed over his shoulder at the other men out on the lawn, then ran inside, calling out the names of his wife and children.

He never stopped to see if Theresa was still alive.

Andy stormed across the kitchen and through the second, smaller archway that led into the rooms on the front left side of the house. As a result of taking this shortcut, he beat Keith to the living room by a few seconds, enabling him to take his brother-in-law by surprise. Andy emptied the rest of the Magnum's rounds into Keith's head and chest. One shot went wild and shattered the large front bay window.

Andy tossed the Magnum aside and pulled both the Mauser and the Walther from his jeans, holding one pistol in each hand. He bolted from the living room, through the dining room, and rounded the corner into the foyer just as Irv hit the top step of the porch.

Andy kicked open the front door. For the next fifteen seconds, while the sky ignited and Lee Greenwood sang how God should bless this country he loved, God bless the U.S.A., the front porch of the Leonard house became a shooting gallery as each of the four remaining adult males—at least two of whom were drunk—came up onto the porch one by one and was summarily executed.

Andy fired both pistols simultaneously, killing his father, his uncle Martin, his older brother Chet, and Tom Hamilton, Jessica's husband.

A neighbor across the street, Bess Paymer, saw Irv's pulped body wallop backward onto the lawn and yelled for her husband, Francis. Francis took one look out the window and said, "Someone's gone crazy." Bess was already dialing the police.

Andy went back into the house and grabbed the rifle off the dining-room table, picked up the Magnum as he passed back through the living room, then headed for the kitchen, where Randy, still alive, was attempting to drag Joseph through the back door. When he heard his uncle come into the kitchen, Randy reached out and grabbed a carving knife from the scattered contents of the cutlery drawer, which Miriam had wrenched free on her way down, then threw himself over his infant brother.

"That was one brave kid," an investigator said later. "Here he was, in the middle of all these bodies, he had two bullets in him so we know he was in a lot of pain, and the only thing that mattered to him was protecting his baby brother. An amazing kid. If there's one bright spot in all this, it's knowing that he loved his brother enough to . . . to . . . ah, hell, I can't talk about it right now."

For some reason, Andy did not shoot his nephew a third

time. He came across the kitchen floor and raised the butt of the rifle to bludgeon Randy's skull, and that's when Randy, in his last moments, pushed himself forward and jammed the knife in his uncle's calf. Then he died.

Andy dropped to the floor, screaming through clenched teeth, and pulled the knife from his leg. He grabbed his nephew's lifeless body and heaved it over onto its back, then beat its face in with his fists. After that, he loaded fresh clips into the pistols, grabbed Joseph, stumbled out the back door to the garage, and drove away in Irv's brand-new pickup.

At 9:21 P.M., the night duty dispatcher at the Cedar Hill Police Department received Bess Paymer's call. As was standard operating procedure, the dispatcher, while believing Bess had heard gunfire, asked if she were certain that someone had been shot. This dispatcher later defended this action by saying, "Every year we get yahoos all over this city who decide that the Kiwanis fireworks display is the perfect time to go out in their backyard and fire their guns off into the air—well, the Fourth and New Year's Eve, we get a lot of that. We had every unit out that night, just like every holiday, and there were drunks to deal with, bar fights, illegal fireworks being set off—M80s and such, traffic accidents . . . holidays tend to be a bit of a mess for us around here. Seems that's when everybody and their brother decides to act like a royal horse's ass.

"The point is, if we get a report of alleged gunfire during the fireworks, we're required to ask the caller if anyone's been hurt. If not, then we get to it as soon as we can. If we had to send a cruiser to check out every report of gunfire that comes in on the Fourth, we'd never get anything else done. I didn't do anything wrong. It's not my fault."

It took Bess Paymer and her husband the better part of two minutes to convince the dispatcher that someone had gone crazy over at the Leonard house and shot everyone.

Francis, furious by this point, grabbed the phone from his wife and informed the dispatcher in no uncertain terms that they'd better make it fast because he was grabbing his hunting rifle and going over there himself.

A cruiser was dispatched at 9:24 P.M.

At 9:27, a call came in from the Leonard house; by noon the next day, that phone call had been replayed on every newscast in the country:

"This is Francis Paymer. My wife and I called you a couple of minutes ago. I'm standing in the . . . the kitchen of the Leonard house . . . that's One-eighty-two Merchant Street . . . and I've got somebody's brains stuck to the bottom of my shoe.

"There's been a shooting here. A little girl's hanging in the hallway, and there's blood all over the walls and the floors, and I can't tell where one person's body ends and the next one begins because everybody's dead. I can still smell the gunpowder and smoke.

"Is that good enough for you to do something? C-could you maybe please if it's not too much trouble send someone out here NOW? It might be a good idea, because the crazy BASTARD WHO DID THIS ISN'T HERE—

"—and I think he might've took a baby with him."

By 9:30 P.M., Merchant Street was clogged with police cruisers.

And Andy Leonard was halfway to Moundbuilder's Park, where the Second Presbyterian Church was sponsoring Parish Family Night. More than one hundred people had been gathered at the park since five in the afternoon, picnicking, tossing Frisbees, playing checkers, or flying kites. A little before nine, the president of the Parish Council had arrived with a truckload of folding chairs that were set up in a clearing at the south end of the park.

By the time Francis Paymer made his famous phone call, one hundred seven parish members were seated in twelve neat little rows watching the fireworks display.

Between leaving his Merchant Street house and arriving at Moundbuilder's Park, Andy Leonard shot and killed six more people as he drove past them. Two were in a car; the other four had been sitting out on their lawns watching the fireworks. In every case, Andy simply kept one hand on the steering wheel while shooting with the other through an open window.

At 9:40 P.M., just as the fireworks kicked into high gear for the grand finale, Andy drove his father's pickup truck at eighty miles per hour through the wooden gate at the northeast side of the park, barreled across the picnic grounds, over the grassy mound that marked the south border, and went straight down into the middle of the spectators.

Three people were killed and eight others injured as the truck plowed into the back row of chairs. Then Andy threw open the door, leaped from the truck, and opened fire with the HK53. The parishioners scrambled in panic, many of them falling over chairs. Of the dead and wounded at the park, none was able to get farther than ten yards away before being shot.

Andy stopped only long enough to yank the pistols from the truck. The first barrage with the rifle was to disable; the second, with the pistols, was to finish off anyone who might still be alive.

At 9:45 P.M., Andy Leonard crawled up onto the roof of his father's pickup truck and watched the fireworks' grand finale. The truck's radio was tuned in to WLCB. The bombastic finish of *The 1812 Overture* erupted along with the fiery colors in the dark heaven above.

The music and the fireworks ended.

Whirling police lights could be seen approaching the park. The howl of sirens hung in the air like a protracted musical chord.

Andy Leonard shoved the barrel of the rifle into his mouth and blew most of his head off. His nearly decapitated body slammed backward onto the roof, then slid slowly down to the hood, smearing a long trail of gore over the center of the windshield.

Twenty minutes later, just as Russell Brennert and Mary Alice Hubert turned onto Merchant Street to find it blocked by police cars and ambulances, one of the officers on the scene at the park heard what he thought was the sound of a baby crying. Moments later, he discovered Joseph Hamilton, still alive and still in his safety seat, on the passenger-side floor of the pickup. The infant was clutching a bottle of formula that had been taken from his mother's baby bag.

6

I stopped at this point and took a deep breath, surprised to find that my hands were shaking. I looked to the ghosts, and they whispered, *Courage*.

I swallowed once, nodded my head, then said to my students, "That baby was me.

"I have no idea why Andy didn't kill me. I was taken away and placed in the care of Cedar Hill Children's Services." I opened my briefcase and removed a file filled with photocopies of old newspaper articles and began passing them around the room. I'd brought some of my research along in case I'd needed it to prompt discussion. "The details of how I came to be adopted by the Conover family of Waynesboro, Virginia, are written in these articles. Suffice it to say that I was perhaps the most famous baby in the country for the next several weeks."

One student held up a copy of an article and said, "It says here that the Conovers took you back to Cedar Hill six months after the killings. Says you were treated like a celebrity."

I looked at the photo accompanying the article and shook my head. "I have no memory of that at all. At home, in a box I keep in my filing cabinet, are hundreds of cards I received from people who lived in Cedar Hill at that time. Most of them are now either dead or have moved away. When I went back I could only find a few of them.

"It's odd to think that, somewhere out there, there are dozens, maybe even hundreds, of people who prayed for me when I was a baby, people I never knew and never will know. For a while I was at the center of their thoughts. I like to believe these people still think of me from time to time. I like to believe it's those thoughts and prayers that keep me safe from harm.

"But as I said in the beginning, this story isn't really

about me. If there's any great truth here, I'm not the one to say what it might be. The moment that officer found that squalling baby on the floor of that truck, I ceased to be a part of the story. But it's never stopped being a part of me."

7

Details were too sketchy for the eleven P.M. news to offer anything concrete about the massacre, but by the time the local network affiliates broadcast their news-at-sunrise programs, the tally was in.

Counting himself, Andy Leonard had murdered thirty-two people and wounded thirty-six others, making his spree the largest single mass shooting to date. (Some argued that since the shootings took place in two different locations they should be treated as two separate incidents, while others insisted that since Andy had continuously fired his weapons up until the moment of his death, including the trail of shootings between his house and the park, it was all one single incident. What could not be argued was the body count, which made the rest of it more than a bit superfluous.)

Those victims were what the specter of my uncle was thinking about as Jackson Davies and Pete Cooper walked through him.

Andy's ghost hung its head and sighed, then took one half-step to the right and vanished back into the ages where it would relive its murderous rampage in perpetuity, always coming back to the moment it stood outside the house and watched as two men passed through it on their way toward a police officer.

8

Russell Brennert looked at the two other janitors who'd come along tonight and knew without asking that neither one of them wanted him to be here. Of course not, *he* had known the crazy fucker, *he* had been Andy Leonard's best friend, *his* presence made it all just a bit more real than they wanted it to be. Did they think that some part of what had driven Andy to kill all of those people had rubbed off on him as well? Probably—at least that would explain why they hadn't told him their names.

Hell with it, he thought. Call them Mutt and Jeff, and leave it at that.

He checked to make sure each plastic barrel had plenty of extra trash bags. Then Mutt came over and, fighting the smirk trying to sneak onto his face, asked, "Hey, Brennert—that's your name, right?"

"Yeah."

"We were just wonderin' if, well, it's true, y'know?"

"If *what's* true?"

Mutt gave a quick look to Jeff, who turned away and oh-so-subtly covered his mouth with his hand.

Russell dug his fingernails into his palms to keep from getting angry; these guys were going to pull something, or say something, he just knew it.

Mutt sniffed dryly as he turned back to Russell. He'd given up trying to fight back the smirk on his face.

Russell bit his lower lip. *Stay cool, you can do it, you need the money* . . .

"We'd just been wonderin'," said Mutt, "if it's true that you and Leonard used to . . . go to the movies together."

Jeff snorted a laugh and tried to cover it up by coughing.

Russell held his breath. "Sometimes, yeah."

"Just the two of you, or you guys ever take dates?"

You're doing fine, just fine, he's a mutant, just keep that in mind . . .

"Sometimes it was just him and me. Sometimes he'd bring Barb along."

"Yeah, yeah . . ." Mutt leaned in, lowering his voice to a mock-conspiratorial whisper. "The thing is, we heard that the two of you went to the drive-in together a couple of days before he shot everybody."

Fine and dandy, yessir. "That's right. Barb was going to

come along, but she had to baby-sit her sister at the last minute."

Mutt chewed on his lower lip to bite back a giggle. Russell caught a peripheral glimpse of Davies and Cooper heading back up to the porch with one of the cops.

"How come you and your buddy went to the drive-in all by yourselves?"

"We wanted to see the movie." *Jesus, Jackson, get down here, will you?*

Russell didn't hear all of the next question because the pulsing of his blood sounded like a jackhammer in his ears.

". . . thigh?"

Russell blinked, exhaled, and dug his nails in a little deeper. "I'm sorry, could you run that by me again?"

"I said, last week after gym when we was all in the showers, I noticed you had a sucker bite on your thigh."

"Birthmark."

"You sure about that? Seemed to me it looked like a big ol' hickey."

"Stare at my thighs a lot, do you?"

Mutt's face went blank. Jeff jumped to his feet and snarled, "Hey, watch it, motherfucker."

"Watch what?" snapped Russell. "Why don't you feebs just leave me alone? I've got better things to do than be grilled by a couple of redneck homophobes."

"Ha! *Homo*, huh?" said Mutt. "I always figured the two of you musta been butt buddies."

"Fag bags," said Jeff, then the two flaming wits high-fived each other.

Russell suddenly realized that one of his hands had reached over and gripped a mop handle. *Don't do it, Russ, don't you dare, they're not worth it.* "Think whatever you want. I don't care." He turned away from them in time to see a bright blue van pull up behind the police cruiser. A small satellite dish squatted like a gargoyle on top of the van, and Russell could see through the windshield that Ms. Tanya Claymore, Channel 9's red-hot news babe, was inside.

"Oh shit," he whispered.

One of the reasons he'd agreed to help out tonight—the money aside—was so he wouldn't have to stay at home and hear the phone ring every ten minutes and answer it to find some reporter on the other end asking for Mr. Russell Brennert, oh this is him, I'm Whatsisname from the In-Your-Face Channel, Central Ohio's News Authority, and I wanted to ask you a few questions about Andy Leonard blah-blah-blah.

It had been like that for the last three days. He'd hoped that coming out here tonight would give him a reprieve from everyone's constant questions, but it seemed—

—*put the ego in park, Russ. Yeah, maybe they called the house and Mom or Dad told them you'd be out here, but it's just possible they came out in hopes of getting inside the house for a few minutes' worth of video for tomorrow's news.*

Mutt smacked the back of his shoulder much harder than was needed just to get his attention. "Hey, yo! Brennert, I'm talking to you."

"Please leave me alone? Please?"

All along the murky death membrane that was Merchant Street, porch lights snapped on and ghostly forms shuffled out in bathrobes and housecoats, some with curlers in their hair or shoddy slippers on their feet.

Mutt and Jeff both laughed, but not too loudly.

"What's it like to cornhole a psycho, huh?"

"I—" Russell swallowed the rest of the sentence and started toward the house, but Mutt grabbed his arm, wrenching him backward and spinning him around.

One of the tattered specters grabbed her husband's arm and pointed from their porch to the three young men by the van. Did it look like there was some trouble?

The ghosts of Irv and Miriam Leonard, accompanied by their grandchildren Ian, Theresa, and Lori, stood off to the side of the house and watched as well. Irv shook his head in disgust, and Miriam wiped at her eyes and thought she felt her heart aching for Russell, such a nice boy, he was.

On the porch of the Leonard house, an impatient Jackson

Davies waited while the officer ripped down the yellow tape and inserted the key into the lock.

"Jackson?" said Pete Cooper.

"What?"

Cooper cleared his throat and lowered his voice. "Do you remember what you said about no reporters being around?"

"Yeah, so wha—" Then he saw the Channel 9 news van. "Ah, fuck me with a fiddlestick! They plant a homing device on that poor kid or something?" He watched Tanya Claymore slide open the side door and lower one of her too-perfect legs toward the ground like some Hollywood starlet exiting a limo at a movie premiere.

"Dammit, I *told* you bringing Brennert along would be a mistake."

"Thank you, Mr. Hindsight. Let *me* worry about it?"

Cooper gestured toward the news van and said, "Aren't you gonna do something?"

"I don't know if I can." Davies directed this remark to the police officer unlocking the door. The officer looked over his shoulder and shrugged, then said, "If she interferes with your crew performing the job you pay them for, you've got every right to tell her to go away."

"Just make sure you get her phone number first," said Cooper.

Davies turned his back to them and stared at Tanya Claymore. If she even so much as *looked* at Russell, he'd drop on her like a curse from heaven.

Down by the trash barrels and buckets, Mutt was standing less than an inch from Russell's face and saying, "All right, bad-ass, let's get to it. People're sayin' that you maybe knew what Andy was gonna do and didn't say anything."

"I didn't," whispered Russell. "I didn't know."

Some part of him realized that Tanya's cameraman had turned on his light and was taping them, but he was backed too far into a corner to care right now.

"Yeah," said Mutt contemptuously. "I'll just bet you didn't."

"I *didn't* know, all right? He never said . . . a thing to me."

"According to the news, he was in an awful hurry to get you out before he went gonzo."

For a moment, Russell found himself back in the car with Mary Alice, turning the corner and being almost blinded by visibar lights, then that cop came over and pounded on the window and said, "This area's restricted for the moment, kid, so you're gonna have to—" and Mary Alice shouted, "Is that the Leonard house? Did something happen to my family?" And then the cop shone his flashlight in and asked, "You a relative, ma'am?" and Mary Alice was already in tears, and Russell felt something boiling up from his stomach because he saw one of the bodies being covered by a sheet, and then Mary Alice screamed and fell against him and a sick cloud of pain descended on their skulls—

"I had no idea, okay?" The words fell to the ground in a heap. Russell thought he could almost see them groan before the darkness put them out of their misery. "Do I have to keep on saying that, or should I just write it in braille and shove it up—"

"—you knew, you *had* to know!" The mean-spirited mockery of earlier was gone from Mutt's voice, replaced by anger with some genuine hurt wrapped around it. "He was your best friend!"

You need the money, Russell.

"Two of 'em was always together," said Jeff, just loud enough for the microphone to get every word. "Everybody figured that Brennert here was gay and was in love with Andy."

Three hundred dollars, Russell. Grocery money for a month or so. Mom and Dad will appreciate it.

It seemed that both of his hands were gripping the mop handle, and somehow that mop was no longer in the bucket.

He heard a chirpy voice go into its popular singsong mode: "This is Tanya Claymore. I'm standing outside the house of Irving and Miriam Leonard at One-eighty-two Merchant Street, where—"

"You wanna do something about it?" said Mutt, pushing Russell's shoulder. "Think you're man enough to mess with me?"

Russell was only vaguely aware of Davies coming down from the porch and shouting something at the news crew; he was only vaguely aware of the second police officer climbing from the cruiser and making a beeline to Ms. News Babe; and he was only vaguely aware of Mutt saying, "How come you came along to help with the cleanup tonight? Idea of seeing all that blood and brains get you hard, does it? You a sick fuck just like Andy?" But the one thing of which he was fully, almost gleefully aware was that the mop had become a javelin in his hands and he was going to go for the gold and hurl the thing right into Mutt's great big ugly target of a mouth—

Three hundred dollars should just about cover the emergency room bill—

Then a hand clamped down so hard on Mutt's shoulder that Russell thought he heard bones crack.

Jackson Davies's smiling face swooped in and hovered between them. "If you're finished with this nerve-tingling display of machismo, we have a house to clean, remember?" Still clutching Mutt's shoulder in a Vulcan death-grip, Davies hauled the boy around and pushed him toward one of the barrels. "Why can't you use your powers for good?"

"Hey, we were just—"

"I know what you were *just,* thank you very much. I'd appreciate it"—he gestured toward Jeff—"if you and the Boy Wonder here would get off your asses and start carrying supplies inside." Russell reached for a couple of buckets, but Davies stopped him. "Not you, Ygor. You stay here with me for a second." Mutt and Jeff stood staring as Ms. News Babe came jiggling up to Russell in all of her journalistic glory.

Davies glowered at the two boys and said, "Yes, her bazooba-wobblies are very big, and no, you can't touch them. Now get moving before I become unpleasant."

They became a blur of legs and mop buckets.

Russell said, "Mr. Davies, I'm sorry, but—"

"Hold that thought."

Tanya and her cameraman were almost on top of them; a microphone came toward their faces like a projectile.

"Russell?" said Tanya. "Russell, hi. I'm Tanya Claymore, and—"

"A friend of mine once stepped on a Claymore," said Davies. "Made his sphincter switch places with his eardrums. I was scraping his spleen off my face for a week. Please don't bother any member of my crew, Ms. Claymore."

The reporter's startling green eyes widened. She made a small, quick gesture with her free hand, and her cameraman swung around to get Davies into the frame.

"We'd like to talk to *both* of you, Mr. Davies—"

"Go away." Davies looked at Russell, and the two of them grabbed the remaining buckets and barrels and started toward the house.

Tanya Claymore sneered at Davies's back, then turned around and waved to the driver of the news van. He looked over, and she mimed talking into a telephone receiver. The driver nodded his head and picked up the cellular phone. Tanya gave her mike to the cameraman and took off after Davies.

"Mr. Davies, please, could you—dammit, I'm in heels! Would you wait a second?"

"She wants me," whispered Davies to Russell. Despite everything, Russell gave a little smile. He liked Jackson Davies a lot and was glad this man was his boss.

Tanya stumbled up the incline of the lawn and held out one of her hands for Davies to take hold of and help her.

"Are those fingernails real or press-ons?" asked Davies, not making a move.

Russell put down his supplies and gave her the help she needed. As soon as she reached level ground, she offered a sincere smile and squeezed his hand in thanks.

Davies said, "What's it going to take to make you leave us alone?"

Her eyes hardened, but the smile remained. "All I want is to talk to the both of you about what you're going to do."

"It's a little obvious, isn't it?"

"Central Ohio would like to know."

"Oh," said Davies. "I see. You're in constant touch with

central Ohio? Champion of the common folk in your fake nails and designer dress and tinted contacts?"

"Does all that just come to you or do you write down ahead of time and memorize it?"

"You're not being very nice."

"Neither are you."

They both fell silent and stood staring at each other.

Finally, Davies sighed and said, "Could we at least get our stuff inside and get started first? I could come out in a half hour and talk to you then."

"What about Russell?"

Russell half raised his hand. *"Russell* is right here. Please don't talk about me in third person."

"Sorry," said Tanya with a grin. "You haven't talked to *any* reporters, Russell. I don't know if you remember, but you've hung up on me twice."

"I know. I was gonna send you a card to apologize. We always watch you at my house. My mom thinks you look like a nice girl, and my dad's always had a thing for redheads."

Tanya leaned a little closer to him and said, "What about you? Why do you like watching me?"

Russell was glad that it was so dark out, because he could feel himself blushing. "I, uh . . . I—look, Ms. Claymore, I don't know what I could say to you about what happened that you don't already know."

The radio in the police cruiser squawked loudly, and the officer down by the vans leaned through the window to grab the mike.

"All right," said Tanya, looking from Davies to Russell, then back to Davies again. "I won't lie to either of you. The news director would really, really prefer that I come back tonight with some tape either of Russell or the inside of the house. I almost had to beg him to let me do this tonight. Don't take this the wrong way—especially you, Russell— but I'm sick to death of being a talking head. Don't ever repeat that to anyone. If—"

"Oh, allow me," said Davies. "If you don't come back tonight with a really boffo piece, you'll be stuck reading

TelePrompTers and covering new mall openings for the rest of your career, right?"

Tanya said nothing.

Russell looked over at his boss. "Uh, look, Mr. Davies, if this is gonna be a problem, I can—"

"She's lying, Russ. Her news director is all hot to trot for some shots of the inside of the house, and he'll do anything for the exclusive pictures, won't he? Up to and including having his most popular female anchor lay a sob story on us that sounds like it came out of some overbaked nineteen-forties melodrama. Nice try, though. Goddammit—it wouldn't surprise me if you and your crew were the ones who tried to break in."

Tanya looked startled. "What? Someone tried to break into the house?"

"Wrong reading, sister. Don't call us, we'll call you."

The hardness in Tanya's eyes now bled down into the rest of her face. "Fine, Mr. Davies. Have it your way."

The officer in the cruiser walked up to his partner on the porch, and the two of them whispered for a moment, then came down toward Davies and Tanya.

"Mr. Davies," said the officer who'd unlocked the door, "we just received orders that Ms. Claymore and her camera-man are to be allowed to photograph the inside of the house."

Behind her back, Tanya gave a thumbs-up to the driver of the news van.

"What'd you do," asked Davies, "have your boss call in a few favors, or did you just promise to fuck the mayor?"

"Mr. Davies," said one of the officers. The warning in his voice was quite clear. "Ms. Claymore can photograph only the foyer and one other room. You'll all go in at the same time. I will personally escort Ms. Claymore and her camera-man into, through, and out of the house. She can only be inside for ten minutes, no more." He turned toward Tanya. "I'm sorry, Ms. Claymore, those're our orders. If you're inside longer than ten minutes, we're to consider it to be trespassing and are to act accordingly."

"Well," she said, straightening her jacket and brushing a thick strand of hair from her eye, "it's nice to see that the First Amendment's alive and well and being slowly choked to death in Cedar Hill."

"You should attend one of our cross burnings sometime," said Davies.

"You're a jerk."

"How would you know? You never attend the meetings."

"That's enough, boys and girls," said Officer Lock and Key. "Could we move this along, please?"

"One thing," said Tanya. "Would it be all right if we got some shots of the outside of the house first?"

"You'd better make it fast," said Davies. "I feel a record-time cleaning streak coming on."

"Or I could get them later."

Russell had already walked away from the group and was setting his supplies on the porch. The front door was open and the overhead light in the foyer had been turned on, and he caught sight of a giant red-black spider clinging to the right-side wall—

He turned quickly away and took a breath, pressing one of his hands against his stomach.

Mutt and Jeff laughed at him as they walked into the house.

Pete Cooper shook his head and dismissed Russell with a wave of his hand.

The ghosts of the Leonard family surrounded Russell on the porch, Irv placing a reassuring hand on the boy's shoulder while Miriam stroked his hair and the children looked on in silence.

Tanya Claymore's cameraman caught Russell's expression on tape.

It wasn't until Jackson Davies came up and took hold of his hand that Russell snapped out of his fugue and, without saying a word, got to the job.

And all along Merchant Street, shadowy forms in their housecoats and slippers watched from the safety of front porches.

9

Even more famous than Francis Paymer's phone call is Tanya Claymore's videotape of that night. It ran four and a half minutes and was the featured story on Channel 9's six o'clock news broadcast the following evening. Viewer response was so overwhelming that the tape was broadcast again at seven and eleven P.M., then at six A.M. and noon the next day, then again, reedited to two minutes, forty-five seconds, at seven and eleven P.M.

It is an extraordinary piece of work, and I showed it to my students that day. I eventually received an official reprimand from the school board for doing it—several of the students had nightmares about it, compounding those about the Utica killings—but I thought they needed to see and hear other people, strangers, express what they themselves were feeling.

The ghosts wanted to see it again, as well.

As did I—and why not? In a way, it is not so much about the aftermath of a tragedy as it is a chronicle of my birth, a point of reference on the map of my life: *This is where I really began.*

10

The tape opens with a shot of the Leonard house, bathed in shadow. Dim figures can be seen moving around its front porch. Sounds of footsteps. A muffled voice. A door being opened. A light coming on. Then another. And another.

Silhouettes appear in an upstairs window. Unmoving.

The camera pulls back slightly. Seen from the street, the lights from the house form a pattern of sorts as they slip out from the cracks in the particleboard over the downstairs windows.

It takes a moment, but suddenly the house looks like it's smiling. And it is not a pleasant smile.

All of this takes perhaps five seconds. Then Tanya Claymore's voice chimes softly in as she introduces herself and says, "I'm standing outside the house of Irving and Miriam Leonard at One-eighty-two Merchant Street, where, as you know, four nights ago their son Andy began a rampage that would leave over thirty people dead and over thirty more wounded."

At that very moment, someone inside the house kicks against the sheet of particleboard over the front bay window and wrenches it loose while a figure on the porch uses the claw end of a hammer to pull it free. The board comes away, and a massive beam of light explodes outward, momentarily filling the screen.

The camera smoothly shifts its angle to deflect the light. As it does so, Tanya Claymore resolves into focus like a ghost on the right side of the screen. Whether it was purposefully done this way or not, the effect is an eerie one.

She says, "Just a few moments ago, accompanied by two members of the Cedar Hill Police Department, a team of janitors entered the Leonard house to begin what will most certainly be one of the grimmest and most painful cleanups in recent memory."

She begins walking up toward the front porch, and the camera follows her. "Experts tell us that violence never really ends, no more than a symphony ceases to exist once the orchestra has stopped playing."

As she gets closer to the front door, the camera moves left while she moves to the right and says, "And like the musical resonances that linger in the mind after a symphony, the ugliness of violence remains."

By now she has stepped out of camera range, and the dark, massive bloodstain on the foyer wall can be clearly seen.

At the opposite end of the foyer, a mop head drenched in foamy soap suds can be seen slapping against the floor. It makes a wet, sickening sound. The camera slowly zooms in on the mop and focuses on the blood that is mixed in with the suds.

The picture cuts to a well-framed shot of Tanya's head

and shoulders. It's clear she's in a different room, but which room it might be is hard to tell. When she speaks, her voice sounds slightly hollow and her words echo.

"This is the only time that a news camera will be allowed to photograph the interior of the Leonard house. You're about to see the kitchen where Miriam Leonard and her two daughters, Jessica Hamilton and Elizabeth Shannon, spent the last few seconds of their lives, and where seven-year-old Randy Hamilton, with two bullets in his small body, fought to save the life of his infant brother, Joseph.

"The janitors have not been in here yet, so you will be seeing the kitchen just as it was when investigators finished with it."

For a moment, it looks as if she might say something else, then she lowers her gaze and steps to the left as the camera moves slightly to the right and the kitchen is revealed.

The sight is numbing.

The kitchen is a slaughterhouse. The contrast between the blood and the off-white walls lunges out at the viewer like a snarling beast escaping from its cage.

The camera pans down to the floor and follows a single splash pattern that quickly grows denser and wider. Smeary heel- and footprints can be seen. The camera moves upward: part of a handprint in the center of a lower counter door. The camera moves farther up: the mark of four bloody fingers on the edge of the sink. The camera moves over the top of the sink in a smooth, sweeping motion and stares at a thick, crusty black whirlpool twisting down into the garbage disposal drain.

The camera suddenly jerks up and whips around, blurring everything for a moment, a dizzying effect, then comes to an abrupt halt. Tanya is standing in the doorway of the kitchen with her right arm thrust forward. In her hand is a plastic pistol.

"This is a rough approximation of the last thing Elizabeth Shannon saw before her youngest brother shot her to death."

She remains still for a moment. Viewers cannot help but put themselves in Elizabeth's place.

Tanya slowly lowers the pistol and says, "The question for which there seems to be no answer is, naturally, 'Why did he do it?'

"We put that question to several of the Leonards' neighbors this evening. Here's what some of them had to say about seventeen-year-old Andy, a young man who now holds the hideous distinction of having murdered more people in a single sweep than any killer in this nation's history."

Jump-cut to a quick, complicated series of shots.

Shot 1: An overweight man with obviously dyed hair saying, "I hear they found a tumor in his brain."

Insert shot: Merchant Street as it looked right after the shootings, clogged with police cruisers and ambulances and barricades to keep the growing crowd at bay.

Shot 2: A middle-aged woman with curlers in her hair saying, "I'll bet you anything it was his father's fault, him bein' a gun lover and all. I heard he beat on Andy a lot."

Insert shot: Lights from a police car rhythmically moving over a sheet-covered body on the front lawn.

Shot 3: An elderly gentleman in a worn and faded smoking jacket saying, "I read there were all these filthy porno magazines and videotapes stashed under his mattress, movies of women having relations with animals and pictures of babies in these leather sex getups . . ."

Insert shot: Two emergency medical technicians carrying a small black body bag down the front porch steps.

Shot 4: A thirtyish woman in an aerobics leotard saying, "I felt that he was always a little *too* nice, you know? He never got . . . angry about anything."

Insert shot: A black-and-white photograph of Andy taken from a high school yearbook. He's smiling, and his hair is neatly combed. He's wearing a tie. The voice of the woman in shot 4 can still be heard over this photo, saying, "He was always so calm. He never laughed much, but there was this . . . *smile* on his face all the time . . ."

Shot 5: A little girl of six, most of her hidden behind a parent's leg, saying, "I heard the house was haunted and that ghosts told him to do it . . ."

Insert shot: A recent color photograph of Andy and Russell Brennert at a Halloween party, both of them in costume. Russell is Frankenstein's monster, and Andy, his face painted to resemble a smiling skeleton, wears the black hooded cloak of the Grim Reaper. He's holding a plastic scythe whose tip is resting on top of Russell's head. The camera moves in on Russell's face until it fills the screen, then abruptly cuts to a shot of Russell in the foyer of the Leonard house. He's on his knees in front of the massive bloodstain on the wall. He's wearing rubber gloves and is pulling a large sponge from a bucket of soapy water. A caption at the bottom of the screen reads: "Russell Brennert, friend of the Leonard family."

He squeezes the excess water from the sponge and lifts it toward the stain, then freezes just before the sponge touches the wall.

He is trembling but trying very hard not to.

Tanya's shadow can be seen in the lower righthand corner of the frame. She asks, "How do you feel right now?"

Russell doesn't answer her, only continues to stare at the stain.

Tanya says, "Russell?"

He blinks, shudders slightly, then turns his head and says, "Wh-what? I'm sorry."

"What were you thinking just then?"

He stares in her direction, then gives a quick glance to the camera. "Does he have to point that damn thing at me like that?"

"You have to talk to a reporter eventually. You might as well do it now."

He bites his lower lip for a second, then exhales and looks back at the stain.

"What're you thinking about, Russell?"

"I remember when Jessie first brought Theresa home from the hospital. Everyone came over here to see the new baby. You should've seen Andy's face."

Brennert's voice begins to quaver. The camera slowly moves in closer to his face. He is oblivious to it.

"He was so . . . *proud* of her. You'd have thought she was *his* daughter."

He reaches out with the hand not holding the sponge and presses it against the stain. "She was so tiny. But she couldn't stop giggling. I remember that she grabbed one of my fingers and started . . . chewing on it, you know, like babies will do? And Andy and I looked at each other and smiled and yelled, 'Uncle attack!' and he s-started . . . he started kissing her chubby little face, and I bent down and put my mouth against her tummy and started blowing real hard, you know, making belly-farts, and it tickled her so much because she started giggling and laughing and squealing and k-kicking her legs . . ."

The cords in his neck are straining. Tears well in his eyes, and he grits his teeth in an effort to hold them back.

"The rest of the family was enjoying the hell out of it, and Theresa kept squealing . . . that delicate little-baby laugh. Jesus Christ . . . he *loved* her. He loved her *so much,* and I thought she was the most precious thing . . . she always called me 'Uncleruss'—like it was all one word."

The tears are streaming down his cheeks now, but he doesn't seem aware of it.

"I held her against my chest. I helped give her baths in the sink. I changed her diapers—and I was a helluva lot better at it than Andy ever was . . . and now I gotta . . . I gotta scrub this off the wall."

He pulls back his hand, then touches the stain with only his index finger, tracing indiscernible patterns in the dried blood.

"This was her. This is all that's . . . that's left of the little girl she was, the baby she was . . . the woman she might have grown up to be. He loved her." His voice cracks, and he begins sobbing. "He loved all of them. And he never said anything to me. I didn't know, I swear to *Christ* I didn't know. This was her. I—oh, *goddammit!*"

He drops down onto his ass and folds his arms across his knees and lowers his head and weeps.

A few moments later, Jackson Davies comes in and sees him and kneels down and takes Russell in his arms and rocks gently back and forth, whispering, "It's all right now, it's okay, it's over, you're safe, hear me? Safe. Just . . . give it to me, kid . . . you're safe . . . that's it . . . give it to me . . ."

Davies looks up into the camera, and the expression on his face needs no explaining: *Turn that fucking thing off.*

Cut to: Tanya, outside the house again, standing next to the porch steps. On the porch, two men are removing the broken bay window. A few jagged shards of glass fall out and shatter on the porch. Another man begins sweeping up the shards and dumping them into a plastic trash barrel.

Tanya says, "Experts tell us that violence never really ends, that the healing process may never be completed, that some of the survivors will carry their pain for the rest of their lives."

A montage begins at this point, with Tanya's closing comments heard in voice-over.

The image, in slow motion, of police officers and EMTs moving sheet-covered and black-bagged bodies.

"People around here will say that the important thing is to remove as many physical traces of the violence as possible. Mop up the blood, gather the broken glass fragments into a bag and toss it in the trash, cover the scrapes, cuts, and stitches with bandages, then put your best face forward because it will make the unseen hurt easier to deal with."

The image of the sheet-covered bodies cross-fades into film of a memorial service held at Randy Hamilton's grade school. A small choir of children is gathered in front of a picture of Randy and begins to sing. Underneath Tanya's voice can now be heard a few dozen tiny voices softly singing "Let There Be Peace on Earth."

"But what of that 'unseen hurt'? A bruise will fade, a cut will get better, a scar can be taken off with surgery. Cedar Hill must now concern itself with finding a way to heal the scars that aren't so obvious."

The image of the children's choir dissolves into film of Mary Alice Hubert standing in the middle of the chaos outside the Leonard house on the night of the shootings.

She is bathed in swirling lights and holds both of her hands pressed against her mouth. Her eyes seem unnaturally wide and are shimmering with tears. Police and EMTs scurry around her, but none stops to offer help. As the choir sings, "To take each moment and live each moment in peace e-ter-nal-ly," she drops slowly to her knees and lowers her head as if in prayer.

Tanya's voice-over continues: "Maybe tears will help. Maybe grieving in the open will somehow lessen the grip that the pain has on this community. Though we may never know what drove Andy Leonard to commit his horrible crime, the resonances of his slaughter remain."

Mary Alice dissolves into the image of Russell Brennert kneeling before the stain on the foyer wall. He is touching the dried blood with the index finger of his left hand.

The children's choir is building to the end of the song as Tanya says, "Perhaps Cedar Hill can find some brief comfort in these lines from a poem by German lyric poet Rainer Maria Rilke: 'Who weeps now anywhere in the world, without cause weeps in the world, weeps over me.'"

The screen fills with the image of Jackson Davies embracing Russell as sobs rack his body. Davies glares up at the camera, then closes his eyes and lowers his face, kissing the top of Russell's head. This image freezes as the children finish singing their hymn.

Tanya's voice once more, soft and low, no singsong mode this time, no inflection whatsoever: "For tonight, who weeps anywhere in the world, weeps for Cedar Hill and its wounds that may never heal.

"Tanya Claymore, Channel 9 News."

11

After the tape had finished playing and the lights in the classroom were turned back on, a student near the back of the room—so near, in fact, that Irv Leonard's ghost could have touched the boy's head, if he'd chosen to—raised his hand and asked, "What happened to all those people?"

"Tanya Claymore was offered a network job as a result of that tape. She eventually became a famous news anchor, had several public affairs with various coworkers, contracted AIDS, became a drug addict, and drove her car off a bridge one night. Jackson Davies remarried his ex-wife, and they live in Florida now. He'll turn seventy-one this year. Mary Alice Hubert died of a massive coronary six months after the killings. Most of Cedar Hill turned out for her funeral. Russell Brennert stayed in Cedar Hill and eventually bought into Jackson Davies's janitorial service. When Davies retired, Russell bought him out and now owns and operates the company. He'll turn fifty-two this year, and he looks seventy. He never married. He drinks too much and has the worst smoker's hack I've heard. He lives in a small four-room apartment with only one window—and that looks out on a parking lot. He told me he doesn't sleep well most of the time, but he has pills he can take for that. It still doesn't stop the dreams, though. He doesn't have many friends. It seems most people still believe he must have known what Andy was going to do. They've never forgiven him for that." I looked at the ghosts and smiled.

"He was so happy when I told him who I was. He hugged me like I was his long-lost son. He even wept. I invited him to come and visit me and my family this Christmas. I hope he comes. I don't think he will, but I can hope."

The room was silent for a moment, then a girl near the front, without raising her hand, said, "I knew Ted Gibson—he was the first person that Dyson shot. He . . . he always wanted me to go to Utica with him to try their ice cream. I was supposed to go with him that day. I couldn't . . . and I don't even remember why. Isn't that terrible?" Her lower lip quivered, and a tear slipped down her cheek. "Ted got killed, and all I could think of when I heard was I wonder what kind of ice cream he was eating."

That ended my story, and began theirs.

One by one, some more hesitant than others, some angrier, some more confused, my students began talking about their dead or wounded friends, and how they missed them, and how frightened they were that something so terrible could happen to someone they knew, maybe even themselves, had the circumstances been different.

The ghosts of Cedar Hill listened, and cried for my students' pain, and understood.

12

Before they left that day, someone asked me why I thought Andy had done it. I stopped myself from giving the real answer—what I perceive to be the real answer—and told them, "I think losing out on the scholarship did something to him. I think he looked at his future and saw himself being stuck in a factory job for the rest of his life and he became angry—at himself, at his family, at the town where he lived. If he had no future, then why should anyone else?"

"Then why didn't he kill his grandmother and Russell, too? Why didn't he kill you?"

Listen to my silence after he asked this.

Finally, I said, "I wish I knew."

I should have gone with my first answer.

I think it runs much deeper than mere anger. I think when loneliness and fear drive a person too deep inside himself, faith shrivels into hopelessness; I think when tenderness diminishes and bitterness intensifies, rancor becomes a very sacred thing; and I think when the need for some form of meaningful human contact becomes an affliction, a soul can be tainted with madness and allow violence to rage forth as the only means of genuine relief, a final, grotesque expression of alienation that evokes *feeling something* in the most immediate and brutal form.

The ghosts of my birth seem to agree with that.

You read the account of the Utica killings in the paper and then move quickly on to news about a train wreck in Iran or a flood in Brazil or riots in India or the NASDAQ figures for the week, and unless you are from the town of Utica or in some way knew one of the victims or the man who killed them, you forget all about it because you can't understand how a person, a *normal enough* person, a person like you and me, could do such a horrible thing. But he did, and others like him will, and all you can hope for is not to be one of the victims. You pray you will be safe. It is easier by far to understand the complicated financial maneuverings of Wall Street kingpins than an isolated burst of homicidal rage in a small Midwestern city.

They are out there, these psychos, and always will be. Another Andy Leonard could be bagging your groceries; the next Bruce Dyson might be that fellow who checks your gas meter every month. You just don't know—and there's the rub.

You *won't* know until it's too late.

I wish you well, and I wish you peace. My penance, if indeed that's what it is, must nearly be paid by now. The ghosts don't come around as much as they used to. The last time I saw them was the night my son was born; they came to the hospital to look at him, and to tell me that I was right, that those prayers spoken by strangers for the baby I once was are still protecting me, and will keep myself and my family safe from harm.

I'll pray, as well. I'll pray that the next Andy Leonard or Bruce Dyson doesn't get that last little push that topples him over the line; I'll pray that these psychos go on bagging groceries or checking gas meters or delivering pizzas and never raise a hand to kill, that the police in some other small town will be quick to stop them from getting to you if they ever do cross the line; I'll pray that no one ever picks up a paper and reads your name among the list of victims.

Because that kind of violence never really ends.

I hold my son. I kiss my wife and daughter.

The story is over.

Except for those who survived.

We continue.

Safe from harm, I pray.

Safe . . .